M000284676

This book is dedicated to my late parents,

Jack and Val Young (nee James)

To Dad, for being the straight-talking Yorkshireman
you were,

and Mum, for introducing me to the 'curse' of
The Crying Boy

Foreword

by Kelvin Mackenzie

A few decades back The Sun newspaper ran a series of front-page stories about The Crying Boy, a painting that would be found undamaged amid the ruins of houses burned down by fires.

So many readers feared the 'curse' of the Crying Boy that The Sun organised mass bonfires of the paintings. The reason I go down memory lane is that author Jane E James has been in touch about the publication of her supernatural novel which is based on these events. It will be a crying shame if it doesn't make it to film as well.

Good luck with the book. Best wishes. Kelvin.

Prologue

'One Year Earlier'

They are close. Closer than they have been before, these foolish near-adults who dare each other on with their whispered obscenities and angry gestures. Do they not see the charred remains of what was once a family home? Do they not brush up against the imposing wire fence and signs that read 'Danger Do Not Enter'?

Clinging to the boards that blindfold the ghostly dwelling are the claws of an old wisteria that now wraps itself around the building. The derelict house cares nothing for the adolescents who trip fearlessly up to its front door. The stench of burnt wire and rubber is already irritating their airways. The house has no neighbours and sits uncomfortably close to the edge of the moor. The landscape resembles an ocean of black ash but the teenagers bring torches and matches with them; things that they know will get my attention. I wonder at their stupidity. It's not as if they haven't heard of the 'curse' before. They are all too aware of who I am.

Am I not the reason they are here now? Why they have been hovering these last few wintry nights, staring up at what is left of the blackened walls as they try to drum up the courage to do only what the reckless young will.

Like them, I, too, have been waiting. I have also been listening out for the sound of their car racing on gravel. I liken myself to a faithful dog grown accustomed to the sound of its master arriving home. But unlike a faithful dog, I do not know what it is to be surrounded by family and a sense of belonging; so when at last I see their torches eerily lighting up the room, I feel no pity.

Suddenly, one of the torch lights swings around to investigate the burned-out remains and there is a sharp intake of breath that I do not think is mine.

'Fuck,' the first boy wears a woollen hat pulled tightly over his ears. The second wears a look of superiority. With them is a young girl with Bambi-sized eyes.

'They say he died right here on the floor.' The superior boy's arrogance leads me to suspect he comes from a privileged background and I despise him all the more for it. Meanwhile, all three gawp at a spot on the floor – imaginations in overdrive as they conjure up delightful images of dead bodies.

'That no matter how hard he tried, he couldn't get out because none of the windows or doors would open.'

'Fuck.' The woollen hat boy is easily impressed and the superior boy relies on his fear, as if it were an addiction.

'The cursed painting was found lying next to him... the only thing to survive the fire.'

'And there's our man... or should I say – boy?' At last, superior boy's torch comes to a dramatic halt on my face.

Bambi-eyed girl buries her head in the woollen hat boy's chest as if she cannot bear to look upon me, even though I was once thought beautiful and admired by many.

'They say anyone who damages the portrait will reawaken the curse and never get out alive.' It dawns on me then that although the superior boy is enjoying himself, he doesn't really believe in the 'curse', not yet. Not like the other two, who at least have the sense to be in awe of me.

Superior boy takes out an aerosol and sprays a green cartoonish moustache on my upper lip. All three wait for something horrific to happen.

And when nothing does – 'This is a load of shit.' Bambi-eyed girl breaks the spell and superior boy collapses with hysterical laughter.

I know little of such laughter. It has been shockingly absent from my life. There have been tears of course and smiles, but a few. I do not know of any kindness, either, but I am aware that the other two have turned away from me (as many before them have done) and only the woollen hat boy's eyes are on me now. I feel such contentment when I see his expression change from relief to horror.

'Fuck.'

The other two swing around, follow his gaze and stare in disbelief as they watch the moustache fade to nothing in front of their eyes.

'No fucking way, man.' The superior boy reminds me of a poisoned rodent with his grey skin, gaunt body and twitching face. He takes out a box of matches from his pocket and shakes them at me.

'Maybe we shouldn't,' Bambi-eyed girl pleads.

'Maybe we should.' Superior boy strikes a match and the scent of sulphur seems to restore his confidence. Although my breath is invisible, it finds its way toward the flame just as easily as any human's. And the light goes out… to be replaced with the muffled sound of a child crying. The sound echoes around the dilapidated building and appears to come from above and below us. I have grown good at this kind of deception as I have had many years to practise. So good, in fact, that I find I can be anywhere at a moment's notice.

'Fuck.'

Bambi-eyed girl grabs hold of the superior boy's arm but he has no intention of saving her. I can see it in his self-serving eyes.

Then, the patter of feet vibrates above us – the sound of a child's footsteps running out of one room and into another. I shut my eyes for a second and take delight in what they must be imagining – the glimpse of yellow hair and flash of cornflower blue iris.

'Fuck.'

All three teenagers stare up at the condemned ceiling and follow the movement around the upper floor. The sound gathers momentum as the owner of those footsteps starts to descend the stairs.

Panicking, superior boy takes out a lighter and with trembling fingers, holds it dangerously close to my face.

We lock eyes and I can see his confusion as it dawns on him at last that I am not just a painting – or a myth.

'Burn, you fucker.'

There is a whoosh of flames as the lighter explodes into an angry ball of fire. Superior boy's hand is on fire. He screams in agony and beats the flames out with his other hand. The Bambi-eyed girl stands among the debris and screams as if she has been practising this moment all her life.

'Fuck. I fucking told you, man.' Woollen hat boy grabs hold of his friend and propels him toward the door. Not wanting to be left behind, Bambi-eyed girl quickly follows.

Now they are gone, the house is mine once again and I wouldn't swap the smell of burning for the finest of perfumes.

I have heard it said by some that the purpose of a painting is to capture a moment in time. Others argue that the intention is to express an emotion. And still others say it is to make a connection with the living. But what if its purpose is to do all three?

Chapter 1

Inside Cleopatra's neon-lit lounge, the plush corner seats are made from blood-red velvet – as if it is a place used to concealing stains – and a shadowy line up of scantily clad women is silhouetted on its walls – women who once worked here but never will again.

A semi-naked dancer is curled around a shiny pole and no wonder all eyes are on her – she has long spray-tanned legs and a mop of dark curly rockstar hair. Wearing a see-through fishnet body and stockings, she does things with her limbs that no ordinary human should.

But for a few unusually well-behaved customers, the place is empty. After all, it is a weekday afternoon, Thursday to be precise, in a side street off Leeds City Centre. The kind of street nobody really ventures down unless they happen to be on a stag night or leaving do.

Judging by their work gear, this group of men are builder types. They sip their beer sparingly, hating to have paid quite so much for it, and study the dancer as she spread-eagles herself on the pole.

Perched on the edge of a sofa and looking as if he might make a bolt for it any second, Clayton Shaw is the only one of the group to remain seated and his John-Boy Walton eyes are anywhere but on the pole dancer. In his mid-thirties, Clayton looks at home in washed denim; the tighter the better, he's been told. His corn-coloured hair might be on the retreat but he clearly has a few more years good looking left in him.

The music changes to 'Need You Tonight' by INXS and the transition acts as a signal for the dancer to disentangle herself from the pole and strut toward the group of men. Her approach is greeted with cheers and whistles from the majority but Clayton springs to his feet; anxious to be someplace else.

'I'm not sure this is a good idea.'

Bearded mate Crusher and silver-haired supervisor The Fox push Clayton back into his seat and playfully hold him down. 'You're not leaving your own leaving do,' The Fox warns.

The dancer wiggles a nicotine-stained tongue at Clayton and gyrates against his leg; a grotesque move that reminds him of a dog humping a cushion. He keeps his eyes on a faulty spotlight on the ceiling that sizzles and flickers. Then, from out of nowhere, he produces a screwdriver.

'I should take a look at that,' he grins foolishly and groans go up all around. The guys know him too well.

'Once a sparky, always a sparky,' Crusher jokingly cuffs the side of Clayton's head. With that, they drag him out of his seat and thrust him 'up close and personal' with the dancer, who just happens to wear the same perfume as his wife – a fact that puts him off even more.

Laughing good-naturedly (he knows when he is beat) and enjoying the friendly ribbing of his mates, Clayton slips a twenty-pound-note in the dancer's G-string.

'My wife is going to kill me,' Clayton warns playfully.

Chapter 2

School children in summer dresses or shorts hurry to put away pencil cases and rulers, eager to escape the confines of the boiling-hot classroom. On the wall behind the teacher's desk is a very large clock. Instead of having numbers, it has numerical sign language – a collection of intricate hand signals printed across its face.

Standing under this clock and leaning wearily against her desk is thirty-year-old Avril Shaw. She has her yellow hair tied back in a wilted ponytail and something about her makes you think of Cinders *before* the Fairy Godmother makeover. Her fine, translucent eyelashes and eyebrows are the colour of cloudy lemonade and the smattering of school-girl acne across her cheeks gives her skin a curdled egg appearance.

She is clearly a woman who could be beautiful if she wanted to be, but prefers instead to hide behind tired, watery eyes and a body that has grown too thin to be thought sexy.

As Avril watches the last of the children scamper away, she rolls her lip as if it is a piece of tobacco she is desperate to make a cigarette from. It's only been a few months since she quit and already she's wondering if it was a good idea to give up smoking so soon after– but she quickly stops herself thinking that way because Clayton wouldn't like that one little bit.

Another thing she can't help doing is kneading the puckered skin on her throat. Conscious that the angry red scarring is often the first thing people notice about her, Avril never lets on that the disfigurement actually goes as far as her belly button. Inexplicably, whenever she meets anyone new she can't seem to avoid highlighting it by pointing it out with nervous fingers.

Only children dare be open about her disfigurement. 'I got a birthmark too, on my finger, miss,' they'd tell her as if it was of no consequence, or 'My daddy accidentally gave me this scar when I was little.' She couldn't tell them *her* scarring wasn't a result of anything quite so innocent.

In a determined effort to stop scratching, Avril glances over to where one of her favourite pupils – a schoolgirl with bright red hair and green cat-like eyes – has deliberately lingered behind, and is now hiding behind her desk lid.

Realising that she now has her teacher's full attention, the five-year-old grins mischievously, gently closes the desk lid as if she knows the banging of it will annoy Avril, and warily approaches. With her bulky fringe getting in the way of her eyes, she holds up her freckled hands and uses sign language to communicate with Avril.

Avril smiles warmly and immediately signs back, saying at the same time, 'I will miss you too.'

The child hesitates for a second and then presses herself against Avril's legs, wrapping her chubby little arms around her waist and not letting go; even when she feels her teacher freeze against her. After a minute or so the child skips casually out of the classroom, taking with her all the goodness that was in it before.

Casting a sad look around the empty classroom, as if it will be her last memory of it, Avril's watery gaze settles on a forgotten chair pushed into a corner and her whole being sinks with the sadness of it.

'He's not here, you know.'

Jumping at this unexpected intrusion, Avril turns to stare at Grace, her robust-looking teaching colleague, who is gazing at her from the open doorway.

'He's in there.' Grace comes over to tap insistently on Avril's bony chest, right where her heart should be, before steering her determinedly towards the door. Avril resents the fact that nobody will leave her alone with her loss.

'Come on. They're all in the staffroom waiting to say goodbye,' Grace tells her, not allowing her one final look back over her shoulder at the empty classroom.

Chapter 3

Made of stone, icy to the touch in the shade and gloriously warm in the sunshine, the house on the moor has now been completely renovated. The wire fence has gone and the boarded-up windows have been replaced with newly painted sashes.

Standing over the building is a large black ash tree that creaks like a smoker's chest. The tree leans and sighs even when there is no wind... like today, under a faultless blue sky. The only thing to spoil such a skyline is where it has been shot through with methodical white lines from aeroplanes.

Rocking back and forth, as if it is about to lull a child to sleep, the tree drops sparse leaves onto the grass, where (despite being recently landscaped) the turf looks as if it already has hundreds of children's footprints churned into it.

The house is long and low and comprises two storeys with a brick archway that leads into a secretive courtyard area at the back. It has black windows, two chimneys and a streak of attic windows built into the roof. Various outbuildings nestle close to it as if they are frightened children clinging to their mama's skirts. A low stone wall, broken in parts, giving the impression of missing molars, grumbles its way around the whole plot.

Avril stands next to Clayton in the driveway of their new home and finds she can't quite look it in the eye. There is something about the house that frightens her, but she feels too foolish to let on. She is wearing a summer dress that is almost transparent in the rays of the midday sun and her coltish legs are visible though the flimsy material.

She feels overwhelmingly small next to Clayton, who is a whole head and shoulders taller than she is. Rattling the keys to their new home in his hand, he is as excited as any schoolboy.

'This is it, Avril,' he tells her, as if she doesn't already know.

Looking down at Clayton's other hand, which should have been holding hers; she notices that their hands have all the *appearance* of touching but their identical fair-blond skins cleverly avoid each other.

'I can't believe Swallow's Nest is actually ours.' Clayton says with fatherly pride.

'Why do you insist on calling it that?' Avril raises her hand to her eyes, partly to block out the sun and partly in an attempt to erase the throbbing in her head. 'It's not a person. It's a house and it doesn't need to have a name.' Because she is secretly jealous of the hold this house has on Clayton, she is harsher than she intended. Although he must be in danger of spotting this, he chooses to avoid conflict and tugs playfully at her loose hair instead.

'Sometimes we're more like brother and sister than husband and wife,' she says haughtily, storming off ahead.

Chapter 4

Avril does not feel this house's embrace as she ought.
Even the sitting room, which is her favourite of all
thirteen rooms, does not offer much of a welcome.
She is afraid the low wooden-beams will catch Clayton out
one time too many. Already he has half a dozen gashes to
his forehead that weren't there yesterday.

There is something about the house that unsettles her;
as if there is a hidden history to it. *But that can't be true,*
she decides, because it has only recently been renovated and
should therefore be considered brand new. Their 'fresh start'
as Clayton likes to call it. But there are too many reproduction
period features for the likes of Avril, who prefers a more
contemporary, clean-living feel. She especially doesn't like
the chimney breast wall that throbs with something like a
heartbeat whenever she puts a hand to it.

If the floor was made from laminate and the wood
painted over with white gloss, she might feel better about
the place but Clayton would never hear of that. His love
of all-things-wood suggests he should really have become
a carpenter rather than an electrician. She supposes that is
what he is doing now: sawing at a bit of wood and turning
it into something useful. When they were first married she
found this habit charming. Now, she finds it irritating.

Men always have to find something to do – whereas she can sit for hours, just thinking, knowing all the time it isn't good for her.

She is meant to be unpacking but all she really wants to do is find a quiet place somewhere and cry her eyes out. In danger of doing exactly *that*, Avril seeks comfort from the things she knows – the squashy brown leather sofa, the collection of paperbacks stacked on the book shelves and the expensive rug given to them as a wedding present. She's forgotten who bought it for them but she can remember they once used to make love on it.

Ignoring the box of ornaments she is supposed to be unpacking, Avril walks over to the selection of framed family photographs lined up on the coffee table that Clayton made out of a door and picks up their wedding day portrait. They look incredibly young, she thinks wistfully, and for once Clayton hadn't up-staged her with his knockout looks. As soon as it is in her hands she can feel the confetti in her hair and the bubbles of champagne up her nose. The sound of the church bells chiming is instantly in her ears, as are the voices of their friends wishing them well. Peering closer, she notices that for once, she looks pretty… almost beautiful.

Running a hand through her messy hair that picks up static and crackles with electricity whenever she enters this room, she reminds herself she ought to make more of an effort with her appearance if she wants to be anything like the girl in the photo again. Then, glancing at the brick wall, she notices for the first time that there is a faded rectangular shape just above the fireplace – as if somebody had once hung a large family portrait there. *How strange*, she thinks.

What is stranger still is that out of all the family photos lined up on the coffee table, there is none of Avril's own family. There is a good reason for this, but it isn't something she wants to think about right now. She hasn't been as lucky as Clayton.

Sniffing, because she can't get rid of the wretched fishy smell that invaded her nostrils the minute she arrived here, Avril's melancholy is interrupted by the unmistakeable grumbling sound of thunder sneaking up on them like a stranger's shadow. All at once the sky outside darkens. Within seconds rain is pattering down on the roof and a sliver of white lightning can be seen in the distance, poking at the moor with its pointed finger.

Covering her ears with her hands, wanting to shut out the sound of the gathering storm, she finally goes in search of Clayton, all the while knowing he won't take her anxiety seriously. While Clayton is adventurous and loves thunder and lightning, she lives in fear of storms. Clayton wants so much for them to be alike. *But it has to be his kind of like, not mine,* she thinks moodily.

He'd annoyed her earlier, on the drive, and she hadn't been ready to make friends quite so soon, but now she has the perfect excuse to go and find him. The truth is she needs Clayton more than anything and this admission scares her even more than the house does. Apart from the other thing in her life she is meant to be putting behind her – the very real threat of losing Clayton is always on her mind.

Chapter 5

Natural light floods in from a matching pair of sash windows that resemble half-closed eyes, illuminating a torturous collection of tools hanging from the walls. Wooden furniture hangs from the ceiling and a rickety wooden ladder disappears into a boarded-out loft space.

This, then, is Clayton's new workshop and he imagines spending a lot of time out here while Avril marks homework in the snug; a bolt hole she'd immediately claimed for herself. He likes to think they'll fall into the habit of meeting up in the evenings for a glass of wine and a sharing of confidences but in reality he knows there is little chance of this happening.

Her mood tonight is as black as the storm gathering over Will's Mother's but he barely notices the thunder and lightning – shame the same can't be said for her frame of mind. She will soon be fretting over the gale outside but he knows better than to go and find her. Best leave her to her own devices. Better that than try, as he's done so many times in the past, to put a comforting arm around her, only to be shrugged off.

He bends his head over the house sign he has lovingly created and gently caresses the glossy wood. As he does so, he realises he can't remember the last time he stroked his wife with the same affection. He knows Avril resents the amount of time he spends 'playing around with wood' but he loves a project. It isn't good for a man to sit around doing nothing, the way gossiping women do. Idle hands and all that.

He still has a hundred-and-one other chores to do and they've barely made a start on unpacking but he desperately wants to finish the sign. Already it has taken shape. Two hand-crafted swallows entwined in flight hover over a miniature replica of Swallow's Nest. All that is left for him to do is paint it before hanging it proudly over the front door.

Clayton hopes Avril will be part of the re-naming ceremony, but somehow doubts it. He has no idea what *does* please her these days. Nor can he tell what is on her mind most of the time, yet they had once been able to finish each other's sentences. Does she still love him? Sometimes he thinks so and others… well he can't be certain. For a while now, things haven't been right between them, but apart from the obvious, he feels this is mostly down to her refusal to talk about her childhood or her past.

Such mystery baffles Clayton because he loves nothing more than clarity and openness. But the same can't be said for his wife who seems to enjoy being as puzzling as a murder-mystery novel.

'If you put vagueness out there, Avril, then vagueness is what you will get back,' he'd once warned her.

Their differences had never mattered before. But now they are growing apart. At least, everything seems to point that way.

He is quick to make new friends but Avril is shy and reserved. She can even come across as being snooty and distant, only he doesn't tell her this; knowing it would hurt her feelings. The desire to protect each other from harmful truths is something they *do* still have in common.

Earlier he'd caught her looking at the family photos in the sitting room, picking them up and turning them over as if clues to who they *really* were would be revealed on the back. Watching her stand there like that, completely oblivious to his presence, made him feel like an unwelcome guest at somebody's wedding. He is horrified by the amount of spying he does on his wife; acting like a sly tom cat that creeps in and out of her life. This is the only way he can find out anything – like *is she alright?*

Where are the pictures of her family? That's what he's always wanted to know but has never dared probe too deep for fear of causing one of those week-long-silences that grows between them like a field of stinging nettles.

Chapter 6

Swallow's Nest might be all lit up like a magical doll's house with its windows throwing out an orange night-time glow, but outside thunder uncurls like a blanket over it and hailstones ping off the new slate roof. Coming from the direction of the moor and running hand-in-hand like schoolchildren, Avril and Clayton dodge the bolts of lightning that hit the ground like angry words.

An explosion of thunder louder than any lion's roar sees them clasp their hands to their ears at the same time and Clayton laughs, something Avril hasn't heard him do in a long while. It makes her glad she agreed to his mad suggestion of braving the storm, although truthfully the bottle of champagne they'd knocked back earlier helped sway her. But it's not until they're tippy-toeing drunkenly over the newly-laid grass, which is spongy and wet underfoot, she dares to hope she might in time grow to like the house.

Avril glances at her husband sideways on and reminds herself that there is something of the caveman about him, even if he does smell like a wet dog. As if he can guess what she is thinking, Clayton shakes himself like a gundog emerging from water, and his sodden jumper sprays her with water. For once she laughs along, not minding. Then, she surprises herself by kissing him full on the mouth. At first it feels like a mistake and she's tempted to pull away but Clayton's arm creeps around her and soon grows in confidence. She's all but forgotten the taste of his lips and the scratchy feel of his skin – but the earthy sawdust smell that lingers on his body is something she would recognise anywhere.

As they sway together, ignoring the claps of thunder and driving rain, she keeps her eyes on the blacked-out moor and likens it to a threat that prowls up and down in the distance. Even though the rain stings her eyes, she fights to keep her eyelids open. She does not close them even when Clayton heaves her up into his arms and stares into her face a lot longer than is comfortable; not because she cannot bear to break away from his intense gaze but because she's fearful of what is waiting for her in the blackness.

Chapter 7

Merging together as if they share the same gnarled branches and limbs, is a man built like a *T. rex* and the towering ash tree that stands guard over Swallow's Nest. The man rests a hand on a walking cane that he keeps close to his side, like a well-trained sheepdog. He has a lived-in face and grinds his jaw as he spies on the newcomers to Swallow's Nest. *People who have no business being here,* he thinks. *People who don't belong here,* he decides.

He watches the tall young man pick up the blonde woman in his arms and carry her towards the house. They don't appear to notice how unforgiving and hostile the building appears at night. Although the woman is slight, he notices that the man stumbles often as if he is drunk. They are an extraordinarily handsome couple. But being attractive won't save them. No more than being in love will.

As they come closer still, he takes a step back, losing himself in the deformed branches of the tree. They pass by, just ten or twelve feet from him, and he catches the scent of the woman – a delicate floral fragrance that doesn't anger him the way some women's perfumes do. Although his face is as ragged as a crumbling cliff edge, he's nobody's grandfather and is not immune to the sight of a pretty woman (even if this one does have an aura of impenetrable sadness about her). She has him remembering the legs, arms and soft pink flesh of women he once knew. Women that are now lost to him. The memories are painful and before he's even met the young woman on the moor, he's disgruntled with her. But meet her he will. He has no more choice in this than she does.

He sees them go into the house and hears them bang the heavy oak door behind them but it does not close completely and they do not notice. *Anyone could creep in behind them*, he thinks. Even from here he can see their trim shadows in the hallway as they pause to kiss. And when the man eases the woman's sweater away from one slim shoulder and puts his mouth to it, he likewise cannot stop himself from wondering what she tastes like. Milk and honey, he'd like to bet, with the smell of grass and mint in her hair.

Closing his eyes, he imagines swapping places with the young man, and for a second or two he's someplace else. But then, all at once he's transported back to another more terrifying moment. Fighting to block out the disturbing memory, he realises *nothing* (not even a beautiful woman) can prevent him from going back in time.

***

Swallow's Nest burns. Clouds of black smoke swirl upward into the night sky while bursts of orange flame flicker in and out of the building like a persistent dragon's tongue. There is a crackling of wood, of explosions mimicking shotgun fire and the heat of the fire can be felt from afar.

The house creaks and leans first one way then the other before sighing like a frustrated old woman incapable of reaching her own cobwebs. The windows then explode, spitting deadly splinters of glass into the crowd, reminding them that this isn't a cheerful Bonfire Night get-together.

He has seen houses burn before, even if most of the crowd here hasn't. But not like this. Never like this.

He was the first to arrive on the scene and he had called the fire brigade at the first opportunity but the remote location and difficult terrain meant they couldn't get here in time; unlike the locals who nigh broke their necks to scramble out here. He can see the familiar ship-like vessel heading towards them now, taking the dips in the lane as carefully as a young foal. Its unhurried wailing reminds him of a screeching curlew flying over the moor.

Wishing the firefighters would hurry up, he chooses to keep his distance from everybody else but cannot entirely block out their astonished cries of 'Oh, my God. Oh, my God,' as they pray to a deity he wants no truck with.

Amid the sound of smouldering debris falling to the ground, there are shrieks of fear from those who never expected a house fire to be this noisy. Then, the attic floor of the house collapses, like a fragile ice shelf, and heartbreaking screams are heard inside. At times, the unbearable cries for help sound like a pig having its throat cut.

No one at the scene, other than him, knows who has been left inside the building. But one thing they can all be sure of – is there is no way out for whoever *is* inside. Nobody could escape an inferno like that.

Chapter 8

Her kiss had surprised him almost as much as the unexpected summer storm. Braving the assault of hailstones that had been flung at them like a windfall of apples, he had carried her all the way back to Swallow's Nest in silence, frightened one of them would say something to spoil the moment. And now his heart is pounding with fear at the prospect of making love to his wife.

They are both soaked to the skin – shivering and teeth chattering – as they huddle around a hastily lit fire, which spits and hisses like an angry cat. As the grey smoke curls upwards, making his eyes sting, he watches Avril pour out more champagne and feels comforted by the 'welcome to your new home cards' dotted about the sitting room. They remind him of people he knows and trusts.

His wife might look as if she grew up bottle-feeding newborn lambs but there is a dark side to her past. One she refuses to talk about. And if he ever presses her on the subject she completely blanks him. Sometimes for days on end.

He takes a sip of champagne and watches her stir up the fire with a poker. He's never been able to start a fire properly, not in the way she can. As the orange embers from the logs dance in the air and settle as ash on the oak floor, he realises they are kneeling on their special rug – which they shagged on like rabbits for the first two or three years of their marriage. Back then, Avril had been up for it as much as he was, he remembers fondly.

Smiling to himself, because he knows she won't want to be reminded of this, he fights back the urge to sweep a wet lock of hair from her face and instead pictures her naked. The reality of her body never fails to blow him away and he keeps a picture postcard image of it in his head as a painful reminder of what he is missing.

Although she is painfully thin, the roundness of her belly always surprises him. It does not seem to belong to the same woman who has ribs as prominent as the keys on a piano. Having secretly watched her undress more times than he cares to remember, he knows that nowadays the triangular V-shape between her legs is overgrown because she no longer bothers to wax it. It is heart-breaking to know she has let herself go.

Her skin is the colour of home-made custard, he observes closely, the kind his mother used to make, but his eyes are drawn to her ring-less wedding finger. No matter how many times she tells him 'It's too big and will slip off,' it still hurts like hell.

As for the scarring on her body that he is not allowed to mention, made all the more obvious by the firelight flickering on her skin, he would give anything to be allowed to touch it. He suspects it has ridges and knots… like roughly sawn wood. But Avril has trained his fingers to avoid it at all costs. She is like a living doll that has been rescued from a fire, he thinks sentimentally, and feels something twist inside him. He'd like to protect her forever, if she will let him.

***

She doesn't know or care if it is real champagne or a much cheaper alternative – all she wants is to get it down her as fast as possible. Knocking back another glass full, she immediately refills her glass and glances nervously at Clayton, who has that familiar lovesick look on his face that has come to worry her.

He can't seem to take his eyes off her and she knows it is something to do with the way her damp clothes cling to her body. Realising she won't be able to put him off much longer, and reprimanding herself for not being thought too thin or too prickly, she closes her eyes and fights back the rising panic that threatens to overwhelm her. The last thing she wants to do is yell and lash out at him again, the way she did the last time they tried to do this.

My God, she loves this man. There has never been any doubt in her mind about this and the truth of it is written on her face. *So, why does the thought of making love to my husband repulse me?* she asks herself. Then, sensing him lean toward her, she feels his breath against her hair. It is the touch of a warm and generous man who would help a whole street full of homeless people if he could.

'Avril?' His voice is urgent.

There is always something that somebody wants from me. Something I don't want to give, she thinks tetchily, secretly hating him for putting them in this situation and blaming herself for having first started it out on the moor.

'Avril?' he says again.

She kisses him back, pretending at a passion she doesn't feel, and silently berates him for making her do this. She wants to make him happy. Really she does. Hasn't she already proven this by agreeing to move to this Godforsaken desolate spot? All the while pretending nothing bad has happened to them. But deep down a part of her is sick of trying to please and the threat of a rebellion keeps bubbling to the surface.

When his hands move down to her breasts, or what there is of them, her body freezes but he doesn't notice and this selfishness makes Avril want to take a bite-sized chunk out of his mouth.

'It's been a long time,' he says, plunging an uninvited hand between her legs.

What makes him think I want this? Why would he think I'd want to, after everything that has happened? She wants to scream.

'Are you sure?' he *needs* her permission to continue but even as she gives him the gentlest of nods, they are both aware her consent is given reluctantly. Pulling him on top of her, *best get it over before I change my mind*, she feels him tugging off her pants, while outside the storm does its worst. Jealously she listens, wishing she could howl out her pain.

Keeping her eyes closed, she wraps her legs around Clayton and prays that she won't think about *the other thing* while they are at it, all the while knowing it is impossible not to, especially during intimate moments like this. *How can I not think of him? And I don't understand how Clayton can do this, not when he knows how I feel.*

It has been a long time since they last had sex and Clayton is as red-blooded as the next man, so she feels she has no choice but to satisfy his sexual desire. *Yet whenever I am in need of a hug he is nowhere to be found,* she thinks miserably. Having to open her legs in order to keep her own husband from straying makes Avril feel resentful as hell.

Likening Clayton's lovemaking to the build-up of the storm; she feels him thrust into her in perfect harmony with the peals of thunder outside and it seems to her that somebody somewhere is mocking her. Then the lights inside the sitting room begin to flicker and she struggles against him, terrified the electricity will go out altogether. There the lights go again; flickering off and then on again. Wriggling beneath Clayton, unable to call out because his mouth is covering hers, she would deny him the pleasure of orgasm if she could, but it's too late. He is there. She can tell by the way his body spasms. It feels so wrong. She wants to tell him so; remind him of what they have been through. *How can you take pleasure from my body when it is dead?*

That's when the lights go off completely and they are left with nothing but the sound of their own breathing.

She cannot bear this blackness or the silence that has descended on them and all at once she finds herself clinging desperately to Clayton's damp body. Whereas moments ago she would have liked to kill him, now she will not let him go, even though he resists her clutches.

The lights come on briefly only for a light bulb to pop, causing the rest of the lights to immediately trip out again. As Avril acclimatises herself to the blackness, she feels Clayton move away from her. But he is stopped in his tracks by a different sound altogether – something wholly unrelated to the storm. There it is – a crash, followed by a thump… thump… thump… coming from directly above them.

'What is that?' Avril grabs hold of whatever bit of Clayton she can.

'It's just the storm.'

'No it isn't, Clay,' she insists. Again, he tries to pull away from her but she holds on to his soggy sweater and listens for the sound to recur again. And when it does…

'See.' She tells him.

Thump… Thump… Thump… the sound continues, no closer and yet no more distant than before.

'Stay here,' Clayton tells her firmly and recognising the determined tone of his voice, she is too scared to do anything other than obey.

Chapter 9

Shining an invasive torch light into the doorway of their tomblike bedroom, which is full of incriminating shadows, Clayton all too readily closes the door again. Not easily spooked, there is nevertheless something about what he is doing that does freak him out – but whatever *it* is – it continues to evade him.

Wherever the sound is coming from, it is definitely not from any of the four main bedrooms on the first floor. He is ready to give up the search and go back downstairs when he hears it again – closer this time – a fluttering sound followed by a thump... thump... thump... the same sound that lured him up each tread of the staircase. The same sound that gave Avril the perfect excuse to push him away just as he was about to ejaculate inside her.

Sensing the racket is coming from immediately above his head, Clayton glances up at the loft hatch and fights back an ill-fated feeling.

He pulls down the loft ladder and then climbs warily into the unknown, swinging his torch first one way and then the other; watching it pick out cobwebs and clutter. Feeling reassured by stuff he'd expect to find in a loft space, he shakes off the jumpiness he felt earlier and steps into the attic. Wondering how dead leaves could have got in here, he hears them crunch under his trainers and lowers his head under the wooden rafters. The attic runs from one end of the house to the other and at one end there are three windows that look down on the front driveway.

The rafters, though freshly sawn, do not have the usual agreeable aroma of freshly cut wood. In fact, for a newly-renovated property, it is incredibly dark and dusty and the musky smell suggests the place is already overrun with mice. Reminding himself to buy some traps the next time he's in town, Clayton suddenly finds himself cowering with fear as two birds fly out of nowhere and dance erratically above his head.

'Shit.' Clayton ducks again and again; childishly protecting his head with his hands as they dive bomb him. It takes him a minute or two in the darkness to work it out, but he's pretty sure these are swallows. *Wait till I tell Avril!* He is pleased to have solved the mystery.

'But how the hell did you get in here?'

Searching around for clues, his glance falls on one of the half-open attic windows and at last the penny drops. He'd been wondering where the draft was coming from. He shoos the birds toward the window and they dodge him at every opportunity. In the process their wings flutter across his face and he's not sure he likes the sensation. Eventually they make their escape. They may not have a clue where they are going in the dark, but at least they are unhurt. Tomorrow, he will have to see about making the attic bird-proof. Then, just as he is about to shut the window *something* outside catches his eye; *something* that causes every hair on his body to stand on end.

Not wanting to believe what he has just seen, or thinks he has seen, Clayton moves closer to the glass and stares out into the blackness. There. Under the tree. He sees it move again. A pale hand in the dark. *Jesus Christ.* He knew he hadn't imagined it. There really is someone out there.

Chapter 10

Clayton takes a step back from the misted pane of glass that bears his handprint and shakes his head in confusion. He can no longer be certain he saw anything at all, let alone a person. There certainly isn't any evidence of anyone out there now – he hasn't seen a flicker of movement in the last five minutes. Could he have been mistaken? And why would anyone want to be out there, given the time of night and the bad weather? Unless they were taking shelter from the storm.

'Too many glasses of bubbly, old man,' he reprimands himself, keen to shrug off the whole unsettling incident.

As Clayton backs away from the window, his unlaced trainer knocks against something on the floor. He pulls away a sheet of tarpaulin and is surprised to find an old portrait hidden beneath. He picks up the painting and wipes away the build-up of dust that he knows should have taken years, not weeks or months, to accumulate. As more of the painting is revealed, he stares fiercely at it, as if trying to outwit it in an arm wrestling contest.

He hardly dares believe what he sees. It can't be. It isn't possible. He now recognises this is exactly what he had been fearful of and why he had been on edge earlier, long before he set foot in the attic. The impression that something predestined is about to happen is upon him again – and the fear of not being in control is alien to him. He needs to know he can be relied on to handle a crisis; that he is capable of protecting his wife. He hopes he has done so by insisting she stay downstairs. She doesn't need to see this.

'What is it, Clay?'

Jumping in alarm, Clayton spins around to see Avril's head poking out of the loft hatch. Although she has given him a real fright by creeping up on him, any leftover anger he might have felt towards her disappears as soon as he sees her anxious face. It's a face that somehow looks at home in hospitals and at funerals, but never at parties.

'I told you to stay downstairs.' He might have forgiven her but he doesn't want her to know this. Then, doing exactly what he doesn't want her to, she climbs into the attic.

'What have you got there?'

'Nothing,' he says, swallowing the lie, knowing she will see straight through it. 'Just some dumb old picture.'

'Let me see.'

'There's nothing *to* see.' He is too stern and he immediately realises his mistake. Now nothing will stop her from getting her own way.

'I want to see, Clayton.' She comes to stand right beside him. In the dark he feels her eyes boring into him, as she attempts to work out what the lie is doing here. He has never been able to deceive her the way she does him.

Suddenly the electricity comes back on. *Give me a break*, he thinks dismally, realising nobody is on his side tonight, least of all the Northern Powergrid company. They stand side by side, watching the lurking shadows grow more distant as light floods in all over the house.

Avril immediately recognises the boy in the painting; just as he knew she would. No amount of dust can hide the fair hair and blue eyes that were once so familiar to them. But it is only a resemblance, he reminds himself; nothing more than a cruel trick. He can only hope the peasant-style clothing the boy wears and his dirty tear-streaked face will reassure Avril the likeness is nothing more than a coincidence – but judging by the way her body trembles violently, he doubts it. Watching her eyes fill with tears brings him almost to his knees. When she finally wrenches her eyes away from the painting – her accusing glance falls on him.

'It's him!' she whispers croakily as if she has just lost her voice. And then again, even more distraught this time 'Tommy!'

Chapter 11

Avril realises she will never figure out how the vast double range works. "She can't even look at it without thinking it resembles a spaceship. She is used to cooking on a nice simple electric hob and the fuel burning relic in front of her remains an enigma.

The only good thing about the room is the floor-to-ceiling window that offers panoramic views over the moor. Perched in front of that window is a friendly-looking couch with a faux fur blanket thrown over it. How it got there, she doesn't know, but the throw reminds her of a dead animal; a thought that makes her feel queasy. There is also an island, that stands as alone and isolated as she feels, with swivel bar stools pushed up against it. It saddens her that she's unlikely to spin around in any of them, sipping an exotic cocktail that tastes of coconut and mint.

Other than that, all she can see is hateful pine. Pine units. Pine flooring. Pine furniture. There are even pine beams over the windows. This dull, rustic world of orange pine makes her feel as if she has walked into a second-hand furniture shop; somewhere she wouldn't normally be seen dead in. For the life of her she cannot comprehend where all this awful furniture has come from. Most of their old stuff hasn't even made the move, she can see that now. She blames herself. God knows where her head has been these last few months.

'This kitchen will be great for parties,' Clayton had told her when they first came to view the house; but she hadn't bargained on it being the first thing on their agenda. Yet here they are, before they've even had a chance to unpack properly, planning exactly that.

She has been given the responsibility of blowing up balloons with a pump that doesn't work correctly. She looks at the un-inflated balloon in her hand and lets out a deflated sigh. *If one balloon can defeat me so easily, I'm not going to get very far,* she realises despondently.

Through the open doorway, which leads into the boiler room, she can see Clayton perched on a stepladder fiddling with a smoke alarm on the ceiling. After last night, they are not talking. *We are talking,* Avril corrects herself, *just not about the painting or Tommy.* She can't think why this should surprise her – this is nothing new.

Every so often the smoke alarm goes off – inflicting a high-pitched beep, beep, beep sound on her already heightened senses. She's not sure if the alarm is faulty or if Clayton is just testing it, but the racket puts her on edge all the same.

'Who's idea was it to have a housewarming party, anyway?' Clayton jokes, keen to 'move forward' as he likes to term it.

'Certainly not mine,' Avril mutters under her breath. Then, on hearing the deafening sound of the alarm going off again she pulls a face and starts to massage her forehead.

'Can't you just take the batteries out?' she asks impatiently, fighting off the first symptoms of a tension headache.

'How many times have people done that and paid for it with their lives?' Clayton is at once in serious work mode, talking to her as if she was an apprentice on a youth training scheme. But before he can get too enthusiastic about lecturing her, a habit of his she has grown used to, somebody rings the doorbell and for once Avril is glad to receive a visitor.

Chapter 12

As soon as Avril walks into the sitting room, her hair ripples with electricity and the fishy smell is once again in her nostrils. Hoping the woman following her doesn't notice either of these peculiarities, she turns to face her, giving her a nervous smile.

'And this is the sitting room.' Avril shouts above the din of the alarm. The noise is doing her head in but at least she's making an effort. The same can't be said for Mrs Davis, who shows a general dislike of everything. Under such scrutiny, Avril feels herself blush.

Then, seeing the woman's shifty eyes lock on to something that really does make her face recoil in horror, Avril follows her alarmed gaze and sees that she is staring at *The Crying Boy* that now hangs on the chimney wall – exactly where the faded rectangular shape had been. It hangs there as if it has always belonged there, Avril is pleased to see.

At long last the beep, beep, beep of the alarm stops and Avril sighs in relief. 'I can't believe my husband wanted to throw it away,' she tells the woman, unaware that her own glance softens every time she looks at the painting.

'There's been a mistake. Sorry.' The little woman barks, startling Avril, who physically jumps at the sound of her voice. Mrs Davis then clamps her lips shut as if she has said too much. Doing a military about-turn she heads toward the door, looking as if she will knock down anybody who gets in her way. Panicking, Avril skips after her, wondering what on earth she could have said to offend her.

'You'll have to find somebody else,' the woman warns her, hurrying past Clayton who chooses that moment to saunter in.

'I managed to fix it,' he says out loud, rather expecting a round of applause and is nonplussed to find the woman has left the room without introducing herself.

'What happened to our new cleaner?' he wants to know.

The sound of the back door crashing shut is all the answer he is going to get and right now Avril would seriously like to poke him in the eye with a pen. Then, to top everything off, the alarm goes off again. Beep, beep, beep...

Avril covers her ears but nothing can drown out the terrible wailing. 'I can't stand it any longer,' she yells. Then, pushing past her bewildered husband she exits by the back door, just as Mrs Davis had done.

Chapter 13

The sound of the smoke alarm has followed Avril onto the moor, where she sits on a rocky outcrop staring at a dilapidated old barn that looks as homesick as she feels. Although she has left the piercing beep, beep, beep noise behind her, she keeps her hands clasped to her ears because out here it still feels unbearably real to her.

Avril feels exhausted by the terrible memories that haunt her but she cannot ignore the horrific images that leap through her mind. Nor can she forget the nightmares that cause her to wake up at night, screaming and crying, while Clayton lies beside her, pretending to sleep. Aware he does this not to be cruel, but because he cannot bear to have her reject him if he reaches out to her, she does not hold this against him.

Knowing Clayton will not follow her out here does not make her feel more alone. Nothing can. The emptiness inside her will never go away. Nor will the beep, beep, beep sound.

***

Back then, Avril had been younger, prettier, plumper and happier than she'd ever been. Didn't she have everything a woman her age could wish for? A great career, a wonderful home, an adoring husband, a beautiful–

It was a day like any other. The day *it* happened. She can remember every moment as if it were yesterday. Having woken up at ten minutes past six, they'd started the day arguing over whose turn it was to make breakfast. They were both running late and parted without remembering to kiss each other. Not a great start to the day, but nothing too out of the ordinary.

At lunchtime she'd popped to the local shop for fresh bread and milk and a good-luck bottle of wine for the two of them… for later. They were trying for a baby but neither wanted to make a big thing of it. She must have been looking particularly good that day because when she exited the shop she received a wink and a wolf whistle from a lorry driver parked outside. He was sat in his cab with the door half open, rolling a cigarette from a pouch of tobacco on his lap. She remembered this only because it made her want to smoke too, but she'd made a promise to give up for good. They couldn't afford to take any risks. Not after last time. They wanted this pregnancy, if it happened, to be plain sailing.

She'd clocked off work a few minutes later than usual but again this was of no consequence; life as a teacher meant this was always happening to her. As always, he was waiting for her at the school gate – looking a little worried perhaps because she was late. But as soon as his hand was in hers, everything was right again, they were both complete.

By chance, she'd been talking to one of the mums when it happened. Across the road from where she worked there was a development of new starter homes being built and a heavy goods lorry was churning up mud and cement in the otherwise nice middle class street. Its roar drowned out the conversation she was having with Sylvia, whose six-year-old son she taught. Glancing up, Avril thought she saw the driver remove a roll-up from his mouth and nod to her as if he recognised her. But she didn't know any lorry drivers. It was only when he winked at her she realised he was the same man from outside the shop.

Because she was distracted by the driver and the sound of his lorry's reverse warning lights going beep, beep, beep – as well as half-listening to Sylvia's unwarranted concerns for her son's development, Avril did not notice his hand slip out of hers. She certainly did not feel him shuffle away from her and it wasn't until Sylvia looked up, her face growing suddenly grey with fear, that Avril glimpsed him out of the corner of her eye.

'Tommy,' she screamed. 'Tommy.' Again and again she screeched his name out loud, but of course he didn't... couldn't hear her. The sound of the lorry's screeching hydraulic brakes filled everybody's ears, not just Avril's, as she broke away from Sylvia's grasping hands to dart across the road. But it was too late. She was too late.

Chapter 14

Tommy. Gone. In the blink of an eye. Or in her case, the wink of a distracted driver trying to get the attention of a pretty girl. But not just any pretty girl. *Her.* And she couldn't deny having enjoyed the attention at the time; stupid, vain, silly girl that she had been. How could she ever forgive herself for allowing her own son to slip away from her unnoticed? She should have been paying more attention. She should have known he would have wanted to cross the road to see his best friend Josh, who had been walking with his dad on the opposite side of the street. How could she forget the last time she saw him alive; the final glimpse of school uniform disappearing under the dirty wheels of a lorry.

Clayton's answer to all this was the move here to Swallow's Nest and no more talk of babies or pregnancies and she suspects this is because he has seen their son's dead body and she has not. He might be keeping the terrible reality of Tommy's crushed corpse to himself but she has her own dark secret to guard. He still does not know about her connection to the driver; the man who ruined all their lives, including his own. Clayton will never know how grateful she is to the man, whose name she cannot say out loud, for keeping quiet about their ill-fated encounter.

Although her husband loves to second guess her, he does not need to know everything.

He certainly does not need to know that the beep, beep, beep sound of the smoke alarm isn't the only thing to have followed her onto the moor. Tommy is here too. Ever since they discovered the painting in the attic she has felt his presence. Odd that she'd never felt him before and never at their old house; only since moving to Swallow's Nest. Of course she realises the crying boy in the painting is not her son; even if the likeness *is* striking. But it feels as if Tommy has somehow inhabited the painting and is now trying to connect with her on some level. She realises how ridiculous this sounds but there is no denying they share the same lemon-coloured hair and cornflower blue eyes; even Clayton had spotted this. Another thing they have in common is the matching frown and downturned mouth, which reminds Avril of when her five-year-old son had been in a pet. It makes her sad to remember how often he was angry and unable to express himself in the silent world he inhabited. Tommy didn't hear the lorry because he was profoundly deaf. The lorry driver didn't see him because he was too busy flirting with her.

Realising that her fingers have been raking on the ground and churning up soil and heather – she stops – frightened by what she has unknowingly done. Seeing that her nails are clogged with dirt and her balled up fists are coated in wool from the carcases of dead sheep – she gets to her feet and looks about her; worried somebody will notice her distress and come over to interfere, as they usually do. But apart from scattered sheep bones she is completely alone on the moor.

Avril dusts her hands together and sighs. It must be time to go back to Swallow's Nest. Soon it will be dark. As if in agreement, a lone crow lands on the crumbling stone wall that was once used as a sheep pen and caws crossly at her. Avril has never seen one this close up before and she's not sure whether to run from it or fling a stone at it. Flapping its wings in annoyance, the crow leans its head on one side before taking off again. She watches it fly awkwardly, one wing pointed lower than the other, and then land on top of the dilapidated barn before disappearing into its open roof space.

Although she has been staring across at it this last hour, she hasn't noticed it properly until now. Grim and grey and made from York stone, the barn leans onto a rugged stone mound on the moor. Its wooden slatted doors have rotted away in places to reveal gaping holes that look as if a giant has punched his fist through them. Each door hangs slothfully off its hinges, she notices, and the black shadowy void she glimpses inside is too daunting an entrance for most moor walkers. Even so, there is a used pathway through the grass that suggests *somebody* is coming and going from the disused building.

Shuddering, because the old barn gives her the creeps, she is about to head home when she hears something unusual. Something that doesn't tweet, croak or hiss like the rest of the wildlife surrounding her. Cocking her head to one side, she imitates the crow without realising it, and listens again, more acutely this time. There it is… The sound of laughter. A child's laughter. Echoing around the moor.

And that's when she glimpses him out of the corner of her bewildered eye – a small child with a shock of pale yellow hair – running over the open moorland. He moves awkwardly, like the crow, and every so often he stumbles and Avril's hand flies to her chest. He could so easily fall and hurt himself.

'Tommy?' Avril holds her breath without knowing she is doing so. Meanwhile, his scent bounces off every wilted blade of moorland grass.

'Tommy?' The fragrance of his bath time hair is in her nostrils and the sugary odour of his breath is against her cheek. Nobody's child smells the same. What mother wouldn't recognise the precious scent of her own child? Not even sheep get this bond wrong.

But why is he running away? Tommy would surely run into my arms, not away from them. Perhaps he wants to show me something. Perhaps he needs me to follow him.

Casting an apprehensive look back over her shoulder in the direction of Swallow's Nest, she is conscious of the fact that Clayton wouldn't want her to do this. She'd go so far as to say he'd probably forbid it. Her old therapist would agree, saying 'You're not ready for this, Avril.'

Who says I'm not? Avril thinks rebelliously; but she is torn between her husband and son. It has always been this way, she realises.

What if the child running over the moor is real and not just a figment of my loneliness and imagination? What if it is Tommy? Avril asks herself. She can't leave him out here alone on the moor. She couldn't do that to any child. She'd never forgive herself if anything happened to him. She wants to know if this child, who looks and sounds like Tommy, has the same smattering of golden freckles across his nose or the familiar gap between his two front teeth; but she knows there is only one way to find out. As if hypnotised, Avril watches the boy run toward the barn, all the while chuckling to himself the way Tommy used to. He then slips through a gap in the barn doors and disappears inside. Swallowing back any lingering doubt, Avril follows.

She moves determinedly over the undulating ground and covers the distance as easily as any athlete. Then, without hesitating she presses an eye to a crack in the wooden door and peers inside. At first she sees nothing but blackness. Then rainbows of diminishing light shine through the open roof to pick out rusted machinery and sagging bales of straw. She can already feel dust particles settle on her pale eyelashes, turning them grey. The flakes irritate her nose, making her want to sneeze, making her want to blink. Over there in the corner, hiding behind one of the giant bales of mouldy old straw – she can just about make out the shadowy silhouette of a child; no longer laughing but whimpering. Seeing him cowering and crying like this – as if he is afraid – makes her heart fill with a fiercely protective emotion that isn't new. *I must get to him.* She is about to try yanking open the doors when she senses a shadow looming behind her.

'Did you lose someone?'

Spinning around to face the giant standing in front of her, Avril immediately looks for a way past him and a chance to escape his frightening bulk. Sensing that he wants something from her – she experiences terror. This man could be a madman, a rapist, a serial-killer or perhaps all three. What had she been thinking of coming up here on her own?

'I thought I saw a little boy go in there.' Nervously Avril nods her head in the direction of the barn and sees a flicker of fear appear in his snake-like eyes.

'A little boy alone the moor?' He appraises her coolly. 'I don't think so.' His voice is weighted down with scorn and loaded with West Yorkshire.

Feeling safer, because local men don't usually turn out to be murderers, Avril switches her attention back to the barn. Now that she no longer fears him quite so much, she puts her eye back to the gap in the wood, determined to find out if the boy, *Tommy*, is still inside.

'But I could have sworn…'

She feels him move behind her; hears his walking cane grind against the exposed rock and suddenly he's towering over her like an ugly block of flats.

'Like I said. I don't think so.' He places an arm as wide as her whole upper body across the barn door, blocking her.

Cowardly, she backs away and he doesn't try to stop her. This is off-putting because he doesn't seem to do or say any of the things she imagines madmen, rapists and serial killers do. Even so, as soon as there is enough distance between them she makes a break for it and flees – her heart pumping with adrenalin as she bolts like a frightened hare over the moor.

Chapter 15

There are four speckled eggs in the nest, and while he is busy pushing the nest material back under the eaves, the anxious parents circle above his head. From the ground, Clayton originally thought it was a wasp's nest because it appeared to be made of wood pulp. It wasn't until he got the long ladders out and climbed all the way to the top of the house he realised it was a swallow's nest. But the nest has been damaged by the storm and hangs dangerously close to the edge. He is surprised to find it intact at all.

Perched high up on the well-maintained ladder that has been positioned at exactly the right angle for the height, which he's calculated to be one unit *out* for every four units *up* according to the Health and Safety Executive guidance, Clayton is not afraid of falling. He's only ever fallen once before – and that was for his wife. The thought amuses him and he finds himself grinning as he watches her come back from her walk on the moor. Seeing her struggle with the five-bar gate makes him conscious of just how frail she has become these last few months. Whenever she leaves the house she looks as if she's lost another dress size by the time she comes back.

She is dishevelled, as if a gust of wind had viciously grabbed hold of her pony tail and tugged her all the way home. He watches her come to stand hesitantly at the bottom of the ladder where she looks up at him with apologetic eyes. Bang goes his plan of staying angry with her until she apologises. These days he can't open his mouth without being accused of something or other. He hardly knows how to act around her any more.

Sometimes this makes him angry. Angry enough to want to pack his bag and leave. Not forever. Just for a few days perhaps. But he only has to take one look at her troubled face to know he could never do this. How many times has she begged him never to leave? The thought of losing her terrifies him, too. He can't make it on his own. She is much stronger than him, even if she doesn't realise it. And when she sobs into her pillow at night, he wants to let her know how much he wants to *be* her pillow. Afterwards though, when she cries herself to sleep, he watches over her. It comforts him to see her chest rise and fall and to know she is still part of his life. Because when she stops breathing in her sleep, as she sometimes does, and her face goes all grey and ghostlike – he has to move away from her in the bed because she reminds him of… God no. He can't even think the word 'corpse' without being reminded… without seeing…

'You came back then.' Stating the obvious is something he's always been pretty good at, so he sticks with it.

'What are you doing?' She is actually smiling at him. A tad coyly perhaps, but it's a start.

'A bird's nest. Four swallow's eggs.' He sounds more of an expert than he is but he likes to impress her.

'You're not going to destroy them?' She is immediately protective. It doesn't take much for her maternal instinct to kick in.

'I'm actually making the nest safe,' he explains tolerantly. But she's not listening.

'This is as much their home as it is ours, Clay.' Now she's looking at him as if she's his mother; annoying the crap out of him again. *When did she get to be so whiney?*

'You always think the worst of me,' he tells her.

'I don't.'

'You do.'

She knows he's right and that there's no point denying it so he watches her search for something else to say instead.

'You should have come too.' She nods shakily in the direction of the moor. He can't tell if she means it or not.

'I didn't get an invite to *that* party,' he jokes. Then, as he comes down the ladder he is surprised to find her still waiting for him at the bottom. She even treats him to a grateful smile. He is pleased she is not going to continue with the argument; especially over something so small.

'Oh my God. The party,' she squeals suddenly, remembering that their guests are due in less than two hours.

Clayton shakes his head in astonishment as she disappears into the house; bellyaching about how much she still has to do. *How could she forget something so important?* he wonders.

Chapter 16

The gable end bedroom has three tall windows joined together that look out on the giant ash tree at the front of the house. The tree sheds leaves on the sills and takes up most of the window space. Its branches brush gently against the glass, as if unwilling to hurt it. The action reminds Avril of a mother brushing her child's hair, but she has no such fond memories to look back on.

Somebody, one of the removal men she suspects, has mistakenly left her wooden rocking chair in here – the one she usually reads in late at night when she can't sleep. She was going to have it in her own bedroom but it somehow feels right in here. *Sometimes furniture has a habit of choosing for itself and the sooner you realise it the better,* somebody once told her (Grace, probably). The ceiling is high and the walls are painted dove grey; a shade trending with most developers right now. But it is a callous colour, devoid of any warmth. *A colour that should only be used in morgues and funeral parlours,* she thinks morbidly.

Although it is well-lit and airy, the room has a false brightness, as if it is trying to hide a sadness only she can detect. Nevertheless, she feels at home here. The only thing she doesn't like is the sound of her slippers shuffling along the wooden floor. The shushing sound reminds her too much of Tommy's plimsolled feet in gym class.

Gazing around the room, Avril realises it isn't completely empty after all. A few unopened removal boxes have been pushed into a corner. Her heart speeds up when she realises that the one of the boxes has 'Tommy's things' written on it in bold black letters. Her mouth drops open when she sees that *Tommy's* box has already been opened and a child's fire truck pokes out of the top. It was one of his favourite toys, she remembers wistfully. They had spent many hours hunting for it when it was lost – under beds, in cupboards, in the garage, in the garden.

Tearing her eyes away from the gruesome reminder, Avril feels her skin prickle as she looks down and sees something in her hands that wasn't there a moment ago. Or perhaps it was? She has no idea. All she knows is, the blue woollen child's jumper she is holding is very precious – but she has no recollection of removing it from the box.

As she inhales on Tommy's jumper and fights back tears, Clayton appears in the open doorway. At first he has a hopeful smile on his face but this disappears as soon as he sees what she is doing. The disappointed look on his face is as familiar as her morning cup of tea.

'We talked about this.' He looks at the jumper in her hands as if he would also like to touch it but she knows he will never do this.

'Just this one. That's all I kept.' She hates how wheedling she sounds.

'We have to move on, Avril.'

She wants to ask *why?* Why is it so important they move on? Why can't they stay as they are now? grieving and mourning as if it only happened yesterday. The closer to grief she is, the closer she is to her son. She doesn't want it to lessen, because this would mean...

'I know,' she tells him instead, lowering her eyes so he will not see the untruth in them. She keeps the lie from him as she does so many other things.

'It doesn't feel right though, having the party without him.' She wants him to feel it as much as she does.

'It's too late to cancel now.'

Suddenly he is cold and distant. A stranger. Not the man she married. Not the proud father either. *But that reaction only lasted only until he found out Tommy was deaf,* Avril reflects bitterly. Avril has never met the Clayton that really matters. He's certainly never played his hand at the grieving father of a deaf child.

These days it's as if he wants to shrug her and Tommy off and revert back to his bachelor lifestyle; out with the guys from work – drinking and sending each other up all night. But he isn't as young or as fit as he used to be. *He will party himself to death if he isn't careful,* Avril realises sadly. And then a terrible thought enters her head that has never been there before. *That might not be such a bad thing,* the voice tells her. *Then, it would be just you and Tommy. Then, you would be free to grieve for him as much as you like.*

Glancing fearfully around the room, as if searching for the person who put such a dreadful idea in her head, Avril doesn't understand why her thoughts are spiralling out of control. If anything, before she came here, her therapist said she was doing much better. *How can I think such terrible thoughts about my own husband? I'd never want anything bad to happen to Clay.*

'This would have been his room.' The words are out of her mouth before she can stop them and she sees Clayton recoil as if he had just received a punch in the stomach. She gets the feeling that he wants to walk away but something is stopping him. There is something he *has* to know.

'We are okay, aren't we?'

What he really means is – is *she* okay? Or is she in danger of losing it again? He wants to know if he should call Dr Ribbons and have a quiet word. *I've lost a child. There is nothing wrong with me. Why can't anyone see that?* She wants to scream the words out loud but crushes that thought. If she starts any of that, he really will call her therapist.

'Of course,' she nods back at him, realising he doesn't believe it any more than she does.

Before either of them can do or say anything else, they are rescued by the sound of someone knocking at the door. The angry sound makes Avril jump.

Clayton throws her a smile that doesn't quite reach his eyes and walks away.

Still cradling the jumper, Avril crosses the room to peer out of the window. To her surprise, she sees their caller is none other than the man from the moor. Infuriatingly, he stands on her doorstep as if he has every right to be there.

Then, as if he knows he is being watched, he steps back from the porch and glares up at the window.

'Oh shit,' Avril jumps out of sight, not wanting his criminal glance to fall on her. But their eyes collide. She is surprised to find his are accusing as if she has stolen something from him.

How dare he darken my door. What on earth can he want? Suddenly realising Clayton is about to come face to face with this monster, she decides she'd better get downstairs to warn him of what he is up against.

Placing Tommy's jumper back in the box, Avril berates herself for not mentioning any of this before. Why didn't she tell Clayton about the big scary man from the moor when she had the chance? Intent on righting that wrong, she heads toward the door.

'Clayton,' she calls out in warning. Maybe he hasn't quite got to the door yet? She can't hear any voices in the hallway.

Then, without warning the door bangs shut, barring her way. It closes so viciously; Avril feels the cold draft slice across her face. She comes to an abrupt standstill. The door has not shut by itself, she realises.

Chapter 17

The man from the moor is in her kitchen. Having hoped never to set eyes on him again, she can hardly believe they have come face to face for the second time today. Only this time she is on home ground and he is the trespasser – except it doesn't feel that way. He might have convinced Clayton he dropped by to do his neighbourly duty, but he doesn't fool her. Arms folded crossly, Avril leans against the sink and eyes him suspiciously – hating the way he looks as if he belongs here. As he casually twirls a cigarette over in his fingers she notices how unruffled he appears under the glare of her hostility.

He looks like a wounded stag about to collapse by the side of a road, she thinks huffily. The smell coming off him reminds her of game being hung up to mature and his hands are scraped at the knuckles as if he has recently been in a fight.

When she first came downstairs to find him sitting in her kitchen, her first reaction was to feel relief that no blood had been shed and that Clayton was unharmed – but even so – she knows this man is bad news. She feels it in her heart. Further evidence of this is the way he sits at the kitchen table looking as if he is the head of a family about to carve up a Christmas turkey. She is glad they haven't yet got around to unpacking their set of carving knives.

'You'll have to go outside if you want to smoke.' She barks, surprised by her own daring. But her words have little effect on a man the size of Everest. The bulk of him even overpowers the enormous kitchen, making her feel small and inconsequential.

'Oh, I don't smoke. Not any more. I'm saving this...' he points the cigarette at her as if it is a gun, 'for when the world comes to an end.'

Watching him slip the cigarette back behind his ear, Avril darts a sly look at the door, on edge in case Clayton comes back in and on edge in case he *doesn't*. Realising he will think her barmy if she tells him about the door shutting in her face upstairs – she is even more reluctant to explain how she came across the man from the moor; and why she never mentioned him before. *Has it become so normal for me to keep things from my husband that I no longer know I'm doing it?*

Knowing her sensible other half is bound to come up with a logical explanation for what happened upstairs, when she struggled for a full five minutes to open the door before it finally opened by itself, she is equally sure it *cannot* be rationalised. *Something or someone wanted to keep me in that room. I am convinced of it. But as yet I cannot understand why.*

The man from the moor distracts her by shuffling uncomfortably in his seat and she watches him stretch out a leg as if is something he has to do often. She doesn't know his name yet, but when she does, she knows she will always think of him as *the man from the moor*. He isn't the kind of man who wants to be sat down for long, Avril supposes, not with that gammy leg. He is clearly in pain and trying to hide it. Sensing he is almost as disfigured by his rheumatic limbs as she is by her physical imperfections, Avril's fingers flutter unwittingly to the scars on her chest.

Although she suspects the man from the moor is not as dangerous as he first appeared, she still fears him and cannot find it in her heart to drum up any pity for him. Not just because she considers him an ogre; but because he can take pain relief to disguise his wrecked body and she cannot. His scars are not on public view the way hers are. But now she knows he is as human as the next person and that there is no danger of her dying at his hands today, she decides she no longer wants Clayton to find out what happened on the moor.

How the hell am I supposed to ask him not to mention anything? she wonders desperately, worried Clayton will come back in the room any second.

'About earlier…' she runs out of words too quickly.

'Alone on the moor, your mind can conjure up all sorts of peculiar things,' he says, in a voice not meant to carry. *Is he talking about the boy? Did he see him too?* she wonders.

'You being one of them?' she raises a cynical eyebrow.

'Touché.' He salutes her playfully as if he doesn't mind losing to a woman; but Avril can tell by his bogey-man smile that he doesn't like a smart arse.

She waits for him to say something else. His mouth opens to do just that and then it closes again. She is spellbound by the wet tongue that flicks out of his mouth, because it looks as if it's not in a hurry to be anywhere.

Clayton comes back in. His hair is ruffled and he has a bird dropping on the shoulder of his T-shirt that she hadn't noticed earlier. With one expert glance she can tell that his top hasn't been ironed; he's grabbed it out of the laundry basket and put it straight on. It dawns on her that he looks uncared for and this knowledge saddens her. *Why haven't I noticed this before?* Even so, next to the man from the moor, he appears clean, fresh, kind and good. Her Clayton... happily bouncing around like a beautiful Golden Retriever.

A dog with a twinkle in his eye, she corrects herself, because he has a bottle of whiskey in one hand and two glasses in the other. As Clayton clinks the glasses together and indicates the bottle, she watches the old man's eyes light up.

'Queen of The Moorlands. Best single malt as promised.' Clayton talks nineteen to the dozen as he pours out the whiskey and takes a seat at the table. When he gestures for Avril to join them, she shakes her head and his eyes cloud over a little. Unlike her, he doesn't seem worried by the old man. In fact, she suspects the reverse is true.

As she watches the old man take his first slug of the honey-coloured liquid, she is surprised to see a flicker of disgust pass over his face that he doesn't quite manage to hide. *If he doesn't like the taste, why doesn't he just say so?* she wonders irritably. At a couple of hundred quid per bottle, Moorland whiskey isn't cheap. Or maybe he just has more expensive taste? But judging by his rough country clothing and convict haircut she somehow doubts this. Feeling irritated by the pair of them – they are now discussing Yorkshire Ales from God's Own Country' and getting on like a house on fire – she decides she has heard enough. She can't stand around all evening worrying about an old man's drinking preferences.

'If you'll excuse me, I really am quite busy,' she announces in what she hopes is a sure fire way of getting their attention. *I want him out of my house, now...* she attempts telepathy on Clayton but this goes unnoticed.

Realising none of her tactics are going to work, she marches purposefully to the door. *To hell with it,* she fumes with every step; realising they are going to keep on ignoring her. It's only when she puts her hand on the doorknob to turn it, that the man from the moor pulls himself to his feet in an old-fashioned 'ladies present' sort of way. He makes a right meal of it, she notices. Even Clayton puts out a protective hand to steady him. *He was not like this on the moor*, she reminds herself. Out there he moved quickly and silently.

'Sorry if I spooked you earlier, on the moor.' The old man says, at last.

Hearing him apologise doesn't make up for anything; because now Clayton's questioning eyes are on her.

Chapter 18

The open windows let in the distinctive grassy aroma of the moorland, the smell most locals wish they could bottle, and the slight breeze carries with it garden scents such as mint and rosemary. The summer evening also brings with it a regular influx of bumble bees that swing wearily by, pausing on the window sill to rest their pollen-laden legs, before flying away again.

Doing her make-up in front of the dressing table mirror, Avril keeps a vigilant eye on the bees. As a child she believed they only made a buzzing sound when they were angry and can remember howling, 'Why are they always so mean?' and being comforted by a random adult, having been chased yet again by the stripy little blighters. The happy memory makes her smile. She has few such recollections of her childhood.

As yet there are no curtains flapping at the window and she likes it this way. Even with the windows open it is unbearably hot inside the bedroom but the sound of the grasshoppers chirping outside is getting on her nerves. Although it is still light and will be for another few hours, they will not be hoodwinked by summer daylight saving time. They still know when it's seven o'clock. She has always been intolerant of certain sounds and there must be a million grasshoppers out there right now all forming an orchestra to serenade her. For a minute she wonders what they can have to say to each other. It's not as if they lead very interesting lives. But they certainly like to gossip a lot.

Her antique dressing table mirror has a crack in it and the glass has gone misty, making it more difficult than it needs to be to do her make-up. It is as flawed as she is and this is just one of the reasons why she keeps hold of it. More importantly, it was gifted them by Clayton's parents, Pat and Colin, whose house is full of more of the same antiques and artefacts. Clayton calls them hoarders but really they are collectors of imperfect things and she's glad of this because they took her in as one of their own the first day she was introduced to them. One day, not too soon from now she hopes, they will inherit their bursting-at-the-seams Cornish cottage. It no longer saddens Avril that she has no such family heirlooms to inherit. She doesn't generally like old stuff anyway. She's often wondered about the family who owned her dressing table. They were living breathing people, too, at one time. People who loved and lied just as she and Clayton do now. She wonders if anyone else kept things hidden in the locked drawer the way she does. As she enjoys the distorted mirror's blurring effect on her reflection she remembers that this locked drawer is the other reason that she made the dressing table her own.

Viewing the rest of the room from its reflection in the mirror gives it an illusory feel; making their king size bed look squashier and more inviting than usual. She'd much rather curl up in it with a book and a glass of milk than have to go to a party, let alone host one. It's the last thing she feels like doing and Clayton knows this.

The embroidered patchwork quilt that straddles the bed was given to them soon after Tommy was born. It had taken Pat the whole nine months of Avril's pregnancy to stitch it by hand. There are a lot of memories wrapped up in the quilt. Sometimes she holds sections of it in her hands and breathes in the past, imagining the scent of her son's white towelling nappies or his spilt milk. After once spilling coffee on it, Clayton suggested they get it professionally cleaned and Avril had almost bitten his head off. *It would be like getting rid of a part of our son*, she'd protested.

They would often have Tommy in bed with them even though they'd been advised against it. Due to his deafness and other disabilities the doctors at Tommy's hospital said they should encourage their son to be independent but Avril had fiercely opposed this. Although she and Clayton often rowed about it, she loved nothing more than having her two favourite guys in bed with her at the same time.

There are no pictures of Tommy in this room. Both Clayton and Dr Ribbons agreed it was better that way. Once they had all moved on, they could start gradually introducing photos and keepsakes. Nobody knew that she kept a photo of him inside her reading book. She kept it in the locked drawer of her dressing table and looked at it whenever she was on her own. She doesn't need to slide the drawer out now to be staggered once again by how much her dead son resembles the child in the portrait downstairs. They are identical. Like twins. Avril knows there is a reason for this; but as yet she hasn't figured out what it means.

The sound of running water disturbs her thoughts. She'd almost forgotten about Clayton in the en suite bathroom. Supposing she'd better hurry up and finish her make-up, she applies the rest of her vivid blue eye shadow. Eighties chick transformation complete, she is surprised to find she likes her deliberately messed up blonde hair and piglet-pink cheeks.

'Pretty amazing guy I'd say. He must have a hundred and one stories to tell, being an ex-fire-chief and all,' Clayton calls out loudly from the en suite.

'The Chief! What a self-glorified name. I bet he gave it to himself.' Avril rolls her eyes at her husband, even though he cannot see her. There is no response from the bathroom other than the sound of Clayton turning off a tap. His silence makes her feel ashamed. It's not like her to be cruel or unkind. But… and it's a big but… 'He gives me the creeps. You didn't see the way he was… out on the moor.'

'The way he told it, you were the one who scared the hell out of him.'

Avril stares at her reflection and sighs. Her pout is every bit as impressive as the person she is meant to be – Debbie Harry. She then gets to her feet and admires her outfit. *Not bad*, she thinks, smacking her glossy lips together.

Then Clayton struts in to steal her thunder – looking as gorgeous as the real Simon Le Bon from Duran Duran with his mullet wig and oversized designer jacket with authentically rolled up sleeves. Underneath the jacket he wears a T-shirt with 'Wild Boy' printed on it.

'Just promise you didn't invite him to the party,' Avril grumbles.

'I promise,' he says throwing her a kiss that doesn't come anywhere close to landing in her direction.

Chapter 19

Avril stands alone with a glass pressed to her lips. She hopes nobody is going to try to rescue her. Doesn't know half the people here and the ones she does recognise... well they are Clayton's friends really, not hers. Suddenly feeling like an oddball at her own party she starts to jiggle her head to Blondie's track, 'The Tide Is High' hoping this will help her to blend in. If nothing else, she is determined to show Clayton she is capable of having a good time. Even if she's not talking to him right now.

She keeps one eye on the *reason* she isn't talking to him – The Chief – who mingles happily with their other guests, looking as if butter wouldn't melt.

He fits in better than I do, she observes crankily, watching The Chief's every move. Her observation ceases abruptly when something fast, blonde and giggly collides skittishly into her. Before Avril knows it, the only other person to have come as Debbie Harry, is clinging on to her as if they are old friends that go way back. The kind that share lipstick, perfume and tampons. Avril has never had such a friend before and doesn't need one now.

'Oops sorry,' the other Debbie Harry laughs tipsily, slipping her arm through Avril's and hiccupping loudly.

'But I couldn't help noticing we are practically twins dressed like this.'

Avril is aware that nothing could be further than the truth, and she does not like to be touched by strangers. She especially does not like to be touched by strangers who look as though they will keep on smiling even when they are dead. Sometimes she can barely tolerate her own husband's hands so it takes a lot for her to disengage herself without being rude.

'I'm Suzie,' the girl says in earnest, as if she rather thinks Avril should know this already.

'Of course you are.'

Suzie. Fun, flirty and definitely under thirty, Avril groans inwardly, already disliking her for having messier hair, glossier lips and pinker cheeks – not to mention a far sexier outfit. Suzie is as cute and playful as a kitten and Avril wishes she could shove her out of a cat flap and lock her out for good.

Avril is bothered by the way Suzie can't stay still, even for one minute; seeming able to talk, drink and dance all at the same time. When Suzie leans across Avril to point excitedly across the room, Avril avoids her Kitekat breath.

'Who's he? He's very good-looking isn't he? I wonder if he has an owner.'

Only mildly interested at first, Avril glances across the room to see *who* Suzie is pointing at, and is not that surprised to find her own husband is the one to have caught her eye. Her jealousy instantly aroused, Avril wishes Clayton didn't have such pulling power. *Clayton's mouth is a place where a lot of women would like to be.*

'Yes I suppose so,' she agrees stiffly.

Clayton is the life and soul of the party. He can't help be anything other than the centre of attention because people naturally gravitate toward him. Avril watches him pat The Chief on the back and sees how the old man's eyes light up.

Watching him and The Chief leave the room in search of Clayton's bawdy drinking mates, Avril becomes aware of somebody trying to get her attention and is relieved to see Grace hovering uncertainly in the doorway; looking horribly out of place in a long Kaftan, with a waist-length plait running down her back. *More 70s hippy than 80s party girl*, Avril groans inwardly. Nobody needs rescuing more than her best friend, she decides.

'Excuse me,' she is curter than intended with Suzie.

I don't like her, Avril thinks resentfully, as she hurries toward Grace, whose friendly full-moon face is all the more welcoming in a room full of husband-stealing strangers.

Chapter 20

Garlands of fairy lights hang from the large balcony at the back of the house. Although it looks directly out on the moor the landscape is invisible. It has faded to black in the background. The aroma of candles lingers in the air, mingling with the more traditional night-time scents of Yorkshire. Meanwhile, guests huddle around an outdoor fire which rages aggressively in a contemporary metal orb-shaped fire pit. Its bright orange flames reach out greedily – like the hands of needy children.

Grace and Avril stand apart from everybody else and stare at Clayton. He is surrounded by a group of his close friends. They each have a Special Brew in one hand and a tall story in the other. They are boozy and loud and only one man looks the odd one out, Avril realises with satisfaction.

'Who is that?' Grace asks in her cross Brown Owl voice.

Over the years Grace has met all of Clayton's friends so Avril doesn't have to guess which one she is referring to.

'You know Clayton, with his waifs and strays.' She shrugs dismissively.

Grace looks more closely at Avril, then back again to The Chief, who bothers her in the same way a late-night knock at the door might.

'People are often kinder to stray animals than they are to the people who matter most,' she says with significance.

'I'm so glad you're here,' Avril sighs contentedly.

Knowing Grace remains loyal to *her*, no matter how fond of Clayton she is, is what counts. They both owe her a lot. Look at how she helped them through their loss – cooking, shopping and mowing the lawn. She'd even left casseroles on the doorstep when Avril refused to get out of bed or answer the door. The Chief can laugh at Clayton's jokes all he likes but he will never take Grace's place in their heart.

Unnervingly, their eyes meet. Hers and The Chief's. And it seems to her that he can read her thoughts because he looks at Avril as if he'd like to get his own back on her for thinking such thoughts. Then, in a split second he's back in character – a harmless old guy who is trying to fit in and make new friends.

'When do you start the new job?' Grace wants to know.

'Two days' time – and I'm absolutely terrified.'

'Don't be. You've got nothing to be afraid of'

Avril's gaze lingers pointedly on The Chief and her smile vanishes. *I'm not so sure that's true,* she thinks uneasily.

Chapter 21

From where he is standing, on the opposite side of the balcony to his wife, Clayton can see what she cannot – a thousand stars twinkling in the distance. To him, they appear like silver coins on a black jewellery cloth. Although his knowledge of the galaxy is limited, he would like to bet if his wife was an astronomical body, she'd be made of dark matter. He doesn't resent Avril for holding onto her grief as if it is her only friend, but he'd much rather be the one to hold her hand.

As it is, he is surrounded by people who no longer matter. Once upon a time his friends might have been important to him, but not anymore. He doesn't mind hanging out with them now and again and having a laugh but he can do that with strangers any night of the week. He's always been able to make friends instantly. Some of the old crowd sense his detachment. Crusher, for instance, who has always been needy and dependent, has gone all sulky and weird on him. Clayton suspects he is also jealous of the attention he is lavishing on The Chief. But he will have to deal with it. They are no longer the men they once were. Crusher is already twice divorced and bitter enough for a dozen jilted men. *He wants to stop moaning about how much child support he has to pay for his kids,* Clayton complains inwardly. *I'd give anything to have to cough up a few hundred quid each month for the chance to see…* he stops himself there, before it hurts too much. Before he really does tell Crusher a few home truths.

Listening to The Chief is better than watching an episode of *Crimewatch* but Clayton can't help wondering how much of the heroics are really true. Could he really have rescued so many people from house fires or come across as many dead bodies in blazing buildings? For a moment Clayton finds himself conjuring up images of smouldering corpses that have been burnt to death. *What an absolutely agonising way to die*, he reflects morbidly, imagining what it must be like. But thinking of dead bodies isn't good for him because he only has to close his eyes to see his son lying there…

Chapter 22

The last twenty-four hours have seen Avril's world change in more ways than she bargained for. Suddenly there are two people in her life that weren't in it before – The Chief and the walking mantrap that is Suzie. When the kitchen door opens and The Chief comes in, she groans inwardly and goes on impaling cheese and pineapple on cocktail sticks. Why hadn't she and Clayton made the most of every moment together when they had the chance? Their first night at Swallow's Nest might not have been the resounding success they wished for but she longs to have it back again – like a souvenir in her pocket.

Although she has her back to him, she is highly sensitive to The Chief's movements and senses, rather than sees, him scrape back a chair and sink gratefully into it. When she turns, his look of exhaustion already feels as familiar as the antique knife in her hand. The one with the gleaming copper blade.

There is a peculiar taste in the roof of her mouth that she cannot spit out. Even her saliva tastes of smoky wood. Every time she inhales, it feels as if smoke is filling her lungs, causing her to panic. *It must be the outdoor fire.* Even her hair has gone all frizzy as if singed and the make-up on her face is wilting fast. It feels as if the house has been put on a stove and is slowly bubbling away, waiting to boil over and erupt at any minute. The thought frightens her.

Before The Chief came in, she'd been stabbing at the cheese and pineapple in exactly the same way a jealous wife might attack a rival, but now she is much calmer. It wouldn't do for him to see her take her anger out on the finger food. But it still hurts that Suzie has stolen her gloomy, grieving thunder. *I was meant to be the only Debbie Harry at the party*, she thinks murderously.

'Clayton told me what happened. What you've been through,' The Chief is the first to break the silence.

'Well, he shouldn't have.' She will not let him see her surprise, even if her arched back speaks for itself. *Clay never talks about Tommy to anyone. Why would he choose to spill his heart out to this crotchety old man?*

'It's not good to bottle things up,' he says.

Now, Avril does turn around. Just in time to catch him pushing his beer away. Once again there is a look of revulsion on his face as if he can't stand the taste. She wonders why he drinks at all if he doesn't like it. *He does it to fit in*, she finally realises. Putting down the knife, she folds her arms and gives The Chief her full attention.

'And when Clayton told you all this… did he say *it*… this thing… happened to us, or just me?' When Avril sees the old man's eyebrows meet in the middle of his grumpy forehead, she laughs cynically. 'He did, didn't he? I'm right.'

At that moment the door flies open and a line of conga dancers headed by Clayton and Suzie tumble in. Before the beat of Black Lace's 'Conga' even registers in her mind, Avril's scolding glance seeks out Clayton's hands. She'd burn them off Suzie's waist if she could. Although Clayton grins and waves at her and The Chief in passing, she is quick to notice that his smile doesn't reach his eyes.

As the conga procession exits out of another door, Avril leans against the island in the centre of the room and sighs despondently. Clayton has found Suzie. Just as she knew he would. Or perhaps Suzie found him? It doesn't really matter which way around it happened.

She grabs a tumbler from the dishwasher, goes to the black coffin-like fridge freezer and fills it with milk. She then takes it to the table and places it none too gently in front of The Chief so that it spills onto the table. She takes away the beer bottle and goes back to standing at her island.

'It's not me who's holding it all in. Pretending it hasn't happened.' The words are out of her mouth before she can stop them. 'That's what's so scary.'

For a long time, he doesn't say anything. She watches him take a tentative sip of the milk; soon followed by a more confident gulp. Seeing the white frothy liquid on his whiskery face reminds her of a kitten tasting milk for the first time. *But he is no playful pussycat,* she reminds herself cautiously.

'Sometimes when you're scared of something, the feeling gets so bad you want to take it by its throat.' The Chief tells her, pausing for effect. He doesn't need to. His words mesmerise her. Thrill her even. 'Then, you have to put it out of its misery like you would a rabid dog.' The Chief squeezes his hands together as if he really would like to press them against somebody's windpipe... hers, most probably. It's as if he has personal experience of what he is describing and this thought sends a chill down Avril's spine. 'And the fear goes with it.' He snaps his fingers as if nothing could be simpler.

Is he suggesting I kill Clayton? Avril's mind whirls with panic. Yet the idea doesn't seem quite as outrageous as it should and this scares her even more than his words.

'What are you suggesting?' she demands fiercely, determined to get back on track. It's up to her to put him in his place. It's her house. Her party. Her husband. Her fear.

The Chief leans back in the chair and appraises her. For a moment, she thinks he's about to put his bad-tempered old legs up on the table but he doesn't quite dare.

'Just saying.' He shrugs his shoulders and throws back the last of the milk before belching silently. 'And what about Clayton? What is it that scares him?' he asks casually.

Avril shakes her head as if to imply nothing on this earth could frighten her husband. She isn't about to feed him everything on a plate like it's his Sunday roast. She must keep him guessing a little longer even if Clayton has filled the old man in on most stuff anyway.

'Not even losing you?' The Chief isn't easily fooled.

'Ever since he found out Daleks can't climb stairs he hasn't been afraid of anything.' She says this with a hint of a smile, enjoying the way The Chief's face screws up into a scowl that reminds her of a clenched fist.

'Just saying,' she says innocently, turning her back on him once again.

Chapter 23

The house has not yet imprinted itself on Avril. She is still to count the exact number of steps on the stairs and work out how to open and close the sash windows without losing a finger. She might not yet be able to find her way blindfolded around the upper floor but one thing she can sense is its growing acceptance of her. So far, every step she has taken has seemed to offend it. Every touch of her fingers has made it flinch. But tonight, filled with so many strangers, it seems to be reaching out for what it finds familiar. *It doesn't welcome this intrusion any more than I do*, she realises and this knowledge makes her warm toward it.

The music of Michael Jackson's 'You Are Not Alone' vibrates ironically around the house and she can't help thinking, *Not true. I'm always alone. Even at parties.* Especially now Grace has gone. For the third time tonight, she checks that their bedroom door is locked. She can't bear the thought of anyone wondering in here or sitting on the bed where Tommy used to lay his head. It still breaks her heart to remember the times when his frustration made him violent or when Clayton had to hold him down to prevent him lashing out.

Now that Tommy is no longer with them – it's Avril who finds herself wanting to lash out. Just seeing the door at the end of the landing (the one that would have been Tommy's), makes her angry. She is tempted to go inside and shut the door on the rest of the world so she can sit in the rocking chair and stare out at the large ash tree instead. *But that's not what I came upstairs for*, she reminds herself, fearing she will risk upsetting Clayton if she abandons their guests. *But as usual he is nowhere to be seen.* She doesn't want to think about what he could be up to.

She peers over the wooden balustrade to see if she can spot his blond head bobbing about below. But all she can see are two 'Frankie Goes to Hollywood' types snogging on the bottom step of the stairs. Their fake moustaches make it difficult for them to kiss properly and impossible for her to tell what gender they are. Although this shouldn't matter, Avril finds herself wondering what Clayton can have in common with such people. *This party is a joke*, she seethes. *It's not like we're in our twenties anymore. I bet he doesn't know half of the people here either.*

Her sweat-soaked hand almost slides off the stair rail as she descends the stairs. The fear of rejection and humiliation nudges her down each step like badly-behaved twin sisters. *I've never known it so hot*, Avril protests inwardly, wiping the perspiration from her brow. She hates the crush of bodies and the way the music grows louder as she squeezes past the leather-clad couple on the bottom step. The thumping beat of the music vibrates through her entire body until even the little toes on her feet start to arch in protest. There is an overwhelming smell of sweat and bad breath that reminds her of school shower blocks. It is far worse than the fishy smell that gets up her nose every time she enters the sitting room. She heads in that direction now without thinking. *I can't stand this heat and noise.* Avril tosses her sticky hair, hoping for the slightest of draughts to cool her down.

For someone like Avril, who doesn't like to touch or be touched by strangers, it is doubly hard for her to push her way through a room full of people. She watches the grey fog of cigarette smoke leave people's mouths in sarcastic swirls and can't make out one shadowy face from another. Most of their guests are aware of the house ban on smoking but this is being ignored and she rather suspects the seaweed smell invading her nostrils means somebody has also dared light up a joint. She blames Clayton. If he was here their guests wouldn't be taking such liberties. Avril is about to protest when somebody turns the music up again and she is forced to clasp her hands to her head. Her ears might be small, like an arctic fox's, but they are highly sensitive to sound. She remembers the beep, beep, beep of the truck and fights against the memory.

That's when she notices the vibration of the music is causing her arrangement of framed family photographs to bounce up and down. Even the juddering ceiling lights seem to object to the sound and flicker on low power one minute and full the next. She's sure the bulbs are about to explode and rain down on their heads but nobody else seems to notice. As usual, whenever she enters this room, her hair has gone static with electricity and the fishy smell is back in her nostrils; fighting for supremacy over the cigarette smoke – and winning.

Her eyes are drawn to *The Crying Boy* portrait on the wall. It judders with every thump, thump, thump of the music and once again her heart skips a beat. TOMMY. And then… *Not now. Not now,* she warns herself. *Time enough for that later. Right now I really need to find Clayton.*

'Has anybody seen Clayton?' she shouts nervously; aware her high-pitched voice is drowned out by the beat of the music. But her plea falls on deaf ears; even though they are all hearing people. She touches the shoulder of a guy dressed like Boy George, but he shrugs her off as if he objects to being mauled by her nasty fingers. 'I was just wondering if you've seen Clayton?' she says apologetically.

'Who is Clayton?' *His voice is as sharp as a pocket knife,* Avril decides, watching him turn his back on her. Once again, she asks herself, *Who are these people? And why did Clay invite them?* Then, taking a few steps back from the party-goers, Avril finds herself back in the same corner of the room she started off in. *Why did Grace have to leave so early?* Fighting back tears, Avril tries to zoom in on a friendly face but there is nobody in the room she can turn to. Nobody except– but she has to stop her imagination running riot. She knows it is not possible for a painting to be willing her to look its way.

Wearily, she closes her eyes, longing to be anywhere else but here. That's when she hears it…

Suzie. Suzie. Suzie.

The ghostly whisper wraps itself around Avril, like an expensive fur coat might. She is burning up. She can't breathe. Eventually, the music backs off like a timid guard dog, all bark and no bite. People are breathing on her. Hands are pawing her. The blackness she fears is almost upon her.

Chapter 24

Huddled around the outdoor fire, Clayton and Suzie watch its twin flames entwine intimately like a couple on a dance floor. Everybody else has gone inside, beaten off by blood-thirsty mosquitoes that have fled back to wherever they came from with big satisfied bellies. Clayton has never met anyone quite as playful as Suzie. She reminds him of a young Marilyn Monroe because underneath the false eyelashes and fake tan she is adorable.

He watches her inhale on an extra-long cigarette which has her bright pink lipstick stamped on it. She looks up at him in a very practised way and blinks innocently, delighted with her own flirty behaviour. Really, she could be the poster girl for any dating campaign but the really touching thing about her is that she does it inoffensively. Everything about her behaviour suggests that she doesn't take herself seriously.

'What are you thinking about right now?' She points an intoxicated finger at him and the tip of her painted nail slides down his shirt very close to his nipple, making him shiver involuntarily.

That I'm a married man. That I love my wife. That I need to sober up, Clayton thinks to himself. But rather than bore Suzie with all this detail he simply smiles apologetically.

'That we should go back inside,' he tells her.

But when he next looks up, she is so much closer than she was before and he suspects this has always been her intention. He feels her hot breath on his arm and his skin prickles pleasurably. It doesn't matter what his mind is saying. His body is telling him something completely different. But he's no longer a teenage boy ruled by hormones, he reminds himself sternly. He's a grown man with responsibilities.

'Suzie,' he protests, trying to unhook himself from her clutches. Then, aware that she is studying him, he watches her already dark blue eyes turn the colour of midnight. She sighs heavily as if she likes being in the circle of his arms and he senses that she is in need of some protection. Her vulnerability is far more dangerous than her other more obvious female attributes.

She reaches for her glass and takes an unfeminine gulp of something fizzy, before clumsily wiping the sparkly residue from her mouth. There are pink lipstick marks all around the rim of the glass so that it looks as if half a dozen women have been drinking from it. She knocks back the last of her drink, as if to suggest she is going to be busy doing other things for the next half hour, and then balances the glass precariously on the fire surround. In spite of the compromising position he finds himself in, Clayton wills the glass not to fall. He cannot bear this reckless kind of behaviour. The glass could overheat and burn her beautiful mouth the next time she picks it up.

Unaware of what dull thoughts are racing around his overcautious head, Suzie leans into him. Unlike Avril, she is not excessively thin. She has curves in all the right places and judging by the way the blue material stretches over her chest – she is not flat-chested like his wife. As soon as this treacherous thought enters Clayton's head he berates

77

himself. *How can I think such things? What an arsehole.* But he cannot shake off the truth. He is more than a little tempted because he is more than a little drunk. It's okay if this happens and he does nothing to encourage her, he tells himself.

Suddenly aware that the tempo of the music coming from inside has changed, he realises that Duran Duran has been replaced with a more current Leona Lewis track that definitely didn't make his 80s party soundtrack. He wonders momentarily who has put it on? But as Suzie seems to like it he decides it doesn't matter.

'You don't like people getting close to you, do you?' she mews like a disappointed kitten, 'especially uninvited ones.' He assumes she is referring to the fact she has somehow gate-crashed this party, but he doesn't want to be reminded of this right now. All he can think about is her touching him again. She knows this. He can see it in her eyes. He also knows she will not go any further without some sort of invitation. He has been rumbled. Transparent fool that he is. He realises now that he hasn't protested nearly enough for a married man.

'Sometimes I like it very much,' he says at last, wondering if her mouth will taste of sparkling wine.

***

Avril stares at *The Crying Boy*. It stares back. She mouths the words to the song playing on the hi-fi and remembers it is by Leona Lewis. The title of the track is 'Fire Under My Feet' and she remembers it being played on the radio during the car journeys they made back and forth to Swallow's Nest. Both she and Clayton had liked the song, she recalls, but he had sung along to the words and she had not. They both knew this was because she hated leaving behind the town house in Wellington Road, Leeds, and he did not.

The crowd in the sitting room has quite disappeared and Avril is alone with the street urchin in the painting, whose eyes reveal real torment. There is such a look of persecution and fear on the boy's vagabond face that Avril can't help wondering what he has endured. For one so young and innocent, there is an equal measure of spite and hostility in the watery blue eyes and she is once again reminded of Tommy when he was in a pet. When she closes her eyes, Avril isn't at all surprised to find the darkness of her mind is now occupied, not by Clayton, but by the boy in the painting *and* her son.

Suddenly there's an almighty rumble followed by the sound of a woman screaming and both the candles and the sitting room lights go out. Avril's eyes fly open in time to see *The Crying Boy* portrait crash to the floor. Among confusion and fear, the party-goers rush outside to find out where all the screaming is coming from and Avril finds herself involuntarily carried along with them. Although she remains at the back of the throng crowding onto the balcony, she arrives in time to see Clayton patting Suzie's arm and trying to console her. It comes as no surprise to Avril to find her husband out here alone with Suzie. All along she had known where to find him.

'It's okay, folks. Her sleeve caught on the fire, that's all.' He tells everyone reassuringly, although his voice is unmistakably shaky.

'*That is not all.*' Avril thinks angrily, refusing to respond to the appeal in Clayton's guilt-ridden face as his eyes seek her out in the crowd.

Chapter 25

Although the house is still in chaos, all of their disgruntled guests have now dispersed due to Clayton's black mood, which engulfed him as soon as the lights came back on. Now that the 80s decorations have been ripped down – the only evidence that a party took place is the trail of trodden in peanuts and cigarette ash.

Deciding it really doesn't matter where her own ash falls, Avril inhales rebelliously on a cigarette (left behind by one of their guests), and gazes at *The Crying Boy* that has been re-hung erratically on the wall. She tips it to one side and takes a step back to make sure it is straight.

Clayton comes to a halt in the doorway and his downcast eyes are immediately drawn to the cigarette in her fingers but for once she doesn't care. Tonight the cigarette is more important than his disappointment.

'I thought you'd quit, given up?' he quizzes her.

'I thought *you* had.'

Clayton is the first to lower his eyes. They both know they are not talking about something as simple as a cigarette.

'Nothing happened.' Clayton says, continuing to hover in the doorway as if he needs permission to enter.

'I'm gutted for you,' Avril sucks hungrily on the cigarette, hating the way the smoke gets in her eyes, making them water unexpectedly.

As if he would bury his head in her lap and plead for forgiveness, Clayton cautiously enters the room. *Cap-in-hand, like a regular unfaithful husband*, Avril can't help thinking.

'I've never cheated on you, Avril.'

Before either of them can misunderstand the other or turn their faces away through fear of conflict or irreconcilable differences, there is a tap on the sitting room door.

'Any chance of a nightcap?' The Chief limps into the room. Frustrated by this unwanted interruption, Avril is annoyed at how relieved Clayton is to see him.

'We thought everybody had gone.' Clayton says nervously, not wanting to meet Avril's eyes.

'Taking a walk, that's all. Good for the old rheumatism.' When he's finished drawing attention to his limp, The Chief looks around for a seat and when he isn't immediately offered one he frowns in the way confused pensioners do when they don't understand what is happening to them.

He'll have to do far more than that to gain my sympathy, Avril wishes she could turn off the spiteful thoughts in her head. Since coming to Swallow's Nest she hardly recognises herself. When did she get to be so mean and vindictive?

'Coffees all round then,' Clayton says awkwardly, just before exiting the room.

Avril pointedly turns her back on The Chief and gazes at *The Crying Boy* instead. Although mesmerised by the boy's piercing blue eyes, she is aware that The Chief continues to observe her closely. This reminds her of the way the doctors and Clayton used to look at her after Tommy died.

'His name was Don Bonillo,' The Chief says from behind her, surprising the hell out of her. He is so close she can feel his gamey breath on the back of her neck and it makes her skin crawl. Wondering how he can have gotten so close without her knowing, she turns around to confront him. Her eyes burn with curiosity at the sudden revelation. *Don't stop. Don't stop.* She wills him to go on.

Chapter 26

Clayton has fallen drunkenly asleep at one end of the sofa; his head turned away from the heat of the log fire. When his mouth twitches momentarily into what looks like a smile, Avril's blood boils. *He'd better not be thinking about Suzie.* She never again wants to smell the girl's cheap perfume on her husband's shirt. Despite everything, she still loves him. She wonders if there is anything he can do that would make her stop. They have been through so much together. Surely they can outsmart one drunken night of temptation.

If The Chief wasn't here she'd be tempted to crawl onto the sofa next to him and pull his head into her lap. She used to love whispering her secrets out loud to him when he was asleep. In those moments she felt close to him. No matter that he couldn't hear her. Hearing isn't all it's cracked out to be. She and Clayton had found this out together.

The firelight dances on Avril's face, warming her cheek. The chill of the moor at night creeps into her bones, making her crave warmth. She is wearing Clayton's hand-knitted sweater, which smells of him. Not Suzie, she's relived to find. Her legs are tucked up under her on a single armchair and her alert eyes are settled on The Chief who sits at the opposite end of the sofa from Clayton,

83

massaging his rheumatic leg. She notices The Chief's eyes keep flickering to *The Crying Boy*, whose own eyes appear to have narrowed in temper. This is exactly how Tommy used to look when he needed a nap.

'Go on, Chief.' She is unable to hide her frustration at how slow he is to reveal his story. She finds this surprising when her role as teacher requires unending patience. The Chief certainly brings out the worst in her.

'He was a street urchin found wondering around Madrid by the artist known as Bragolin. Anyway…' The Chief sighs dramatically as if it is a struggle to go on but Avril senses he is playing with her. He clearly wants to tell his story. He just wants to do it at his pace. Not hers. 'A local Catholic priest told Bragolin the child had run away after seeing his parents die in a blaze.'

On hearing this, Avril's pity for the child is immediate. The agony of what he has been through is something she can entirely relate to. *This can't just be a coincidence*, she tells herself. She can see him now, in her head, hiding among bales of straw with tears running down his dirty face. He has run into a barn to escape the blaze and the unbearable sight of his parents calling out for help as they burn.

'He told the artist to have nothing to do with the runaway because wherever he settled fires would mysteriously break out.' Again The Chief's hooded eyes are drawn to the boy in the painting and this time Avril sees real fear in them. She wriggles in her seat, desperate for him to go on. 'Because of this the locals called him Diablo, or devil,' he tells her.

Realising that superstition and fear must have played a huge part in all of this folklore, Avril still finds it difficult to comprehend how anyone could have treated an innocent child so cruelly. *How could anyone give such a name to a baby?*

'Ignoring the superstitious priest, Bragolin decided to beat the curse out of the boy.'

Oh my God, it just gets worse, Avril thinks miserably. Somehow she has acquired one of the squashy cushions in her lap and she hugs it for comfort. She can picture Bragolin taking off his belt and lashing out at the cowering child.

'He painted him anyway.' The Chief stabs a finger at the portrait. 'The paintings made Bragolin rich but one day his studio burned to the ground and the boy was accused of arson.'

Liking this turn in the narrative, Avril delights in imagining Bragolin roar with anger as he watched his paintings go up in flames. Before she even has chance to ask, *what happened to the boy?* The Chief second guesses her.

'He ran off crying and was never seen again. Turns out he never spoke and was thought to be a mute.'

'So he was deaf, like Tommy?' Stunned by this discovery, Avril locks eyes with the boy in the painting.

'What happened to him?' She whispers anxiously; her eyes roaming over to Clayton, who is in no danger of waking up just yet. For this she is grateful. He wouldn't like her hearing this. On that thought, she realises The Chief has deliberately saved the best for last.

'Then, from all over Europe came the reports of the *cursed* Crying Boy painting causing fires. Bragolin was regarded as jinxed and nobody would look at his paintings again,' he tells her. 'And in 1976 a car exploded on the outskirts of Barcelona. The victim was burnt beyond recognition but a driving licence confirmed it was 19-year-old Don Bonillo.'

A log on the fire suddenly splinters and crackles. Flakes of red hot wood spit into the room, narrowly missing The Chief. He looks suspiciously at the portrait and shudders.

'Nobody ever came forward to claim the body.'

Chapter 27

Wearing an oversized shirt of Clayton's that has been discarded because it is missing some buttons, Avril is in the middle of a big clean-up operation. She wears rubber gloves and scrubs at the kitchen table, not liking the ashy taste on her tongue caused by last night's smoking. Her throat burns, too, as if she's coming down with something, and when she comes into contact with leftover food she gags as if she has just swallowed a dead mouse.

She hears Clayton's whistling long before he comes into the room and can only suppose he's going to keep up this fake cheerfulness until she forgives him. It's his way of reassuring her they are on track. Grabbing a mop, she moves it over the floor, wanting something else to look at when he comes in. But when he does breeze in, she can't help noticing how unruffled he looks in a crisp shirt and conservative slacks. This is such a different look to his everyday work wear that she can't help wondering what he might be up to. Then she remembers their appointment and immediately feels guilty.

Avril watches Clayton open the fridge door and drink straight from the milk bottle. Unlike most wives, she does not mind. Out of the two of them Clayton has always been way fussier than her. But she does stop mopping to stare at him, feeling very much like Cinderella in rags compared to his Prince Charming. It is only when he starts to walk across her just-mopped floor that he comes to a surprised halt, as if he has only just noticed her.

'What's the hurry?' He points at the mop in her hand. 'I thought the new cleaner was starting today.'

He has no idea how difficult it has been to find a cleaner willing to trudge all the way out here. Three of them had walked into the sitting room, glanced around, spotted *The Crying Boy* and skedaddled. Avril had no choice but to take on a woman with no references who demanded double the hourly rate for her trouble.

'I don't want to frighten her off like the others.'

Clayton shrugs and moves away. As far as he's concerned, he's done his duty, shown an interest.

'Clay? About last night?' She stalls him. Watches his back stiffen and his shoulders freeze.

'I've already told you nothing happened with Suzie.' He still won't meet her eye, she notices miserably. 'I was just a bit drunk, that's all, and I've already apologised.' He might as well have said 'I don't know what else I'm supposed to do.'

Stop flirting with other women, she wants to scream, but doesn't. Strange how she's already over this. Usually she'd drag out something like this for days, if not weeks, making sure she got her money's worth out of Clayton's slip-ups. But suddenly his near-infidelities don't concern her anywhere near as much as they used to. Or at least they're not top of her priority list right now.

'I meant about The Chief. What he told us last night about *The Crying Boy.*'

'You didn't believe any of that rubbish, did you?' Clayton laughs derisively.

'You're the one who said he was worth listening to,' she reminds him tartly.

Juggling the mop, she folds her arms crossly, wanting him to know how annoyed she is that he won't take her seriously. But instead of apologising, she watches his eyes crinkle at the corner in an amused way. Sometimes, like now, she'd like to wipe the smugness from his face. Aware she has so much ammunition to hit him with, in order to do just that, she guiltily retracts this thought.

'I've got to go. Catch you later.' He tells her, blowing her a kiss.

'You haven't forgotten our appointment, have you?' she can't resist checking, just in case.

Clayton pauses. Of course he's forgotten. But she'd been so sure he hadn't. Why else would he be dressed in smart trousers and a shirt instead of the usual jeans and T-shirt?

'It's in my diary,' he assures her, tapping his shirt pocket. It's true. She can see the indent where his pocket-sized diary is kept. She must have read him wrong – misjudged him – but she will not apologise for this.

'Enjoy your last day of freedom,' he says as an afterthought, ruffling her already messed-up hair before exiting the kitchen. It infuriates Avril, the way he treats her like she's his sister. Frustrated with him. Herself. The move. The Chief. Suzie. And a hundred-and-one other things. Avril glances around the trashed room and feels overwhelmed.

Her ears prick up when she hears the sound of Clayton's van start up. But then, another quite different and totally unexpected racket has her jumping out of her skin. Beep, beep, beep – the smoke alarm has gone off again. Avril screws up her face until it's as wrinkled as the mop she's holding.

'Not again,' she groans.

Grabbing a tea towel from the drainer she marches into the boiler room and wafts the fabric under the smoke alarm's nose.

Chapter 28

Glancing at the Gant watch Avril bought him for his thirtieth birthday, Clayton drives along the Halifax Road wondering how on earth he's going to fill his day. He has nine whole hours before he can return home, and so far, he only has two appointments lined up. One is to do a rewiring quote for a local builder in Keighley and the other is to install a new circuit board for a landlord in Pudsey.

Of course he has no real intention of keeping his other appointment; the one Avril couldn't resist reminding him of. He figures she knows this anyway. It is just a charade they play each time something like this crops up. They both know he will duck out of it at the last minute. Later, Avril will no doubt tick him off but she won't really want him to feel bad about not turning up. Some things she is better at, *like talking*, than he is. His own father is the same. Neither of the Shaw men like being coerced.

Yet that is exactly what he had allowed to happen to him last night. Avril might not believe it, but he had already made up his mind *not* to kiss Suzie when that blasted painting crashed to the ground and all the lights went out, causing Suzie's sleeve to catch on fire. If he didn't know better, he'd swear the creepy painting did it on purpose, just so he'd get caught red-handed. He knows it wasn't fair to lead Suzie on the way he did and it certainly isn't fair on Avril who has been through so much. It is hardly her fault she ended up marrying some dumb egotistical bloke who can't turn down the advances of a pretty woman. *What an idiot I've been*, Clayton groans, pulling a face at himself in the rear view mirror.

I'll make it up to her, he promises himself. *I'll take her home something nice. Something really special.* Just as he's racking his brain to think of an original gift, Clayton spots a sign outside a pair of pebble-dashed houses and pulls alongside so he can read it in more detail. He is pleased to observe a twitching behind the curtains which means somebody is at home. Clayton figures he can get Avril's present sorted right now and collect it on the way home. She is always urging him to be more spontaneous and he figures he can't get more spur-of-the-moment than this. So without stopping to think, he gets out of the car and makes his way up the path to the house with the sign. Already he can see the figure of a woman coming to the door behind the decorative glass.

'Avril will love it,' he thinks, congratulating himself for settling on something so perfect so soon.

Chapter 29

Having given up any pretence at clearing up, Avril stands in front of *The Crying Boy* portrait and stares into the child's suffering eyes. Constantly drawn to the dirty urchin's face, she hasn't moved for the last five minutes. She can't stop thinking about how similar their pasts may have been or how he must have suffered all the way through his miserable childhood.

Now she knows his name, the barriers between them have been broken down. The child in the painting is not Tommy, she knows this now. Nor is her dead son trying to communicate with her through the painting as she first imagined. But that doesn't mean the crying boy isn't in need of her pity and love, the same as any child. *The fact that he looks like Tommy only makes me warm to him all the more.* She tries out the Spanish sounding name on her mouth 'Don Bonillo' and it feels weirdly familiar; as if she has spoken it out loud many times.

She has a bin bag full of party leftovers in her hand but doesn't notice when some of the contents spill out on to the floor. So far today, she has retched at the first whiff of leftover prawn sandwiches but all she can inhale now is smoke. The smell is everywhere, she decides. Up her nose, in her hair and on her clothes. Aware that the closer she gets to the painting, the hotter she becomes, Avril has to convince herself this is real. *I am not imagining this.* Now they are almost touching – face to face as it were – and her face glistens with sweat. Already her hair is full of static electricity and has lifted off her shoulders as if it has a mind of its own. The fair hairs on her arms curl up, as if they have been caught in a ball of fire. Life with Clayton has left her unsure of many things. Yet today, she has never felt more confident in what she is seeing and feeling. For once she does not doubt her own thoughts. The child is imprinting on her. She knows this. She senses it. She even welcomes it.

She does not experience fear, only awe, as her hand reaches out to touch him. Her shaky fingers settle on his face and she gently caresses the tears in his eyes.

'What did they do to you?' she asks, taking one step back from the overwhelming heat.

The painting then judders against the wall and an angry sound rages above her, as if a whirlwind has gotten into the house. A terrifying crashing comes from upstairs and the vibration is felt throughout the entire building. Never before has Avril heard anything quite so furious with itself and she wants to run from it but finds she cannot. It is the same noise they heard on their first drunken night at Swallow's Nest. The night they first unearthed the painting. *The Crying Boy* had called out to them that night, just as it is doing now, she realises in astonishment. In recognition of this, her hand flies to her heart and she is reassured by its agitated beating.

'Deaf and mute. And never shown any pity. I wonder if you ever learned to–'

As Avril's heart fills with compassion for the child, her very active mind begins to mull something over. An idea has just occurred to her that most normal people would consider insane. But to Avril it makes perfect sense. *Why on earth didn't I think of it sooner?* Then, making a decision she will not be able to undo – if she's right (and it's a very big if) – she uses sign language to communicate with the portrait.

'Do you like to play?' Avril signs and speaks at the same time, using facial expressions to liven up an otherwise silent language, just as she's been taught to. As she waits for a response – *please make it happen* – she becomes aware of a deathly silence settling on the room. She has never known the house be so quiet. There is no leaking tap, no hum of the fridge freezer coming from the kitchen and no bird song echoing down the chimney. Then she realises the house is holding its breath and waiting – just as she is.

There is a long pause during which nothing happens and Avril begins to doubt herself again. *Maybe I did imagine it after all?* There must be hundreds of people like her, she realises, who can feel the eyes of a portrait following them around the room, or sense it trying to connect with them. She is also aware there are many more others (like Clayton), who could gaze at the same painting for hours at a time and never see or feel a thing.

The sudden loss of the child in the portrait mortifies her; reminding her that grief is never very far away. It's not one of those emotions that get left behind in houses like an old sock or forgotten ornament. *I've already lost one little boy and now I've lost another,* she whimpers miserably.

Then, right out of the blue, a current of warm air scampers past Avril, almost touching her. The wave of movement against her bare skin immediately gives her goose pimples. She is unwilling to move in case she frightens it… him… away and there is no denying his ghostly presence is here in the room with her. This time she is not mistaken. She would swear this on Tommy's life, if only that were possible. She holds her breath in suspense as she listens to the sound of a child's footsteps running across the wooden floor. The scurrying footsteps are accompanied by the unmistakable sound of a boy's excited giggling. Avril is wide-eyed at first, hardly daring to believe… and then a slow smile of acceptance settles on her face as she realises what is happening.

Chapter 30

There is an insistent tapping at the back door that keeps on being ignored; visible through the frosted glass is a shadowy figure with its face pressed up against the pane. Eventually, the door opens and a woman pokes her head in. This is Mrs Mills, the cleaner with cloak and dagger eyes that Avril has been forced into hiring; the only candidate not to have turned her down flat. Now that she's in the kitchen, Mrs Mills loses no time in making herself at home. Taking in the chaos, she tuts and sighs loudly. The accompanying expression seems at home on her face.

'Ay up,' she says in deep Yorkshire to nobody in particular. She then walks over to the vintage clock on the wall and turns the minute hand forward by half an hour. Chuckling to herself, she slips off her coat as if she might actually mean business. Her black hair might be tinged at the edges with white, but she is extremely fit for her age. Years scrubbing floors for other people and wiping young ones' arses has seen to this. She places her oversized bag on the table. It's cheap but practical, she'd have you know, if you took the time to ask her. And it's full to the brim with stuff she's accumulated from other people's houses. Stuff she daren't leave at home in case one of her own lot accumulates it from her. She pulls out a pinny which has all the appearance of being home-made and very old.

'I'd better gi' it some pasty,' She slips the pinny on and pats its pockets flat as if it is a neighbour's old dog she is used to greeting. She then eyes up the greasy baking trays in the sink. And she really is about to get her hands wet, no word of a lie, when–

'Am I getting warmer?' She hears her new employer call out excitably from another room. For a minute, Mrs Mills wonders if the good-looking husband is home. If so, she wouldn't blame Mrs Shaw for taking full advantage of this. Even at Mrs Mills' ripe old age, she wouldn't say no to a little rumpy-pumpy with him. Shame he isn't a doctor, though. She likes doctors best. There is no fun to be had saying you work for an electrician or a sign-language teacher. Mrs Mills wonders what's wrong with being a proper teacher.

If the young couple *are* up to mischief that is definitely something she wouldn't mind seeing. If they *have* forgotten about her coming today, she means to give them a fright they won't forget in a hurry. It won't be the first... or last time... that has happened in this house. On that ghoulish thought, she crosses herself before inching open one of the internal doors that go off the kitchen.

***

'Come out, come out, wherever you are.' Avril calls out playfully. Hide-and-seek had been Tommy's favourite game, too, and so far, she's looked behind curtains and in every corner; places a small boy might be waiting to be found. That's when she hears the creak of the door being tentatively pushed open and realises their game has been disrupted and that he cottoned on to this before she did. *Clever boy!*

But the proud motherly smile is soon wiped from her face. *Who is in the house with us? Who has been listening in on us?*

Her mind races with all kinds of possibilities but the fear of Clayton returning home early is the very worst scenario. She'll be back in the loony asylum before she knows it at this rate. She knows she isn't supposed to call it that or even talk about her so-called *voluntary* stay at The Specialist Mental Health Care Unit in Leeds but she can't think of a better name for it.

There is a discreet cough and Avril visibly relaxes. Clayton doesn't have a discreet bone in his body and certainly isn't the kind to hide in the background, waiting to be noticed, like this person is doing.

Awkwardly, Avril backs out of her wedged-in position behind the sofa and her face reddens when she sees Mrs Mills standing in the doorway, glaring at her.

'Mrs Mills! I didn't hear you come in.' Secretly Avril is annoyed. Why does the woman have to creep around? Why can't she make herself felt and heard like a normal person? Really it's all Mrs Mills fault she has been found in such a compromising position when she'd worked so hard to create the opposite effect. Avril had even mopped the floor in advance of her coming!

'And I didn't know you had a bairn,' Mrs Mills says accusingly. Clearly not a fan of young children, she nods toward the sofa as if to imply one of the ghastly creatures might be hiding behind it. 'Nowt was said to me about cleaning up after bairns.' As if experiencing a sudden onset of whiplash, Mrs Mills cracks her hen-like neck. It's a horrible sound. Like someone breaking the wishbone on a chicken carcass.

Avril waits for Mrs Mills to tell her 'it's more money for bairns' but she doesn't. As always, she is guilty of thinking the worst of people.

'I can explain,' Avril tells her; playing for time. Until Mrs Mills has been reassured there are *no* children in the Shaw household to clean up after, she's not about to lift a finger.

Chapter 31

Having suggested they go through to the kitchen to have a cup of coffee and a chat, Avril is annoyed to find she cannot get Clayton's Krups espresso coffee maker to work. He had bought it on a whim, she recalls, and paid over £700 for it. Avril really prefers plain old Nescafé out of a jar but she's never come out and said so because she doesn't want to hurt his feelings.

Mrs Mills has made herself at home at the kitchen table. If she notices Avril's lack of expertise with the coffee maker, she doesn't mention it. Out of the corner of her eye, Avril watches her turn the pages of a *Woman's Weekly* and thinks to herself, *I will get this damn coffee maker going*.

'I always read my magazine if I'm on an official break,' Mrs Mills informs her, without turning around in her chair. 'And I take it this *is* an official break?'

'You won't have to make up the time later, Mrs Mills. I can assure you of that.'

Realising this official break could go on indefinitely if she doesn't soon resolve the coffee crisis, Avril takes down the jar of Nescafé. Within minutes she is handing a perfectly good cup of coffee and a plate of Bourbon biscuits to Mrs Mills, who promptly dips one in her drink.

'Ooh brand biscuits, no less.' Mrs Mills marvels that a teacher and electrician are able to afford such luxury.

Turning her back on the woman, Avril rinses off the baking trays soaking in the sink and feels annoyed that she didn't get out of doing this unpleasant chore. *Here I am washing and drying up pots while she takes the weight off her legs. All because she walked in on something she doesn't understand but wants to take full advantage of,* Avril fumes. At the same time, she sneaks sly glances at Mrs Mills and wonders how best to explain herself.

'When you came in earlier, I was trying to catch the swallows so I could let them out of the sitting room window.'

'Swallows, you say.' Mrs Mills' face twists with doubt.

'Yes.' Avril nods encouragingly. 'They get disorientated and fly in through the windows.'

'So they manage to remember the 7,000-mile route from South Africa and then get lost? Lose their sense of direction once they get to Swallow's Nest? Is that what you're telling me?' Mrs Mills demands.

'You seem to know a lot about birds,' Avril can barely keep the animosity from her voice; hating the way this woman has so easily rumbled her. *But she doesn't know what I was really doing in the sitting room. There is no way she can guess at the truth. Nobody must ever find out about this.*

'Birds and bairns are all the same. Once you've had them you never get shot of them. Sooner or later they come home to roost and there's nowt you can do about it,' Mrs Mills warns.

Chapter 32

Having scraped her long unruly hair into a French twist, Avril comes into the kitchen wearing a cool-blue linen trouser suit. She is completely unaware that the fabric is an exact match for her eyes. Usually she sticks to wearing black, because it's a way of publicly mourning her son without people questioning it. If Clayton has a sneaking suspicion of this, he doesn't say anything.

Having wasted thirty minutes trying on clothes, she'd finally settled on the one outfit that didn't completely drown her. Mind you, just to keep the trousers up, she'd had to dig out another hole in the belt for her narrow waist. A skirmish with the scissors means she now has a plaster taped around her finger, concealing a rather nasty cut. It feels strange having a band of any kind on her finger as it's been such a long time since she wore her wedding ring. Realising she can't remember when she last saw it, Avril becomes flustered. She may choose not to wear it but she certainly doesn't want to lose it. Then she remembers seeing it in a glass dish on her dressing table and relaxes. Clayton may not object to her not wearing his ring but he would go mental if she actually lost it.

There is an overpowering smell of bleach in the room which must mean Mrs Mills is finally getting on with her work. Avril is at first optimistic and then down-in-the-dumps when she realises it is taking Mrs Mills forever to dry up a single glass. The woman doesn't even attempt to speed up when she sees Avril watching her. Sighing, Avril guesses this is how it is always going to be. She doesn't say anything – not because they've already got off to a bad start – but because she's too much of a coward. *A bad cleaner is probably better than no cleaner at all*, she convinces herself. There is no way she is going to let on to Clayton she has made a terrible mistake.

Avril slips on a pair of court shoes and hobbles around the kitchen, collecting keys, purse and handbag as she goes; all the while watching Mrs Mills unhurriedly put one wineglass down before picking up another, which she dries at a snail's pace. *She's not about to bust a gut for anyone*, Avril grumbles inwardly. Then she happens to glance at the wall clock and immediately panics.

'Is that the time? I'm going to be late.' Avril checks her watch. 'Mine must be slow,' she tells Mrs Mills. Avril then makes a point of winding her watch on because she wants to impress on her the importance of good timekeeping.

It is a simple Timex with a stretchy silver strap, which she's had since she was seventeen. It was the first thing she ever bought herself. Who would have thought troubled-teen Avril Croft with her tragic start in life would ever keep down a job and be earning money before she turned eighteen? The watch might be badly scratched and one of the hands keeps catching on the other, making it lose time on occasion (such as now), but she wouldn't part with it for anything. Clayton is always threatening to buy her a fancy new one, to match the expensive one she'd bought him, but this makes her angry. 'I'll refuse to wear it, if you do,' she'd warned him. Realising that the watch has now stopped altogether, Avril heaves a sigh. Maybe she should let Clayton buy her a new one after all? What is the point of being sentimental about a watch when her own son is dead?

'I'll be back before you go, Mrs Mills.' Avril is worried about leaving Mrs Mills alone in the house but right now she has other pressing matters to attend to; the appointment for one thing. So she exits in a hurry, and her heels sink into the gravel as soon as she's out of the door, making it difficult for her to walk with anything like authority across the drive. Certain Mrs Mills has already stopped work in her absence, Avril approaches her car and wonders (not for the first time), what she was thinking of the day she bought it.

There is nothing nice about the ugly Fiat sitting in the drive. It doesn't have any cuddly animals on the back seat or a tree-shaped air freshener hanging off its rear view mirror. But it does have a dent in the driver's side door which she's never gotten around to fixing; and this gives the car a hurt look as if it knows how unattractive it is. *Now I know why we're such a good match for each other*, she thinks cynically.

Then, feeling the hairs on the back of her neck stand up, Avril comes to a crunchy halt in the gravel. She feels compelled to turn around and when she does, her eye is immediately drawn to the upstairs window. This is the room that would have been Tommy's. Hadn't she pointed this out to Clayton, just the other day?

In the window, Avril can make out the small figure of a child. The boy's hand is touching the glass and she senses that he is sad to see her leaving. His breath fogs up the glass and she can tell he has been crying. *It's not Tommy. It's not Tommy,* she reminds herself harshly.

'I won't be long. I'm coming back.' She signs and speaks, glad to have someone miss her. Then, realising anyone

103

can see her out here in the open, she checks the lane for Clayton's van. She wouldn't put it past him to come home unannounced, claiming to have forgotten something. Checking up on her is a habit he fell into when Tommy died. She scours the downstairs windows for incriminating shadows but thankfully there is no sign of Mrs Mills. For now, her secret, *their secret*, is safe.

Chapter 33

Mrs Mills' eyes narrow suspiciously as she watches Avril wave to an upstairs window before getting into her car and driving away. Only when she's sure it is safe to step back from her hiding place behind the kitchen window, does she do so. Rather than sit down immediately for a rest, she looks up at the ceiling and frowns.

'If there are no bairns, then who the devil does she think she is waving at?' Mrs Mills speaks her thoughts out loud. This is a habit she's gotten into from working alone in people's houses. Most employers prefer to be out of the house when she cleans, worried she will want to gossip her hours away, and Avril Shaw is no exception. Mrs Mills has known a dozen other such types who think they are better than her because of their fancy educations and big houses. But once Mrs Mills gets to know all about the people who employ her, it soon becomes clear they are no better than they should be. As far as Mrs Mills is concerned, 'They can all wipe my arse.'

Mrs Mills will learn all of the Shaw's secrets in good time but right now there is something going on she doesn't understand and she means to get to the bottom of it.

'Time for an unsupervised tour, I think,' she says, pulling open the door into the hallway.

On her way upstairs she notices that almost every wooden step creaks noisily which is enough to freak most God-fearing folk out. And it's that dark on the landing she has to cling onto the wooden balustrade to guide her along. She daren't put on any lights because she is only meant to be doing downstairs today and doesn't want to get caught out by Mrs Shaw arriving home unannounced.

At the end of the landing is a door she hasn't yet seen the other side of. When Mrs Shaw first showed her around, she made up some excuse about the door being locked and not having the key on her; but Mrs Mills could smell the lie a mile off. Now that her eyes have become acclimatised to the dark, she realises the door at the end of the landing is the gable end room. The one that looks out on the big ugly tree. Making up her mind that nothing is going to stop her going inside, she finds her heart racing ahead of her.

The handle turns easily in her hand and Mrs Mills' tongue rolls out of her mouth in greedy anticipation of what she might see. She is rather put out to find the door doesn't creak eerily on its hinges.

'You're not so scary after all.'

Taking a few wary steps inside, she immediately feels how parky the room is, even though it's baking outside. Yorkshire is having one of its hottest summers on record and she for one can't wait to see the back of it.

Taking a closer look around, she soon realises it is completely devoid of any furniture or knick-knacks, save a toy fire truck, a rocking chair and some removal boxes.

'It's a shame that,' she tuts to show her disappointment. 'Because it could be a nice enough room with those three windows at the end. Mind you, that tree ought to come down, because it's as dark as Bob's arse is in here.'

Not that she sees much of her old man's arse. Since she had the mastectomy ten years ago he hasn't wanted to see her naked. It reminds him too much of the cancer, he says.

On that depressing thought, Mrs Mills tippy-toes over to the triple window and peers out. The tree, which is as tall as the house, directly faces this window and its gnarled old branches prevent the sunlight from seeping in. Although the room might be well lit at any other time of the day, the late morning sun doesn't seem to want anything to do with it. Mrs Mills decides that this is definitely the same window she caught Avril waving up at, yet there is nothing here apart from the rocking chair. She nudges the chair so that it rocks, however begrudgingly, and then notices there is condensation on the glass that could have been caused by someone breathing on it. As if it offends her, Mrs Mills rubs at the mist with the sleeve of her jumper until it is gone. She then walks over to the corner of the room where the removal boxes have been abandoned. Noticing that one of the boxes has 'Tommy's things' written on it, she scratches her chin and wonders who Tommy is. There's something about this Avril Shaw that unsettles her even more than the house does. And when you've spent your whole life in Yorkshire, there's only one word to describe someone like her.

'Barmpot,' Mrs Mills says out loud.

Chapter 34

Avril sits in one of a pair of leather chairs drawn close together and waits. The enormity of the chair makes her feel small, like a child, and she is reminded of being back in school, fearful of being told off. Her legs dangle ridiculously off the end of the chair and the sweltering leather sticks uncomfortably to her skin. The waiting is unbearable but it has to be better than the interrogation that will surely follow.

She's afraid of being asked questions she may not know the answer to, in case they judge her and start to murmur about 'specialist units' again. Just thinking about this makes her feel panicky. Her hands are clammy enough as it is and when she flaps her blouse in an attempt to cool down she gets a whiff of her own body sweat. Her foot wiggles nervously, lost without the steadying anchor of the floor, and she keeps glancing at the empty chair beside her.

'What frightens you, Avril?' She's been asked this question many times before. Even The Chief threw that one at her, right out of the blue, but she has never given an honest answer. She wonders what they would say if she told them the truth. *My mind frightens me. I have no idea where it is taking me. If you had any idea of what I have been up to this afternoon, you would have me locked up. But I'm not going to tell you any of this because Clayton wouldn't like it and I don't want to make him or anyone else suspicious.* For this reason alone, Avril must play along as best she can.

A tall woman comes into the room wearing expensive perfume and a lopsided smile. This must be Emma Watts. Avril has already become acquainted with the name and likes it. It is so ordinary sounding. Not at all like her last therapist. Avril still resents Dr Ruby Ribbons for having witnessed her crying like some snotty-nosed infant.

Emma is a huge surprise to Avril. Not least because she is so young. The girl is probably as tall as Clayton and pretty enough to be a model. Dr Ribbons had been middle-aged and didn't pay attention to her appearance. Avril only ever saw her in jumpers covered in cat hair. But Emma wears a white frothy blouse and a brown leather skirt that fondles her hips the same way a man would. Her hair is the colour of dark chocolate and her make-up is minimal. Avril notices all of these things long before Emma opens her mouth. Even before they've been introduced Avril decides to give her a chance. She'd like to bet this girl gets underestimated a lot because of her age and the way she looks.

'Sorry to keep you. I'm Emma.'

Avril gets to her feet and they shake hands. Emma's touch is light and feminine and Avril likes her all the more for it. Emma glances at the chair next to Avril as if it is a person she cannot wait to get to know. 'Still not arrived then?'

'I'm really sorry,' Avril says, all the while thinking, *Just once, I would like to make somebody's acquaintance without first having to apologise.*

She is about to start explaining what she is sorry for when her mobile phone rings.

'That'll be him now. Calling to say he's too busy.' Avril volunteers lamely.

***

Wearing dark sunglasses and looking extremely shamefaced, as if he doesn't want to be seen in this particular street, Clayton keeps his head down and leans against his work van, all the while holding his mobile phone to his ear. He has parked outside a block of newly-built terraced houses which boast alternating bright red or dark green front doors – all in the same design – a sure sign that this is a social housing development for people on low incomes. But that isn't the reason he doesn't want to be seen here. He isn't a snob. God knows he's got nothing to be superior about. No. The real reason for his discomfort is standing in the open doorway of one of those red doors.

As he waits impatiently for Avril to answer his call, his eyes flicker guiltily to number thirty-three's doorstep where Suzie kills time waiting for him. Seeming ridiculously happy to see him, she tries to hurry him along by clinking two glasses of iced drink together in greeting. She waves enthusiastically whilst attempting to balance the drinks in her hands and he groans when he sees she has on the teeniest of torn denim shorts and a revealing bikini top. There is zero chance of him not noticing how her perfectly-formed breasts bounce in time with the jiggling ice. Her brown fake-tan belly reminds him of the colour of iced cola and suddenly he is very thirsty.

***

Avril glares accusingly at the mobile phone that continues to ring long after she's retrieved it from the bottom of her bag. Usually it would have cut off by now or gone straight to voicemail but today when she wants it to do exactly *that* – it rings persistently as if it wants to annoy her. She could kill Clayton for this.

'Aren't you going to answer it?' Emma wants to know.

'It's easier for him if I don't.' Avril admits. 'He'll be happier leaving a message. No confrontation that way.'

As the words leave her mouth the room becomes blurred and Avril sees stars in front of her eyes. All she can see through this sudden fog is a shadowy line up of books on shelves nobody ever reads. She can tell nobody reads them by the upright way their spines are stored, like soldiers who have never been to war. The fact that she can no longer see doesn't frighten her. She's used to experiencing moments of blurred vision; the aftermath of what happened to her as a child when the corneas in her eyes were severely damaged. *People see me and think only of the visible scars. They don't realise there are other less obvious injuries too,* she thinks bitterly.

Avril only relaxes when the phone finally stops ringing. Now that there is no longer any danger of having to speak to Clayton in Emma's presence, her vision clears. Soon everything is back in focus and she is able to watch Emma sit down in the chair intended for Clayton. She is irritated to find that Emma doesn't look as awkward as she does, because her long catwalk legs reach the floor even when crossed. Avril looks at her own stunted legs and likes Emma a little less than she did five minutes ago.

'What about you?'

These are exactly the sort of questions Avril hates. No matter how many times she steels herself for them they always seem to wipe the floor with her. Avril looks down. She doesn't want Emma's eyes on her when she tells her first lie.

'What about me?' Avril shrugs as if she is of no consequence. As if she doesn't matter. They may as well be talking about her old self.

Emma leans forward in her chair and reaches across to rest her hand on Avril's knee. Normally, Avril would shy away from any physical contact so she is somewhat surprised to find she likes having it there. For a moment she is seduced by the notion that Emma could be her friend and not just her therapist. The sympathetic hand on her knee makes her feel safe but just as she has this thought, Emma removes it.

'Are you happier avoiding confrontation, Avril?'

Avril senses there is no right or wrong answer to the question and this gives her the confidence to take the lead.

'Has the session started yet?' Avril glances at the alarm clock strategically placed on the table next to Emma. She's had enough of these sessions to know how things work and refuses to talk longer than she has to. An hour is all she agreed to.

'If that's what you want, Avril.' Emma picks up the old-fashioned alarm clock and sets it for one hour's time. The faint ticking sound is a disappointment. *A clock like that should tick loudly to remind us how doomed we all are*, Avril reflects. She can tell by the way Emma handles the clock it does not belong to her. It has probably lived in this room for the last twenty years. It belongs here in a way that Avril does not. *I've lost a child. There is nothing wrong with me. Why can't anyone see that?*

'What is it you're missing about Clayton right now?'

At first Avril is staggered by this question. But then she reminds herself that Emma doesn't know her yet. Not in the way Dr Ribbons did. 'Nothing,' she responds angrily and immediately takes herself in hand before anything gets written down. *Patient becomes aggressive when questioned about her relationship with her husband.* Avril can picture the words appearing on the page even before Emma has picked up her pen. And then she takes Emma even more by surprise when the next words rush out of her 'Myself. I miss myself. The girl I used to be… before Tommy. Before either of them.'

Chapter 35

Mrs Mills is now poking around in the Shaw's bedroom, where she has no business being. She flicks a duster over some framed photographs on the dressing table, as if intent on cleaning them, but really she's just being nosey. There are no pictures of Mrs Shaw she notices and wonders why not. After all, there is no denying the lass is pretty even if she is as skinny as a whippet and badly scarred. There's plenty of photographs of the husband though, more than enough for any wife to have to put up with; but she supposes this must always be the case for couples without bairns.

A ring left in a glass dish on the dressing table soon takes her mind off the photographs and within seconds she has it in her hand. Holding the ring between her thumb and index finger she scrutinises the hallmark; but without a jeweller's eyepiece she is unable to tell if it is made of platinum or silver. If it is platinum, it will be worth a bob or two. She tries it on for size but it is so small it won't pass over her work-worn knuckle. The wedding ring clearly belongs to Mrs Shaw and Mrs Mills can't help wondering why she no longer wears it. Placing the ring back in the glass dish, she twirls her own cheap gold wedding band around on her finger. It might not have cost much but she wouldn't be seen dead without it. She is starting to think the Shaw's may have more secrets than an Agatha Christie novel.

Wondering what other skeletons they have in the closet, she tries to pull out the dressing table drawer but it won't budge. On edge, in case she gets found out – after all that Avril Shaw isn't right from the ankles up – she yanks the latch more firmly but it still won't slide out. She daren't be too rough because the old fashioned dressing table looks as if it's about to fall to bits. Feeling rattled, she scrabbles around in other drawers for a key. Finally, as she picks her way through a mountain of fancy underwear that doesn't look as if it's seen the light of day in years, her fingers stumble across it. She wastes no time in getting the drawer open and is hugely disappointed to find a solitary paperback inside.

Realising it's one of those erotic books women are meant to be so fond of, she flicks through its pages. Pulling a face at the well-known title, she can't get her head around why any woman would want to be cable tied to a bed and spanked. She would beat Bob over the head with a rolling pin if he ever tried any of that nonsense. Mrs Mills supposes Mrs Shaw has a good enough reason to keep it locked away and is about to put the book back when a photograph slips out of its pages, landing face up in her hand. The photograph is of a young boy with blond hair and blue eyes. There is nothing disturbing about the picture, yet Mrs Mills' hands shake as she holds it. She immediately recognises the boy in the photograph. Did so the second she saw his face. This is no ordinary bairn. It's the same child that's in the painting downstairs. The one that's said to be cursed.

A faint sound on the landing causes Mrs Mills to freeze in fear. There it is again. The sound of somebody climbing those spooky unlit stairs. But these are no ordinary footsteps, she realises. Those light cautious steps are more like what you'd expect from a child sneaking around in a game of hide and seek. For some reason this makes her go cold all over. She hears the creak again, closer this time, and holds her breath. Soon it will reach the top of the stairs. Soon it will be on the landing.

When the door to the Shaw's bedroom squeaks open an inch Mrs Mills screams with fright and then jumps almost out of her skin when she catches sight of her own reflection in the dressing table mirror. Her hand automatically goes to her racing heart as she waits for the door to be thrown open.

Chapter 36

Avril stares mesmerised at the stones in her lap which catch the light in a certain way and bounce shadows off the walls. One is large, at least the size of her hand, and the other is much smaller (the size of a pebble). She likes the smooth marble-like texture of one but not the abrasive touch of the other. It feels unfinished, like a work in progress and this makes her feel anxious, in case she is expected to do something about it.

'And what does the large stone represent?' Emma's voice comes from nowhere, like a car in the fog. It startles Avril.

'Noise. The sound of traffic. And screams. My screams.' Avril pauses as if winded and struggles momentarily to get her breath. 'The lorry was owned by a company called Double Days. I know that because the name was repeated twice on the cab door. I see the logo every time I close my eyes. Hear the lorry's brakes. And I can't escape the sound of its reverse alarm beeping.' Avril puts her hands over her ears and bows her head. 'Most days I want the world to stop but it just keeps turning without Tommy in it.'

She wants to cry properly but she can't. Today she can only drum up a few pathetic tears for her son and this is nowhere near good enough. Nevertheless, she pulls out a tissue from her bag and dabs at her eyes. She is desperate for Emma to know how much it hurts. That it wasn't her fault.

'He couldn't hear the lorry. That's why he died. He could hear certain noises, usually high-pitched ones, but not that day. All he could think about was crossing the road to see his friend.'

'Is Tommy the reason you became a sign language teacher, Avril?'

'I wanted to help him and others like him.' Avril is unaware that her face lights up as soon as she starts talking about teaching. 'It was a way of coping I suppose.'

'And Clayton? How did he cope?'

'He never got used to the idea. Because Tommy's hearing loss was genetic he ended up blaming himself. He was born that way, you see, and Clayton had trouble acknowledging it.'

'Was the deafness proven to be on Clayton's side then?'

Avril shakes her head. 'I don't have any family so it couldn't be proven either way.'

'No family at all?'

'No.' Avril is blunter than she intended.

'That's rather unusual, isn't it?'

Avril doesn't answer. *This is none of her business. I won't talk about this,* she decides stubbornly, before giving Emma the same look she gives Clayton whenever he probes too deep. Although she won't mention her family out loud, nothing can stop her remembering them and all at once the strong scent of chrysanthemums overwhelms her. She is unable to remember her parents without the repulsive odour being present. Clenching her knuckles, Avril remembers coming across a bunch of chrysanthemums on her parents' grave, left there no doubt by someone who didn't know them the way she did. She had been so angry about this she had ripped their skinny petals to shreds but their earthy smell remained on her clothes for the rest of the day. As usual, whenever she thinks about *them* she sees their blurred faces through a grotesque halo of flames. It is too much. She cannot do this. Ever.

'And the smaller stone?' Emma has changed tack; knowing better than to persevere with a subject that clearly makes a patient uncomfortable.

'Silence. No more noise. No more footsteps.' Avril's sadness sits wearily on her face. She looks like somebody who hasn't slept in a long time. But then, unexpectedly, her face lights up at a more pleasurable memory. 'He might have been deaf but he still knew how to create noise.' She pauses again, unsure as to whether she should go on, because all of a sudden she's remembering bad stuff about her son and this makes her feel disloyal.

'At times he would get angry.' Avril admits guiltily. Suddenly the temperature in the room dips and the sunlight disappears. It feels as if Tommy's sulky shadow has just stormed into the room. No matter that he could sometimes be a handful, Avril wishes she could once again feel the spiteful nipping of her son's fingers digging into her flesh.

'Other children would play happily on the slide or get their parents to push them on the swings. But Tommy wasn't allowed to join in and this sometimes caused him to scream and lash out. The other parents would look at us in disgust and I could tell they were thanking God he wasn't theirs.'

Avril takes a sip of water and wonders why she hadn't noticed the glass by her side before. The ice hasn't quite melted and the water is still cool and refreshing. She glances quickly at Emma and is touched by how engrossed she appears to be in her story. She can't remember the last time anyone listened to her quite so avidly.

'I would brace myself for these attacks and take a firm hold of Tommy just in case he hurt another child. He would struggle while I restrained him, of course, but I wouldn't let go until he exhausted himself. Until he was forced to remain still. I hated having to do this. I couldn't stand him thinking I wanted to hurt him in any way. But I did. Sometimes there would be bruises.'

'What would happen next, Avril?'

'The other parents would gawp at us as if they couldn't believe their eyes but I wouldn't let them see me cry. Instead I'd throw my arms around Tommy and fight back the urge to throw things. I wanted to hurt those people. Damage their perfect lives until they understood.'

Avril looks down at the two stones in her clenched hands. Her hands feel sore from holding them for so long.

'He could be very difficult. Especially when Clayton was around. If Tommy saw us arguing…'

'What did you argue about back then?'

'Tommy mostly,' Avril shrugs as if this was never a huge issue. 'Clayton refused to use sign language so he was unable to communicate with his son. It was another way of refusing to accept Tommy's condition.'

'And now?' Emma sounds concerned.

***

Mrs Mills hasn't yet dared leave the sanctuary of the Shaw's bedroom. She is still not convinced whoever or whatever it was on the stairs has gone away. But thankfully, all she can hear now is the reassuring tick of a clock from somewhere inside the room. It reminds her of a second heartbeat.

When nothing else happens she sinks onto the bed in relief and scolds herself for having such an overactive imagination. Bob warned her against working in this house, after what happened before, but as always she thought she knew best. She makes up her mind not to tell him about this. He is always telling her she'll frighten herself to death one of these days. Her with her dodgy heart an' all.

Keeping an ear out for the faintest noise on the stairs, she pulls back the patchwork quilt and exposes the sheet underneath. She then runs a critical eye over the spotlessly clean sheet and follows it with a probing finger, testing for damp spots. She pulls a poisonous face and clucks out loud like an excitable hen heading for the pot.

'Nowt going on in there then,' she states bluntly. 'No wonder 'er bladder's too near 'er eyes.'

***

The lack of sex is also on Clayton's mind, which is why he can't tear his eyes away from Suzie's breasts. They look so full of life in that tropical print bikini top. Just a moment ago when she handed him his drink, they'd come so close to his face he'd been tempted to touch them. He imagines sucking on them. He'd like to bet he could get a whole nipple in his mouth if he wanted to. To his horror he feels his penis start to stir. *Fuck*, he thinks. *How embarrassing is this? Get a hold of yourself man.*

That's when the child comes running into the room and his semi erection vanishes along with his fantasy of Suzie being sexually carefree and childless. He watches the black-haired boy leap into his mother's arms and for a few churlish seconds he is jealous. Then, when he sees the spattering of freckles across the boy's face he is instantly reminded of his own son. Although this boy doesn't look anything like him, he does have the most amazing green eyes he's ever seen. The kid is beautiful in a way his son never was.

Clayton knocks back his drink and grins stupidly at the kid. He's a little shy, he can tell, because he turns his face away and buries in it his mother's cleavage. *Exactly where I wanted to be a few minutes ago*, Clayton sighs wistfully. *But the boy does have more of a right to his mother's chest than I do*, he concedes. Right now though, he needs to make his excuses and go. He watches Suzie pat down her son's wayward hair and realises he will never know what it is like to be touched by her. She will never smile at him the way she does her son. All women are the same when it comes to motherhood. But that's a good thing, he reminds himself, because for a few mad moments he'd been sorely tempted.

I am just a man, he reminds himself, as if this detail somehow exonerates his behaviour; but he's not mug enough to really believe this. *I'm no more than a stupid red-blooded male who thinks with his dick*. If he could undo his previous lurid thoughts about Suzie, he would. If he could stop thinking about sex, he would. But the truth is, he isn't getting enough of it to prevent his thoughts spiralling dangerously down this route. And it isn't just sex he misses, he realises belatedly. It's intimacy too.

These days Avril is so cold and distant, it's like sharing a house with a porcelain doll. The kind that's stored away in a box. *Christ*, he finally realises how close he came to actually cheating on Avril (always supposing Suzie would have been up for it if the kid hadn't been around), when only a few hours ago he'd promised her he'd always be faithful.

Clayton looks at the boy wriggling around in Suzie's lap. He has white chubby legs and a way of staring right back at him that implies he knows exactly what kind of thoughts he has been having about his mother. The kid must be four or five years old – around his own son's age.

'Want another?' Suzie asks him.

'A kid? Me? No. No way.' Clayton is at once on his feet.

'I meant a drink.' Suzie laughs, as if everything is funnier than it actually is. Feeling a little foolish, he supposes this habit of hers might irritate him after a while.

'Best not.' Clayton gestures to Suzie's arm. 'I just wanted to check on the burn, that's all.'

Suzie puts the child down and gets to her feet. She is frowning and Clayton can tell she doesn't believe that's all he came around for. *What a shit I am*, he thinks.

'You'll come again, won't you?' There is a plea in her voice he can't ignore. She's young and beautiful and probably has loads of different men chasing after her; but for some reason she has latched onto him. She really likes him, he can tell. And she is just as lonely as he is. Most men would have trouble walking away from such a lethal combination.

Chapter 37

Avril cradles her bag in her arms and thinks once again of her loss. For five years she held Tommy like this and now her arms have no purpose. She may as well cut them off. Clayton is no substitute. In many ways she resents him for even trying. Why would she want to hold him when she cannot do the same for her son?

'So you'll speak to Clayton? Try to get him to agree?'

Emma is keen for Avril to move forward. Something she's not quite ready to do yet. Furthermore, Emma's question has surprised Avril because it hints at a naivety she wouldn't have suspected her of. Clearly, she's never been in a long-term relationship herself or she wouldn't have suggested such a thing. Avril has never been able to change Clayton's mind about anything, let alone something as important as having another child.

'He would never agree.'

'But if you explained to him it's the one thing that could make you happy again? He might–'

'There is more than one way to have a child.' Avril says more sharply than she intended.

'I'm not sure I understand what you mean.' Noticing how Avril's eyes have gone all secretive and guarded, Emma shifts uncomfortably in her chair, not liking this unnerving change.

Avril is just as mystified by her own response. She had never intended those words to slide out of her mouth. *There's more than one way to have a child*, she'd told Emma casually, as if obtaining another child without Clayton's consent was completely acceptable. But how else was she meant to get her hands on another child? If Clayton won't agree to them having a child of their own, he would never consider adoption or fostering. Then, it finally dawns on her. The idea is not new. She has in fact been nurturing the possibility all along. From the moment she first set eyes on the boy in the painting, she has thought of nothing else.

***

Mrs Mills stands in the middle of the sitting room and glares at *The Crying Boy* as if trying to stare it out in a battle of wills. Her glance flickers between the photo in her hand, the one she took out of the dressing table drawer, and the boy in the painting.

'Like peas in a pod,' she mutters before slipping the photograph in her pocket. She mustn't forget to put it back where she found it before she leaves. She then takes out a duster from her pinny and begins to swat it aimlessly around the room. But she's not able to concentrate on housework for long. Instead she casts a long mean look around the room, trying once again to figure things out. But it's no good. She can't get to the bottom of things. Not yet. The only thing Mrs Mills *is* certain of is, Avril Shaw was not searching for birds when she walked in on her.

'Swallows, my eye,' she shakes her head in denial. But if that had been a lie, what had she really been doing? That's what Mrs Mills wants to know.

She puts her hands on her hips and sighs in frustration. Then she catches sight of the boy in the painting again and this time she's positive he looks more spiteful than before.

'Don't you be giving me no evil eye now.' Mrs Mills throws her duster at the portrait.

Chapter 38

She has already insisted he take it back but he seems hell-bent on refusing to take her seriously; no doubt believing she will eventually come around to the idea. More fool him. Because she never will. Avril cannot even bear to look at the pointy black head poking out of the neck of Clayton's shirt, let alone bring herself to touch it. He can see how furious she is, yet he continues to stroke its glossy head and makes encouraging noises at it, certain all the fuss will die down in the next few minutes.

'I lost my son and you think you can replace him with a kitten,' she says through gritted teeth.

'I thought it might cheer you up.' He ignores the sting in her words and pulls an injured face.

He's so used to getting his own way she can tell it hasn't once occurred to him that she might not back down. Knowing her husband as well as she does, Avril can guess what he's thinking. 'What's not to love?' he'll be asking himself. 'Who couldn't take to a cute ball of fluff like this?' Well *she* can't, clearly, although he refuses to recognise this.

'You thought it might cheer me up?'

At last he catches the cold deadly look in her eyes. She can tell that her anger worries him. It's something he doesn't like to witness. She glances at *The Crying Boy*. *At least somebody is on my side,* she thinks.

'He was my son too.' Clayton stumbles on his words, realising his mistake too late.

'Not that you'd notice. You never talk about him. You never even say his name out loud.' She is harsh. It feels good. She will not feel sorry for him.

'What's the point?' Clayton's temper stirs at last. 'He never heard me when he was alive.'

'You couldn't even be bothered to turn up today. That's how much our son means to you.' She finally throws at him what really matters. The very thing they've been avoiding saying to each other. She cannot do this without bursting into tears.

'Our son,' Clayton laughs bitterly. 'I can't even remember what he looks like, yet you want me to discuss him with a complete stranger. Do you have any idea how that feels?'

'Oh, Clay.' Avril feels herself weaken.

'I'll take it back now.' He is deliberately cold. He wants her to know how disappointed he is in her. He might as well have said, 'What sort of wife wouldn't love a kitten?'

Instead he says, 'It was stupid of me. I realise that now.' But the red spots on his cheeks indicate that he doesn't believe this. He thinks she is in the wrong and nothing will convince him otherwise. He is so damned infuriating.

By now the kitten's eyes are wide with fear and the fur on the back of its neck is raised. Clearly it came from a nicer, less argumentative home than the one it now finds itself in. It crosses Avril's mind that they are not fit to be cat owners, let alone parents. When the frightened kitten hisses at Clayton, he stomps toward the door.

'That's it. Walk away, like you always do.' Avril calls out pettily, aware of how childish they are both being. *Stay,* the better half of her pleas.

'Do you want me to take the kitten back or not?'

'That's not what I meant and you know it.' Avril hates it when he deliberately misunderstands her, the way he is doing now.

'I just thought it would be nice to have a pet, that's all.'

Clayton screws up his face as if the kitten means everything to him but she knows this is not true. As usual, he's just trying to make her feel sorry for him so she will relent. When she doesn't show any immediate signs of doing so, he walks out, banging the sitting room door with such force their wedding photograph falls over.

The next thing Avril hears is the back door slamming, followed by the rattlesnake sound of Clayton's diesel engine starting up. She absent-mindedly straightens a cushion on the sofa before righting the picture of her and Clayton. She doesn't look at it. Doesn't want to be reminded of how happy they once were. But then she asks herself, *were we ever really happy?* Because even then her lies came between them. *Poor Clay,* she thinks. *He really had no idea what he was taking on when he got involved with me.*

The fishy smell is in her in her nostrils again, making her want to throw up the small portion of granola and almond milk she managed to keep down this morning. The revolting smell is always at its most powerful in the sitting room and she wonders why nobody else can smell it. Clayton has tried to persuade her it is the lingering smell of singed wiring but she doesn't think this is the case. He accuses her of being over-sensitive but he doesn't know all the facts. She believes the smell has been with her since childhood and that it has followed her into her adult life.

What she hasn't told Clayton is that it's not just the burnt wiring she can smell. There is a stench of charred bodies too. It seeps from the walls of the house like cigarette smoke.

***

She'd taken the kitten home knowing they would be furious with her. They'd never had a pet of any kind before. Her parents were always saying they couldn't afford it. But it didn't stop them smoking and drinking. She would keep the kitten hidden under her bed for now, while it was still little. That way there would be no risk of her dad booting it up the backside the way he had Jamie. She can still remember the way her mum went for him over that and for once he'd almost looked sorry. Like he knew he'd gone too far.

On the night of the fire, when her dad really had gone too far, she'd managed to get Jamie out but not the kitten. Named Robbie, after her favourite member of Take That he was so tiny she was able to hold him in the palm of her hand. He had sad weepy eyes and an orange coat that was sticky in places and he had difficulty holding his head up, she remembers. She didn't know then that he had been taken away from his mother too early and would probably have died anyway.

Out on the street, Jamie had been hugged by neighbours who usually refused to have anything to do with them, while somebody else rolled her over on the pavement in an attempt to put out the flames. There was nothing left of her nightdress, she remembers. Although her eyes felt like they were on fire and her body raged in agony, she had, along with everybody else on the street, watched their house burn. It was only when she saw the kitten at the window mewing for help that she remembered Robbie. But no matter how hard she fought, they wouldn't let her go back for him. Since the night of the fire, when her home burnt down and she lost everything, including the skin she was born in, she has never been able to bear the sound of a cat's meow without being reminded of her loss.

Chapter 39

Clayton's van is parked once again outside Suzie's house, only this time he's sensible enough to remain inside. He's been here long enough to watch each of the street lights come on and to know that all of the children who were playing in the street earlier have now been called indoors. It was the sight of them that froze his hands to the wheel. If his own son had been alive, it would never have entered his head to come here. But his boy *is* dead and there is nothing he can do to change this.

From across the street he watches Suzie come to the window and look out. Even from here she looks sexy as hell. He sees her nibble her thumbnail, as if she's nervous, and he wonders what's troubling her. Him probably. He knows she likes him. More than likes him.

He's sure she'd love the kitten, which lies asleep in a box beside him on the passenger seat, but he can see he had been wrong to come here again. As embarrassing as it will be, he has no choice but to take the kitten back to the house he got it from. *The Avril I used to know would never have turned a kitten out onto the street,* he can't help admitting. He looks at the sleepy ball of fluff and wonders for the umpteenth time, *what is wrong with my wife?*

***

Avril has found herself standing outside the door to the spare room, Tommy's room, without knowing how she got here. *What is wrong with me?* she can't help wondering. Her eyes are as jumpy as she is, out of control and darting here, there and everywhere. She avoids her reflection in the landing mirror – lest she sees someone she doesn't recognise; but she can see a shadow there that she doesn't think belongs to her. That's when the ceiling light above her head starts to flicker. *Turn around and go back downstairs*, she orders herself. But just as she is about to obey her inner self, the door creaks open.

The doorknob is deathly cold in her hand but even this does not disturb her dreamlike state. Finally, she pushes it open and peers into the unlit room. *I don't have to go inside*, she comforts herself. She has not forgotten the last time she entered this room, when she was imprisoned against her will. How could anyone forget something like that?

She feels for the light switch just inside the door. It takes a few seconds for the energy-saving bulb to get going. *Come on, come on,* she thinks impatiently; hating having to stand alone in the dark. When the light does finally come on, Avril can hardly believe her eyes.

The rocking chair bucks wildly, as if being ridden by a devil child, and the contents of the removal boxes have been strewn across the floor. But perhaps more chillingly, there… in the centre of the room, is Tommy's fire truck. As soon as it spots Avril, it starts heading her way.

It's not possible. This can't be happening. She's not through telling herself this when the truck comes to a stop at her feet and toots its horn. It does so in a jolly sort of way as if none of this is terrifying for her. She inches away from the truck, only for it to follow. Eventually she finds herself in the middle of the room, praying that the truck will stop of its own accord. When it does, she finds herself even more frightened than before. In the silence, she can hear somebody else breathing. She hardly dares raise her eyes, frightened of what she might see. Suddenly, the light bulb above her head explodes and shards of glass rain down on her, forming a sparkly crown in her hair.

'Don Bonillo.' Avril calls out in alarm.

Chapter 40

A persistent hammering and the sound of muffled shouts finally gives Avril the courage to move from her cowering position. By now, the rocking chair has fallen still and the room is back to how it should be; with Tommy's things neatly packed away in boxes. Looking around for broken glass, anxious not to cut her bare feet, Avril is not unduly surprised to find the light bulb still intact.

Seconds later, she makes a dash for it and as soon as her feet hit the carpeted landing, she recognises Clayton's impatient hollering. She has never been so relieved to hear his voice. Never thought she'd escape that room or the child that isn't Tommy *or* the ghostlike playful one she encountered earlier. This is a house full of children, she realises. Although she senses they are one and the same, only Don Bonillo's presence frightens her.

Running barefoot through the unlit downstairs rooms, she switches on lights as she goes. *How did it get to be so dark?* Maybe they'd had an electricity cut? That could account for the lights flickering, she supposes, but quickly dismisses the idea. She must stop pretending she doesn't know exactly what was in that room with her. She makes up her mind that she must not keep this to herself any longer. Tonight, if it's the last thing she does, she must talk to Clayton. Even if he doesn't believe her; even if he threatens to have her put away, she has no choice but to come clean. In her rush to let him in, she skids on the tiled floor. As soon as she sees his familiar face through the glass door she feels in safe hands.

'There she is.' She hears him say, just as she turns the key in the lock and manages to get the door open. And in he comes, throwing an apologetic smile to The Chief who dawdles behind, hidden in the shadows.

'At last,' Clayton grumbles half-heartedly as the two men pile into the kitchen, crowding Avril. Instinctively she takes a step back, momentarily floored. This isn't what she was expecting at all. The Chief is the last person she wants to see right now. She wrings her hands and notices that bits of fluff from Tommy's woollen jumper cling to her palms, yet she cannot remember having held it.

With a boyish smile, Clayton breezes past Avril as if they are still on the best of terms. Avril is unable to stop herself suspiciously sniffing the air where he passes; hunting down any hint of perfume that might belong to another woman. Detecting nothing unusual, she breathes a sigh of relief.

'Why did you lock the door?' He asks casually, for something to say more than anything, she guesses.

'I didn't,' she tells him.

Clayton knows better than to question her but The Chief raises an overgrown eyebrow. He'd challenge her if he could. She feels she cannot breathe with his bulk filling the room. He seems somehow to bring the vast space of the open moorland inside with him. She reminds herself that she must stop thinking of him as the man from the moor. He doesn't deserve such a noble title.

Clayton is keen to create an impression that all is forgiven, especially in front of their guest. Deceit is something they've both become good at, she realises cynically. *In some ways we are perfect for each other*.

'I asked The Chief back for supper.' Clayton nods in the old man's direction and Avril follows his gaze, knowing he's really warning her to 'play nice'. She should be furious with him, but now that she's had chance to think, she is relieved. Now they have company, her chat with Clayton will have to be postponed. Perhaps she was being too hasty earlier? She needn't tell him anything at all if she doesn't want to.

'If you don't mind?' The Chief is talking now, she realises belatedly, and is awaiting her response. This rings alarm bells in Avril's mind because she keeps disappearing inside herself, drifting off to places no one else goes. When this happens, she has no idea what else is going on around her. She sees his eyes dart from her to Clayton in a way that implies there is something peculiar about her behaviour and hates him all the more for picking up on this.

'There's always room for one more,' she says with a fake smile. 'That's our motto, isn't it Clayton?'

If they were alone, Avril would remind Clayton of the times Tommy insisted on climbing into bed with them; when they'd joke 'There's always room for one more,' before budging up to make room for him. Because of this, he deliberately avoids eye contact with her but she can tell he is not fooled by her false cheeriness any more than the old man is.

The Chief can look at the floor all he wants, so long as he doesn't suspect her of anything more sinister. If he ever touches her, even in passing, she will jump out of her skin. His wart-ridden hands must be as tough as a pair of old boots. Avril has no idea why she hates him so much. But whenever he's around, she feels threatened. She's sure he is looking for ways to divide her and Clayton and as things stand at the moment, that wouldn't be difficult to achieve.

Chapter 41

Clayton never tires of watching her. Sometimes, he thinks he hates her. Other times he's overwhelmed with love and sympathy for her. Only Avril has the ability to make him feel guilty and responsible for all that has happened, including their son. Understandably, this makes him resentful. He might not have been there on the day his boy died, but she was. Perhaps this is why she blames him.

Right now, she may only be doing something as simple as tossing a salad around in her hands but he finds her mesmerising. He wonders if grief has ever suited anyone quite so much as it does her.

The pale skin, the watery blue eyes, the tiny waist a man could break with one hand – all make him think he was mad to consider going to bed with Suzie. Hand on heart, he's not sure he ever really intended to. He is convinced he was just toying with the idea in a spoilt, childish attempt at getting back at Avril for making him feel worthless. Suzie might be a nice enough girl, if a tad annoying, but Avril is the real deal. The love of his life. No matter how much they might fight.

Like any other couple, they are preparing dinner together tonight, but unlike most other couples they are not talking. In his mind, this isn't a bad thing. Sometimes silence has a way of straightening things out.

They are outside on the balcony and candles have been lit all around them. As ever, there is a real night time chill in the air and this makes Clayton glad of the hot barbecue coals he's leaning over. He flips over a sad-looking trout and his eyes immediately start to run from the fishy fumes. He takes a swig of cold beer, liking the taste too much. Just lately, he's been drinking more than he should and he resents the fact his wife can make it through a whole week without turning to alcohol. In his weaker moments he suspects Avril is too good for him and always has been.

He glances over at The Chief, who is squashed into one of the narrow rattan sofas and appears to be broodingly studying the moor. Like Clayton, he also has a chilled bottle of beer in his hand but doesn't put his lips to it.

Clayton presses a spatula on the fish and holds it down until it sizzles and spits angrily. It feels good to take his frustration out on something.

'Be with you in a jiffy, Chief.' Clayton starts to plate up the fish. The Chief raises a hand but does not take his eyes away from the moor.

'You'd rather have him over than be alone with me,' Avril suddenly hisses in his ear.

'The alternative was much worse,' he warns her, thinking of Suzie's openness and warmth. But when he sees the bemused look on his wife's face he wishes he could take his words back. He was being intentionally mysterious, knowing it would provoke her. She doesn't probe, no doubt guessing she might not like what he's got to say.

'You're so full of grief, Avril. Sometimes it's difficult to deal with.' He means well. Perhaps she will understand where he's coming from.

'If I come across full of grief. It's because I am,' she tells him, snootily drawing herself up to her full height.

He wonders what made Avril this way? What happened in the twenty-two years, before he knew her, to make her so wary? Although she has always refused to discuss her childhood with him, he regrets not making enough of an effort to find out more; especially since their son died and she withdrew into herself. He's never suspected her of keeping secrets before but now her world seems full of them.

Having a child might have changed Avril but he rather suspects they were happier *before* they had him. When their son died it destroyed her in a way he couldn't have anticipated. It doesn't help that she's got no other family. Her grief is made worse because of it. He's sure of this. Didn't people always say that blood was thicker than water?

Convinced she must have a blood relation out there somewhere, he decides to do a bit of investigating. He's heard of sites people go on to discover long lost family and if he can hunt down a distant relative, it might make Avril feel less alone in the world. Might even earn him some brownie points while he's at it. Wondering why he hasn't resolved to do anything about it before now, and forgetting momentarily how bad he is at coming up with ideas, Clayton makes up his mind to put the wheels in motion as soon as possible. Without Avril's knowledge, of course.

Chapter 42

Aware that Avril continues to study him intently, The Chief rolls his emergency cigarette around in his fingers before putting it back behind his ear. He knows she can't stand the sight of him, and that's not surprising considering their run-in on the moor; but he's sure the atmosphere between her and Clayton has nothing to do with him. He wonders what caused the argument and who is going to apologise first. Judging by how much whiskey Clayton is getting down his neck and the look of revulsion on Avril's face, he doubts either of them will.

There's a mist brewing over the moor that is the same colour as strong Yorkshire tea and soon it will hang over their heads like a bad headache. Avril lit the outdoor fire some time ago but he chooses to keep away. Fires and him have a habit of not getting along. Each time he takes a sip of the Queen Of The Moorlands, Clayton keeps raving about, it makes his eyes bulge. Revolting stuff. Avril's got the right idea with the cup of hot milk she's hugging. A right innocent she looks, sitting there wrapped up in a blanket with only her toes on show.

Up to now, he's been keeping them enthralled with his stories and they've fallen for every one, hook, line and sinker. As a young lad, brought up on these very moors, he grew up around older men who all claimed to have done things they hadn't, in the hope of inspiring awe. Nowadays, he's just as good at fabricating a story. But some things are true, he reminds himself. Some stories don't need any embellishment and the one he's currently telling happens to be one of them.

'And there were over fifty of these fires, all told?' Clayton asks excitedly. 'All during the eighties?'

The Chief keeps his audience waiting with a longer than average pause. He knows this habit of his annoys the hell out of Avril. Her impatience was one of the first things he noticed about her and he pauses all the more, just to irritate.

'In most cases the houses were completely destroyed and only *The Crying Boy* remained untouched.' He tells them, enjoying the look of disbelief on their faces.

'Did anyone die in the fires?'

The Chief figures it's natural that Avril should want to know this; that she should get straight in there with the one question that matters. This is one of the first things he'd ask too if he were her. If he was living in *this* house. She knows better than anyone else that it doesn't take a painting to burn down a home. He's done his homework on Miss Avril Croft, that was.

'Some argue that the curse will only come into effect if the owner of the painting becomes aware of it, whilst psychics claimed the painting was haunted by the spirit of the boy.'

He watches Avril's eyes climb up into her head as she takes this information in. Is she afraid? She should be. But he has a hard job reading her. Unlike Clayton, who is as open as you like. And dumb too, judging by the drunken way he is imitating a ghost behind his wife's back. While he feigns terror, Avril acts as if none of this matters. But he knows this to be a lie. He's watched her. Seen her. He has an idea of what she is up to. She also has an idea of what Clayton is up to behind her back and is not the least bit impressed. 'It's the drink talking,' she'll be telling herself.

'But did anyone die?' She insists on knowing, all the while batting Clayton off.

Clayton stops fooling around, bothered by his wife's intensity, perhaps, and now they are both looking at him expectantly. They will have a long wait on their hands if they think he's going to spill the beans so soon. This, he will do in his own time. When it suits him. *It doesn't exactly suit me to think of it now*, he admits wryly, *but I can't help myself*.

As he stares into the blueness of Avril's eyes, he thinks about the night that continues to haunt him. He will never forget stumbling across the man's body lying face down on the floor. How could he? Considering what they meant to each other. The stench of burnt flesh was strong in his nostrils, he recalls, and lying next to the man was an untouched *Crying Boy* portrait that nobody wanted to look at.

They all jump when they hear the chilling sound of a fox in the distance, calling for its mate. After another premeditated pause, The Chief breaks into a grin.

'You shouldn't let the facts get in the way of a good story, Avril,' he chuckles, letting her know she's been had. That he's been joking all along.

'He really had you going there.' Clayton points to Avril and laughs too loudly. The drink again.

'In other words, without any mystery, there would be no curse.' Clayton sums it all up in a few words and The Chief laughs along with him, if less exuberantly. He is very much aware that their boyish humour excludes Avril. It is meant to.

'*In other words,*' Avril stresses, 'I shouldn't worry my pretty little head about it, is that it?'

She is well pissed off. But he had seen it coming. The signs were there. So he is not at all surprised when Avril gets to her feet and lets the blanket fall to the floor.

'You don't need language to interpret what a person means,' she says pointedly to him. Clearly, she is taking his part in the wind-up personally, even though her husband was a co-conspirator. Nose in the air, she storms toward the house, huffy as anything. *Given half the chance I'd take some of the stiffness out of her,* he thinks loutishly. But then, just as she goes by, the flames in the outdoor fire soar upwards and just as quickly decrease in size again. The Chief and Clayton raise their eyes at each other, momentarily startled.

'Spooky,' Clayton says, looking worried.

'The breeze. Nothing more,' The Chief says, even though the night is as still and calm as you like. Soon they are sniggering conspiratorially again, like naughty school boys who have just played a prank on their teacher.

'Mind you, that's just the kind of hysteria that provoked *The Sun* newspaper to invite its readers to send in their paintings for a mass bonfire.' The Chief taps his nose, implying he doesn't share this sort of information with just anyone and Clayton nods seriously, as a mark of respect.

They silently digest this information and stir again only when an upstairs light comes on. Together they watch Avril's silhouette moving around as she prepares for bed.

'And thousands did. Can you believe that?' The Chief says it like he can still hardly believe it; even after all this time. But that doesn't stop his eyes from locking on to Avril's figure moving around the bedroom. He'd give anything to see her naked. He's no longer sure he'd want to touch her or be touched by her. That would be a sacrilege. Dangerous too, in the current situation. To look would be enough.

Too late, The Chief senses Clayton is observing him in a wary way, no doubt made uncomfortable by the way he's ogling his wife. He'd better watch himself. Clayton is not as drunk as he thought. He's also more intelligent that he originally gave him credit for. Finally, The Chief tears his eyes away from the sight of Avril undressing and focuses on the flames coming from the fire. Instantly, he feels Clayton relax.

'As supervising fire officer I made sure they all burned beautifully. A few of my officers listened out for muffled cries but all we heard was the crackle of burning paint.' The Chief pulls a melancholy face, indicating he is done. Clayton stares thoughtfully into the fire and The Chief follows suit. They do not realise that they are both imagining the eerie sound of muffled cries coming from the flames.

Chapter 43

Everywhere is in darkness. He knows the light switch is somewhere on the landing but his groping hand cannot find it. Instead, he uses the wall to guide him down the stairs. His head hurts and he's not sure what is going on. A clock ticks somewhere – loudly, slowly and methodically. He can't remember having heard it before. He's unsure of a lot of things but one thing's for certain – he hasn't been this scared in a long time. Then he remembers their first night in Swallow's Nest, when he went into the loft and found the painting. He'd practically shit himself that night, too.

Unlike Avril, Clayton understands that the similarity between the boy in the painting and their dead son is a coincidence and nothing more, but that doesn't stop him wishing they'd never come across it. There is something about the portrait that plays on his wife's mind. Avril certainly hasn't been the same since she saw it. Obviously, the likeness to the boy has disturbed her. It did him, at first. Clayton might not be the most sensitive person alive but even he realises the portrait means more to Avril than it should.

Nowadays she's as jumpy as a long-tailed cat in a room full of rocking chairs. And her twitchiness is catching too, because if he listens really closely, even *he* can make out the sound of a child's laughter echoing around the hallway. As Avril must have done so many times before him, he imagines the laughter belongs to their son. He wonders if this is how it is for her all the time.

At the bottom of the stairs, his fingers finally stumble upon the light switch and the ghostly laughter ceases as soon as the hallway floods with light. *Just my imagination then,* he reassures himself. Clayton rubs the sleep out of his eyes and gets his bearings. The way he's been drinking lately, huge gaps appear like sinkholes in his evenings when he can't remember a thing. Right now, with Avril acting the way she is, he can't get any shut-eye without first having a drink. It's either that or lie awake all night, tossing and turning.

He'd woken up parched and after drinking two glasses of tepid water from the glass usually reserved for his toothbrush, he'd come out of the en suite bathroom to find Avril wasn't in bed either; hence his coming to look for her.

Noticing that the door to the sitting room is slightly ajar, he walks over to it and pushes it fully open. It takes a few seconds for his eyes to adjust to the darkness and then he sees her... She wears a silky nightdress and nothing more and he's horrified by how thin she has gotten, even in the last few days. Her ribs poke out of the material like kindling in a net. She stands in the centre of the room and stares, just stares, at *The Crying Boy* on the wall.

'Avril?' he calls out softly. This isn't the first time he's caught her sleepwalking and he knows better than to alarm her. The door squeaks in his hand and he holds his breath in case she turns on him the way she did last time, when he found her talking to herself in the corner of the bedroom. 'I'm not talking to you. I'm talking to them,' she'd hissed nastily, without even seeing him, before turning back to the wall. But Avril remains rooted to the spot. Impossible to reach. It's almost as if she has become hypnotised by the painting and this makes him shudder all over.

Not knowing what to do, Clayton shakes his head sadly and wonders, *when did my wife first start acting like a ghost?* Even as this thought crosses his mind, he knows he is not being completely honest with himself because even before he opened the sitting room door he had been dreading finding her like this. All along he'd known where he would find her.

Chapter 44

On the whiteboard somebody has written 'Welcome Mrs Shaw' and underneath the same words have been drawn on in sign language. Avril teaches the two-handed finger spelling alphabet to a small group of hearing impaired children while others are helped individually by classroom assistants. In this environment Avril is at her happiest but her mind still races with doubt, because only she knows what an imposter she is. At work or at home, the fear of being exposed never leaves her.

How did I get here? she wonders, glancing at the nice middle-class volunteers who don't smoke, drink or swear but *do* go to yoga and host dinner parties for their friends. These days they look up to her and even defer to her. After all, she is Mrs Shaw, a teacher and a professional in her own right. But she can't help wondering what they would think if they knew the truth. *I'm not who you think I am.* She'd love to shout the truth at them in her old Avril Croft voice.

Having come from the poorest, most run-down council estate in Cambridge, where poverty amongst children was at its highest, she'd managed to pull herself out of the gutter and turn her life around by the time she turned 15. A model pupil, she had later gained a degree in educational studies at Leeds Trinity University as well as developing a taste for culture and the arts. But she couldn't have done any of this without June Croft, who not only provided her with a home when she needed one, but who mentored her too. Avril had been turned down by other prospective foster parents because of her horrific scarring and destructive behaviour, but June, herself a retired teacher, wasn't going to be outwitted by a terrified teenager.

The wealthy widow had been left a rambling old house and a generous pension and the two became thick as thieves in a very short space of time. June was not an affectionate woman but Avril doted on her all the same. Sadly, she died not long after Avril turned eighteen, having had one form of cancer or another for as long as Avril could remember.

Along with the five-bedroomed property in York, Avril also inherited June's small fortune. But she couldn't bear the thought of living alone in her foster mother's house and sold it; donating half the proceeds to the Children's Regional Burns Unit in Yorkshire. She was sure this was what June would have wanted. The remainder she kept for herself.

She still has £80,000 in a savings account that Clayton knows nothing about. She can't tell him about the money because she doesn't want him to find out about her past or where she came from. *She* might have been born among a family of benefit scroungers but her husband wasn't. Clayton's parents are wealthy, middle class retired academics and when Clayton informed them he didn't want to go to university, they were nothing but supportive. They'd even coughed up half of the money to buy Swallow's Nest. It often strikes her as odd how she has all the *appearance* of being middle class, recognizable in her voice, clothes and profession – but Clayton is the real deal. He might act like a man of the people, somebody very ordinary, but he's always been out of her league.

When she notices her new headmistress observing her through the glass pane in the door, Avril stops daydreaming and gets on with her work. This is a good school and she is very lucky to have been offered this position. She can't afford to screw up again. Already, she's caught several of her new colleagues stealing glances at the scarring on her throat and chest. She'd rather they commented on it than ignore her as this only makes her feel more isolated. Like a leper. Still, she should be used to this reaction by now. What's worse is them knowing about Tommy.

This is meant to be their new start. *My new start*, she reminds herself. Yet this seems an impossible task when everybody already knows everything about her. Avril feels overwhelmed by the responsibility placed on her shoulders. A new home. A new job. Fitting in. Making friends. It is all too much. Her eyes start to sting and her ears buzz with that familiar beep, beep, beep sound. *How is it possible to make a new start without Tommy or the chance of having another like him?* She can't imagine a future without children. She supposes this is why she finds herself turning to *The Crying Boy*, so she can fulfil her yearning to be a mother again. Being a mother is what she was born to do. She glances at the bobbed heads of the children in her care and realises that being a teacher is never going to be enough.

Then, she notices that the headmistress is waving at her through the door, trying to get her attention.

'Are you alright?' the woman mouths silently, obviously concerned by how immobile Avril is. Usually, any teacher worth her salt is tripping over the children in her care with never a moment to stand still.

Avril nods back and sends her a reassuring smile before turning her attention back to the blond-haired boy who she's sure is the same height as Tommy was when he died. She strokes his hair, unaware that she is applying too much pressure to his head and wishes the assistants would hurry up and leave the room. She loves being alone with the children. She cares about this even more than she does her class teaching stats. Everyone here knows she is a conscientious, caring teacher and that the children are safe in her hands. 'Too safe,' her last headmistress had suggested after Avril claimed one of her pupil's was being abused at home. Convinced he was at risk, Avril had been hell-bent on having him removed from his parents' care. But after much investigating it turned out Avril was wrong and the head had never let her forget this.

'You mustn't allow yourself to become too involved,' she had been warned. The head had even dared suggest childless teachers were more prone to this type of hysteria than those *with* children. *I do have a child. He might be dead but I am not childless. I am a mother.* Avril had wanted to scream all of this and more in the woman's face and nobody was more surprised than she was, when she later found out she *had*. Afterwards, she'd been made to go and lie down in the children's sickroom before Clayton arrived, looking like a sombre undertaker, to take her home.

Chapter 45

Despite drinking loads of water (something of a novelty for him), *and* taking painkillers, Clayton's head is still throbbing from last night. It's just as well he doesn't have any appointments today because he's probably still over the limit and the thought of losing his licence is enough to make him stay home. Besides, he's determined to fix this damned smoke alarm before Avril throws it at him. Sometimes, she overreacts to the slightest thing, like the sound of the alarm going off, but last night she had every right to be upset.

What with getting pissed and joining in with The Chief winding her up about those fires, Clayton realises they both acted insensitively. Today he intends making up for it by completing chores around the house, like the squeaky door in the spare bedroom. The one with the faulty latch that keeps closing on itself and sticking. With all that talk of burning buildings, especially as the very house they are standing up in was once burnt down, it's no wonder Avril has started sleep walking again.

As always, everything in his workshop is neat and orderly. His workbench has been cleared so that it only contains the tools he needs – a screwdriver and an electrical testing device, along with some additional wiring. It's going to be a fiddly repair job, he can tell. Doesn't help that every five minutes he keeps seeing a shadow out of the corner of his eye that breaks his concentration. There it goes again. He catches only a glimpse of it as it passes. A bird perhaps? Or a shadow magnified by the powerful midday sun? He stops what he is doing and wonders who he is trying to kid. He may not want to believe it but he can't shake off the feeling that he is being watched. It's an unsettling thought. He remembers Avril once telling him she felt as if she was being watched all the time, but he hadn't taken this claim seriously. She'd even gone on to say she didn't know what it was like *not* to feel that way, which was kind of weird. Exactly the sort of talk he doesn't like. Anyway, as he's not as easily spooked as Avril, he soon convinces himself he is mistaken and goes back to the job in hand. Until he sees it again. This time he puts down the screwdriver, walks over to the doors and peers outside.

'Anybody there?' he calls out, almost hopefully. He'd much rather arrive at a satisfactory and logical explanation than not. But no one is there.

Feeling irritated, Clayton goes back to the workbench and stares at the faulty smoke alarm as if *it* is to blame for the way he is feeling. He's really not in the mood for this. Something is niggling him. He's not himself. And it's not just the hangover. This afternoon he's planned on doing a little research on his wife's maiden name to see if he can come up with any clues about her past, but he's already dreading the outcome. What if he doesn't like what he discovers? What if she finds out what he's up to behind her back? He wonders if the risk is worth taking.

When he next looks up and sees the formidable black shadow of a man standing directly in front of him, Clayton's heart packs such a wallop he almost shrieks like a girl.

'Jesus,' he growls. 'You didn't half give me a fright,' he tells The Chief, who looks as if he has been standing there some time, observing him.

'Sorry. I didn't mean no harm.'

If The Chief notices how twitchy Clayton is, he shows no sign of it. Limping into the building, his stubborn old eyes fix on a selection of chisels, all honed to vicious perfection and he lets out a whistle of admiration.

'This is amazing.'

'It's getting that way,' Clayton admits, still reeling from the fright. *I'll end up as jittery as Avril at this rate*, he warns himself. *Not a good habit to get into.*

'You know, I never thought I'd see anyone living in this place again.' The Chief removes the cigarette from behind his ear and twirls it around in his fingers.

Clayton notices that it's not the same wrinkled one as before. This one looks new, as if it's just been slid out of a packet. He wonders why he keeps buying them if he really has given up smoking.

'You mean because of the fire?' Clayton wants to know.

The Chief shakes his head and frowns, indicating he no longer wants to talk about this. Yet last night Clayton couldn't shut him up, even when he could see it was upsetting Avril. He might have been as guilty as The Chief was, but that doesn't mean he doesn't know when a joke has gone too far. And it obviously did, hence the sleep walking.

'So far off the beaten track an' all, is all I meant.' The Chief pauses. 'For most people that is.'

'We're not most people.' Clayton tells him. 'I'm glad you popped by, because there's something I wanted to say to you.' Clayton swallows nervously, feeling like a nipper again in the shadow of this much older and frankly much bigger man.

'Well, spit it out son. It's the best way, as far as I can tell.'

'About Avril,' Clayton clears his throat. 'She was a bit spooked last night. Not that she said anything, mind,' he adds hastily; not wanting The Chief to hold anything against her. 'It's just that… well… with you putting all that stuff in her head about the picture, I think she's becoming a bit obsessed.'

'So you'd rather I didn't mention it again?' Although he seems surprised by the question, The Chief shrugs innocently, as if to say 'is that all?'

'Yes, mate.' Clayton nods.

'No problem at all,' The Chief says, looking bored.

Clayton doesn't know why, but he rather expected a show of resistance on The Chief's part. But then he realises that The Chief isn't deliberately making things easy for him; he just isn't up for discussions about irrational women. Clayton can't say he blames him.

Chapter 46

Avril can see Swallow's Nest in the distance. It sits in a scooped-out dip on the moor but the top of the tree and its two chimneys are still visible on the horizon. This is the first time since moving here it has felt anything like returning home. A morning spent teaching must have done her the world of good because today she feels more positive than she has in a long time. She won't admit it, even to herself, but she's hoping to have the house to herself when she gets back. *Will I see Tommy or the other child today?* she wonders. *It doesn't really matter which one,* she is surprised to find out, *as long as it isn't Don Bonillo.*

She is only about half a mile from home when a large man steps out in front of her, causing her to brake a little sharper than she should. It's The Chief. *He's probably been skulking around on the moor just so he can frighten me,* she thinks. She watches him limp sluggishly toward her. He has a gun slung over one shoulder and carries two dead rabbits with glazed-over eyes. She hopes they died instantly and didn't have to be finished off by his giant hands. She wonders if the gun is armed and if the safety catch is on. What if his rotten old leg trips him up and the gun goes off in her face? The gun frightens her even more than The

Chief does. Nevertheless, she winds down her window and musters up a smile.

'Hi, Chief.' Her words sound false, even to herself.

He leans into the window, invading her space, and all at once she feels ridiculously small. Her pint-sized car offers no protection at all because he could pull the door off with one hand if he wanted to. Close up, he's even more gruesome than she thought. He has pock-marked skin and a greenish tinge to his stubble.

'How's it feel doing a full day's work again?' He sneers, feigning just as much interest in her as she would him.

'Only half a day so far,' she corrects him and regrets doing so almost immediately. *Why can't I speak to him without resorting to criticism? Normally, people don't rub me up the wrong way as much as he does*, she reminds herself. They both seem intent on riling each other up.

'I thought I'd pop back for lunch. Surprise Clayton.' Without knowing why, she feels the need to explain. 'You're welcome to join us.'

'That's not what I hear,' he barks. 'Besides, I've got my own.' He shakes the bloodied rabbits at her, smearing her car.

Realising this is not the same man from last night who wanted to scare her with his tales, Avril shrinks back from him. This is not even the same man from the moor who frightened her into running away. This man is angry, wild and dangerous. She feels it in her bones.

'And if you want to know about that there picture of you'rn, you'll have to look up old newspaper archives. They should tell you all you need to know, because to tell the truth, I don't much feel like talking about it anymore.'

Like a bear with a sore head, The Chief then stomps away, having said all he's going to. He does not take the pot-holed lane that isn't really a road at all. Instead he heads toward the moor. Avril watches him go, puzzled by his ever-changing behaviour. There's no working the old codger out. When he is alone with her, he is a completely different person to the one he is when he's with Clayton. Once he's out of sight Avril starts up the car. She can't even remember stalling it.

***

The Chief doesn't know how he managed to keep smiling throughout that exchange with Clayton, or how he managed not to give his true feelings away. But afterwards, he'd taken his temper out on the wildlife, shooting far more rabbits than he could eat and using the butt of his gun to put an injured deer out of its misery. Usually, he takes no pleasure in an animal's death, but today he had to vent his rage on something.

As if one run-in with a Shaw wasn't enough for one day, he'd then spotted her car coming along the pot-holed lane to Swallow's Nest. From his position on the high ground, it appeared like a toy car with a Sindy doll at the wheel. The one good thing to come out of his conversation with Clayton was knowing his plan was working. Freaking her out about the painting and the curse was exactly what he'd intended.

Having watched the slow progress of the car as it came around the bend, he realised she liked to take things nice and steady as if she was some timid little thing that wouldn't say boo to a goose. But that was just for show. Right from day one he'd sensed there was an anger inside the real Avril that she couldn't shake off, no matter how hard she tried. He got the feeling she was just looking for someone to take it out on and at first he had hoped it wouldn't be Clayton. Now he knows he needn't have worried, because he was the scapegoat. Although he's trying not to, he feels he is in danger of getting too attached to Clayton. The guy is too good to be true. The Chief has never met anyone so generous and open before. It isn't the Yorkshire way. That said, he isn't about to let emotion get in the way of his plan.

Chapter 47

Avril places her handbag on the kitchen table and notices how empty and tired it looks, rather like how she feels. There's not much inside – just a purse with a broken clasp, a crumpled up emergency sanitary towel and a nude-coloured lip gloss. She's seen a lot of women grope around in their overstuffed handbags unable to find what they are looking for, but she doesn't need a physical reminder that she is missing something from her life. The handbag might be old but she will not part with it. It was one of the first things Clayton bought her and it would be cruel to toss it away now, just because it is no longer fashionable. She sighs, wondering if things will ever improve. *I doubt it, if an empty handbag can bring me almost to tears,* she thinks.

Habit makes her switch on the kettle before giving the place the once over. Straight away she notices the dishes haven't been washed up. Nor has the table been cleared. Clayton's crusty toast remains are scattered over the worktop and there are coffee stains on the floor.

Gritting her teeth, Avril disappears into the hallway. 'Mrs Mills? Mrs Mills?' She calls, unable to keep the frustration out of her voice.

There is no response. No sound of shuffling feet coming down the stairs or of the woman swearing under her breath, the way she does when she thinks no-one is listening. Avril marches back into the kitchen and turns on a tap, splashing cold water on her face and neck. It's unbearably hot indoors. She pushes open one window then another. In the distance she thinks she can see a child playing alone on the sun-scorched moor and holds her breath for longer than is good for her.

Hearing the back door open, she spins around to see Clayton standing there with a foolish look on his face. She can't think why he should look so pleased with himself when the house is such a mess. His hair is ruffled as if a loving parent had just run a hand through it and the smell of freshly sawn wood has followed him into the kitchen.

'Where's Mrs Mills?'

'You mean "Tuts and sighs"?' he laughs mischievously and rolls his eyes. For a second he is fun-loving Clayton again. The one she misses most when her mouth is full of pillow; when she's trying her best not to cry at night.

'You mustn't call her that,' Avril snorts, recognising that he always did have a unique way of summing people up.

'She said she'd come back later when it was more convenient *for her.*' Clayton shrugs, impressed by Mrs Mills' bluntness. His face breaks into a grin again and Avril's heart does a somersault. 'At least that's what I think she said.'

They share a rare smile and suddenly there's warmth between them. It's true the woman is impossible to understand and Avril is glad they have come to the same conclusion.

'Come on, I'll give you a hand.' Clayton attacks the pile of washing-up while Avril continues her inspection, opening up the door to the washing machine and rummaging in the bin.

'She's done nothing I asked her. She hasn't even put the washer on. And the list I left her is in the bin.'

'Why don't you sack her, then, if she's no good?' Clayton asks in a disinterested sort of way. Avril stares back at him and realises none of this matters. The only thing that is important right now is the way Clayton is smiling at her.

'Sack Mrs Mills? I couldn't possibly do that,' she plays along innocently, biting her bottom lip.

'You mean you daren't,' Clayton teases. He is spot on and they both know it. Deliberately ignoring him, she grabs a loaf of wholemeal bread, a half cucumber, an iceberg lettuce, a bag of celery and some low-fat spread from the fridge.

'Perhaps you could have a word?' she suggests, spreading the bread with margarine and layering it with lettuce.

'Oh no, you don't.' Clayton throws her a warning glance over his shoulder and unwittingly drips soapy water on the floor. 'I'm not having anything to do with it.'

'She could be a lot worse, I suppose.' Avril bites into a stick of celery and struggles to swallow even this stringy morsel.

'Yep. So far she hasn't managed to burn the house down.' It's the wrong thing for him to say, but this time Avril doesn't pick him up on it.

'Talking of *fiery* personalities…' Avril deliberately lets her words hang in the air. 'I ran into The Chief on the way home.'

'Oh?' Clayton is cautious. 'And what did he have to say?'

'Nothing much,' Avril tells him, wondering why her husband looks sheepish all of a sudden.

Chapter 48

Normally, Avril loves spending time in libraries where the smell of books stirs up memories of her favourite childhood stories; but today she is hunched over a laptop in the school's ultra-modern building, which is an altogether different experience.

Everywhere she looks there are reminders of what it means to have a hearing impairment; from the sign instructing visitors to 'Please ensure your hearing aid is set to the T position' to books featuring deaf characters. Everything is specifically designed to help children and their parents deal with new or demanding situations, but today Avril finds all of it depressing.

The room has bright orange furniture and blue chairs that look as if they have only just been unwrapped. The white walls are decorated with a selection of pupil's work and in one corner there are scatter cushions on the floor where children normally sit cross-legged with books balanced on their laps. The room smells of bleach rather than old books and the floor squeaks like her old school gymnasium used to. Not only that, the glossy book covers seem to compete with one another for her attention.

Being small, Avril doesn't find it uncomfortable to sit in one of the child-sized chairs. The air conditioning is working and she feels almost cool. For once, her hair is dry and does not stick to the back of her neck. Another plus is that the school-issue laptop is fairly modern and the internet connection is fast. She hasn't got long, she reminds herself, darting a quick look behind her to check nobody has crept in after her. She could get into trouble for being in here, as strictly speaking she should be back in her own classroom preparing for tomorrow's lesson. What she is up to isn't exactly work-related either. Even so, she'd rather get found out by one of her colleagues or even the headmistress than have Clayton cotton on to what she is up to.

Having simply tapped in 'The Crying Boy' to the search engine she now scrolls through the multiple web pages that have come up. The words 'cursed', 'haunted', 'paranormal' and 'myth' fill her screen. It's not long before Avril has read all about Sandra Rush, who claimed to have seen the jinxed painting swing from side to side hours before her house burnt down. Then she reads the report about Grace Hopper, who was hospitalised with severe burns after her house caught fire. Although the poor woman's home was burnt down, *The Crying Boy* painting was later found undamaged. Another unnamed woman blamed the death of her husband and three sons on the crying boy 'curse'. Roy Wilkins, secretary of The Folklore Society speculated as to whether the artist had mistreated his model, resulting in a vengeful curse. *So, The Chief was telling the truth the other night*, Avril realises with a jolt, *even though he tried to make it sound like a joke afterwards. But it isn't a joke. None of it is. And he wanted me to know this. Why else would he tell me look up old newspaper archives?*

She doesn't know whether to feel vindicated by what she has uncovered or afraid. She suspects the answer will come to her at a later date. Putting her concerns aside for now, Avril reads about Malcolm Robinson who attempted to destroy a neighbour's Crying Boy painting only for his own house to catch fire. She glances through similar snippets of information until she comes across something that strikes her as even more significant.

'A 43-year-old man died in a house fire in which the room was gutted but an unscathed Crying Boy painting was found on the floor near the deceased's body.'

But it's not the report itself that puts the fear of God into her. It's not even the digitally modified picture of the crying boy with his eyes on fire. No. It's the faded black and white photograph of the deceased man. He is a lot younger and slimmer of course, but even so, she is certain that it's him.

'The Chief.'

Chapter 49

Oblivious to the beep, beep, beep sound of the smoke alarm coming from the boiler room, Clayton stands back to admire the Yorkshire moors painting that hangs on the sitting room wall. It is grey and wintry in the painting, unlike today, and the moors are wet with Wuthering Heights rain. He can't wait to witness the changing seasons from Swallow's Nest. So far, they've only known what it's like to live here in a hot, sulky summer.

When he hears the back door in the kitchen slam to, he realises that Avril is home already and this means trouble for him because he still hasn't managed to fix the smoke alarm.

'The noise,' Avril complains, walking into the room with her hands over her ears. She looks beat, he notices. Hot and exhausted. It must be hell teaching other people's kids all day when your own is... He stops. These days he's becoming almost as morbid as she is. Avril's mood is more catching in these surroundings. Grief and heartbreak become like lost dogs in a city the size of Leeds, where you are never alone. But here on the moor, he feels the difference.

'I thought I'd fixed it. Then I got waylaid doing something else,' he holds up his hands in surrender but she's in no mood to laugh this off. Earlier this afternoon she'd been in much higher spirits. He doesn't know what has happened to her in the meantime but she has her arms folded defensively and looks as cross as a cat with its tail caught in the door.

'You've had all afternoon to sort this out, Clay,' she whines in a way she wouldn't do with her naughtiest pupil.

'It's only just this minute gone off again,' the edge to her voice is catching. Now *he's* feeling a little hard done by. 'Besides, I think the batteries are stuck inside.'

'Then you'll have to take it down again,' she states the obvious. He wonders if she does this on purpose, just to annoy him. Then he reminds himself what a sneaky bastard he has been this afternoon, going behind her back. The time wasted searching her family tree on the internet could have been put to better use, considering he found out absolutely nothing. He might as well have made a proper job of the smoke alarm and finished off his other chores while he was at it. He wonders how she would react if he walked over to her now and kissed her full on the mouth, by way of an apology. Before he's made up his mind whether or not to wade right in, he realises Avril is now glaring past him – at the painting.

'What's that?' She looks knocked for six, not exactly the reaction he was looking for.

'What do you think?' He moves away from the chimney breast so that her view is unobstructed. He wants her to be every bit as impressed as he was when he first saw it.

'I think it looks like the same view I see every day from my window,' she shrugs impatiently.

Okay, so it's clear she's not the slightest bit impressed, he realises dismally. But he doesn't have a Plan B.

'I bought it from an antique shop in Keighley a few days ago and as they delivered it this afternoon, I thought I'd put it up as a…' he runs out of steam.

'A surprise,' Avril finishes his pathetic sentence for him. Her frown is also big enough for the both of them.

'Do you like it?' He dances on his toes, suddenly desperate to take a piss.

'Where is *The Crying Boy*?'

'I thought you might prefer this,' he points at the painting of the moor in case she hasn't really looked at it properly. 'It has nice white sheep in it. You like sheep.'

'Clayton, where is my picture?'

'I put it in the garage,' he hesitates, 'for now.'

'You were going to throw it away.' She squawks in alarm, and presses a hand over her mouth. 'It's bad luck to take it down,' she hisses, in a way that makes him think she is frightened of being overheard. But by whom?

'Surely you don't believe in all that—'

'*The Crying Boy* picture... my *picture* stays,' Avril interrupts rudely, before he has chance to finish.

The sound of a crash – something being dropped in the hallway – makes them both jump. They listen to the rustle of scheming feet moving away from the sitting room door; on the retreat now they've been rumbled.

'Mrs Mills,' Clayton whispers, secretly pleased that there is somebody even more stupid than him around. With that, Avril rolls her eyes and storms out of the room.

Chapter 50

Stepping into the kitchen, Avril notices that Mrs Mills is bent over the sink, attempting to scrub it clean. In her panic to look busy, her arms are going ten to the dozen. Avril doubts Mrs Mills has ever worked this hard in her entire life. *Who does she think she's fooling?* she scolds silently, wishing she had the guts to say so out loud.

'Mrs Mills?' Avril holds her head high and waits patiently. She must be firm but fair. That has to be the way to go on. There can be no more repeats of today. If things go to plan she will say nothing about the woman listening in at the door just now or shirking her responsibilities.

'Ay, I'm just finishing up here.'

Mrs Mills isn't in any hurry to face her either, Avril realises. This is welcome news.

'Mrs Mills? I must insist we have a little chat.'

Mrs Mills huffs and puffs as if everything is too much trouble but she does eventually turn around.

'Oh well. If you *insist*,' she sighs. 'But it's not as if I haven't got a hundred and one other things to do.'

Avril notices that Mrs Mills' eyes refuse to settle on anything for too long. In particular, she seems to have trouble looking Avril in the eye. *If I didn't know better, I'd say she was afraid of me, but I find that hard to believe. How could anybody be scared of me?*

'I don't think things are working out very well for either of us at the moment.' Avril is pleased to find her voice doesn't shake as much as she thought it would.

'Looks like things are working out for one of us.' Mrs Mills rolls her mean little eyes around the expensive kitchen. Finally, Avril understands that the older woman resents her for having the big house. After all *she* is the outsider; not even from these parts. She wishes she could tell Mrs Mills that she never wanted to live here. But as she is no longer of this mind, she does not let on.

'I appreciate you may be used to managing your own workload, Mrs Mills, but it's really important to me that you follow directions–'

'Me ears. You'll be wanting to pay me compensation for me ears, if I'm to go. All this racket,' Mrs Mills complains belatedly, covering her ears with her hands.

That damned smoke alarm! I could kill Clay. I really could, Avril thinks. *I bet he's got his nose up against the door right now, listening in and enjoying every minute.*

'I won't be made a fool of, Mrs Mills.' Suddenly Avril is tough, surprising even herself. 'By anyone,' she warns, glaring at the kitchen door where she knows Clayton is hiding. 'But I *am* fair. And that means I'm prepared to offer you a further week's trial on the condition you follow my instructions to the letter. I won't ask more of you than is physically possible but I do expect you to finish all the items on the list I give you. Is that understood?'

'You're not sacking me then?' Mrs Mills lowers her hands and eyes her employer warily. Avril can't decide if the woman is pleased or not. She's not one to give much away.

'As I said, we'll give it until Friday and see how things go. I can't say fairer than that, can I?'

'If you say so, Mrs Shaw,' Mrs Mills exaggerates a dip in her knee, and Avril's face reddens in embarrassment. *Did she really curtsey to me just then?*

'There's no need to call me Mrs Shaw. Just Avril.'

'If you say so.' Mrs Mills turns her back on Avril and empties more bleach into the sink, making Avril's eyes water.

'And my husband, Clayton... will have the smoke alarm fixed by the next time you come,' Avril promises; although she suspects the beep, beep, beep sound doesn't bother the woman anywhere near as much as she says it does.

***

Clayton is perched one-footed on a stepladder, struggling to re-hang *The Crying Boy* on the wall. It's never an easy job to do on your own but as soon as it *is* back on the wall, the beep, beep, beep sound stops. *No way*, he thinks and finds himself gazing at the boy's tormented face. He searches for something in the watery eyes, but doesn't know what he expects to find... except how much he is reminded of his son. This alone is enough to make him hate the painting, without taking into account what effect it is having on his wife... who isn't falling apart as much as he thought, judging by the way she tore into Mrs Mills just now.

He was dead proud of her when she came out with that line 'I won't be made a fool of by anyone.' Because of course he'd been listening in at the door. He hadn't been able to resist. But as soon as their dispute was over, he'd beaten a stealthy retreat back to the sitting room because even he didn't want to bump into the terrifying Mrs Mills.

Once again he finds himself staring at *The Crying Boy* portrait. He thinks he detects a slight movement on the boy's face and peers closer still. When he sees the child's mouth twitch in an upward motion, as if about to break into a twisted smile, Clayton leans back in amazement. Woah. *That did not happen. I swear he just smiled at me – but not in a good way.* He knows this isn't possible. But he also knows what he saw. Or what he thinks he saw. Avril's twitchiness must really be getting to him.

'You don't like the cleaner either, huh?' he jokes, deciding his imagination must be playing tricks on him. Just to be doubly sure, he takes one last look. As his body leans toward the painting, Clayton's own eyelashes sweep against the boy's cheek. That's when he sees the child's pupils dilate into terrifying pools of blackness. Taken aback by this, Clayton leans too far back and unbalances the stepladder. He tries to steady himself as it wobbles beneath him, but it is too late. The stepladder and Clayton swing sideways and clatter to the floor, landing sideways on.

Before he has chance to right himself, the door opens and Avril comes in. Her concern is not for him however. Her eyes swing straight to the painting, checking it is unharmed. When her eyes do eventually come to rest on him, they are accusing.

'I did it,' he gestures feebly at the painting and rubs his bruised elbow.

'So I see,' Avril folds her arms in that schoolteacher way of hers that always makes him feel like a small boy.

'Dinner will be in an hour. *If* you're finished messing about by then.' She shakes her head despairingly, then exits.

'Yes, miss,' he grumbles as soon as she's out of earshot. Then, leaning heavily on one arm, he pulls himself up from the floor and his hand scratches against something sharp. *Shit, that hurt. And it's drawn blood,* he realises, looking at his palm. He licks the blood away, not minding the taste, and with his thumb and forefinger he prises a rusty two inch nail out of a groove in the wooden floorboards.

The nail had been sticking upwards, right where his head landed after the fall.

Straightaway he thinks, *Christ. How lucky am I?* Then, his glance falls suspiciously on *The Crying Boy* portrait and he starts to question his own sanity. *Don't be daft, man. It's just a painting and the near miss with the nail is nothing more than a coincidence.* He doubts himself for only a few seconds more before his logical mind takes control again.

'You nearly had me going there,' he says jokingly to the painting, all the while shaking his head at his own foolishness. 'Load of old mumbo jumbo.'

Chapter 51

The walls of the snug are lined in pale stone, the kind used in cellars, but the room is surprisingly cosy. In one corner, there is an unlit wood burning stove with a basket of fragrant logs next to it. A fake animal skin hugs the floor and a glass hurricane lamp casts a golden glow around the room. The effect reminds Avril of a pair of sunset-coloured Swarovski earrings she once owned. She may still have them. She really can't remember. One day, when she's feeling better, she may look for them.

She's sitting in a vintage chair in front of a battle-scarred desk that was another 'gift' from the in-laws. If it wasn't pitch black outside, she'd be looking out onto the pretty courtyard garden at the back of the house. She minimised her open web pages as soon as she heard Clayton's Caterpillar booted feet approaching, and the computer screen in front of her is also black.

In he comes, bringing a glass of white wine in one hand and a cold beer in the other. He smells of cedar wood deodorant and something new. She glances up and sees that he has changed into a checked shirt she hasn't seen before; the kind farmers wear. She resists a smile at his expense. Clayton has always dreamt of growing his own fruit and vegetables; even though he's not at all green fingered. He must have showered already, she realises, and hopes this doesn't mean he is expecting a repeat performance of their first night at Swallow's Nest. She really can't face the thought of sex right now or even another row about it. She doubts she has the energy for either.

She barely ate anything for dinner, just a few mouthfuls of quinoa while Clayton happily munched his way through a plate of pulled pork in barbecue sauce. Every slovenly mouthful he took made her want to retch. Not satisfied with this, he went on to spend the whole meal checking out the right pronunciation of 'quinoa' on his mobile phone, while she stared at his forehead wishing she had a bullet for it. When she couldn't take any more she got up, placed her plate in the sink and walked out. Until now, the rest of their evening had been spent in solitary confinement – him sulking; and her getting on with some uninterrupted research.

She takes a polite sip of her wine. She's just going through the motions. As soon as he's gone, she will take it to the downstairs cloakroom and flush it down the toilet.

'No rest for the wicked, huh?' he asks, gesturing at the paperwork on her desk. She smiles politely but does not respond. She really doesn't want to encourage any further conversation. But he is not put off by her silence. He proves this by parking his bum on the corner of her desk; unaware that he is invading her precious space. *A place he has no right to be*, Avril feels.

This is not his first beer of the evening, she's quick to notice, recognising the familiar puffy redness of his face. Tonight his eyes are more grey than blue; another indication that he is drinking too much. She should care more. Have it out with him. But she is too tired. Other concerns, like the history of *The Crying Boy* consume her more. She smiles at Clayton again, only this time there is real pity in her heart for him. Somewhere inside this heavier, drunker version of her husband is the Clayton she fell in love with. The one she *would* have died for. *Would* have done anything for. *Would, would, would,* Avril's own words torment her.

Pretending he hasn't noticed the blank screen until now, Clayton gestures toward it.

'Not much marking going on there,' he remarks casually.

'Confidential pupil files,' she tells him. There's no reason why he shouldn't believe her. She often has to access sensitive information and asks him not to look at it or touch it; not that he'd want to. She could get into a whole lot of trouble for sharing personal data on vulnerable children.

'I've often wondered what secrets a five-year-old can have, that you can't share with your husband,' he says dryly, before taking another noisy gulp of beer.

Tommy was five, and he lived in a world full of secrets and silence, she wants to throw this knowledge at him. But she smiles sweetly instead, cottoning on to the fact he is being unusually suspicious. This is not like Clayton. He hardly ever questions her. Or if he does, it's usually to do with her mental health. It's as if that's all he's been concerned with in the months since they lost their son.

'Not checking up on me, are you?' Avril teases. She dares not be too breezy with him, in case he mistakes her friendliness for flirtation.

'As if I dare,' he grumbles, getting up from the desk. As he gets to his feet, the blond hairs on his forearm brush against her own skin and it sends the invisible hair on her arm into a frenzy. She cannot believe he still has the power to make her tingle like this.

'I won't be long,' she assures him, careful not to make it sound like a promise of anything.

She doesn't get a response. Not even a word of parting. Things have got progressively worse since moving here, she realises despondently. And yet she sometimes feels like her old self again and when this happens they become close for short periods of time. But these moments don't last. Her emotions are so up and down she hardly knows herself at all. *So much for our new start,* she thinks.

Wanting to forget about Clayton and their marital problems, at least for now, she maximises her windows and brings up the newspaper report she was reading earlier.

A Yorkshire fireman's own brother ignored the warning of The Crying Boy 'curse' and fire later destroyed his home; but the painting remained unscathed. Avril eagerly soaks up this information, yet there is nothing unusual about it. She has by now read many other stories like it; but something in particular keeps making her come back to this one. There is something going on here she doesn't understand. Flicking back to the report she came across earlier this afternoon in the library (the one with The Chief's photograph) she reads it again. *A 43-year-old man died in a house fire in which the room was gutted but an unscathed Crying Boy painting was found on the floor near the deceased's body.* Ignoring the image of the crying boy (the one with his eyes on fire), she goes back to studying the photograph of The Chief and runs her fingers across the screen, tracing his familiar features. As well as being younger and slimmer she is now able to detect a warmth to this person's eyes that is definitely absent in The Chief's. Perhaps this isn't The Chief they know, she deduces. *My God, I think I am looking at his brother,* she realises at last. *He's the one that died in the fire.* Deciding she has learned enough for one night, she closes down the computer and wonders why he has never spoken of it.

***

Having figured out Avril is up to no good on her computer, and deciding two can play at that game, Clayton has done a Google search on his smart phone and still can't find any evidence to suggest his wife, the former Avril Croft, ever existed. He's done with family history and genealogy sites as they take too long to research and so far, he's discovered there are three Avril Crofts on Facebook. This is a whole lot better than the blank he drew this afternoon. Unfortunately, one of them is from The Philippines and the other two have private Facebook accounts. Neither has yet responded to the friend requests he sent them.

Realising they are both swatting up on something they shouldn't, without the other's knowledge (a sad state of affairs), Clayton cancels his search and slips his phone in his pocket. He takes another gulp of beer from the bottle (his fifth tonight), and throws a dart at the makeshift dartboard he's set up in the workshop. *I have no idea why she is being so secretive. But I hope it isn't anything to do with another man. I could bear anything but that. That would be even worse than losing the boy,* he realises with a jolt. This knowledge makes him feel shit. *What sort of father am I? How can I even think that about my own kid?* he wonders sadly.

He's had his suspicions before tonight. Just the other day he found her out on the moor with a hopeful look on her face that disappeared as soon as she saw him. *Was she meeting someone up there? Is that what she's up to?* The very thought of this makes him feel physically sick.

Historically, Avril has always been the jealous, insecure one and secretly he used to enjoy it; not that he'd ever admit this to her. Because of this, he supposes he's grown overly confident where she is concerned, but now it's his turn to feel jealous he doesn't like it one little bit. The thought of another man touching her body makes him want to kill someone. *My God*, he thinks, *has Avril had to live with a similar fear all this time? How could I have left her alone in a place like that; worrying her over the likes of Suzie and other women.* Clayton is the first to admit he could have done more to reassure her, especially after what happened.

If Avril *is* seeing anybody – and he intends to find this out pronto – he already knows he will forgive her. He really doesn't have a choice. *But if I get my hands on the man responsible, there's no telling what I will do,* he fumes. This sudden all-consuming anger comes as a surprise to Clayton, who up until now has always been easy going and mild mannered. The sudden desire to hurt someone is new and it overshadows everything else. For instance, he no longer cares that he can't find any evidence of Avril Croft being born. It's way down on his list of priorities. He wouldn't even care if his wife really was a ghost. Living or dead, he loves her.

Chapter 52

The sun sneaks through gaps in the newly hung cotton curtains and outside the open window, swallows chunter away and fat nectar-fed bees buzz by. These are the morning sounds Clayton and Avril usually wake up to. But not today. Because today there is also a loud knocking at the door that sees Clayton leaping anxiously out of bed, wondering what on earth is going on. Avril is soon on his heels, but still finds time to slip a flimsy dressing gown over her exposed, badly scarred body. When Clayton peers out of the window, she sees him visibly relax.

'When you said first thing, I didn't think you meant *first thing*,' Clayton shouts down at whoever is on their doorstep and then laughs; letting Avril know they are in no danger of being murdered in their beds.

'Whoever is it, Clayton?' she asks irritably, watching him slip a crumpled T-shirt over his naked torso. But he's too busy wiping sleep from his eyes to reply, so she goes over to the window to look for herself. She might have known. No wonder Clayton didn't want to say anything. It's The Chief. And he's waving a heavy spade in his hand.

'What's he doing here so early?' Avril pulls the belt of her dressing gown tighter, as if that might protect her from The Chief's prying eyes.

'He's offered to put in some raised vegetable beds for me,' Clayton confides, looking more than a little embarrassed. She watches him dance his way into a pair of denim jeans and then stumble upon a mismatched pair of socks. Avril cannot pretend to be anything other than amused.

'You? Growing vegetables? Well, I wouldn't *raise* your hopes too much, if I were you,' she says with a smirk.

He pulls a face at her and tosses her a boyish smile, 'Ha ha,' he bites back playfully, before exiting the room.

***

Avril has changed into a floral tea dress and summer cardigan and her hair is nipped into a tight, painful ponytail. She wears a pair of flat pumps and a single strand of pearls at her neck to disguise the puckered skin on her throat. This look completes her usual drab working uniform. She might not go all the way and wear prim glasses but all the same she looks very timid and mouse like.

In her hand she carries a thick cream envelope with a Cornish post mark. It is a letter from Clayton's parents. She's on her way to give the letter to Clayton when she sees Mrs Mills pull up in a battered old Volvo estate.

'Mrs Shaw,' Mrs Mills nods stiffly, getting out of the car and putting her foot on the cigarette she had been smoking. Avril wants to tell her to pick it up but feels this might be considered pedantic. It's not Mrs Mills fault she doesn't have much willpower when it comes to lighting up. Should Avril suffer a particularly bad night, she might be tempted to fish that dog end out of the gravel and smoke it herself. As Mrs Mills slams the car door shut, Avril catches a glimpse of the interior. It is filled with junk, carrier bags and an overflowing ashtray.

'Mrs Mills,' Avril is just as formal.

It's clear they are never going to be friends. Warily, they skirt past each other; Mrs Mills on her way to the kitchen to let herself in the back way and Avril through the brick archway that leads into the courtyard garden.

Here she spies Clayton and The Chief showing off parts of their body to each other in some strange male bonding ritual. Scattered around them are planks of wood and freshly dug soil. The soil is crumbly and dry, and has exposed roots in it. Avril feels pity for the torn roots, which asked nothing from the world except the right to exist; but she feels none for The Chief, whose hooded eyes frighten her. The smell of earth invades her nostrils. It reminds her of freshly dug graves. The thought makes her shudder. Tommy's grave was pathetically small. No bigger than the hole these two men have dug. Close to where he was buried there were similar sized graves. It was a consolation knowing she was leaving him in the company of other boys and girls. She doesn't believe in God. Never has. Not before or after Tommy. But she wants to believe in the afterlife for his sake so she says prayers for her child, never asking anything for herself. She suspects all parents of dead children do this.

She is rather intrigued to see The Chief has one trouser leg rolled up, showing off a large burn mark on his calf. The rest of his leg is a mixture of yellow aging skin and ugly varicose veins, Avril notices. Not to be outdone, Clayton has rolled up his T-shirt and now points to a small scar under his ribs, which is barely noticeable.

'This is where the screwdriver slipped and pierced me,' he boasts. 'I had to have six stitches.'

'Except they weren't real stitches, were they Clayton? They were butterfly strips,' she informs the puzzled-looking Chief, without meeting his eye. When nobody laughs, Avril feels obliged to break the awkward silence.

'So that's what you're up to? Swapping old war wounds.' Avril has never been any good at being one of the boys. Not like Suzie from the other night who would have had the pair of them eating out of her hand in seconds.

'You should see some of The Chief's scars,' Clayton tells her animatedly. 'It's no wonder he never made it to retirement.'

She can tell he is deeply impressed. *It's a man thing*, she thinks witheringly.

'Another time perhaps,' she says scathingly. 'Just remember though, while you're swapping horror stories, I can beat either of you, hands down.'

As she speaks, Avril's hands flutter involuntarily to the scars on her chest and throat. *They have no idea what it is really like*, she thinks without bitterness. Then, she sees that this reference to herself has mortified them. The Chief looks at his scuffed old boot, the one resting on the spade while Clayton fakes an interest in the letter. Her comment has certainly lowered the mood. But in her book, that's not such a bad thing. She doesn't want Clayton getting more pally with The Chief than he has to. She'd rather see him kicked out of their lives altogether; make no bones about this, but she can also see this isn't going to happen in a hurry.

Clayton opens the envelope and digs out the paper that smells of bath salts. He's not a great reader. He only ever skims the pages. Usually he relies on Avril to read snippets out to him so he can get the gist of what his mother's lengthy monologues are all about.

'From Clayton's mother,' she tells The Chief, 'just in case you're wondering.' Her eyes then swing guiltily away as she tackles him with the question she's been rehearsing in her head. 'We don't hear you mention family much,' she tries to sound as causal as possible but he gives her a strange look, second guessing her as always. Nothing much gets past him. She has always known this. His steely eyes let her know he's not about to be interrogated by her or anybody else.

'Which makes me wonder, do you have any relatives hereabout?' her voice wavers nervously. She's determined to go on, no matter the consequences.

'Now what made you wonder a thing like that?' The Chief looks as if he'd like to tear her apart with those brutal hands of his. Yet he keeps his voice neutral enough for Clayton not to notice; proving once again how crafty he is.

Avril blushes and looks away; unnerved by The Chief's fierce gaze. She wishes she had never said anything now. *He will want to get his own back on me for this*, she fears. She looks to Clayton for back up but she can tell he is oblivious to the charged atmosphere.

'Yeah, come on, Chief. Are there any more of you?' he asks innocently.

'A brother. We don't speak no more.' The Chief takes his time responding.

'That's sometimes the way it is with families.' Clayton nods thoughtfully but his eyes rest on Avril; waiting to see if she gives away anything about her own past.

'Was he a firefighter too?' Clayton wants to know.

My husband is obsessed with all action hero figures, Avril groans inwardly. Sometimes she'd like to box him around the ears for being so easily star-struck. *You're twice the man he is*, she wants to scream.

'No.' The Chief doesn't seem to mind being questioned by Clayton. It's only Avril's curiosity he objects to.

'And does he live local?' Avril gets in quickly, while they still have The Chief's cooperation.

'You could say that.' The Chief replies moodily, turning his back on them to stare at the open moorland.

She hears his bones creak as he reaches for the cigarette behind his ear.

***

The Chief watches Avril drive away in her car. She might be as light as a feather but the flimsy piece of junk leans sideways as it bounces along the rough moorland track. Although she has her nose in the air and won't glance his way, she still has the audacity to pip as she passes. The tooting of the horn sounds friendly enough but he knows she is secretly wishing him miles from here. Resting his aching hands on the spade, he resists the urge to pick up a clod of earth and throw it after her. *Stuck up bitch*, he cusses, spitting a stream of ugly phlegm into the freshly dug soil. *How dare she check up on me? Who does she think she is?* Avril's snooping complicates things. He's not yet sure how much she knows, or thinks she knows, but it's clear he is going to have to increase his efforts if his plan is to succeed. It *has* to succeed; he corrects himself grimly. He doesn't need any reminders of what will happen if it doesn't.

Somehow or other, the Shaws keep getting in the way of what he wants. He never imagined they would be so complicated or that he would grow to like at least one of them very much. On the surface, they appear like an ordinary enough couple but they continue to surprise him. He'd counted on having them out of Swallow's Nest in no time at all. *Why are they still here?* he wonders. Most sensible couples would have fled the place the first night they stayed here; when they discovered the painting. Why isn't Avril more terrified of *The Crying Boy*? He's dropped enough warnings about the curse to scare most folk away. But sometimes she looks at the painting with something like affection. He just can't figure it out.

He doesn't want to use the information he has on her just yet. He's saving that as a last resort. Besides, once he lets that out of the bag he'll have no more influence with Clayton. Also, he's not entirely sure what to make of this hard-come-by knowledge. The only thing he knows for certain is her real maiden name *wasn't* Avril Croft; and from what he's found out so far, she's certainly got nothing to be stuck up about.

He throws the spade to the ground and sighs. His whole body aches like buggery. *Face it, you're old and worn out. And you can't keep up like you used to.* Three days ago he turned 60. Nobody remembered to send him a card. He's glad about that because he doesn't need any reminders of how many birthdays Ted has missed out on. He can't believe he only died five years ago. Time has slowed down since then. His younger brother would now be 48 if he were still alive. Ted had been the better person. Happier, kinder, smarter, better looking. *Not a loner, like me.* He had a family too; a beautiful daughter. The Chief's sullen glance takes in Swallow's Nest and the empty moorland that surround it. Over yonder, where the giant ash tree stands, is where he scattered his brother's ashes.

Chapter 53

Suzie's nightdress has a red heart printed on it and her braless breasts lead a life of their own underneath it. The nightdress is also daubed with ketchup stains from last night's fish finger sandwich. She never goes to bed early; preferring to stay up late watching movies. That's why she looks such a fright this morning. Her hair is as fluffy as candyfloss and yesterday's mascara has run, giving her a clown-like appearance. Toby might have tugged her out of bed at seven o'clock this morning to get his breakfast but she still feels half asleep.

She watches her son dipping soldiers into his boiled egg and noisily sucking the runny yolk from the toast. Without fail, he has the same breakfast every morning. Just like he has the same ham sandwich and Quavers for packed lunch and the same chicken nuggets for tea when he gets home from school. He goes to bed at 7pm and she never hears a word out of him again until 7am the next morning. He might be beautiful. Everyone says so. But there is something wrong with her son. She must get out of the habit of thinking this. It's not something wrong, just something different. When he's finished his breakfast, he'll collect his school bag and carefully check he has everything he needs for today's math and PE lessons. He doesn't watch TV or play video games like other children.

Right on schedule, at 7.30am, Toby takes his plate to the drainer and scrapes his eggshell into the bin. He never allows her to do this for him. He then throws her a lop-sided yolky grin, grimaces at the envelope on the table that isn't usually there (she can tell its presence bothers him) and goes out. He won't call for her again until 8.25, by which time she'll have pulled on a pair of tight-fitting jeans and a T-shirt, so she can walk him the short distance to school. As always, he will insist on walking on her right and will not allow her to talk to anyone on the way. Her son's increasingly obsessive, compulsive personality is what really keeps her awake at night, not the TV, and it's time she faced this.

Suzie sighs at the complexity of her son and looks at the envelope stuffed with twenty-pound notes. It is more money than she's seen in a long time. There must be two or three thousand pounds in it. She almost dropped the envelope in fright on first opening it.

'If you don't want to do it, just say so,' The Chief gets up from the other end of the table and drains his mug of coffee. His voice is stern but his eyes are kind.

'Couldn't you just tell them the truth?' Suzie nervously bites her lip.

'Nobody knows what the truth is.' The Chief tells her.

He's looking tired and old, she notices, this uncle of hers, who has done his best to take care of them since her dad died five years ago in that horrible house fire. She was pregnant with Toby at the time, which means Uncle Frank is the only 'grandfather' figure her son has known. She is grateful to him for all he has done; but what he is asking her to do scares the hell out of her.

'You could get him in to see a specialist.' The Chief slides the envelope toward her.

'Is this what dad would have wanted, do you think?' Suzie hates herself for picking up the envelope. For holding it in her greedy little hands.

'He wouldn't want us to do *nothing*.' The Chief shrugs.

'I already tried once and it didn't work. He's never going to fall for it... me... again.'

'I wasn't thinking of *him* this time,' The Chief coughs uncomfortably.

'You mean? You're kidding me right?'

The Chief looks at his boots; letting her know he most certainly isn't kidding. Her heart sinks. She doesn't want to do this. But he's been good to them and he's never really asked anything of her before. She thinks the world of her uncle. And he's right. She does need the money. For Toby.

'It doesn't matter if you can't. Take it anyway,' he gestures to the pile of cash and stoops to kiss her on the cheek. 'I'll just say goodbye to the bairn.'

'No.' Suzie calls him back. 'I'll do it.'

Chapter 54

The primary school in Haworth is in a quiet village street and it has railings running all the way around it. The building itself has the appearance of a cottage bungalow and has hanging baskets outside. Children in polo shirts run around on artificial grass and climb colourful playground equipment. The rubber safety surface means they will never know what it is like to scrape a knee.

When the decision was made to move from Leeds to West Yorkshire and Avril had to look for another job; she applied for a position at this school because of its excellent in-house Deaf Education Programme. Today, she is on morning supervision duty and prefers this to sitting in a stuffy staffroom listening to her colleagues discussing salaries and strategies.

She can't resist keeping more of an eye on the blond-haired children though; the deaf ones too. She feels she's earned this guilty pleasure. Then, out of the corner of her eye she spies a woman waving at her through the metal railings. Curious to find out what she wants, Avril abandons her position and walks over. The woman has an adorable black-haired boy with her. He has intense, know-it-all eyes and clutches on to the woman's hand. It's obvious that the boy doesn't want his mum to stop and talk and this makes Avril smile inwardly. Tommy was just the same. He would often demand her undivided attention; a claim that used to annoy Clayton. Made him feel shut out, he said. But Avril believes it is natural for sons to act protectively around their mothers. Even bad mothers like this one, she thinks unfairly; because by now she has recognized Suzie.

'It's Avril, isn't it?' Suzie clears her throat and casts nervous eyes around the playground; as if fearful of being seen here.

'And you're Sharon?' There is no way Avril is going to give Suzie the satisfaction of being remembered. Not after the way she chased after Clayton.

'Suzie. From the party.' Suzie is rattled. Clearly she's used to leaving a more lasting impression on people.

'Oh yes. I remember you now. You burnt your arm in the fire.' Avril watches Suzie subconsciously stroke her arm; a reminder of the scare she received.

'This is my son, Toby,' Suzie smiles down on her son's shiny black head and waits for Avril to praise his good looks. If she'd said out loud 'This is my son, Toby, *who is still alive*,' Avril couldn't have hated her more. Avril waits for Suzie to go on. She knows there is more.

Suzie stuffs her hands in her jean pockets and sways from side to side. An awkward moment that Avril simply isn't going to help her out of.

'I was wondering if you could give me Clayton's mobile number? I appear to have lost it.' Suzie cannot quite meet Avril's eye when she says this.

'Of course.' Avril immediately starts to scroll through the contact list in her mobile phone. She always keeps it with her when she's on supervision duty, just in case of an accident. 'I can give you the home telephone number and his email address as well if you like,' she offers innocently.

Suzie looks stumped and Avril can tell this is not exactly the response she'd been hoping for. *What a cold fish she must think I am. If only she knew how used I am to women coming on to my husband.*

'Don't you want to know why I need it?' Suzie asks.

'I'm sure you're about to tell me.'

Suzie darts a sly look around her, then lowers her voice to just above a whisper 'Not here. Somewhere more private.'

'I'll be home by four thirty. Why don't you pop and see me then?' They both know this is not the friendly invitation it appears to be.

'Will Clayton be there?' Suzie bites her lip a lot. This is not a habit that would ever endear her to Avril. She has an attractive enough mouth as it is without constantly drawing attention to it.

'I thought you wanted to speak to me alone. Wasn't that the whole idea?'

When Suzie nods uncertainly, Avril is hopeful. Perhaps Suzie has already started to realise she has bitten off more than she can chew. Suzie isn't anywhere near as clever or as brave as she'd like to be.

'I'll see you later then.' Avril tears her gaze away from the boy with the all-seeing eyes; resisting the unfamiliar desire to leave a mark on him. *I've never hit a child in my life,* she reminds herself sternly, *so why am I having such thoughts now?* Yet as she returns to her post in the playground she senses that the slut is still staring after her. *Oh my God, I've never used that word to describe anyone before either. What on earth has come over me?* she wonders shamefully. Something tells her that it is something more than her jealousy of Suzie and her perfect son.

Chapter 55

Avril has her feet curled up under her on the sofa and sips from a cup of refreshing cup of green tea that she balances on her lap. She has made the effort of making it in a proper china cup and saucer, believing it tastes better this way. She looks at her watch; nowhere near as composed as she'd like to be. She then glances at *The Crying Boy* portrait on the wall and feels herself unwind.

She finds it reassuring to have his protective eyes on her. Suzie might have her precious black-eyed boy but she has *him*. In addition, she senses nobody can really hurt her while he is watching over her. And watch over her he does. She's sure of it. She wishes she'd had something – *no someone* – like him around years ago, when she was a child in need of protection. When she first found out the boy in the painting was deaf, like her dead son, and she'd used sign language to communicate with his spirit, she feared becoming lost in a ghostly world that was a product of her imagination. But now she must face up to the grisly realisation that 'fire' is what really connects them. Deep down she has always known this.

Once again, her eyes seek out the crying boy's face. There is a warmth to his eyes that wasn't there five minutes ago. He wants her to tell him her story. She feels this very strongly. *I will sign it to you,* she whispers, *even though I have sworn never to talk about what really happened.*

Taking up her bony hands, she uses fingers, palms and facial expressions to tell her story.

My parents, Alfie and Evie Roberts died in the fire that badly disfigured my body. I was thirteen when this happened. Although the loss of my parents at such a young age was tragic; I want you to know this still isn't my most terrible of secrets. You might not be of this world but I am still not ready to reveal everything to you.

My dad was already dead when I walked into the room. Half of him was badly burnt and he was still in flames. His hand, still unburnt, rested on the arm of the old horse-hair sofa where the fire first started. I remember that the black smoke swirling around him smelt of dusty horses and that I was in my nightdress. I'd only come in to say goodnight. Mum sat in the armchair opposite, sliding pieces of her jigsaw puzzle in place as if nothing untoward was happening. She was either stoned, drunk or both.

'Go back to bed, Avie,' she screamed when I tried to pull her to her feet. Back then everybody called me Avie.

'I swear I'll take a slipper to your backside if you don't leave me alone.' Mum was oblivious to any danger.

So I went to save Jamie instead. It was easy to convince myself that I could go back for her later; that there was still time. But there wasn't. And it turned out Jamie was just as reluctant to escape the flames as she was, so by the time we got out the whole house was on fire and Robbie the kitten was clawing at the curtains. The fire fighters found mum hunched over her jigsaw puzzle.

My parents smoked like chimneys and we stank of fags wherever we went. The kids at school used to bully us for this. Not only that, we lived in a grubby council house that was infested with rats. Sometimes the rats chewed on dad's slippers while he slept. Sleeping was the one thing he was good at. No matter what dad ate, he never put on any weight; due mainly to his forty-a-day habit, I think. I can't once remember seeing my mum eat but she always had a drink in her hand. A pint of cider or a glass of sherry, if she was lucky.

I pretty much brought up Jamie myself; changing his nappy when he was a baby and giving him bottles of milk and Guinness to keep him quiet when they were 'at it'. He was seven years younger than me and as he got older I would find ways to scrape together his favourite meals. Sometimes a neighbour would take pity on us and offer us leftovers; but not without giving us a lecture on dad being a 'waste of space'. We had to listen to such attacks on our father but they were careful not to say anything to his face. He was known for having a nasty temper. He might not have been able to hold down a job but he could finish any crossword in record time and he had a photographic memory. I suppose I take after him in that respect. I suspect he was naturally gifted and could have been anything he liked; but his temper held him back.

Mum didn't die of her injuries straight away. Like me, she was airlifted to the special burns unit, where we laid side by side for the first time in our lives. No matter how hard I cried for my little brother, nobody would bring him to me. So I began to fear the worst. I wouldn't find out what really happened until much later. Unsurprisingly, I started to feel at home in the dark world of sedation that was inflicted on me. The thought of being brought back to consciousness and having to face the pain again was unthinkable. Yet, I did come around when I heard the beep, beep, beep sound of the heart monitor machine flat-line. I was horrified to discover it was my mother's life that was ending, not mine.

This was the first time I had seen her uncovered and when I caught a glimpse of her peeled-back face, I felt myself flinch.

It looked like a gruesome strawberry sundae with straws sticking out of it. I wanted to ask the nurses if I looked as bad; but I was too much of a coward. When a doctor draped my mother's body in a blood stained sheet, it immediately stuck to her oozing skin. I couldn't cry — not from love or pity — because my eyes had also been damaged in the fire. From that moment on, I knew I had to live, for Jamie's sake. With both parents gone, I could not leave him alone. And so began the rehabilitation process that took eighteen long months.

When Avril hears Suzie's car ploughing through the gravel, she sighs wearily and unfolds her legs. This encounter is not going to be pleasant, she realises. Yet with that weight off her chest, she feels surprisingly calm. Clayton was absolutely right when he promised her the move to Swallow's Nest would be good for her. *Nobody can hurt me now;* she comforts herself with this knowledge. *Even if Clay were to leave me for somebody like Suzie, I would be able to cope. All I really need is Swallow's Nest and The Crying Boy.*

Chapter 56

Suzie wishes she had never come. Even before stepping a foot inside Swallow's Nest, she realised what a bad idea this was. But she had no idea how 'wrong' it would feel until she was made to sit down at the table and wait. She looks around her at the familiar layout of the house; a vague reminder of the past. She's only been back here once since it burned down and that was for the party.

Sitting wide-eyed at the table, she can't shake off a terrible sense of foreboding. She's dying for a cup of tea. Something to calm her nerves. Her throat is as dry as a desert. Although there are two cups and saucers lined up on the worktop, each with a teabag in, every time Avril goes to make a brew she gets interrupted. By what, Suzie has no idea. First of all, she pretends to hear something and goes out of the kitchen. This is followed by a whacking noise, which to Suzie's ears sounds like a door being banged shut. Next comes the unmistakable sound of smothered laughter and then Suzie is finally able to make out Avril shushing someone.

She watches Avril come back in. She doesn't look at all flustered. Just apologetic.

'Sorry about that.' Avril is cheery.

'I thought we were on our own,' Suzie's voice sounds whiney, even to herself.

'We are.' Avril frowns as if she is at a loss to understand what Suzie means. 'Except, I don't suppose we are ever truly alone, are we?'

Deciding that Avril can be as deep as she likes, so long as she hurries up and pours her out a cup of tea, Suzie struggles to maintain eye contact with her. She hardly knows Avril, but even *she* can detect a dramatic change in the woman's appearance and behaviour since the night of the party. She is surprised her uncle hasn't mentioned it. Avril looks gaunt and ill; like a recovering cancer patient. She could have sworn her eyes were once as blue as her own, yet today they appear grey and blank; making Suzie feel nervous and uncomfortable. *Why did I ever agree to this?*

Finally, Avril hands Suzie a cup of tea. Not tea exactly, Suzie notices. Just some green watery liquid that has a peculiar flowery odour. Suzie cannot stop her hand from shaking as she takes the cup from Avril. Thankfully, Avril does not join Suzie at the table; choosing instead to lean against the sink. Suzie wonders if the tea is poisoned but under Avril's intense glare feels obliged to taste it. She is not at all surprised to find that it tastes disgusting. *How can anybody drink this rubbish?*

'So, going back to what we were saying a few minutes ago... you're telling me Clay didn't turn up for his appointment with me because he was with *you*?' Avril is matter-of-fact.

'It's not as bad as it sounds.' Suzie watches Avril put the cup to her mouth and pretend to swallow. Realising that Avril is merely putting on an act and that she must really be feeling this news acutely, Suzie hates herself for what she is doing. What has the poor woman ever done to deserve this?

'Isn't it?' Avril glares at Suzie. 'You have no idea what that appointment meant to me. Us.'

Suzie watches the cup and saucer tumble elegantly out of Avril's hand. It travels in slow motion and scatters into delicate, scratchy pieces as soon as it hits the floor. The sound is tinny and abrupt; like bird song. Neither Avril, nor Suzie look at the broken pieces of china on the floor. Neither of them speak. The silence settles eerily on them, like mist on the moor.

Slowly, Suzie gets to her feet and skims a glance at the back door. The cold, impassive look on Avril's face is really starting to frighten her. *Nobody else knows I am here*, she realises with sudden stomach churning fear.

'Look, nothing happened between us. This was just a friendly warning, that's all.

'The best warnings always are,' Avril laughs unpleasantly; ignoring the trail of saliva that trickles out of her mouth.

The fact that Avril makes no attempt to wipe the dribble from her chin freaks Suzie out far more than the smashed cup and saucer.

'You already have a beautiful healthy son. Wanting anything more is just plain greedy.' Avril warns, fixing glazed eyes on a point just behind Suzie. Instinctively, Suzie wants to turn around to see what Avril is staring at but doesn't quite dare... not even when she hears the creak of the inner door opening behind her. Not even when she feels the hair on the back of her neck prick up. Not even when her skin starts to crawl.

'I would never let a man or anybody else come between me and my child.' Avril folds her arms as if she is through talking and smiles at whatever is standing behind Suzie.

I will not turn around. I know there is someone there but I will not look, Suzie vows, inching her way to the back door; never once taking her eyes off Avril's hellishly creepy face. She doesn't get too close mind; just in case Avril suddenly decides to stick out a leg to trip her up. If that happens, Suzie suspects she will never be allowed up again.

Then, just as she thinks she is free; when her hand is on the doorknob ready to throw open the door... something happens to make Suzie scream. At first she is only aware of a blurring of blood and feathers in front of her eyes. It takes her a few seconds to realise that a swallow has collided into the outside of the door. She watches the bird's wings beat frantically against the glass before taking off again. Only then does Suzie become aware of Avril's crazed laughter in the background. This makes her angry enough to forget her fear.

'There's something wrong with you, Avril.' Suzie spins around to confront Avril; relieved to find there is nobody else in the room with them. 'You should get some help.'

'Oh I have.' Avril stops laughing. 'More help than I could possibly need,' she adds mysteriously.

Chapter 57

The darkness is like a sickness she doesn't want to catch. She fears stepping into it. In her dream, Avril is alone on the moor. In the shadows she sees and hears things no person should. *Alone on the moor, nobody can hear you cry. Alone on the moor, nobody can hear you cry.*

She knows that whoever is with her in the darkness is waiting for her to make a break for it. It wants to chase her over the moor; into the unknown. She feels something soft brush against her bare leg and she whimpers out loud. *I must not scream*, she warns herself. *If I'm quiet, it may not find me.* But her thunderous heartbeat gives her away and it moves closer still. *I will not move. I will not run*, she chants, sensing that it is moving around her in a slow circle. It roots around like a rabid dog, inhaling her scent. Then, more terrifyingly still, she feels it lean against her; seemingly at home there. Finally, a small hand nudges hers. It feels cold and clammy to the touch. *I will not be able to bear it if it touches me again*, Avril holds her breath. The hand then tentatively slides into her own frigid palm. When she feels its sticky little fingers squeeze hers, she pulls away.

Now she is running. And it is behind her. Her rejection has angered it. She can tell this by the heat it generates.

If it catches up with her; *when* it catches up with her – it will show her no mercy. Already, her nightdress is on fire. The flames are spiralling upwards towards her belly and her throat. She is burning up. She cannot breathe. Her bloodied feet graze against heather and rock and she stumbles often. Somewhere out there, not a stone's throw away, is Swallow's Nest. If only she could see it, find it, touch it – she would be safe. But she is in a world of blackness; of silence and stillness. Then her feet go from under her and she is floating; like a black crow hovering over lost lives.

The fall does not kill her but her broken fingers will never mend properly. The skin on her face, elbows and knees is torn and bleeding. She spits out a broken tooth that glistens like the white of an eye in the blackness. Her hands cling onto a stone object that she knows won't save her. It is in the shape of a cross and is smooth to the touch; except where words have been carved into it. *It is somebody's gravestone*, Avril realises with dread. She screams; no longer caring who hears her. In her panic to claw her way out, Avril slides deeper into the open grave. When Avril finally hits the bottom, she finds herself staring up at a swirling black sky.

Willing herself not to look at the body lying next to her, she realises she has woken up in her dead son's grave. Having to witness his crushed pitiful body, the way Clayton did, is the thing she dreads most in the world. She cannot, *will not* look. But when she senses unnatural movement close by; followed by an awful bone crunching sound, her eyes track its progress around the grave. When she sees her son's rotting corpse start to sit up and reach out for his favourite blue jumper; she faints.

She cannot open her eyes. It is as if somebody has placed a pile of coins on each lid, weighing them down. She can hear someone breathing heavily next to her. Sensing that she is lying on the edge of some precipice, Avril fears falling. To save herself, she edges closer to the body lying next to her. It is surprisingly warm, as if a heart beats there, but she knows this cannot be. There is also an unmistakeable smell of smoke in the air, yet her nightdress is no longer in flames. Somebody gently removes the weights from her eyes and she can see again. Recognising the shadowy images of familiar objects – the antique dressing table with the cracked mirror and the glass dish holding her wedding ring, it dawns on her that she is back in her own bedroom. She has come home. *Home.* The word feels unfamiliar on her lips.

The bed is soft and welcoming, just like an old friend, and she has a handful of patchwork quilt locked in her hand. Its familiar scent reminds her of sleepless nights nursing Tommy; with Clayton looking on sleepily. As comforting as this is, Avril remains paralysed with fear; even when she sees flames flickering under the bedroom door, searching for a way in. Unable to do anything to stop the smoke spilling into the room; Avril watches it curl its way around the bed, settling on the person lying next to her. Clayton has taken her dead son's place and as usual, his body takes up too much space in the marital bed.

She draws her knees up to her chin and buries her face in the pillow; not wanting to hear the sound of the child's ghoulish laughter oozing out of every corner of the room. Next, she hears footsteps bouncing across the floorboards. The child is on the run. Soon it will be tugging at her nightdress; pleading with her to come play with him. But it is Clayton who stirs beside her; coughing as the smoke enters his lungs. She cannot save him. Her body simply refuses to move. This realisation makes her angry. Angry enough to fight back when she feels the dreaded hand pulling at her body.

'Get off me. Don't touch me.' Avril is astonished to find she is able to move at last; that she is able to throw the hand off. The physical contact seems to have released her; broken the spell. Suddenly, she is sitting bolt upright in bed, wide awake, and with everything as it should be. She scours the room, terrified that her nightmare may not yet be over. But the smoke and the flames have vanished. *He is gone.*

She turns to look at Clayton and sees his limp hand resting on the bedcover. *It was his hand that reached out for me, not the boy's*, she is relieved to find. She watches it move toward her again and this time she does not push it away.

'What is it, Avril?' Clayton mumbles without opening his eyes. Avril can tell he is only half awake; barely conscious at all. He is unlikely to remember reaching out for her in the middle of the night and being pushed violently away.

'Go back to sleep,' she tells him, swinging her legs out of bed and slipping on a dressing gown.

Chapter 58

Avril is spying on Clayton through a gap in the curtains. It might only be eight o'clock in the morning but he has already told his first lie of the day. *Impressive*, she grumbles, wishing she could make out exactly what he is saying; because this is clearly not a work-related call. She can tell this by his face – secretive one minute and stormy the next – the classic signs of a guilty man. Besides, why would he need to go outside to take the call if it was just a customer on the other end? Already, she knows the answer to this. *Suzie.*

Having spent a restless night on the sitting room sofa, Avril is overly crabby this morning; but the fear of waking up in the same nightmare had prevented her from going back to bed. Due to the lack of sleep, she has dark shadows under her eyes and her head throbs in time with her heartbeat. In comparison, Clayton looks as fresh as a daisy. Right now, he has his mobile phone pressed tightly to his ear, as if he wants to be close to the person on the other end. She watches him run a hand through his freshly showered hair before sinking it in his jean pocket. When he starts pacing up and down the drive she knows he is being put on the spot.

He goes out of sight and she is left with an unbroken view of the moor. The smell of heather is heavy in the air and for good reason – its pungent purple carpet stretches for miles. Avril longs for a crisp dusting of frost. She'd give anything to be rid of this hot, dusty summer that drags on like a worn-out extramarital affair.

When Clayton comes back into her line of vision he stares directly at the sitting room window as if he knows she is watching him. From here she can tell his eyes are screwed into mean little bullets and that he has a suspicious look on his face. This makes her angry. *I'm the one being hoodwinked here*, she fumes, *and I will put you straight on this if I have to.*

Before turning away, she notices that the sky is as blue as Tommy's eyes once were. As blue as Clayton's used to be, before he started drinking heavily. On this depressing thought, Avril's eyes fill with tears and a desperate sob escapes her. Her glance then falls on *The Crying Boy* portrait. *His eyes are the bluest I've ever seen*, she marvels.

When the portrait starts to swing from side to side, in a hypnotic, rhythmic motion – she reaches out to steady it – and her fingers brush accidentally against the boy's cheek. She feels his eyelashes flutter against her skin and when her hand comes away – her fingers are wet. *Real tears to match my own.* This does not shock her anywhere near as much as it should.

Chapter 59

Clayton pours boiling water into two almost identical mugs that were part of a Valentine gift bought many moons ago. As usual, it's strong coffee for him and green tea for Avril. He knows she hates being served it in a mug but it will have to do. His fingers are too big and clumsy for delicate bone china. He then turns his attention on the toaster – thin wholemeal bread for her and white doorstep slices for him. She'll have hers with a thin scraping of low-fat spread and he'll have heaps of butter and jam. *Says it all,* he thinks glumly, darting a glance at his troubled wife who leans against the kitchen sink as if it is the only thing keeping her upright.

Actually she doesn't look so much troubled as properly sick; like she's about to throw up. He's really worried about her, he doesn't mind admitting, and the visit from Suzie obviously hadn't helped. He still can't get over the fact she came *here*, to this house, yesterday, to grass him up. Before this morning, when he first got the call from her, he'd never suspected her of being a troublemaker.

He thought he'd made his position clear, but obviously he was mistaken. Next time he sees Suzie – and he fears there has to be a next time if he's ever going to clear this mess up – he will make sure she is under no further illusions about him. He isn't interested. He never really was, even from the start. He's been an idiot, no doubt about that, but he isn't about to let Suzie spoil things for him and Avril. It's not as if anything happened between them, so she had no right coming here and interfering in their business. He'd told her so over the phone and she hadn't liked that one little bit. Made up some story about how she was trying to help, but that didn't wash with him; even when she started sobbing down the phone. Perhaps, in hindsight, he needn't have been so angry with her, but he is worried sick about Avril. He doesn't need anyone telling him how erratic her behaviour is. He is all too aware of this, and hearing it from strangers, people outside his family, is not something he takes kindly to.

There's no telling what damage Suzie's visit may have done. Only last night Avril had thrust him off her in bed; screaming at him to 'Get off' when all he was trying to do was wake her up from her nightmare. Then this morning, he caught her spying on him through a gap in the curtains; no doubt imagining him up to all kinds of trouble. Soon, they will have to sit down and talk. Things are coming to a head.

Agitated, he stirs a spoon around the mugs and boiling water spills out to lick his hand. *Shit. That's hot*, he swears under his breath. Out of the corner of his eye he sees Avril grin. *She's not too sick to take the mickey out of me, then.*

'You should be more careful,' she tells him.

It sounds like Avril. It certainly looks like Avril. But there is a meaning to her words he can't fathom. Likewise, the blank, unreachable look in her eyes.

He hands her the mug of tea and she takes it without thanking him. Rather than look up, she seems fascinated by the liquid inside the mug. She sloshes it about, creating waves, until he's sure she is going to scald herself.

'I'm worried about you, Avril. Is there anything you want to tell me?' That gets her attention. He locks eyes with her, but somehow she evades him. Already she is someplace else. He watches her glance toward the inner door and he can tell she is thinking about that damned painting again. He'd like to smash it to pieces. *See it burn.* For one horrific moment an image of the painting pops in front of his eyes. He can't escape it or shake it off. In his mind he sees it rocking from side to side. But instead of tears, flames streak down the child's cheeks. The crying boy's eyes are on fire. The illusion feels so real, so terrifying, Clayton can taste burning on the back of his tongue. He can even smell smoke.

'The toast, Clay. The toast.'

Clayton stumbles, as if out of a dream. Was he swaying along then, in time with the painting? He can't be sure. He's confused at first. *What is Avril on about?* Then, he sees the toast has caught on fire. Black smoke circles the ceiling looking for a way out.

'Do something.' Avril barks, making him jump out of his reverie.

'Alright. There's no need to shout.' Clayton hurries over to the toaster, switches it off at the mains, and starts wafting the smoke away. This only seems to make things worse.

When the smoke alarm goes off, Avril storms out; leaving Clayton in a quandary. *I've got to stop drinking, else I'm going to end up in the loony bin like… no, that's not fair, I mustn't think such things. But the vision, the painting, it felt so real.* The only way Clayton knows how to fix things is to do something with his hands, so he takes down the smoke alarm that goes beep, beep, beep in his ear, deafening him.

Chapter 60

A wailing ambulance with flashing lights pulls into Moorland Way. As the driver switches off the engine; abruptly killing the siren – two paramedics in green uniforms run up the pathway of number thirty-three and let themselves in. Then, almost every door in the street opens and neighbours congregate in gossiping groups on the pavement, curious to know what is going on.

Inside number thirty-three, Suzie is on her knees, clinging to her sobbing son, who continues to resist her hands, no matter how much pain he is in. She forces his head to turn one way, then the other, for the benefit of the paramedics. All down one side of his face the skin is already starting to blister and peel. Suzie's own face is awash with tears. She is so upset she can barely speak. Underneath her gaping dressing gown, she is naked, but the paramedics are used to this sort of thing and look away.

'It's my... my... fault,' she stammers. 'I was late up. He only wanted his breakfast but I told him it wouldn't hurt him to wait for once, but he–'

Suzie points to the electric cooker and one of the paramedics goes to investigate. A saucepan of still-bubbling water with an egg inside sits on top of the oven. Water has spilt everywhere, staining the hob. The other paramedic gently prises Suzie away from her screaming child but she continues to eye the saucepan as if *it* is to blame for her son's injuries, but really she knows it is her fault.

'I should never have let him come down on his own.' Suzie sobs. 'My son. My beautiful son.' She tries to hold on to him, even as the first paramedic starts cutting off the boy's pyjamas with a pair of scissors. The other paramedic talks quietly into his radio.

'Shouldn't we put him in a cold bath?' Suddenly, Suzie becomes aware of her indecency and she gets to her feet, pulling the belt of her dressing gown around her.

The paramedic with the radio stops talking about 'third degree burns' and smiles at her kindly. 'I'm afraid there is a risk of him going into shock if we do that. All we can do at this stage is apply a cool compress and get some painkiller into him, then get him to hospital as soon as we can.'

'Is it bad?' Suzie asks, fearing the worst.

The paramedic touches her on the arm. She pulls away. She will start bawling again at the first hint of sympathy.

'He's going to be fine.' The paramedic means to sound reassuring but his eyes betray him.

'Fine but scarred for life, is that what you mean?'

All too soon, they are bundled into the ambulance. Suzie tries not to look at the neighbours who have piled into the street. They mean to be kind, shouting out words of support and good wishes. *If they knew what really happened, they would throw glass bottles at me,* Suzie fears. Whilst her son whimpers and cries only a few feet away, she is prevented from comforting him. She has been told she must let the paramedics do their job.

This gives her plenty of time to dwell on her failings as a parent. The ride to hospital, even at break-neck speed, takes the longest eight minutes of her life.

She'd been sat on the bed, twirling a lock of hair in her hand and admiring her reflection in the mirror, talking to Clayton on the phone. He was surprised to hear from her, she could tell, but he didn't ask her where she got his number from. By making Avril doubt her own husband, Suzie had only been doing what her uncle asked. But somehow this plan had backfired on her. At the time, she'd assumed Clayton would want to know his wife was going barmy; that he might even be grateful to her for getting in touch. But rather than *thank* her he had been dead shitty instead. That had come as a big surprise. Where was Mr Nice-Guy-Next-Door when you needed him?

It was during her rather heated conversation with Clayton that Toby appeared in the doorway, frowning at her. She was already late up and her son was impatient for his breakfast. For one minute only – just one, mind – she had forgotten how important his daily schedule was; and shooed him away. She might have known he would go down without her and make a start on his own breakfast. As soon as she heard the metallic clang of the saucepan, followed by her son's screams, she knew something was horribly wrong. She will never forgive herself for what happened and wishes she could swap places with her beautiful son, who is beautiful no more.

Suzie blinks away tears and tries not to think of Avril's words, which keep coming back to haunt her. 'You already have a beautiful healthy son. Wanting anything more is just plain greedy.' Had Avril been trying to warn her something like this was about to happen? But how could she guess, know? *It was wrong of me to make a play for Clayton. I should have known better,* Suzie berates herself. *And as God is my witness I'll never go after another married man again.*

Chapter 61

Walking into the village shop in Haworth is like stepping back in time; a wholesome, pleasurable experience that never lasts quite long enough. There is an abundance of home-made cake and jam; as well as old fashioned sweets that still get weighed in pounds and ounces on a vintage scale. The bunting gives the shop a jolly, post-war feel and customers are greeted by a trio of pretty sisters who all wear the same shade of lipstick. An old fashioned bell rings out each time a customer comes or goes – and this is the only thing Avril is not overly fond of.

The smell of fresh bread makes everybody linger, but having taught her body to starve as a way of punishing herself for being alive, Avril is immune to the sight and smell of food. She is far more interested in the young mothers who bring their armies of children with them. Avril smiles at the children ogling sweets in jars. The mothers are all very pretty, suntanned and sure of themselves. *Very like Suzie*, Avril observes jealously.

Patiently, Avril waits her turn in the queue. She has a basket of uninspiring cleaning products in her hand, which she rather hopes will encourage Mrs Mills into more productivity. But in front of her – a young, tired looking mother loads the counter with cupcakes, crisps, Scotch eggs and bottles of fizzy pop. Every so often she switches the hefty little girl she's carrying from one hip to another. Wrapped around the woman's legs are two primary school-age children. They dart shy looks at Avril and grin through gapped teeth when they think she isn't looking.

The young mother reaches for her children's matching heads and guides them closer to the counter. Clearly, she doesn't let them stray too far from her sight and Avril feels overwhelmed by an attack of guilt. *Why didn't I look after my own son, better?*

Then, becoming aware of Avril's close observation, the woman in front of her smiles cautiously.

'Lovely day for a picnic, isn't it? Now they're on a bit of a break from school.'

Avril nods and smiles. She so wants... needs... this woman to keep chatting away normally to her as if she were an acquaintance or even a friend.

'Me too. I'm a teacher,' Avril explains.

'Oh lovely,' The woman instantly loses her reserve and smiles back, warmly this time. This always happens when Avril tells people what she does for a living.

'Do you have children too?' The woman asks innocently, busily packing her shopping into bags.

'A boy. Tommy. He's five.'

'Same age as my Nathan then,' the woman prods her son forward. He grins foolishly as if he deserves a prize for being picked out. 'Everyone's going over to the Dragons Den play centre this afternoon. You should come. Bring your boy.'

'They've got go-karts,' Nathan tells her, keen to have another boy tag along.

'Maybe I will,' Avril says, looking into her own uninspiring basket of window cleaner and bleach.

***

When Avril comes out of the shop, her basket is full to the brim with bottles of fizzy pop, pretty cupcakes, Scotch eggs, crisps and prepared sandwiches. Outside, the cloudless sky is a piercing blue and the sun is as yellow as it's ever been. The smell of cottage garden flowers fills her nose and across the street a small boy throws a ball for his pet dog. Smiling like Mary Poppins, she holds the door open for an old lady entering the shop, and freezes when she sees who is waiting for her outside. The Chief.

Today, his skin is the colour of smoked haddock and his eyes are as bloodshot as hers were first thing this morning. Perhaps like her, he has suffered from a long, sleepless night.

'People who play with fire end up getting their fingers burned. You of all people should know that, Avril.' He lumbers toward her as if he might grab her by the throat and she takes a step back; discreetly glancing around to see if there is anybody nearby, just in case she should need help

'What's that supposed to mean, Chief?' She keeps everything light, for now, but her eyes narrow all the same.

He might have caught her off guard, but she will not let him have the satisfaction of knowing this. She cannot afford to fall apart, even if she *is* panicking like mad inside. *What does he mean by saying 'people who play with fire end up getting their fingers burned?' What can he know?*

'I suppose you're going to tell me you don't know what's happened,' The Chief barks, making the dog across the road drop his ball.

He can grind his hands together all he wants but Avril can tell The Chief is not as sure as he was a few seconds ago. Now that she comes to think of it, she realises his anger is just a smokescreen. It dawns on her that he is trying to hide his real feelings from her – fear. But fear of what? Of whom?

'I don't know what you're talking about. Has something happened?' Immediately she thinks of Clayton and starts to fret. 'Clayton?'

'It's not like you to go worrying your pretty little head over him, or anyone else for that matter, is it Avril Shaw? Or should I say Roberts?'

The blood drains from Avril's face. She cannot breathe. Cannot move. She's back in the nightmare again, waking up next to her dead son. The Chief's words chill her like no bad news can. This is the moment she has been dreading all her married life; when somebody finally stumbles upon her secret and exposes her. She feels as if she is being suffocated. That she might die, here on the spot. *Pull yourself together, Avril. Don't let him win. Get a grip.*

'You might know my real maiden name, Chief. But you don't know anything else about me,' she gets off to a shaky start but her confidence grows when she sees fresh doubt creep into his eyes. 'Besides, that's old news to anyone except you and people around here.'

He sneers because he doesn't know everything. Not yet. He can't. Or he would already be on his way to find Clayton, to tell him the news – that his wife is not who she says she is. That she is a *murderer.*

Chapter 62

Mrs Mills scowls at the courtyard garden at the back of Swallow's Nest. From the window of the snug she can see that the grass is dying and the cottage flowers have been allowed to grow wild. Soon they will take over everything. This pretty much sums up how she feels about the Shaws, who have taken over what by rights should be Yorkshire folks' territory.

A pain in her left side causes Mrs Mills to double up. Resting her weary face on the desk, she massages the circle of flesh where her breast used to be. After ten years, she still hasn't got used to it not being there. She's only once looked at herself fully naked in the mirror since the mastectomy and Bob has never been able to bring himself to do the same. She doesn't hold it against him. They still have sex most Saturday nights but it's been a long time since he touched her in a sensual way. The feel of her face against the smooth wood is as close to a caress as she's ever going to get, she realises. The thought nigh makes Mrs Mills blush and she sits up too quickly, making the blood go to her head. If Mrs Shaw could hear her prattling on about sex, sensuality and caresses when she is supposed to be giving the snug the once-over, she'd be shocked. This thought makes Mrs Mills chuckle.

Not for the first time, she wonders why Mrs Shaw doesn't buy some decent furniture. It's not as if they can't afford it. Instead they have this pockmarked old desk that has people's names carved into it. Noticing that one of the drawers has been left partially open, Mrs Mills slides it out and is delighted to find a shiny blue cash tin inside.

'Thank you,' she murmurs silently when she sees that the key has been left inside the lock.

Making sure the door is shut behind her, Mrs Mill removes the cash tin. Mrs Shaw is meant to be going out for a walk but Mrs Mills can't say for sure if she has already left. She could still be in the house. It's big enough for both of them to hide in. Unable to resist, she goes ahead anyway and opens up the tin, wary of its razor sharp edges, and gasps when she sees money bags stuffed with notes and silver coins. Staring greedily at the cash, she expertly does the maths in her head, and reckons there must be at least £150 inside. She could feed her family for a month on that – but right now she'd settle for a tenner to treat Bob and the boys to a six-pack of beer. Money has been tight since Bob's disability benefit was cut.

The sound of a door slamming makes her jump. Stuffing the cash tin back in the drawer, she steals over to the window for a better look. When she sees Avril heading toward the moor, Mrs Mills' thumping heart slows to a more regular pace. But her relief is soon swamped by envy.

'It's alright for some with their half-days and holidays, while the rest of us are slogging our guts out,' Mrs Mills tuts and sighs.

Admittedly, she's never been one for walking on the moor; alone or otherwise. *Too dangerous by far. Especially around here. And not just on the moor, either,* she reminds herself ghoulishly. *Look what happened here, in this very house*. But she feels entitled to the same opportunities as Avril Shaw.

Then, it dawns on Mrs Mills that there is something odd about Avril's behaviour. Not only does she keep glancing furtively back at the house, as if she knows she is being watched, but there is also an unnaturalness to her gait. This only makes sense when she realises Avril is weighed down with a blanket and a basket which cause her to stumble often.

Mrs Mills eyes crinkle up suspiciously. She can think of only one reason why any lass would be sneaking around on the moor and doesn't waste time wondering if it's Mr Shaw she's planning on meeting; because in her experience wives only venture onto the moor for people they *aren't* married to.

'Walk be damned! She must think I were raised ont' darn train.'

Chapter 63

The moorland grass is dusty and dry; good for nothing except finger cuts. Its harshness reminds Avril of knotted hair. The weather remains perfectly hot and still – but it always feels wild and windswept on the moor. The land rolls gently underfoot, leading you first in one direction and then in another. Avril knows better than to trust its advice. Grey and lonely, the moor is no friend to anyone. From here, Swallow's Nest is visible in the distance. But the house itself looks less than inviting. Empty. Barren. Isolated. Avril knows how this feels.

The house might have become more of a 'home' than she'd ever dared hope; but when Clayton is lurking in its corners she still feels like a prisoner inside its walls. At times she suspects he is watching her for signs of madness but she gives nothing away; except perhaps her indifference. Every day sees her grow more distant from him. She doesn't know how to stop this. Doesn't know if she *wants* to. Sometimes she thinks Clayton doesn't actually want her to get well again. She doesn't know what he'd make of the fact that out on the moor, alone with her thoughts, she enjoys a sense of space and freedom she can't get anywhere else.

How can one truly belong to a place if you weren't born here? Avril wonders. Yet the very cragginess of her surroundings feels appropriate to her scarred leathery skin. Everything seems to belong to her. Even the dilapidated old barn watches protectively over her. Sunlight leaks through the building's gaping holes, and its gapped toothed grin reminds her of the sticky-faced children in the village shop. On that thought, she cannot resist a quick glance behind her to check the picnic basket is still where she left it. The untouched pop, sandwiches, crisps, cupcakes and Scotch eggs have been laid out on a tartan blanket that looks as if it has been chewed at the corners by a pet dog. A family picnic on the moor should conjure up a happy scene, but too many people are missing from this one to attract a smile.

Avril kneads the frayed end of the blanket between her fingers and stares at the familiar brown rooftop of her house. It is easy to get caught up in the dark, brooding atmosphere of the moor and she has been sitting here too long, staring at nothing. Her bones ache and she is surprisingly cold. *I have not left my body at home, then, as I first imagined.* This realisation surprises her; because when she is up here it feels as if she has slipped herself off, like a coat on the floor.

He is coming. She can hear the coarse grass splitting under his feet as he approaches. She senses him getting closer. As do the birds who go quiet in their ground nests. When the shadow of a child slides onto the grass beside Avril, her eyes cloud over with a foggy acceptance. She jerks out a hand as if she'd been ordered to do so and waits. But this time his shadowy hand does not reach out for hers. For a moment she is confused, then with a mother's intuition, she realises what it is he wants. This time he wants *her* to make the first move. She slides her hand into his and closes her fingers around the coolness of his skin. She is rewarded with an impatient nudge. Recognising that he wants to play, Avril scrambles awkwardly to her feet. Now, when she looks down, she can see two shadows on the grass, one tall and lean (hers), the other small and chubby (his). Somewhere high above them a crow shrieks its abhorrence.

Hand in hand they walk towards the edge of an outcrop where the stone is slippery and wet. Avril tilts her head to listen to the sound of a waterfall trickling into the gulley below. Realising how easily they could fall to their deaths, she tightens her grip on her charge's hand and leads him to safer ground, where the flattened grass rolls away to form a hard-wearing hill. Bidding him 'stay' she dips out of sight to investigate the protruding boulders that push up through the grass like unwanted tombstones. Finding a trail that she considers safe enough, she climbs back up and slips off her summer cardigan; demonstrating that she means business. Not giving herself time to change her mind, she lays down on one side, tucks her head in her hands, and rolls recklessly down the grassy mound; picking up speed as she approaches the bottom of the knoll.

On the way down, everything goes by in such a rush, Avril barely notices the number of times the rocks graze her elbows. When she eventually reaches the bottom, she gets unsteadily to her feet, and laughs when she finds her land legs no longer work. Enjoying the sensation of dizziness, she raises her arms out to the side, and imitating an aeroplane, twirls around on the spot. Soon, she's diving and swooping like a regular fighter jet – the kind little boys want to play with – because by now *he* has joined her at the bottom of the hill.

Suddenly, Avril stops what she is doing and frowns. Turning her head first one way and then another, she listens out for something. Her head swivels slowly, like a creepy doll's might, and her eyes narrow into black slits. Although she can see nothing in front of her, Avril is convinced somebody is out there spying on them. Now that their fun has been spoilt by some onlooker who chooses to remain hidden, she uses the secrecy of sign language to warn her companion.

Chapter 64

Mrs Mills scribbles a hasty note. 'Dear Mrs Shaw. Am leaving today. Please forward money owed to–' and suddenly finds herself out of breath. Just writing to that barmpot is enough to bring her out in a sweat. What was she thinking of, going to work for outsiders? And in a house like Swallow's Nest. Bob had warned her right from the start but she hadn't heeded him. Now she is paying the price.

'Only mad people talk to themselves. Everybody knows that,' Mrs Mills grumbles, pocketing Clayton's stylish pen. Her magpie ways will follow her to the grave, she realises. She takes a last look around the kitchen that cries out for a large noisy family to fill it. But the Shaws don't have any family, least not around here. Nor any friends to talk to neither. And the way Mrs Mills sees it, signing is the same as any other language. It doesn't matter if Mrs Shaw believed there was somebody out on the moor with her, Mrs Mills knows different.

Deciding she doesn't care if she never sees the inside of this house again, Mrs Mills takes out her car keys and zips up her heavier-than-usual bag. She's about to walk out the door when she hears a noise coming from the hallway.

Might it be Mrs Shaw back already? Mrs Mills can't help fretting. She could have snuck in another way in order to creep up and frighten her. After what she saw on the moor, she wouldn't put anything past her. *I'd best mind her,* Mrs Mills realises gloomily, popping the note in her pinny pocket. The less Avril Shaw knows about her intentions, the better.

'Mrs Shaw, is that you?' Mrs Mills calls out in a deceptively innocent voice. *If it is her, and Lord knows, I hope not, I can't let her know I was up on the moor.*

A fluttering sound, followed by a soft thump, comes from somewhere inside the house. A door opening and closing perhaps?

'Mrs Shaw,' Mrs Mills calls again, this time in a louder, more insistent tone.

Mrs Mills creeps stealthily into the hall, not liking the tinny echo of her own footsteps on the tiled floor. She looks up at the dark landing and is relieved to see there are no shadows looming there; she doesn't think the hammering pain in her chest could stand this. The house is now as silent as a sleeping bairn. All the same, she's unable to stop the search just yet, not till she susses out exactly *what* the noise was. She walks toward the sitting room door and opens it; feeling the door close behind her as she steps inside.

At first, she sees nothing out of the ordinary, except that one of the sash windows is partially open, though it had been closed earlier when she went into the room to clean. Had Avril Shaw climbed in through it? Is she lurking somewhere in this room, behind one of the sofas? Until now, Mrs Mills hasn't realised just how much she hates the Shaws. *Maybe I can persuade my boys to give her a fright the next time she's alone on the moor. See how she likes it,* she plots venomously.

That's when something lands on her shoulder and she simultaneously spots the fluttering of a bird's wings out of the corner of her eye. Realising she has been shat on by a trapped bird, Mrs Mills stares agog at the swallow frenziedly flapping around the sitting room.

'Well, I'll be damned.' Mrs Mills is about to shoo the bird out of the window when it finds the opening itself and flies out unaided. How long it had been flying around the room, shitting everywhere, she can only guess. The good news is she won't be the one having to clean it up.

That's when she notices *The Crying Boy* painting is hanging askew; no doubt knocked that way by the bird. On autopilot, she goes over and rights it, then crosses to the window and closes it. She doesn't know why she's bothering. It's not as if Swallow's Nest is her responsibility anymore. When she next turns around, she notices that the picture has moved again and now hangs at an odd angle.

When it starts to rock from side to side, Mrs Mills gasps out loud and zealously crosses herself. Her eyes widen in fear as the boy's eyes blaze first with fire and then devilment.

'Diablo. Devil,' Mrs Mills clutches at her arm and lets out a strangled cry. The sound reminds her of a rabbit caught in a wire snare. As she crumples to the floor, coins spill out of her pinny pocket and roll across the floor. Her last thought before passing out is that she ought to pick them up before somebody else finds them. But by now her arms and legs have turned to jelly, so she falls instead against a coffee table made out of a door; sending a bunch of photographs and a table lamp crashing to the floor.

***

Kneeling by the side of one of the raised vegetable beds that Clayton and The Chief created, Avril plucks out plant after wilted plant and stares into space. She can't help thinking he must already have grown tired of gardening judging by how neglected and thirsty the plants are.

A little while ago she thought she heard a crash and the sound of screams coming from the house but the noise wasn't able to reach her in the way it should. Nothing seems to anymore. In her confusion, people are always coming and going from her world. There are times when she isn't even capable of remembering she was once mother to a boy called Tommy.

Chapter 65

An oxygen mask covers the lower half of Mrs Mills droopy face and she greedily sucks in air while rolling her eyes under paper-thin lids. Heavy blankets swamp her small wiry frame and she appears as fragile as a small doll in the oversized hospital bed. Her pale liver-spotted wrist rests limply on the cover, dropped there by a smiley-faced nurse who popped in earlier to check her pulse.

Sitting closer to each other than they have in weeks, Avril and Clayton perch uncomfortably on a pair of hard plastic chairs that have been drawn up to the bed. Avril's eyes are filled with pity for Mrs Mills' condition but Clayton avoids looking at the patient and flips through her medical notes instead; unaware he is breaking patient confidentiality.

'These notes say one thing but her eyes tell a different story,' he suggests in a bored-stiff voice.

'What's that supposed to mean?' Avril nudges him with her elbow and darts him a sharp look.

Clayton opens his mouth to say something, but thinks better of it. Instead, he rubs his arm where Avril's elbow caught him.

'I wish her husband and sons would hurry up. It doesn't feel right, us being here.'

'She works for us, Clay.'

'I know. It's just that…' his voice drops to a whisper 'it's not as if we know her very well… or even like her.' There. He's said it. He's happy now.

'She was in our house when this happened. We're responsible for her.' Avril's opinion brooks no argument.

They both stop their childish eyeballing when Mrs Mills begins to mumble incoherently.

'There, there. It's alright Mrs Mills. You're fine. You're in hospital,' Avril reaches out for the woman's hand and pats it.

Sensing movement around her, Mrs Mills turns her head in their direction and groggily opens her eyes. When Avril sees that one eye is facing the wrong way and the other is fixed dazedly on her, she quickly drops Mrs Mills' hand and wipes her own palm on her dress.

'She's trying to say something,' Clayton says, jumping to his feet. He doesn't know how long he can stomach looking at the woman's foamy mouth without having to throw up.

'Poor woman,' Avril says, with a quiver to her voice. 'What is it, Mrs Mills? What are you trying to say?' Avril leans closer and speaks louder, but Mrs Mills' confused ramblings still make no sense at all.

'Since when did we understand a word she said, anyway?' Clayton shrugs.

'This is not the time for jokes.' Avril throws him a disparaging look. But every time she glances around, he seems to have moved closer to the gap in the curtain; so eager is he to make his escape. This makes her smile inwardly.

She takes pity on him. 'Why don't you go and find a nurse? See if you can find out what's happening. They might have heard from her family by now.'

Every inch of Mrs Mills' body objects to being left alone with Avril, but as she is unable to voice her concerns, Clayton is allowed to slip away. He's always hated hospitals but Avril can't think why; not when his fairy-tale upbringing hadn't been touched by death or tragedy the way hers had.

As soon as he is gone, properly gone, and Avril can hear him talking to the smiley-faced nurse in the corridor, she picks up Mrs Mills' hand again and leans over the bed so that their eyes meet properly. Almost immediately Mrs Mills opens her mouth to protest, but no sound comes out.

'Probably best you don't talk about what happened. Not to Clayton, not to anyone,' Avril suggests sweetly, all the while keeping a concerned smile on her face that would easily fool the nurse should she decide to come in; but not Mrs Mills, who is clearly terrified. At this moment in time she'd agree to anything. She does so now by shaking her head violently.

'I know it was you, out on the moor, watching me.' Avril tells her matter-of-factly, as if it is of no real significance; yet her grip on the older woman's wrist tightens and the desire to press down harder becomes overwhelming.

'Same as I know it was you who changed the clock that day, making me think I was late for my appointment with the therapist. Yes, that's right. I have a therapist. All mad people do you know.' At this point Avril chuckles.

Mrs Mills tosses her head to the side, avoiding Avril's eyes, and starts to whimper.

'Shush now. There is nothing for you to worry about. So long as you promise to stop spying and playing tricks on people. And you do promise, don't you?'

Mrs Mills nods as best as she can. By now her frog-like eyes are bulging in her head.

'And as for this silly note, I think it's best we disregard it.' Avril takes a screwed up piece of paper out of her cardigan pocket and unravels it. Straightaway, Mrs Mills recognises her own handwriting and she gasps for air.

'I like things just the way they are, Mrs Mills and I won't hear of you quitting. After all, it's not good for children to experience too much change. Especially in their home life.' Avril screws the paper into a ball, pops it into her mouth and starts to chew. She then digs around in her other cardigan pocket and pulls out a pen and some pound coins. Never taking her eyes from Mrs Mills' face, Avril places them on a cabinet next to the bed.

'I believe these are yours,' Avril talks while she is eating, a thing she never usually does. 'Or at least they are now. I think you've earned them, don't you?'

Mrs Mills won't be still. One look at the stolen money has her thrashing around in the bed. Without warning, Avril pulls the oxygen mask away from Mrs Mills' face and calmly watches her struggle for breath.

'I've already lost one little boy and I'm not about to lose another.' Avril is suddenly fierce.

Only when Mrs Mills' face turns a dangerous shade of blue, does Avril replace the mask, but not before allowing it to ping painfully against the woman's skin.

Chapter 66

The Chief watches smokers stamp on still-smouldering cigarette ends before slipping through the hospital's automatic doors. Most shove their hands in their pockets and hunch their shoulders before going inside. Nobody need remind him how depressing hospitals are. He's seen enough of this particular one in the last six months. But today isn't about him. Today he's come to visit Suzie's boy and take over for an hour while she nips home to shower and change. At least that had been his intention, until he saw Clayton and Avril exiting the building.

Having followed them all the way to the car park, he'd watched them walk side by side without once speaking, until they stopped to get into separate vehicles; Clayton into his work van and Avril in the ugly Fiat. As far as he could tell, they didn't even say goodbye to each other. *What a strange couple they are,* he thinks. Even stranger that they should be here at the same time as him. *What were they doing here?* he wonders. They can't have come to see the boy. Suzie would have screamed the place down if Avril so much as showed her face on the children's ward. Turning back in the direction he's just come from, The Chief realises he isn't going to get any peace until he figures it out.

Now it's his turn to dig his hands in his trousers pockets and hunch his shoulders as he passes through the automatic sliding doors. It's baking hot inside and he can smell his own body sweat. As usual he's wearing too many clothes. And his leg is killing him today. He doesn't like admitting how tired he feels, even to himself. Wiping his face on the sleeve of his jumper, he is about to limp over to the reception desk to make enquiries when he spots a familiar face in the crowd; a small stooped fellow wearing a flat cap.

Coming from the same village, he knows all there is to know about Bob Mills and his family. They might be more Yorkshire than most, but they are a dodgy thieving lot. The Chief suddenly remembers that Mrs Mills works for the Shaws and alarm bells go off inside his head. He's not one for coincidences. Never has been. So, with that, he joins Bob in the lift.

Nodding gruffly at each other to own their acquaintance, they share the restrictive floor space with an overly chatty porter who pushes a young boy in a wheelchair. The kid has lost all his hair and has a beaten expression on his face. When they exit on the first floor, The Chief and Bob hitch up to make room for an older woman who clings to the sides of the lift and refuses to make eye contact with anybody. The Chief can't quite make up his mind if she's terrified of lifts, people; or both.

'Who are you here for Bob?' The Chief pointedly ogles the bunch of flowers the old timer is hugging.

'The missus. You?'

'Suzie's lad had a bit of an accident.'

'Sorry to hear it.'

'The bairn is going to be just fine. How about the wife?'

'I'm not so sure.' Bob looks down at his feet and his whole face seems to collapse into a pile of wrinkles.

'I told her not to go and work at that house; especially for outsiders. Warned her no good would come of it. We all know what happened out there. You, more than most.'

Here, Bob pauses to stare accusingly at The Chief, as if he holds him personally responsible for all that has happened.

'But she wouldn't heed the curse.'

Chapter 67

After their trip to the hospital, racing after the ambulance carrying Mrs Mills, he'd gone on to the Old Silent Inn in Stanbury to quote for a re-wiring job. Whilst there, the landlord treated him to a pint of Yorkshire ale on the house and proceeded to tell him all about the pub's creepy past. Apparently, many ghostly sightings had been reported in room ten, which was often let out to hikers who swore they heard two children giggling together at night. For once, Clayton listened; because suddenly the idea of a haunted pub didn't seem so ridiculous.

One drink led to another and his mood had lifted long before he left the pub, so he was a bit put out to find The Chief waiting on his doorstep the minute he got home. Avril pulled into the drive soon after.

Getting out of the van and stretching his long rugby-player's legs, Clayton greeted him pleasantly enough, 'How are you doing, Chief?'

But the old man wasn't having any of it. 'First Suzie and now Mrs Mills. You've got to open your eyes to what's going on around you, son.'

'Woah,' smiling stupidly, because he's a little bit tipsy and no doubt due a bollocking from Avril because of it, Clayton holds up his hands in playful surrender.

'Why don't you start from the beginning, Chief? Or better still, come on in for a drink.' Clayton extends a hand, meaning to pat The Chief on his arm, but he is shrugged off.

'This is no time for drinking. And by the smell of you, you've already had enough for the both of us.'

This stern reminder is enough for Clayton to start taking the old man seriously. He doesn't want to be reported to the police. He's sure he's not over the limit, but you never can tell. Besides, something about The Chief's fear-filled eyes has sobered him up.

'What happened to Mrs Mills was no accident. Nor Suzie's boy,' The Chief garbles.

'What? Now wait a minute. I have no idea what you're talking about. Mrs Mills had a stroke and a possible heart attack. We called for the ambulance ourselves.'

'You're not listening to me. There's something about that painting, your wife–'

'Don't go there, Chief. You have no idea how crazy you sound right now.' Clayton is no longer amused. He won't stand for any attack on his wife. Not from anybody. And he's heard enough rubbish about that painting to last a lifetime.

'Well, what about Suzie then? I suppose you're going to tell me that was an accident too.'

'Suzie? From the party?' Clayton scratches his head in confusion.

'That's right. She's me niece.'

'Well, if that's the case, why haven't you mentioned this before?' Clayton doesn't like the way this conversation is going; not after what nearly went on between him and Suzie. Then he is reminded of the old man's words and he is naturally concerned.

'Is she alright? What did you mean by accident?'

'Not her. The boy. He got badly scalded and taken to hospital.' The Chief's bloodshot eyes fill with watery tears, but again he shakes off Clayton's arm.

'Is he going to be alright?' Clayton is hopeless in these situations. He never knows what to say. A part of him wishes Avril would come over to join them; but he recognises this is the last thing The Chief would want.

'People get hurt around her.'

Clayton is about to ask 'who?' when he realises The Chief's eyes are fixed firmly on his wife. He'd be a fool not to notice the loathing on the old man's face and for a moment he too shudders and feels the hair on the back of his neck curl up with electricity. Avril might have her car boot up, pretending to nose around inside, but she knows she is being watched.

'First Tommy, then Mrs Mills and now Suzie's boy.'

'That's enough.' Clayton's anger is like a flash flood that will disappear as quickly as it arrives, but right now he is as menacing as any cursed painting. 'Go home, Chief, before you say anything else you might regret. It's clear you're upset and not thinking straight.'

The Chief's chin wobbles and he opens his mouth as if to argue his point, but when Clayton shakes his head at him again, he falls silent and his face drops on his chest.

Clayton watches him go, wondering what the hell that tirade was all about. Perhaps Avril was right to have her doubts about him. He can understand why most women wouldn't take to him, but nothing could have prepared him for The Chief's outburst. It was out of character, to say the least.

Not knowing what to think, Clayton digs his hands deep in his pockets and meanders over to Avril. As he approaches the car, she quickly closes the boot, as if she has something to hide, but she's not quick enough; he's already spotted the tins of paint, paintbrushes and rollers inside. He won't ask what they're for. He's got enough to worry about.

'What did he want?' Avril's voice is scathing but he can detect a tremor in it somewhere. She is nervous; afraid of something. He looks down at his feet, wondering if this is a good time to bring up Suzie. *Oh for God's sake, man up,* he tells himself. *Things are much worse than I thought if I'm too scared to talk to her.*

'You remember Suzie from the party?' He keeps his eyes on the dent in the car's backside, wondering how it got there. He doesn't have to see Avril to know she is rolling her eyes in a disinterested way. Reaching into the passenger seat to retrieve her handbag, she continues to ignore him.

'Well, not only does she turn out to be The Chief's niece, but apparently, her son got badly scalded and ended up in hospital.' For a minute he thinks he's got her attention because now she *is* looking at him, but only in a blank detached way, he realises. The beaten expression leaves his face as his anger returns.

'Didn't you hear me? It's likely he'll be scarred for life.' Clayton cannot avoid glancing at the puckered skin on his wife's chest. If she doesn't understand what this means for the child, then no one can.

'Why should I care about her son?'

Her coldness fills him with a dread he has never experienced and he finds himself stumbling backwards.

'What a thing to say, Avril? This is so unlike you. I'm worried about you. The Chief said...'

Now it's her turn to be angry. He watches her eyes narrow and her face tighten. She really can't bear to hear The Chief's name mentioned.

'What exactly did he say?' Hands on hips, she steps forward to confront him.

'I think you should see a doctor. You're not well.'

'And I think you should mind your own bloody business.'

She has never spoken to him in this way before. He is genuinely shocked and also a little afraid; although he doesn't like to admit this. She barely reaches his shoulder and he could easily swat her aside if he wanted to. It's not the physicality of his wife that frightens him, it's what's going on inside her head that concerns him.

'You are my business, Avril,' he says calmly, resisting the urge to restrain her. But he sounds patronising, even to his own ears, like a doctor who has only got five minutes of surgery time left.

'No. You make *everybody else* your business.' She's in his face, yelling now.

Clayton turns away in disgust. He really can't bear to see her like this. He storms toward his work van; determined to get the hell out of here.

'No doubt you'll be playing that slut a visit in hospital later then?' she screams after him.

'No doubt,' he yells back, knowing he will regret his words before he's travelled less than five miles up the road.

Chapter 68

It was almost dusk by the time Clayton got to Suzie's house but there was still plenty of light so he couldn't see any reason for the curtains being drawn. He hoped this wasn't significant. Didn't some people close the curtains as a sign of mourning? Having knocked once, then a second and finally a third time, with no sign of any twitching of the curtains, he'd finally given up and gone to look for her at the hospital. But he hadn't been allowed on the ward. 'Family only,' he'd been told. Although promises had been given that they would get a message to Suzie, he hadn't believed them. The nursing staff were so rushed off their feet; he suspected they'd forget about him in an instant.

So here he is now, back in the van on the driveway, staring into space. Night smells have crept in through the open window and he can pick out the illuminated eyes of a predatory fox out on the moor.

Glancing up, he sees that there is a light on in the gable end bedroom, the room Avril insists would have been their son's if he were still alive. This thought makes him sigh. She must have left it on and forgotten about it. But then, through one of the three tall windows he sees a flicker of movement and his eyes naturally follow it. At first, he thinks it is a shadow; but when he squints harder, he is able to make out the motionless shape of Avril.

She's probably wondering what he's still doing sitting in his van and can almost sense her impatience for him to enter the house. *Just like the old days*, he thinks sentimentally; when Avril would be in the nursery, rocking their baby boy in her arms and eagerly anticipating his arrival home. He sighs again but finds himself smiling now. Drinking in the homely scene of his wife and child waiting for him, Clayton thinks that this must be the most gladdening and natural sight in the whole world.

Then he remembers that the boy is dead and the truth hits him just as hard now as it did the first time he heard about the accident. Accident! Secretly, he's always hated the word used to describe the death of his son. No matter that it wasn't the driver's fault. He'd still like to string him up for his incompetence. When Clayton's mind finally refocuses back on the present, he realises that Avril's shadow is just as it was and her stance is still that of a mother cradling her son. In the present circumstances, this has to be the most unnatural thing he has ever seen.

Once inside the house, he pads silently around the ground floor, wondering when he became so accomplished at going behind his wife's back. Over the past few days he's grown accustomed to righting the wrongs she has committed throughout the day. Yet again, their wedding photograph has been turned face down. He automatically rights it; but this time he notices a crack in the glass that wasn't there before. *Did she throw it at the wall in temper?* he wonders. For the third night running he straightens *The Crying Boy* painting on the wall and just as he's creeping out of the room he turns around quickly, hoping to catch it out in some act of rebellion. So far, thank goodness, it's remained exactly as he left it. The only sensible explanation he has for the mysterious movement of the painting is the vibration caused by them going up and down stairs.

True enough, the stairs moan and groan with every tread as he sidles up them; reminding him weirdly of Mrs Mills' awful lamenting. He keeps his back to the wall though, in case Avril should be lying in wait, about to throw something at him. On safely reaching the top of the stairs, he creeps along the narrow passageway to the gable end bedroom where he sees a light glowing under the door. Pressing an ear up to it, he listens to the sound of Avril's muffled laughter on the other side.

For a second or two he worries that she has someone in there with her. Another man, perhaps? Someone younger and more attractive than him. Does she want somebody else? he wonders. One who doesn't constantly try to control her, one who doesn't drink too much. He wouldn't blame her if she did. Not after the way he has behaved since they lost their only child. Clayton realises he has let himself go these last few months. His eyes are no longer as blue as they once were; no doubt brought about by an over-dependency on alcohol and he certainly has less hair on top than he'd like. Let's face it, his stomach is flabbier than it's ever been and he gets out of breath just running up and down the stairs. Yet he doesn't care enough to do anything about it. *She wouldn't have to look far to do better than me*, he berates himself. Quite rightly, Avril has always accused him of being vain but until this moment, standing outside this door, he hasn't realised just how little he has to be vain about.

Without warning, he throws open the door, hoping to catch her off guard, but it is he who receives the shock when he sees her. When did she get to be so beautiful again? Overnight her teeth have become whiter even than his are right now and her skin has never looked so radiant; even the scarring on her chest glows pink in this light. Although he's always accusing her of being too skinny, he suspects she may recently have put on some weight. It looks good on her.

She surveys him from her side of the room, an expectant half-amused look on her face, as she carries on painting the once dove-grey walls a baby blue. She seems blissfully unaware of the chaos around her or the splatters of paint on her face and clothing. Even the stepladder has been carelessly pulled apart and is not locked securely in place. Itching to right it, it's a few seconds before Clayton is able to spit out what is on his mind.

'I thought I heard you laughing.'

'Something on the radio tickled my fancy.'

He watches her eyes drop guiltily away and wonders why she bothers to lie about something so small. He eyeballs the unplugged silent radio but she does not comment. He has to stop doing this; picking her up on every little thing. *It's no wonder she hates me*, he realises despondently. *If she wants to laugh along madly to herself, that's her business.*

'You never said anything about decorating.' He stays on safe ground.

'Didn't I?' Again, her eyes do not meet his. 'I thought I had. Do you like it?'

He can tell that she really wants his opinion; that it matters to her what he says next. In this moment she is like a child asking for his approval.

'What's wrong with magnolia?' He is programmed to disappoint her. He cannot help himself.

'I like blue.' Her voice is at once frosty. She is so changeable. For once, he does not blame her. He is a pig.

'No. You like magnolia.'

Even Avril cannot argue with this. She knows he is right. So instead she turns away and slaps more paint on the wall.

'I've seen some gorgeous curtains that will go really well in this room,' he hears her saying as he goes out, quietly closing the door behind him. He cannot stay to witness her confusion. Nor does he want to see the fleeting look of hurt that will cross her face when she realises he has gone.

Finding himself back on the other side of the door, he wonders if she will call out his name or even come looking for him. There's no harm in hoping. Neither has yet apologised to the other for earlier. Usually, she's the first to say sorry. Up until recently, this had always been the case. But instead of anything approaching an apology; all he can hear is the sound of her laughter trickling through the door again. So much for his imagining her feeling injured. Unable to resist the urge to spy; Clayton puts his eye against the cold metal of the keyhole and peers inside the room. When he sees Avril lean over the paint dish and press her palms face down into the paint – he steps away from the door. Whatever she's up to in there, he no longer has the stomach for it.

Chapter 69

Sitting up in bed, Suzie rests against a bunch of sagging pillows that have seen better days. Rather automatically, she flips through a glossy celebrity magazine, the kind she usually devours; but tonight she can't concentrate. It's not just Toby she's worried about. The doctors have already indicated his scarring isn't going to be as noticeable as they first thought and tomorrow or the next day he will be allowed home. This is great news and she can't wait. But right now she's more worried about her uncle. Since the accident, he has distanced himself and she suspects this is her fault; for fucking up again.

After all, he did pay her a lot of money to wreck the Shaw's marriage and she hadn't even made a dent in it. So much for supposedly having a way with men. Truthfully, she still doesn't understand why the couple are so important to him; or why it's critical they leave Swallow's Nest. But by not turning up to take his promised turn at Toby's hospital bedside, her uncle had made it clear he wasn't ready to forgive her. Not wanting to leave Toby alone during the day, especially at visiting time, she'd finally crawled in at 10pm; desperate for a shower and some sleep. But now that she is home, all she can think about is one man or the other. Her uncle or Clayton bloody Shaw.

She closes her eyes momentarily and the magazine slips out of her hand and falls onto the floor. Dreamily, she thinks about Clayton's handsome 'boy next door' face and imagines his scratchy hands on her skin. Not for the first time, she wonders what he'd be like in bed. *Avril Shaw has no idea how hot her husband is. Not that I care, though,* she reminds herself crossly, *because I am so over him.*

That said, Suzie can't seem to stop her hand from creeping under the bedclothes to stroke the fuzzy bit of triangular flesh between her thighs. She doesn't feel guilty thinking about sex while her son is in hospital. As far as she is concerned, sex is no different to any other necessary human function. And since nobody expects her to give up food and water on account of Toby being ill; she'll keep right on pleasuring herself, too, thank you very much.

The phone rings, making her snatch her hand away... well from her... snatch, but when she picks it up she is disappointed to find it is Jill from three doors along; no doubt ringing to find out how Toby is doing. Sulkily, Suzie tosses the phone to the bottom of the bed. She really can't face yapping to her for hours on end; and then immediately retrieves it again. If Clayton should ever ring her... want her... need her... she doesn't want to miss his call.

Sighing once again and settling back on the pillows, Suzie gives up all pretence at reading or masturbating; finally owning up to the fact that she is eaten up with jealousy over Avril Shaw. The woman has everything that she doesn't – the house that once belonged to her family, a good job, financial security *and* an adoring husband.

'How is that fair?' Suzie moans. *I live in a crappy council house and can barely afford to pay the rent, never mind the bills. Plus, I'm pretty, or meant to be, and can't find a decent man. Not one who is unattached at any rate.* Right now, Suzie doesn't want to think about how mean she is being about a woman who has lost a child. She does not owe Avril anything, not her pity nor her loyalty, either. Besides, no matter how ludicrous it sounds, Suzie still can't help holding her responsible for what happened to Toby. Hadn't she warned her outright, 'You already have a beautiful healthy son. Wanting anything more is just plain greedy,' just before the accident happened.

It hits Suzie that although Avril might have Clayton Shaw all to herself – he is not the adoring husband he makes himself out to be. No matter how much he might try to deny it, something very nearly happened between them. *If he can nearly stray once, what are the chances of him doing so again?* she wonders cynically.

At the time of Toby's accident, she'd made a promise to herself never to go after a married man again and she meant it. In future, any married guy that comes on to her will get very short shrift indeed. But Clayton is a different kettle of fish. In her mind, a little bit of him already belongs to her. So, it's not as if she'd be going back on her word…

When her mobile phone begins ringing again, Suzie glances hopefully in its direction. *Be him. Please be him.* But of course it's only Jill. Ignoring her friend all over again, Suzie daydreams about ways of getting Clayton to notice her again. Last time they spoke, he'd been a real shit. She knows that winning him back won't be easy but she owes it to her uncle to at least make the effort. In one clean sweep she could win back his trust and have Clayton fall into her lap all at the same time.

But how? It's not as if she has anything on Avril. And she hasn't anything new to tell Clayton that will pique his interest. And then she remembers something. The way Avril was that day in the kitchen at Swallow's Nest. Suzie might not be the brightest kid on the block, but even she knows when she's being had. All that giggling, closing of doors and whispered conversations behind her back could only mean Avril had somebody else with her. Hadn't Suzie sensed, all along, that there had been someone hiding in the shadows?

At first, Suzie had thought Avril was simply going mad – talking to an imaginary person and making things up – but now everything makes sense. *Now I come to think of it, it's pretty obvious she was hiding someone in that house. Somebody she didn't want me or anyone else to know about. Another man, I'll bet.* The very idea of Miss Goody-Two-Shoes actually having sex, let alone cheating on her husband, disgusts Suzie more than it should. She doesn't know why this should be; after all Avril is rather attractive in her own right. *Shame about the scarring though*, the bitchy thought pops into Suzie's head before she can stop it. Rather than be tormented by it, she convinces herself it's no more than Avril deserves.

If Avril has been cheating on Clayton behind his back, and Suzie doesn't have real evidence of this, he ought to know about it. *I owe him that, at least.* And if not true, then… well, the lie can stick in her throat for all she cares.

Chapter 70

Almost as soon as Avril had gone to bed, he'd come up here to the room that would have been his son's. Funny that they no longer call it 'the spare room'. The words just don't sound right on either of their lips. He has mixed feelings about being alone in this room. It almost feels like he's invading someone's privacy. Not Avril's. He's been spying on her too long to start worrying about that. But if not Avril's, then whose?

Taking his time, he gives the room the once over, finding she hasn't done a bad job of painting two of the walls. He's not the least bit surprised though to see the other two are unfinished. She never has been one to finish anything in one go; always giving up far too easily. The blue paint has not yet dried properly and he can still see traces of grey underneath. The colour reminds him of cold gravestones and he wonders if this is why Avril decided to paint over it.

He smiles grudgingly when he spots Avril's blue handprints plastered over one of the unfinished walls. This is just the kind of playful prank she would have pulled years ago. She never could help challenging his OCD tendencies by creating a mess. He misses her hands, he realises sadly, and not just on his body and in the more obvious places. The loss of her touch tears him apart and he's tempted to reach out and touch the next best thing – her imprints halfway up the wall – but he stops when he sees there are other handprints lower down on the wall…

Just looking at these child-sized handprints, that are much too small to be Avril's, freaks him out. They are abhorrent, he realises sickeningly, and senses intuitively that they are not of this world. So, w*ho the hell do they belong to and where did they come from?* Then, noticing there is something quite ghoulish about the way they patter possessively over the wall, Clayton finds himself walking backwards with his heart in his mouth. He has never seen anything to bring him out in such a cold, dreadful sweat as this. Although he can barely bring himself to look, he cannot tear his eyes away either. Whoever made those ghostly handprints must only have been about four feet tall; about the same height as his son – a fact that fills him with horror. They are spread wide and seem to know no fear… unlike him.

As he reaches the door, a cold chill settles on the room but he is suddenly burning up. His shirt clings to his body, making him feel claustrophobic. He hopes he isn't about to throw up. Then, feeling something tugging against his leg, he looks down and is horrified to find the bottom of his trouser leg bunched together – as if being clutched at by a small hand. He kicks out at it and fights back the urge to scream. *How the hell? It isn't possible, yet…*

Suddenly, his phone rings, making him jump. *Jesus, I don't know how much more my heart can take.* Desperate to talk to anyone right now, he fumbles in his pocket for his phone. *I must be going barmy. What the hell is going on in this house?* Although his hands won't stop shaking he risks a quick glance down at his phone and sees a number he recognises. When he next looks up, the child-sized handprints have vanished. Gone. Disappeared. Like they'd never been there at all. *No fucking way.* Placing the ringing phone to his ear, Clayton wrestles open the door. No way is he going to wait around to see if those handprints come back again.

Chapter 71

Although he knows he ought to be looking at Suzie right now, nodding his head to show he's listening and making all the right noises – he cannot stop thinking about the day his son was buried. He hardly remembers how they got through it. Was he polite to well-wishers? Did he sob openly in front of his friends and family? He wonders if Avril has any memories of the day, and wishes he had taken the trouble to ask her. He'd rather think about this, about anything, than stand here listening to Suzie's damning words.

'I'm not lying,' Suzie pouts. 'I'm not making it up.'

Noisily, Suzie blows her nose and rakes a hand through her dirty blonde hair. Her eyes are shrunken from lack of sleep and her face is blotchy. She has never looked less appealing and he ought to feel sorry for her. But he can't. Because here she goes again, making up lies about Avril and expecting him to fall for it.

'And you're a hundred per cent sure you saw him?' Clayton just cannot get his head around what Suzie is trying to tell him.

'Yes I'm sure.' Suzie is yelling now. 'I'd swear it on Toby's life.'

Now she's crying and Clayton doesn't know what to do. He really can't make the physical effort required to put a comforting arm around her. Besides, he doesn't want any part of Suzie clinging to him right now. All he can think is – *Can it be true? Has Avril really been having an affair under my very nose, and in our own home? Maybe even in our own bed. If true, what a kick in the teeth that would be.* Although he may have had his suspicions that there could be someone else, what Suzie is telling him now doesn't feel quite right. He still has his doubts. But then again, Avril *is* always wondering around on the moor alone, perhaps on the lookout for her mystery man and Suzie wouldn't swear on her son's life if it wasn't true. Christ! Has he really been that stupid all this time? He can't believe he has been so easily hoodwinked.

'I saw them kissing through the window and then she must have sent him off to hide somewhere, probably in the living room, because when she opened the door to me there was no longer any sign of him. I told you she was acting oddly all the while I was there, but I didn't put two and two together until I saw them again, coming out of the Old White Lion Hotel.'

'You wouldn't lie about something like this, would you, Suzie? Clayton looks at Suzie with renewed distaste.'

'What do you take me for? Of course I wouldn't.'

'This is so unlike Avril… After all we've been through I can hardly believe she'd do something like this. People who have a child together don't…'

'*Had* a child together.' Suzie's gentle reminder makes Clayton wince.

When she reaches out to touch him, he avoids her. She has to know once and for all that this… them… is going nowhere. It wouldn't matter to him if Avril had cheated on him a dozen times over – he is never going *there* again.

'And you've seen them? Close up? Kissing?' The words tumble out of Clayton's throat, desperate to appear normal, but he is unable to hide his fury from Suzie.

'And touching.' Suzie gulps nervously, as if afraid of him. She can hardly bring herself to meet his eye.

If he gets any angrier she'll likely go quiet on him. Does he want that to happen? Yes. For one terrifying moment he imagines putting his hands around her throat. Shutting her up for good is something he'd like to do right now.

Think. Think. I must think. I'm not myself. Try to remember what she said about the hotel. The Old White Lion is not a place he's heard of before. He certainly can't remember Avril ever mentioning going into any of the hotels in Howarth village. Why would she? Yet how well does he really know her? How well does he know himself come to that? Because right now he's frightened by how strong the desire is to hurt somebody. Not Avril. Never Avril, no matter what she has done. But the man, yes, whoever he is. He can imagine taking pleasure in drilling out his eyes, should he get the chance. Up until now, he thought he knew himself. Hasn't he always claimed to be an open book, in contrast to his ever-mysterious wife. Yet he's starting to realise there are darker elements of his personality that have never surfaced before.

What is wrong with me? he wonders. He must be sickening for something other than the loss of Avril and his child. Look at what had happened to him in that room. Those handprints on the wall. He still doesn't know if he imagined them or not. *But I don't have to lose Avril*, he reminds herself. *She doesn't even have to know that I know about the affair. I won't tell her. That way there's no danger of her walking out on me. I can't let that happen. I thought*

I cared about what happened to Suzie and her child, but I don't. I really don't.

'All this time Avril has been having it off with somebody else and you hardly bat an eyelid.' Suzie is suddenly vitriolic, as if she has guessed nothing she can say or do will ever make him cross the line again.

'Don't say that. I cannot bear the thought of anyone touching my wife.' The words spill out of Clayton before he can stop them. He must not confide in Suzie. Avril would never forgive him. *Alright, I could argue that I shouldn't be worrying about upsetting her too much right now, after what she has done – but I am anyway.* The argument in Clayton's head goes on. When he next looks up, he sees that Suzie has moved closer; that her hand is patting his arm in a comforting way.

'You have every right to feel hurt and angry right now.' The wistful expression on Suzie's face makes him want to push her far away, but he's scared of doing so, in case his anger returns. The way he feels now, he could easily smash up this house and all that's inside it.

'I'm here for you, Clay, if you'll let me…'

The look of longing on Suzie's face tells him that she has mistaken his silence for something else. She has convinced herself that their pairing up is inevitable.

'I have to go. Avril will be worrying.' Unable to hide his disgust, he shakes her off somewhat thoughtlessly.

'Well, isn't she the lucky one?' Suzie is seriously pissed off now and Clayton doesn't blame her.

'I'm the lucky one, Suzie. I always have been.' He is not unkind but he will not allow her to delay him any longer. He walks determinedly toward the door; upsetting her all the more.

'The pair of you are as bad as each other. You both fuck with people's lives. Poor grief-stricken couple. That's what you want everyone to think. But guess what, Clayton Shaw? You've been rumbled because you're nothing but an arsehole. And Avril's no better than she should be.'

'I might be an arsehole, Suzie.' Clayton spins around to confront her. 'But I'm Avril's arsehole, not yours.'

After today, they will never speak to each other again. Even if they see each other in the street they will cross the road to avoid each other. He can't wait for that day to come. He thinks she can't possibly throw anything else at him today that could wound him any deeper. But in the next second he realises how wrong he is.

'But was the kid yours? That's what you've got to ask yourself. For all you know, her affair could have been going on for years.'

Chapter 72

Avril confesses to the affair almost as soon as she is accused of it. She even seems relieved to get it off her chest. There are no hysterical tears, no obstacles being thrown. They are having a proper sit down grown-up conversation for once; the kind he's always hoped for. This is his punishment for wishing Avril would confide in him. 'I love him desperately because he's everything you're not.' She'd told him. 'And I'm leaving you, Clayton. I should have done it months ago. But I didn't want to abandon you straight after...' now her eyes do go all watery, 'Tommy.'

Suddenly, Clayton finds himself sitting bolt upright in bed, relieved to find Avril's walking out on him is nothing but a bad dream. A nightmare in fact. But his reprieve is cut short when he realises he is in a strange bed; a strange room. *What have I done? Please don't tell me I stayed at Suzie's last night.* He scrambles out of bed, grabbing a sheet to cover his nakedness, and pulls open the nearest door. It leads into a hallway that has numerous doors going off it. Every door, including his own, has a number on it. He's in a hotel... no, a pub. Not just any old pub. His local, The Old Silent Inn. As his memory gradually returns, everything about last night starts to become clear.

After his encounter with Suzie, he'd driven on to Swallow's Nest only to sit in the drive for what seemed like hours. Although the house was in darkness he finally saw it as Avril did the first time she set eyes on it. Cold, unfriendly, forbidding. Funnily enough, he senses that she no longer feels the same; that she has in fact warmed to it whereas he has had a complete change of heart. He is beginning to think he was an idiot to up-sticks from Leeds and bring them all the way out here to this Godforsaken wilderness on the moor. *I fit in here less than Avril does*, he realises.

Deciding he couldn't stomach the thought of going inside, he'd driven into Stanbury in the hope of finding a pub open. He'd been lucky. Or not. Depending on how he looked on it; because the landlord had answered his sneaky knock on the back door almost straight away. The rest was history. He'd got hopelessly drunk and ended up sleeping it off in room ten of all places. Clayton couldn't have cared less at the time about spending the night in a so-called haunted room but now he comes to think of it, he does remember hearing the sound of children giggling in corners, just before he went to sleep. He wonders now if he'd been stitched up.

He had polished off a bottle of whiskey with the landlord and now Clayton's head is killing him. Looking at his watch, he realises it is after nine. The sun must be up but it is so dark in here he can hardly see a thing. He tugs open a stubborn pair of curtains and looks at his red bloated reflection in a mirror. There are crumbs in his hair and he has a vague memory of falling asleep at the bar with his head in a bowl of pork scratchings. *It's time to go home and face the music, old man,* he tells himself.

Half an hour later, he's back in the pub lounge but there's no sign of the landlord; just a large surly man at the bar who refuses to acknowledge him. Clayton takes some notes out of his wallet and leaves them on the same sticky table where they'd played a late night game of cards.

'Tell the boss if I owe him any more than that, I'll catch up with him next time,' he says turning to address the man behind the bar. But the man has vanished and Clayton gets the feeling it will be a waste of time searching for him. No human could have disappeared so quickly. He feels the room sway and has to hold onto the back of a chair for support. *Shit. I must have drunk more than I thought.* But hangover or not, he's going to have to head home. His staying out all night will seriously have pissed Avril off. He clings to the hope that she hasn't yet woken up or even realised he's missing. He can be home in fifteen minutes and making carpentry noises in his workshop in no time at all. *She'll never be any the wiser,* he convinces himself.

Chapter 73

It's been a whole hour since Avril managed to track down Suzie's phone number but it has taken her all this time to find the courage to dial it. As soon as it connects, she is tempted to hang up. She knows this conversation cannot go well but she's worried sick about Clayton and really has no choice. It's the only place she can think he might have spent the night. All of their– no, *his* friends, live miles away and he wouldn't have driven all the way to Cornwall without telling her. Even if he had, his mum would have rung and told her. There's no way she would have let Avril worry. And if he isn't at Suzie's, then something terrible must have happened to him. *Please God, let him have shagged her. I can't bear the thought of him being in an accident or lying hurt and injured somewhere, or worse...*

'Suzie. This is Avril. Avril Shaw. I was just wondering if you'd seen Clayton?' Avril coughs nervously to clear her throat. 'He's not with you by any chance, is he?' There is hysterical laughter on the other end of the phone and then the sound of Suzie screaming, 'Leave me alone, you fucking mad bitch,' quickly followed by a dialling tone.

Avril doesn't blame Suzie for hanging up on her. She would have done exactly the same in her place; but she still doesn't know Clayton's whereabouts. If he *is* there, and Suzie lets on she called, he's bound to ring back. So, she waits a good ten minutes, all the while anxiously stroking the scarring on her chest. She's been up since before six, which is unusual for her on a non-work day; having somehow sensed Clayton hadn't come home last night. She's convinced that's what made her get up so early. Looking at the clock on the fireplace mantel she sees that it is now after nine. Three hours of torture already. Just lately she had begun to think she could manage without Clayton, but since waking up this morning she's had a change of heart. Probably it's because she's started eating again and feeling much better because of it. She can't stop munching even now, when she's going out of her mind with worry. An hour ago there was a whole packet of biscuits on the coffee table in front of her and now there are only two left. Picking up another biscuit, Avril polishes it off in a couple of mouthfuls and realises she hasn't thought about *The Crying Boy* or Tommy all morning.

When she hears a tentative knock at the front door her heart soars. Clayton? *Oh thank God, he's alright.* She jumps off the sofa and heads toward the door. Then freezes when she realises Clayton wouldn't knock, not even if he'd forgotten his key. *What if it's the police? coming to tell me he's been involved in an accident; or that he's dead and never coming home again. Oh Jesus, how have we let things get so bad between us? When was the last time we said 'I love you' to each other? I'd want to die if anything happened to Clay. I really couldn't bear it. Why have we been so stupid? Shutting each other out, letting others come between us.* On this thought, her eyes swing accusingly to *The Crying Boy* painting on the wall. She narrows her eyes at it. It's stupid to blame a painting. She knows that. But then again, she hasn't been herself lately. She doesn't know what came over her, only that she quite suddenly stopped feeling unwell.

Bracing herself for the worst, Avril walks into the hallway and tentatively approaches the front door. She takes a couple of determined breaths before yanking it open.

'Chief,' Avril is ridiculously pleased to see him. It's not as if she dislikes him any less than usual – she's just relieved to find he's not somebody in uniform. He doesn't smile back at her. She doesn't expect him to. As usual, he's slow off the mark. Takes his time to spit out what he wants to say. She is reluctant to ask him if he's seen Clayton. He'll be unbearable enough when he finds out she made that call to Suzie. Besides, she's feeling more confident now she knows the police aren't knocking her door down. She was getting herself into a right state just now, thinking the worst. She's sure Clayton is fine. He will come home when he's good and ready.

'I heard you were missing somebody,' The Chief sneers.

'I suppose Suzie called you already.' Avril crosses her arms defensively.

'Word travels fast in these parts,' he tells her somewhat pompously. Any fool can see he is enjoying himself. But Avril is no fool.

'This is no time to play games, Chief. Have you seen him? Is he in... town?' She will not give him the pleasure of saying Suzie's name out loud.

'Not for me to say,' he clicks his tongue and winks.

Avril shakes her head in annoyance and starts to close the door. 'I really don't need this today.'

'But a little birdie did tell me something...'

Avril sighs in exasperation but he has her right where he wants her and they both know it. There is more to come and she has no choice but to listen.

Chapter 74

Avril has her back to Clayton, and refuses to turn around, even though she knows he is standing immediately behind her. As Clayton watches her angrily stuff items into a holdall, his teeth grind together in pent up anger. *I've lost her. I'm too late. I have no idea what to do. What to say.* Although he's desperate to *make* her stay, another part of him thinks she might be better off without him. Perhaps it would be a kindness to let her go. In his next breath he thinks, *Screw that. She's my wife. And I mean to fight for her. Even if I have to take the blame for her having an affair.* Making up his mind that he won't let her leave him for someone else, no matter what, he realises he has to do something, say something, now… before it's too late.

'I hated him when he was born.'

Immediately, her shoulders slump. Next, her arms slow down and stop what they were doing. She turns warily to face him. Her face is washed out and ghostly; but her eyes are narrow slits. He has never seen her this angry before. Even her cheeks twitch with temper; just as their son's used to whenever he was in a pet. Before he's through talking, she's going to get even angrier.

'You're not doing this. You don't get to do this *now*.' She is impressively fierce.

'I thought you *wanted* me to talk about him. Isn't that what you're always going on about?' Despite telling himself to remain calm, Clayton's resentment builds with each word.

'You've had months to do this... Why now?'

'You've never got around to packing a bag before.' He states matter-of-factly.

'Is it any wonder after what The Chief told me?' Avril flounces across the room, pulls out a dressing table drawer and begins an erratic search for something that is clearly none of his business.

'What *did* he tell you? If it's about Suzie...'

'Not everything is about that woman.' Avril screams. 'For once this is about me. And the fact that you lied, Clayton Shaw, something you promised never to do.'

Clayton waits, uncertain where this is going. He hasn't done anything wrong. She can't have anything on him.

Sensing his puzzlement, Avril lets him have it. 'You never once mentioned the fact that this house burnt down the same day Tommy died, did you?'

Clayton feels his face start to burn. She hasn't quite got her facts right, but all the same...

'It was just a bizarre coincidence, Avril. You remember the architect told us the house was torched by vandals when the house was already a ruin; just a few months before they started renovating it.'

'But that wasn't the first time it burned, was it? The first time was on April 13th, more than five years ago, the day I gave birth to your son.'

'I didn't think the dates would matter.' Clayton shrugs in defeat.

Suddenly, she's in his face, pounding her clenched fists on his chest. 'You knew and you never told me.'

He willingly accepts the blows, knowing that she will tire soon. He'd give her a knife to slit his throat with if he thought it would make her feel better.

'You're a liar. You knew nothing on God's earth would have convinced me to move in here, knowing this, let alone step through the door. How could you?'

'I'm sorry, Avril. I should have told you. You're absolutely right. But I thought this place would be good for us. I couldn't have been more wrong.'

'That's why nothing felt right from the start.' Avril darts a hostile look at the walls and shudders in disgust. 'And did you also know that a man died downstairs on the sitting room floor?'

Clayton knows alright. He has the grace to bow his head and glance away from the disappointment in Avril's eyes. Her disillusionment cuts him to the bone.

'No wonder they had it in for us. The Chief and Suzie. Knowing we'd moved into the house where his brother and her father died.'

'What? I don't know where you've got that from, Avril but I swear that part isn't true. Who told you that?'

'I already had my suspicions but he admitted it when he came around earlier to gloat.'

'The Chief's been here? And he said that? But he would have told me something like that.'

'Not such a good friend after all, is he?' Avril laughs at his wounded expression

'All this time. He... *they've* been playing us.' Clayton's anger gets the better of him and he grabs the holdall from the bed and hurls it across the room.

'Oh very grown up.' She shakes her head at him as if he were some unruly pupil, but he has already spotted the photograph in her hand. She holds it close. Clearly she doesn't want him to see it but he can just about see the curling up edge of it. He wonders if it is a photograph of her lover. Has it been in this house the whole time?

'It's me that should be leaving after what you've done.' There. He's said it. Done exactly what he promised not to. He can't help himself. What an idiot.

'You're the one who lied about this house *and* stayed out all night.' She pauses as if it still hurts her to think about this. 'I don't even want to know where.' She cannot look at him as she says this because they both know this is exactly what she wants to know.

'And what about you, Avril? What secrets are you hiding?'

'I don't have any secrets.' Avril looks sick with worry, he notices, and her eyes are all over the place. She couldn't look less guilty if she tried.

'So, who is in the photograph?'

Avril gazes dumbly at the photograph in her hand as if she doesn't know how it got there. Her shoulders slouch some more and her eyes fill with tears.

'Is it him?' he's desperate to know.

Nodding tearfully, Avril walks dejectedly across the room and places the photograph face down on the bed.

'Why can't you say his name?' Avril asks miserably, flopping onto the bed.

I don't know his name yet, he wants to yell, *but when I do, God help him.* And then he frowns, because Avril isn't acting the way somebody caught red-handed with a picture of their lover should. Moving quickly, before she can stop him, he goes over to the bed and flicks the photograph over.

Although he is relieved to see that it is his son in the picture and not another man, he is once again struck by how similar he is to the boy in the painting. Searching for something of himself in his son, it kills him to find none. Unlike the unfortunate dates surrounding their son and this house, he knows this cannot be a coincidence. He doesn't want to face up to the fact that his son might have been fathered by someone else; but what other explanation is there?

'I thought all his photographs had been put away.'

'Not this one,' Avril replies dejectedly.

'Is he mine?'

'What?'

'Is… was the boy mine? I have to know, Avril.'

'What on earth are you taking about?' Avril is looking at him the way he used to her – as if he is losing his mind.

Chapter 75

She has taken Clayton to her favourite spot on the moor, which overlooks the old abandoned barn, and they sit with their legs tucked up under them in the sun-bleached grass. She has already told him too much and as a result her mind is now wondering away from him. A dying sheep, too exhausted to stand, lies on its side and pants heavily; all the while keeping a watchful eye on them. Avril has already made her feelings about the sheep known. She wants to do something to help ease its suffering. But Clayton is of a mind that nature, as cruel as it is, has to take its course. She's not sure she agrees with him but he is not an unkind man and so, reluctantly, she agrees to do nothing.

'I wanted to tell you, Clay, but–'

'I know. I know. Things haven't exactly been easy for either of us.'

'Is that why you spent the night with her?'

She doesn't look at him when she says this. The thought of him spending the night with Suzie cuts her to pieces.

'You're looking at a faithful husband, here,' he tells her. 'I actually spent the night at the pub and I can assure you my head is paying the price.' He smiles inappropriately.

'I'm glad. I don't think I could bear that.'

'What did you mean earlier, when you said you started the fire?' Clayton asks her somewhat churlishly; as if he's already on her case, doubting her again.

His tone is gentle but there is still a disapproving look on his face that terrifies her. She glances away, at something in the distance only she can see.

Somehow, she's always known this moment would come. All those years denying her past and defending her lies have been futile. Now he will know everything and he will leave her, just as she's always feared.

'Everything was my fault, Clayton,' she admits finally. 'I can't blame them for taking my brother away. He wouldn't have been safe with me, they said, not after what happened. He was only six at the time and I was still in the hospital recovering from my... burns when they had him adopted. Before I knew anything of it, they'd given him a complete new identity. I was thirteen and nobody needed my permission.'

'What about your parents?' Clayton's voice quivers with dread and he's absolutely right to be afraid. What she is about to tell him would worry anyone. After today, he won't want to come within a mile of her.

'Dad had fallen asleep in his chair. Drunk as usual. And it was just dangling there between his fingers. Most of the kids at school had already tried it, but I never had. Funny that, when they used to call me "Fag Ash Roberts" because of the smell.' Avril smiles at Clayton's raised eyebrows. It's just like him to be surprised by trivialities, such as her real name. 'I changed my surname to Croft by deed poll as soon as I turned eighteen,' she says by way of explanation. 'It was my way of thanking the woman brave enough to take on a very troubled fifteen-year-old.

'Anyway,' Avril pretends at a flippancy that she doesn't feel, 'I took the dog-end and stole a secret puff or two.

But when I heard Mum coming back in, I panicked and dropped it. It fell down the side of the armchair and I went to hide in my bedroom. Every other Thursday was Giro day for them, and as soon as the cheque was cashed they'd start drinking. To keep Jamie's mind off the fighting and swearing, I would keep him in the bedroom with me until it was safe to come out again. If we were really lucky, they would fall into a drunken stupor by teatime and I would rifle through their pockets for change; so I could take Jamie to the chippy. A battered sausage usually cheered him up,' Avril tells Clayton wistfully.

'You still haven't said what happened to your parents.' Clayton isn't looking at her when he says this.

'They died in the fire, Clay.' Avril bows her head. 'Dad slept right through it. He never felt a thing, even when the flames reached his face. As for mum, she wouldn't let me help her.' Avril puts a shaky hand on Clayton's forearm, bringing his attention back to her face. 'I really did try.'

'It was an accident. A terrible, tragic accident.' Clayton is shaking his head at her as if he wants to be on her side but Avril knows this is impossible.

'I killed my own parents, Clay. I started that fire.'

'You were just a kid. It wasn't your fault.' Even though Clayton's face is wracked with pain he still does not cry. Avril doesn't think she will ever witness him doing so. Not properly. She's seen him well up before, many times, but this is the closest he's come to shedding actual tears.

'I was thirteen. And difficult. Very difficult. At least that's what *they* said. Afterwards… because of what I'd done, it was decided we would be homed separately. My brother got adopted straight away as I knew he would. I'd managed to get him out of the fire unharmed; so he was just as perfect as ever. But I waited two years for someone to come along. Nobody wanted a scarred teenager who refused to communicate. My mother died right next to me in the hospital, Clay, and for two years I couldn't get the image of her burned body out of my head. That's why I never minded what hospital or care home they put me in; and no matter how kind anyone was to me I retreated into a silent world, like Tommy.'

At this point in her story, Avril starts to sob and Clayton awkwardly puts an arm around her. Avril doesn't hold this detachment against him. He's never been good at comforting others. Give him a practical problem to solve and he's able to perform brilliantly; but dealing with tears and emotions has never been his cup of tea.

'And all this time you thought you couldn't tell me something like this?'

Avril nods through her tears and wonders why he's still sticking around. Why isn't he angrier? This is the secret she's been hiding from him her whole life, or at least that's how it feels. She's never dreaded anything more. Yet he's taking it calmly on the chin, as if she'd just admitted to something as innocent as playing truant as a child.

'The truth is ugly, like me, and I was so ashamed of who we were and what I'd done. We were scum, Clayton. That's what people called us.'

'You saved your kid brother's life. That's something you should be proud of. And no matter what anyone else said, you didn't mean to burn down the house or hurt anyone, did you?'

Avril shakes her head; not knowing how true this is. She had hated her parents and can no longer remember if she intended to hurt them or not. This is the part she will never admit to. One more secret she must keep.

'And what about Jamie? Why isn't he part of our lives?'

'If I'd told you about him, I'd have had to tell you everything. The whole story. I was afraid–'

'You think I would have been put off? Jesus, Avril. Don't you know me better than that by now?'

They share a moment of silence, each studying the open space around them. Avril notices that the sheep's breathing has deteriorated. It has one eye fixed on her and seems to be asking for her help. She shudders and looks away. *How can I sit here talking about how horrible my life is when that poor creature is dying right in front of me?*

'He showed up soon after Tommy was born. He'd reached 18 by then and I suppose the adoption agency gave him my details. I wasn't hard to find, apparently. He said he couldn't really remember our parents but he'd never forgotten me. He approached me in the street one day, just like that, out of the blue. I had Tommy with me at the time. He was just a baby then, all tucked up in his pram but I could see he looked just like my brother. He stood there and cried when I told him he was better off without me, that I couldn't be part of his life. He was still the same, sensitive, easily hurt little boy I'd once loved.'

'Oh Avril, why didn't you let him in? He needed you and God knows, you must have needed him. Your own flesh and blood.'

'I know, Clay. I know. But I just couldn't. I didn't want to be reminded of what happened. I saw the way he looked at my scars that day. He blamed himself. I know he did.' Avril's face twists with self-hatred as she makes a fresh discovery about herself, 'I know you won't understand this, but I think maybe a small part of me blamed him too.'

Surprisingly, Clayton nods his head, as if he *does* understand.

'I always wanted to know how you *really* got these, but never dared ask.' Clayton touches the scarring that starts at her throat and snakes its way down to her belly button. 'I think you were incredibly brave to do what you did, Avril.'

Avril's eyes fill with fresh tears. Her capacity for self-loathing means she doesn't feel entitled to his pity.

'Gruesome, isn't it?' she laughs self-consciously and removes his hand from her ravaged skin.

'Not gruesome at all. With or without the scars, I'd love you just the same'.

'How come you want to know about this particular scar and not the other?' she asks suspiciously.

The instant she says this; she senses him draw away from her. This is to be expected. If anyone is a traitor in their marriage – it's her, she realises. She seems resolved on a life of misery for them. There *is* no other way. With their son dead, they cannot expect to deserve any happiness.

'You're referring to our son,' Clayton states eventually, in a leaden voice.

'I let him down, Clay. I let them both down. First Jamie. Then Tommy.'

'No you didn't,' Clayton tells her firmly; before pulling her into his arms. *Will he ever get tired of protecting me?* she wonders. *And is that sheep truly at peace now it's passed?* Without glancing at it, she knows it has gone.

Chapter 76

His hair is white with sawdust and his hands are covered in it too. That's why he hovers outside the sitting room, in case he treads it through the house on the soles of his shoes. He doubts it would bother Avril that much. She's hardly the most domesticated of wives. But the mess would bother him. Although he's noisily made his way through the ground floor, yelling at items he is unable to find and blaming *them* for his anger – he can see he has caught her unawares. So he watches her unobserved from the doorway and it hits him like it never has before that she really has been away from him. He hasn't just imagined this. The difference in her is immediately obvious.

There she is now, knees up on the squashy leather sofa looking relaxed, with her nose in a book. Every so often her hand dips greedily into a bag of crisps and she eats noisily; crumbs dropping down her vest top. He can't remember the last time she ate junk food. She even has a glass of fizzy pop next to her on the table he made; the one she's never liked, because it is made out of 'a smelly old door'.

When she senses she is being watched, she looks up and smiles shyly. The fact that her eyes are full of life and consciousness for once really does give him hope.

Not wanting to give his feelings away, he stumbles on his next words, 'Have – Have you seen my long extension lead?'

Avril raises her eyebrows and shakes her head. He doesn't know why she should seem so mystified. It's a straight-forward question and he wants to tell her so.

'Are you sure you didn't use it in Tommy's room?' he asks irritably; not convinced she hasn't had some involvement in its disappearance. *What is wrong with her? And why is she sitting bolt upright like that and staring at me like she's just seen a ghost?*

'I had a quick look in there but couldn't see anything. What? What is it? Why are you staring at me like that?' He feels a tremor of fear go through him. Just a few seconds ago he'd convinced himself she was herself again but now he's not so sure.

'You said Tommy's room.' Avril stares at him wide-eyed. It's as if she too is seeing him for the first time. Exactly how he felt about her just a moment ago.

'You said his name. I heard you.' She is defensive, keen to stamp on any denial before it has even left his mouth. But he is in no position to argue. As her words sink in, he remains frozen to the spot, incapable of moving.

Then, no longer caring about the trail of sawdust he leaves behind, Clayton stumbles dazedly into the room and flops into an armchair. His face crumbles pitifully as he drops his head in his hands and begins to cry. Sobs rack his body and he makes no effort to restrain them. Deciding it's too late to attempt self-control now, he cries the way a man should over the loss of his son. He doesn't know why it has never happened before, but if Avril is wondering where her strong, reliable husband has gone, he doesn't care. He's always prided himself on being a 'man's man' and has never tried to deny this; but for some reason his belief system is no longer what it once was. He no longer cares what other people think. Realising that Avril has been in ownership of this trait far longer than him makes him feel smaller still.

'I really did hate him when he was born. I wasn't lying or making it up before,' he sobs with all the gusto of a distraught two-year-old. 'I felt so ashamed, I even considered telling people he wasn't mine. I did it once, in the park, when he was going off on one because he wasn't getting his own way. Funny thing is, I didn't feel any shame about that.'

He sees the horrified expression on Avril's face and he can tell she doesn't know what to do. Guesses she's torn between striking out at him or putting her arms around him. Either way, nothing can stop these harrowing thoughts galloping through his mind. When it first began to dawn on him that he may not be Tommy's real father, he was devastated and the relief he felt when he was proven wrong was overwhelming. Only then did he realise how much he had loved his son; and not just 'deep down' either. Now it is clear to him that he loved Tommy just as much as Avril did. Her love had sometimes overwhelmed the kid whereas his love went unrecognised. Avril's all-consuming love for the boy meant there was nothing left for anybody else. Especially him. He knows now that this was not a healthy recipe for a married life together. In essence, she had shut him out – not on the day Tommy died, as she often claims, but on the day he was born.

Now he knows what happened to her – the fire, losing her parents, and Jamie – he understands what made her this way.

'Now I'd give anything to have him back the way he was. I miss him, Avril, all the time.'

From out of nowhere, Avril drops at his feet and draws him into her body so he can feel every familiar bony lump.

'I'm so scared I'm going to lose you, too. It's not too late for us, is it?'

He's saddened by how unsure she looks. He doesn't know why he expected more. He shouldn't be surprised at how estranged they've become. His doing, mostly, he realises.

'I know you know everything about me now and that's a good thing. I can see that. But…' He knew there would be a but in there somewhere. He doesn't blame her for sounding so guarded. 'I've been left on my own for so long, Clayton,' she finally admits. At this, her eyes go fleetingly to *The Crying Boy* portrait and he begins to understand that her preoccupation with it could rekindle at a moment's notice. She may not be as confused as she once was, but she could easily relapse. He can see why she is so tempted to go back to the silent, ghostly world she retreated into as a young woman. She must have felt protected there. Knowing this floors him. He wants nothing more than to make his wife feel protected and safe. *What use am I if I can't do this?* he berates himself.

Not knowing what else to do, Clayton cups her fragile face in his hands and brings her attention back to him.

'Not any more. I promise,' he tells her. 'From now on I'm going to do what I should have done a long time ago, and put you first.'

Choked with emotion, Avril can only nod. But Clayton can tell by the softening of her eyes that his words mean something to her. Her mind isn't clouded right now. Nor is she dipping in and out of the real world as she sometimes does.

'And the first step is getting you well again.' He has every reason to sound cautious because she is at once prickly and defensive. He feels her try to pull away from him, but he won't let go.

'I am well. I'm much better than I was.'

He kisses her forehead and protectively wraps his arms around her, until she eventually gives in and leans into him. She surprises him by placing a hesitant kiss on his mouth. It doesn't stop there. They are both startled by how passionate this kiss turns out to be. The last time he kissed her like this, she was only pretending. This time it is real.

Suddenly, the CD player lights up and the sound of Tiffany's 'I think We're Alone Now' blasts out at full volume, making them jump. Soon, they're laughing and relaxing back into each other's arms; content for now with what they have.

'The CD must have been in there since the night of the party,' Avril says eventually.

'It's been playing up recently. I'll add it to the growing list of things that want doing around here.'

There is a long pause during which neither of them seem to know what to say; each fearful of upsetting the other.

'I'll go and see a doctor, Clay, a proper doctor and not just a therapist, if it makes you happy,' Avril is first to break the enforced silence. 'If you think I need it.'

He'd like to reassure her that it isn't necessary and he hates not being able to do so, but he needs her to do this.

'I think we both do.'

'What are you saying?' she looks up at him with innocent eyes, making him feel like the big bad wolf.

'It wouldn't hurt for me to talk to somebody. Better than bottling things up, don't you think?' *These are words I never thought I'd utter,* Clayton reflects.

He can imagine his father's horror should he get wind of it. *I'm being unfair,* he realises. *Dad would support me in whatever decision I made and he wouldn't judge me for it either.* Until now, Clayton has never realised quite how lucky he is where his family are concerned. He can't begin to imagine what Avril's childhood must have been like. From what she's told him already, it amounts to a lot of neglect and abuse. It's a wonder she didn't lose her mind altogether.

Chapter 77

From the kitchen window, Avril watches the swallows dance high in the sky. Their antics make her want to pull a face, but she resists. A weird clownish grin on her face is the last thing she wants Clayton to see when he comes through the door. Although it's the middle of the afternoon, Avril barely remembers how her day began, only when it ended – the moment the doctor confirmed what she's suspected for some time. She wonders where her bag is and what she's done with her newly-prescribed medicine? Although he tried to assure her that these new drugs should help her condition, he didn't sound very convincing.

Clayton will be devastated when she drops this latest bombshell on him; especially now, when they're just starting to get back on track again. Glancing around, she sees that her bag is on the floor. She remembers now that she dropped it on the kitchen table when she first came in, but it missed and fell on the floor. She doesn't attempt to pick it up again. Her mind is too fuzzy for that. She turns on the tap and appears mesmerised by the water gushing out of it. Slowly she fills a glass and drinks it. She fills it again but does not bring the glass to her mouth this time. Instead, she watches it overfill. *What will I tell him? How will I tell him? How will we deal with what is happening to me?*

A loud bang from above causes Avril to jump in fright and the glass smashes against the side of the sink, slicing into her hand.

'Shit.' Avril presses down on the blood slowly oozing out of her palm but it soon catches up with her accelerated heart rate and begins to squirt freely down the plug hole. *That really was a bloody big bang and I've already had enough scares for one day, thank you very much,* Avril grabs a handful of kitchen roll to mop up the blood. Doing so makes her feel nauseous. She's already had quite enough of it taken from her veins today, for testing, and still feels weakened by it.

There it is again. The banging. It comes from somewhere upstairs and sounds like a door slamming open and shut as if caught in a through-draft. Maybe Clayton left a window open? She'd better go and check before those birds get in again. The mess they made on the day of Mrs Mills' accident was bad enough. Now that she thinks of it, there is something bothering her about that poor woman. But whatever it is Avril just can't seem to put her finger on it. *I'm sure it will come to me;* she is quick to dismiss Mrs Mills from her thoughts. Any mention of her makes Avril increasingly uncomfortable.

***

Avril stands in the middle of what would have been Tommy's room and stares in dismay at its unfinished state. Everywhere she looks there are half-painted walls, paint encrusted rollers, paintbrushes and tins without lids. Sighing, because the thought of putting it all right again drains her, she walks over to the half open window and shuts it. She was right about Clayton leaving it open. *Problem solved*, she thinks in satisfaction, firmly securing the sash lock. She is about to go back downstairs again when something outside catches her attention.

Standing alone on the moor, staring up at the same window she is looking out of, is a child. Avril gasps in fear and stumbles so that her face bumps into one of the glass panes. Luckily, she does not hurt herself, but it's a close call. Enough to shake her up again. Much as she'd like to run away, she cannot take her eyes off this child. Without doubt, he is the same one she followed to the barn on the day she first came across The Chief. With his yellow hair, cornflower blue eyes and raggedy clothing – he's Tommy and *The Crying Boy* all rolled into one. Except her Tommy wouldn't be looking at her that way – with mean, dark little eyes and a crooked, accusing grown-up smile. His presence terrifies her. She thought she was getting better. Hadn't she said as much to Clayton? So why is she still seeing him? It doesn't make sense. He makes her feel ice cold; as if her heart is slowing down. She can't breathe. Just looking at him paralyses her. But eventually she does manage to pull her eyes away and side steps the window, concealing herself from view. She will not look again to see if he is still there. She closes her eyes and counts down from sixty, knowing that she will give in and look before she makes it to half a minute. She won't be able to help herself.

'You look like you've seen a ghost.'

Avril starts at the sound of Clayton's voice. She hadn't heard his footsteps on the squeaky stairs or even sensed he was there in the doorway, watching her. How long he's been there, she can't tell, but she hopes he hasn't witnessed her frantic state. Nothing can prevent her turning troubled eyes on him and bursting into tears.

'Oh, Clay. What was I thinking? I never should have painted this room,' Avril sobs into her hands; at the same time noticing that the kitchen roll wrapping has gone from around her hand. What's more, there is no sign of any blood or cut on her palm. Not even a scratch. *Am I going mad? Please God, don't let that happen again. What is wrong with me?*

Clayton closes in on her, no doubt relieved to find this is one problem he can help her with – a room in need of painting is quite within his capabilities.

'What are you worrying over a silly thing like that for?'

'Silly?' Avril isn't sure whether to be offended or not. She's been prickly Avril for so long, it's a hard habit to get out of. She sniffles into his shoulder, deciding anything is preferable to having to explain to Clayton what just happened – the child on the moor and the blood. They have enough on their plate without him worrying about her mental state all over again. He hasn't even heard the latest news yet.

'What I meant was, you can leave it blue if you like,' he is conciliatory, the adoring husband. The old Clayton. She has never been more glad of it.

'But it might be a girl,' the freckles on Avril's face move about in a surprised way as her brow furrows.

'What are you talking about?' Clayton doesn't take her seriously. Not yet. And Avril hardly knows herself if the words tumbled accidentally out of her mouth or if she always intended letting them slip out this way.

'The doctor– he said–'

'You mean?' Clayton's eyes go suspiciously to her stomach as if it holds all the answers, guessing that it does. Avril's sheepish nod confirms this. In fact, she is busy checking all of his responses. So far so good. He hasn't flipped out yet.

'But you can't be.' He might not be in any danger of losing his temper but it is clear he is stunned by this news. She can see his mind ticking over, figuring everything out. Finally, he gets it. 'The night we moved in...'

'It was the only time we...' Avril points out logically; though she's feeling anything but logical right now. She is in fact so overwhelmed, she feels she could easily pass out.

'It's such a shock. So unexpected.' Clayton is already pacing like an expectant father; but eventually he comes to a standstill and rubs his chin. 'How do you feel about it Avril?'

'How do you?' She might sound noncommittal, as if his answer isn't important, but everything hinges on it.

A lengthy pause creeps in between them, where neither is willing to volunteer their real thoughts for fear of upsetting the other.

'If we keep it, there is every chance it could be like Tommy.' Avril keeps her voice deliberately low and non-judgmental. She doesn't want this news to frighten him.

'What do you mean, *if* we keep it? You want this– our baby, don't you Avril?'

He sounds hurt and this is a good sign. So she nods energetically, frightened of giving too much away. He has no idea that she's already thought things through. He must never know this. The last thing she wants is to trap him, but there is no way she would ever consider aborting this baby. Little does he know that she's already made up her mind to leave him should he ask this of her. Not tomorrow or the next day, but now, this very minute. She would rather die than be responsible for the death of an innocent child.

She watches him scrutinise the room as if he still can't take it all in. He seems undecided. As if he's still thinking about it. Their future is in the balance... in his hands.

'I think I've got some lemon paint in the workshop,' he says at last with a mischievous grin. They share a warm smile that solves everything and Avril throws herself into his arms.

'I love you, Clayton Shaw,' she says, smothering him in excitable kisses.

Chapter 78

Clayton hasn't had a drop of alcohol all night and Avril has never been prouder of him. It must be doubly hard for him to abstain when they have so much to celebrate. Usually, he'd open a bottle of bubbly for the most mundane of reasons but tonight he's concentrating on making the table look nice instead. He's even gone to the trouble of lighting candles and dusting off their best china dinner service. She can't help but be impressed.

In the middle of the kitchen table, he's placed a jug of iced water and Avril helps herself to a glass of this now; pulling a face at the sparse bunch of flowers positioned under her nose. Typically, Clayton shopped for their celebratory meal in a rush and forgot to pick up the roses he'd promised her. Instead, he'd stopped off at a deserted petrol station for this sad offering. She doesn't mind the lack of roses but wasn't able to stop her face from falling when she spotted chrysanthemums in the mix.

The one thing he *has* got right is the dinner. As soon as he asked her what she'd like, she'd replied without hesitation 'Lamb shanks and root veg.' She had ordered it on their first ever date and it had remained a favourite of theirs. Back then, she'd been really nervous about eating in front of him but tonight she is starving. Her newly-prescribed morning sickness pills are already aiding her returning appetite and quite honestly she feels as if she could eat a whole sheep by herself. Remembering the dying sheep on the moor, she feels guilty; but shakes off this thought. Not good for the baby. And concentrates instead on what Clayton is doing.

This is the first time either of them have managed to tame the beast that is their oven and Avril is impressed he has finally mastered it. Resting her hands contentedly on her belly, she watches Clayton slide the steaming casserole dish out of the oven, all the while whistling along to Rick Astley's 'Never Gonna Give You Up.' His eyes crinkle up at the corners whenever he smiles her way.

There is a sudden rapping on the back door that causes them both to raise their eyebrows and in walks The Chief carrying a pack of beers and something wrapped in newspaper. She might have known he would turn up like a bad penny to ruin their evening but at least her skin isn't crawling on first sight of him. She hopes this is a good sign. Maybe they can let bygones be bygones. This thought causes her to smirk. *I never thought I'd hear myself say that.*

'Chief. This is a surprise,' Clayton is immediately defensive, Avril notices, and not his usual easy-going self. But is it any wonder? Obviously, he is still stinging from the news that The Chief and Suzie somehow stitched him up. The fact that neither spoke of their connection to this house or relationship to the man who died here is clearly playing on his mind. Clayton is not one to be duped or made a fool of and Avril doubts he will ever recover from this. The old man may have lost his friendship for good, but at the moment he is oblivious to this fact.

'And so was this beauty.' The Chief chuckles. He is so intent on unwrapping a large trout that he doesn't notice Clayton's change in attitude.

As soon as Avril sees the fish, her stomach starts to churn. Whoever invented the term 'morning sickness' must have been taking the mickey; because in her case the nausea and vomiting had been lasting throughout the whole day and into the night too. *No wonder I turned my nose up at everything that was put in front of me*, Avril grasps at last, pleased to find that she is making up for it now. She can't wait for The Chief to leave so they can eat.

But he shows no sign of doing so. In fact, he seems completely indifferent to the romantic setting.

'Took me the whole morning to tickle it out of the water,' he grunts, stroking the fish as if it were the inside of a woman's thigh. 'Thought I'd cook it up as a treat. You do like fish, don't you, Avril?' he remembers to glance her way, careful to include her, and she is as surprised as he is when she smiles back.

He's got such a shock coming to him, I almost feel sorry for him. When Clay does finally get him alone, he's really going to get it in the neck. Avril can tell this just by the stiff way her husband holds his head and jaw.

'Normally that would be great,' Clayton concentrates on the casserole dish as he says this, 'but as you can see, I've already cooked.' With this, Clayton lifts off the lid and a delicious aroma hits everybody's nostrils.

'Lamb if I'm not mistaken,' The Chief glances regretfully at the fish. 'I guess this'll keep for another day.'

When the Chief plonks himself down at the table and opens one of the beers, Clayton's cheeks fill with colour.

'Actually we're… kind of celebrating.' Clayton tells him.

'A party! Now you're talking.'

Clayton's face is such a picture, Avril has to turn away, for fear of laughing. I *swear the old bugger is doing it on purpose, making it as difficult as possible for Clayton to throw him out. By now, he must have twigged that I've told him everything and he's annoyed Clay has taken my side.*

'Just me and Avril is what I meant.' Clayton tells him moodily. Enough is enough. There's only so far his politeness will extend. Avril know this of old even if The Chief does not.

At this, The Chief's mouth hangs open, but at least he gets up from the table, if a little shakily, stumbling conveniently on his bad leg (the same one that carried him in here with no problem at all), but tonight Clayton does not reach out a hand to steady him. It's a significant moment for The Chief. Avril can see this if Clayton cannot; because this action confirms what the old man already knows – their relationship is at an end.

'Well, why didn't you say so?' The Chief attempts a bravado he does not feel.

At a loss for words, Clayton smiles tightly, and his glance pointedly takes in the door. Still, The Chief dawdles.

'What is it, a wedding anniversary?' The Chief asks disbelievingly, as if he still can't fathom why they want to spend time alone together.

Avril scrapes back her chair and goes to stand next to her husband. 'It's okay. You can tell him,' she looks up at Clayton through pale blonde eyelashes and caresses his arm. In response, Clayton encircles her waist with his arms.

'Avril found out today she's pregnant,' he tells The Chief proudly.

The old man gazes at them in horror. He's quick to try to hide his real feelings but not quick enough for Avril.

'Well, congratulations,' he says grudgingly, looking down at his scuffed boots.

Belatedly, they go through the motion of shaking hands, followed by an awkward silence.

'I expect you'll be wanting to move into the town now then, what with a bairn on the way an all,' The Chief enquires hopefully; as if all may not be lost after all.

'Absolutely not.' Heatedly, Avril stamps on this presumption. 'Swallow's Nest is the perfect place to bring up a child. Isn't that right Clayton?'

In an unguarded moment, Clayton shows his surprise. Only a few hours ago, they'd been discussing selling up and moving back to Leeds. Whatever personal reasons The Chief has for wanting to oust them from this house, they cannot allow him to think he has won. Earlier, they had both been insistent on this; but now Avril can see Clayton is too taken up with the idea of being a father again to care – but he nods anyway to show his agreement.

'I'll be on my way then,' The Chief says dejectedly, 'Leave you two loved-up birds to it.' Painstakingly wrapping the fish back up in the newspaper, he casts watery old eyes on Clayton's back; willing him to turn around – but he does not.

'I'll take me catch with me, though, if it's all the same to you,' he states authoritatively, as if expecting an argument. Then remembering the cold beers, he sweeps them up into his other hand 'and these,' he reminds them.

Your loss, he might as well have implied, Avril thinks comically as she watches him drag his dead leg toward the door. And suddenly it's not funny anymore. She can see that Clayton's rejection has hurt the old man. The confusion and pain in his face appear real at any rate. She does not wish him any real harm and now that Clayton is all hers again, she can afford to be more generous. She's tempted to call him back and invite him to join them for dinner but one warning glance from Clayton holds her tongue. They've always been able to tell exactly what the other is thinking and now is no exception. *We're really special that way*, Avril can't resist crowing, but in the next breath she cowers beneath such smugness, fearful of being punished for daring to think such thoughts. Refusing to allow her superstitions to get the better of her, the old man is soon forgotten, and Avril and Clayton once again only have eyes for each other.

Chapter 79

*T*hey think they're something special. The pair of them.
But they have no idea how 'special.' Bloody fools. And
after the way Clayton treated me just now, I can't help
thinking they're both as bad as each other. The Chief wipes
an errant tear from the corner of his eye and continues
on his way across the moor. Nowadays, it's a real struggle
for him to get anywhere on foot and it's another two-
and-a-half miles to his house, which is at the very edge of
Haworth village. He's never lived anywhere else and has
grown up in the knowledge that the Brontë sisters used
to pass his door every day of their lives. Not that any of
that fancy malarkey has ever impressed him. The tourists
can come all they like, bleating on about the beauty and
magic of the moors but for those brought up here it is a
different place.

All his life he's grafted; often working fourteen hour
days as a fire chief. And for what? A piss poor pension and
little thanks. While Ted was alive, he'd taken satisfaction
in the fact that at least one of the brothers had made good.
There had never been any resentment between them.
They'd always got along even though Ted was everything
he was not – ambitious, sociable and good looking. He
also had a way with the women. Hadn't he boasted of one

day marrying the prettiest, most popular girl in Haworth village? And been proven right. But all that money Ted accumulated from his skip hire business hadn't stopped her leaving him for someone else when Suzie was just a bit of a bairn. Of course, The Chief had been hopelessly in love with her too. Although he never expected anything of her, other than to be near her sometimes, his sister-in-law had teased him mercilessly. She was as quick-witted as Avril in that way. They are in fact very similar, he recognises with a start. He has never forgiven his first love for walking out on him... *them*, he corrects himself; nor will he forgive the Shaws for showing him the door. They might have forgotten about him in a hurry, but they will live to regret it.

By the time he arrives home, he's exhausted. Kicking an assortment of bloodied animal traps out of the way, he collapses into an armchair that still has a handmade doily on the back of it; crocheted by his mum many years ago. The only other bit of furniture in the room is an old fashioned kerosene cooking stove. Here, he fries bits of pheasant and rabbit to keep him going and tries not to listen in on his neighbour's rows. Sometimes, he wonders why they are still living when his own brother is dead. Just lately, he hasn't been able to stop thinking about Ted and he thinks he knows why, even if he doesn't want to face this knowledge just yet. After Ted's wife left him, his brother had muddled along for a while, but his heart was no longer in the business and he was losing money, fast. It was all he could do to keep Swallow's Nest going. In fact, he'd re-mortgaged it several times. The Chief always had a sneaking suspicion he held on to it in the belief she would one day come back. Fat chance of that happening after he'd squandered his fortune. When Suzie left to pursue a life of her own – Ted had fallen apart.

After that, he spent most days drinking and rambling around those empty, outsized rooms, becoming more muddled and confused. In the run-up to his death, Ted convinced himself that *The Crying Boy* painting had cursed him; that it alone was responsible for the loss of his wife, health and business. Some days he would throw bottles of whiskey at it and cuss it. Other days he would lie before it, begging it to bring her back. These are times The Chief doesn't like to dwell on.

He closes his eyes and remembers his parents. A much nicer proposition. He'd looked after them when they were sick and nursed his old dad right up until his death, aged 90. It might be unheard of in these parts for a single man to take care of his elderly parents, but that is exactly what he had done; sacrificing a life of his own in order to do so.

After he lost them, he'd done his fair share of smoking, drinking and womanising, determined not to miss out on life. And when Ted died, things grew steadily worse, until he no longer recognised his own face in the mirror. The Chief has lost count of the number of times he'd passed out drunk on his own sitting room floor, but unlike his brother, he'd lived to tell the tale. But look what that brief sojourn of depravity had left him with. A poisoned ulcerated leg, yellow skin and septicaemia of the liver; not to mention the one thing he keeps close to his heart; a secret he hasn't shared with anybody, not even Suzie.

The biggest of men has never been able to floor The Chief but cancer has him in a strangle hold he can't wriggle out of. He knows he is dying. That he hasn't got long. He has already given up a long list of things that are bad for him, including women and drink, but until he met the Shaws, he was only going through the motions for Suzie and the lad's sake. Knowing what he knows now, that he has just a few months left to live, he has to do one last thing for everybody's sake, including his own. He might not have a clue how he's going to go about it, but having made this promise to himself, he intends to carry it out in true Yorkshire style.

Chapter 80

*A*lone on the moor nobody can hear you cry, Avril reminds herself, using the back of a muddy hand to wipe away the tears running down her face. She is on her knees, looking into a shallow grave, and her hands and fingernails are clogged with soil. There is a slight breeze up on the moor today and it plays with her hair the same way a lover might. She enjoys having its invisible fingers on her face and neck, helping to cool her down. It would be so hot up here otherwise and she's already exhausted from digging the hole. It was a lot harder than she first imagined and the hand trowel she brought along with her wasn't really up to the job.

The hole could really do with being a few inches deeper, she thinks crossly, *but it will have to do. It's not as if I'm burying a body up here*, she's tempted to shout her thoughts out loud. The need to express anger at what she has been through is never far away. Instead, she reaches for her basket and takes out Tommy's blue woollen jumper and the fire truck.

She counts seventeen snags in the wool and remembers that there were only two when she first started counting them. It should have been thrown away weeks ago but she hasn't been able to bring herself to do it. Nor can she bear the thought of doing so now; choosing instead to bury it, along with Tommy's other things. *There will always be a little bit of Tommy on these moors now,* she thinks contentedly.

This will be the last summer I spend as a childless woman; Avril realises in wonder. *I need never be jealous of other women again.* For months now, Avril and Clayton have been arguing about her destructive behaviour. Although he insists there is no need for her to be jealous… she disagrees on a massive scale. *There's everything to be jealous about. Other people's children for one thing.*

Now she has so much to look forward to. A new baby; and a move back to Leeds is also on the cards. *I will never forget Tommy. I won't need any reminders to think of him every day and the child growing inside me will get to know its brother just as much as if he were still alive. Tommy will always be a part of this family, but I have to let him go now, just as Clay has always said, so we can move on.*

Avril has never had a better reason for moving on. She is still amazed at how well Clayton took the news of her pregnancy; having always been adamant he did not want another child. When she asked him to explain his dramatic change of heart, he told her he'd been terrified of going through all that heartache and torment again. He'd also been concerned for her wellbeing, admitting he didn't know if she could cope mentally. On a more selfish level, he was concerned a new baby would drive them even further apart, as Tommy had done. Of course, all that altered the minute he found out she was carrying his child. Now, he can't do enough for her, claiming to have fallen instantly in love with the bump that isn't even visible yet. Clayton says he can't remember feeling this way about Tommy, but supposes that's because he was a lot younger back then and uncertain of what fatherhood had in store for him. Right now though, he has none of those concerns. Gradually, it dawns on Avril how lucky she is. For once, she doesn't think how self-contradictory that sounds, considering she has only recently lost a son.

Sighing, because soon she will have to part with Tommy's things for good, her mind wonders over to the sheep's corpse over by the wall. There are flies buzzing around it and she can smell its rotting flesh from here. *I will not go over and look to see how far it has decayed. This will only remind me that this is the same process that Tommy's body went through.* Fighting back a feeling of sickness, Avril tears her eyes away from the dead sheep and retches into the grass. Thankfully, she does not vomit up her breakfast, just bile. She cannot afford to fall sick again. Thinking such macabre thoughts can only hurt her and the baby, she realises.

Here we go. She inhales the jumper one last time before placing it in the hole. Although she is determined to go through with this, she cannot resist straightening the jumper as if it were a child's body; placing its arms over its chest like one would a corpse. She then places the fire truck beside it, congratulating herself on completing such a milestone. As she gently tucks in the rest of Tommy's things, she remembers back to a day in a playground, some months before Tommy died, when he'd been having one of his turns. She'd had to brace herself against his attack before restraining him the way Clayton had taught her, until finally he cried with frustration and ceased to struggle against her. Her son's temper had been frightening at times and they had to take such steps to prevent him hurting others, including herself.

'Let it go, Tommy,' she'd begged him. And when he was done crying, she'd made him stand tall so that she could sign and talk to him at the same time. 'Let it go,' she'd insisted again. Sensing that he wasn't going to get his own way, he'd reluctantly signed back, 'I let it go,' before falling into her arms, desperate for a cuddle (Tommy could never stand being out of favour for long), and she'd pressed her mouth up against his hot little ear and whispered words he would never hear. 'But I'll never let you go, Tommy. Never ever.'

But she had. She'd let go of his hand on the day he died. Tommy couldn't help his anger but she could have prevented his death. *If only I'd been paying more attention*, she berates herself for the thousandth time. The likes of Grace, Clayton and his parents are all quick to assure her she isn't to blame; that it could have happened to anyone – but it doesn't get any easier – no matter how many times she goes over it. The guilt will never leave her. She's wished him a different death more times than she cares to remember; believing anything must be preferable to what really happened. She's often thought what a blessing it would have been if Tommy had been mauled to death in a playground by a savage dog or had his head bashed against a wall by a school bully. *As it is, I may as well have driven over him myself.*

Scrambling to her feet, unaware of how creased and dirty her bare knees are from sitting so long, Avril takes a handful of soil and sprinkles it on top of Tommy's things. She speaks, signs and cries all at the same time. 'I let you go, Tommy. I let you go.'

***

The Chief stands over a patch of newly patted down earth and absently chews on a blade of grass. There's a quizzical frown on his face and a sliver of blood at the corner of his mouth that he doesn't bother to wipe. He kicks at the mound again and steps quickly back from it, as if afraid something will leap out and grab him by the throat. He knows these moors like the back of his hand and this hole wasn't here yesterday; nor was it dug up by no fox, rabbit or badger either. He's been hunting, shooting and trapping animals long enough to suspect human involvement.

Fiddling with the emergency cigarette behind his ear, he scans the moor for other signs of disturbance. But nope. Nothing else is amiss. Just a rig-welted sheep that must have died after getting stranded on its back, which is now being picked over by crows. All it would have taken was for somebody to roll it over on its side; but instead it had been left to die an agonising death mauled alive by foxes and countless other predators; including the crows. If he had his gun with him, he'd be tempted to take a shot at them. He hates crows.

He pushes the toe of his boot into the freshly turned over soil and it meets resistance. He bends down, groaning because of the pain in his gammy leg and exposes what is hidden beneath – the wheel of a toy fire truck. Is somebody taking the piss? Are they on the moor laughing at his reaction right now? This can hardly be a coincidence, not with him being a retired fire chief an' all. It's only when he pulls out the blue woollen sweater that everything falls into place.

Turning to look in the direction of Swallow's Nest, he realises that Avril has finally done what Clayton has been urging her to do for weeks and got rid of the dead bairn's stuff. In doing so, she has handed him everything on a plate. Realising that it would kill her to know this, The Chief's mouth twists into a spiteful smile. He can hardly believe his luck. As a new plan starts to formulate in his mind, his jaundiced eyes fill with hope. So far, all his attempts to get them to leave have been cack-handed, but now, armed with this discovery, he reckons he'll have them out of Ted's old home before they know what's hit them.

Chapter 81

Hot and bothered, having trampled on several large cardboard boxes, Avril places the flattened pieces in the wheelie bin. The workout has caused her to break into a sweat and she finds herself longing for the endless summer to be over. She can't wait to wrap up in an oversized jumper and spend days on the sofa reading and snacking on pickled onions; a favourite craving from her last pregnancy.

If Clayton could see the state she's in now, he would be angry. *No, not angry. Angry isn't the right word for my husband anymore,* she reminds herself. *He would be concerned.* These days he doesn't want her lifting a finger around the house and is even on the lookout for a new cleaner; just until they decide what to do about moving. But after what happened with Mrs Mills… she is less keen. The woman still troubles Avril, but when she phoned the house to ask how she was, a man, Mr Mills she supposes, rudely hung up on her; intensifying her fear that she is somehow responsible for the woman's accident.

She struggles to close the lid on the crammed bin and has to press her weight down on the cardboard but this doesn't make much of an impact. By now her arms are killing her and she wonders if she dares climb inside the bin so she can jump up and down on the cardboard. But if Clayton came home and found her doing this, he would probably have a heart attack. As she pictures his horrified face, she finds herself smiling. She's doing a lot more of that recently and it feels good. But the smile vanishes when she sees the words 'Tommy's things' on a ripped up piece of cardboard. Realising that this is the last time she will ever have to see those words or think about Tommy's jumper and fire truck, she closes the lid.

Dusting her hands together, she turns to go back inside the house. That's when she spies a man heading toward the moor. Although he's some distance away, his sheer size and awkward gait make him instantly recognisable.

'Chief,' she shouts, unsure if he will hear her from this far away, but he halts anyway and turns to stare in her direction. For a moment, he appears to be looking straight at her but then continues on his way without so much as a wave or gesture to acknowledge her presence. Avril is mystified. She could have sworn he had seen her.

***

Avril comes out of the kitchen swigging water from a bottle and is about to push open the sitting room door when she notices muddy footprints on the hallway floor. They are too big to be her own and Clayton isn't home yet. He rang just five minutes ago to say he would be another hour. Later, they are going to drive into Keighley to drop a key off at the estate agents. Come Monday, it is going back on the market.

Gazing in horror at the man-sized footprints, Avril can't help think Monday can't get here quick enough. She wants to be rid of the place as soon as possible and Clayton feels the same. In the short time they have lived here they have experienced nothing but bad luck. Tentatively, she places her own foot over one of the muddy footprints; testing its size. The owner of these footprints must be a size thirteen at least and, therefore, tall. When she sees that the footsteps lead all the way up the stairs she starts to panic.

'I know somebody's up there. You'd better come down and show yourself.'

The ensuing silence does nothing to reassure her. Her eyes dart toward the door. *It's not too late to run*, she reminds herself. *But wherever I go, the same macabre silence will be waiting for me.* Although terrified of what she might find up those stairs, Avril has no choice but to follow where the menacing footprints lead.

***

Having deliberately saved this room till last, she opens the door to what would have been Tommy's room and peers inside. She gets the surprise of her life when she sees that Clayton has already redecorated it. In his effort to please her, he must have got on the case straight away. It wouldn't have taken him long; no more than an afternoon. She finds herself shivering at the thought of bringing a baby into this environment and comforts herself with the knowledge they will soon be decorating another nursery in a different home.

Suddenly, the rocking chair by the window creaks. It doesn't move exactly. She'd be out of here in a shot if that happened. But it definitely creaked, as if somebody had just sat down in it. Deciding there must be a draft coming through the window or floorboards, Avril isn't about to hang around to find out. Just as she's about to close the door on this scene, she notices a jumble of items spread out around the rocking chair. She'd been too busy looking at the freshly painted yellow walls, wondering where the step ladder and paint tins had disappeared to, to notice them before. Belatedly, she realises there are muddy footprints in here too. These are less visible than the ones in the hallway. By now most of the mud must have worn off the wearer's shoes.

As if it were pushing her aside, her own shadow comes from behind her and falls spookily onto the floor in front of her as she walks into the room. The items scattered around the rocking chair are too familiar for her not to instantly recognise them, but she fights the conviction all the same. The closer she gets, the more her heart hammers in her chest and she fears every menacing creak of the floorboards beneath her feet. *It can't be. Oh please, God. Don't let it be…* she prays. But no amount of pretending is going to make what she is seeing any less true. Her heart is in her mouth as she reaches out for a familiar piece of soiled clothing. *It might not be what I think it is. It could just be a cleaning rag left behind by Clayton.*

Avril wills herself not to glance again at the other things that cannot be so easily accounted for and instead concentrates on the scrap of material she is holding. It is covered in a crumbling mix of dry soil and grass and she can tell that it has been handled roughly. She doesn't need to count the snags in it to know there are even more in it now than when she buried it on the moor four hours ago. By now, her mouth is so dry she doesn't think she could scream if she wanted to. The return of Tommy's blue woollen jumper is not an illusion; any more than the fire truck sitting at her feet is.

Chapter 82

Wrapped in a blanket with a mug of sweet milky tea in her hands, Avril can't stop shivering. Having listened carefully to her garbled account of what happened, Clayton insisted she rest on the sofa while he took a look around upstairs. She hadn't wanted him to leave her, even for a few minutes, but was too scared to accompany him. She's been a complete wreck since discovering Tommy's things and practically threw herself into Clayton's arms when he finally showed up, half an hour later than planned.

When Clayton comes back a few minutes later, looking doubtful, Avril's first thought is that he doesn't believe her.

'You're right about Tommy's things but there are no dirty footprints on the stairs. Or anywhere else for that matter.'

'But I saw them, Clay, with my own eyes. They can't just have disappeared,' Avril protests tearfully and is relieved when Clayton takes hold of her hand. All at once, she is hopeful. 'What do you think happened to them?'

Now he's looking at her in the old, mistrustful way and she is tempted to remind him that they are *supposed* to be putting all that behind them. Instead, she decides to be more reasonable. He *wants* to believe her and that has to count for something.

'Avril, are you sure you went on the moor and buried them?' He asks tentatively.

It breaks her heart that he has to ask this, but she decides not to hold it against him. Neither of them need reminding how wildly erratic her behaviour has been.

'You think I made it up?' she asks quietly.

'I'm not saying that. Buy you're bound to feel a bit up and down at the moment, what with the baby and everything.'

In a childlike manner, Avril holds out her hands for him to inspect. It's terribly important that he believes her.

'I've still got dirt in my fingernails,' she tells him trustingly.

'I don't know what to say,' Clayton screws up his face in bewilderment. He's had so much uncertainty thrown at him these last few months that Avril suspects it is sometimes all too much for him. His hair is grubby, she notices, and in need of a good shampoo. She would love to take him into the kitchen and wash his hair over the sink.

He looks up at her and grins, as if he has guessed what she is thinking. But his smile doesn't last long. Soon, he's scratching his head with frustration and pacing up and down the sitting room floor.

'You think The Chief did this, don't you?' He comes to a sudden stop, as if this idea has only just occurred to him.

'I'm not sure. I don't know.' Avril squirms in her seat. Even she's having trouble believing the man from the moor would be capable of digging up their dead child's things in an attempt to frighten them. 'But it was definitely him on the moor. All I know is he looked at me as if I was a ghost and kept on walking. I put it down to his still being angry with us from the other night.'

'But why on earth would he do something like that?' Clayton wants to know. 'Especially now. I mean he's won, hasn't he? He's got what he wanted. We're leaving.'

Avril is just as confounded as he is. He's right, though. What has the Chief got to gain by scaring them now? But if not him, who else could it have been? Avril's accusing glance falls on *The Crying Boy* portrait.

Chapter 83

Having got back from the estate agents an hour ago, Clayton had gone straight to the snug to catch up on paperwork but has now wondered into the kitchen with food on his mind. Avril has obviously been lured into the kitchen for the same reason, because she has beaten him to it. Nothing seems to satisfy her hunger these days. He watches her nosing around in the fridge, nibbling at this and that, before drinking straight from the milk bottle. Because he's never seen her do this before, he finds himself chuckling.

'Caught you red handed!'

She jumps and almost drops the milk. But he can tell she is only mildly annoyed at being spied on.

'It's not nice creeping up on people,' she grumbles light-heartedly.

'You've missed a bit.' He tells her, tapping his own mouth and pulling a comical face. She swipes her face with the back of her hand but misses.

'You numpty,' he says and they both laugh. Finally, he goes over and wipes away the trickle of milk with his finger.

***

Having got back from the estate agents an hour ago, Avril had gone straight upstairs to run a bath. A good soak in the tub was exactly what she needed. She had only been lured away from it by the thought of food. On her way downstairs she tried to remember everything the agent had told them. Clayton seemed to grasp financial and legal matters much better than she did. She'd simply been pleased to learn that the value of their house hadn't gone up or down in the short time they'd lived here and no awkward questions had been fired at them. She couldn't be happier that the agents were going to market the house straight away and were confident of getting a quick sale. After a day like Avril has just experienced, she is feeling surprisingly positive.

At least she was until Clayton came into the kitchen and caught her drinking milk straight from the bottle. Not that there is anything wrong with that. He does it all the time. And of course, he hadn't meant to frighten her. But what he doesn't... can't... know is that one of them is repeating what has already happened. She glances at the clock and sees that it is now 7.05pm. In a second, Clayton will point at his mouth and come over and wipe the milk from her chin. How does she know this? Because he's just said the very same words to her he said five minutes ago, at 7.00pm.

'You've missed a bit,' he tells her, tapping his own mouth and pulling a comical face. Only this time she does not attempt to wipe the milk away herself; nor does she join in with his laughter when he calls her a 'numpty.' Here he comes now, with his finger and she backs away, terrified. *Is my own husband deliberately trying to make me think I'm going mad?*

She watches him go to the fridge and take out a giant beef tomato, which he places on a chopping board. When he picks up a large serrated edge knife and teases his finger along the blade, she edges even further away.

'What?' He laughs at her startled expression. His eyes are gentle. His expression kind. This is the same man who rescued the swallows from the loft and rebuilt their nest. He wouldn't hurt a fly, she realises, and she was a fool to believe otherwise. *I love my husband and my husband loves me, so if Clayton isn't deliberately playing with my mind, then it must be me who is doing this.*

Avril walks over to the table, scrapes out a chair and abruptly sits down. When she next looks across at her husband, she sees that he is frowning. As ever, whatever she does seems to surprise the hell out of him.

'I need to tell you something,' she tells him.

'Okay,' he puts down the knife, wipes the tomato juice from his hands and walks over. Pulling out a chair, he sits down next to her. She doesn't respond to his smile. He still thinks they are joking around.

'I think I hurt Mrs Mills,' she says hanging her head.

'Of course you didn't, Avril.' Straight away he babies her, lifting up her head and stroking her hair.

'I need to tell her that I didn't mean it. That I haven't been myself lately.' Avril's panic runs away with her and her face collapses into her hands.

Clayton peels her fingers away from her face. 'You didn't do anything.'

'But how do you know?' she demands.

'Why would you even think such a thing? It was an accident. Everybody said so. Oh…' As usual, Clayton is quick to grasp at anything that exonerates her. 'Is this about Tommy? Are you still blaming yourself for what happened and indirectly doing the same with Mrs Mills?'

'No.' She snaps her head away from him. Why must he paw her like a child when she's trying to tell him something this serious? 'What if I never buried Tommy's things on the moor? What if we're blaming The Chief for something he didn't do? What if I hurt Mrs Mills without knowing I did it?'

'That's a whole lot of "if's", Avril Shaw.' He is incredibly gentle with her. Kinder than she deserves, if what she is suggesting is true.

'If I did make any of it up, then I must still be ill,' she states decisively, grabbing his nearest hand and kissing it before holding it to her heart. 'I'm not getting any better, am I Clay?'

'There is nothing wrong with you, Avril. I may not be able to explain any of this right now but I do know you haven't hurt Mrs Mills. You couldn't hurt anyone.'

Thinking of her mum and dad, the kitten Robbie, brother Jamie, The Chief, Suzie and her beautiful boy, and her own dead son, Avril allows Clayton to pull her into his lap but all the soothing in the world won't convince her she isn't somehow responsible for all that has happened.

Chapter 84

Although the estate agent had warned Avril not to expect too much, she cannot help be excited by this morning's viewing and the prospect of an early sale. Even Clayton left the house smiling, and he's got a lot on his mind at the moment; what with The Chief and Tommy's things turning up again. She wonders who their potential buyers might be and feels a tremor of guilt run through her. *What if they're a young couple like us, with a baby on the way? And if so, should I warn them? But what could I possibly tell them that is tangible and believable? They'd think I was mad!* Besides, Clayton would be furious with her if she did that. Although he is adamant this house is no more cursed than the painting on the wall, she is less certain.

Instinctively, her eyes go to the painting and she remembers the effect it had on the woman who came to be interviewed for the cleaning job. If one glance at it was enough to send her running, who's to say it won't have the same effect on the people coming to look around?

Deciding she can't risk this happening again, Avril goes over to the picture and lifts it off the wall. It is not as heavy as she imagined, but it is cumbersome, and she has to wrap her arms around it, in order not to drop it. This close up, she cannot avoid looking into *The Crying Boy*'s tear-streaked eyes and feels a pang of regret.

'I'm sorry,' she tells it. 'But you are just a picture when all is said and done. Not a living breathing child.'

She pauses in the hallway when she hears the sound of a radio being played upstairs. From here, she can tell it is tuned to a loud rock station; the last thing she wants her buyers to hear when they step over the threshold. So far this morning, she has baked bread and arranged flowers in vases in order to seduce them into thinking this is the perfect family home, and she's not about to have this impression ruined by a poor taste in music. Clayton must really have a lot on his mind if he can't even remember to turn the radio off. Grimacing, because the buyers will be here in less than twenty minutes, she puts *The Crying Boy* portrait down and plods upstairs. *Honestly, I could kill Clay sometimes.*

Chapter 85

She should have known she would end up back in this room sooner rather than later. Just hovering on the threshold to what would have been Tommy's room is enough to freak her out; and that's before she's stepped foot inside. She can't help glancing around for evidence of muddy footprints and is relieved to find there aren't any. *Thank God for that.* Ever since Tommy's things made a sudden reappearance she's had a phobia about coming in here; insisting on keeping the door closed at all times.

But now it is open and the radio is playing inside, on the windowsill. *What is wrong with Clay? Why does he keep coming in here when he knows how I feel about this room?* His persistence is starting to annoy her. In the back of her mind, Avril knows that the music is not exactly Clayton's cup of tea and that he wouldn't deliberately tune into the kind of station that plays The Prodigy's 'Firestarter.' Nor would he have turned it up this loud. But she'd much rather feel angry with him than contemplate the chilling alternative – that somebody else is to blame.

Pushing the door wide open, just in case somebody is lurking behind it, Avril casts a wary look around before stepping inside. Refusing to look from right to left, she walks quickly, shuddering as she goes, and her fingers shake as she unplugs the radio from the wall socket. Once done, she heads straight for the door.

She almost makes it... when the thing she has secretly been dreading... happens. The door bangs shut in her face; cutting her off from the rest of the house. Since first stepping inside the room, Avril sensed it wanted to imprison her. Yet she continues to resist this terrifying realisation; her mind insists there must be a perfectly good explanation for the door closing on her again. Determinedly, she tries the handle. Of course, it won't budge. *Who am I kidding?* Avril groans. Behind her, the half open sash window beckons. *Was it open when I first came in?* Avril nervously scratches at the scarring on her chest. She really can't be sure.

She heads for the window and peers out, hoping to catch a glimpse of Clayton's van rattling along the pot-holed lane. He did say he would try to make it back in time for the viewing but there is no sign of him. Although her buyers are not due for another fifteen minutes, Avril clings to the hope that they will arrive early. At least that way, she will be able to get their attention from the window. But the thought of being locked in this room for that long makes her feel physically sick. It doesn't feel safe for her to look around or explore. In fact, she gets the feeling that this will be frowned upon. Keeping her eyes fixed on the floor, she can't help noticing that Tommy's things have gone; no doubt thrown away by Clayton. Not so long ago, this would have felt like the ultimate betrayal of their son's memory but now all she cares about is protecting the new life growing inside her. For that reason, she remains perfectly still and quiet – fearing any movement or noise created by her will only antagonise *it*.

When the sash window suddenly slams shut, Avril panics and throws her weight at the door.

'Let me out, God damn you.' Avril wrestles with the handle, but the door still refuses to budge. Avril's outrage at this unnatural occurrence makes her want to lash out.

'I'm not afraid of you.' She stands her ground, feeling less brave than she sounds.

Then, spying the rocking chair again – she grabs hold of it and hurls it across the room; slamming it into the nearest wall. This feels good only for a second or two... until the sound of a child's laughter eerily fills the room. It creeps in from underneath the wooden floor boards and oozes from every crevice and corner, making Avril sweat with fear. It's a sound she recognises. Or thinks she does. *The Crying Boy. Don Bonillo. Diablo.* As soon as the boy's name pops into Avril's head she doubles up in agony and cries out in pain. *Oh my God. It's as if something is punching me in the stomach. The pain is unbearable. Aghh... there it is again.* Avril is convinced the spiteful jabbing is brought on by a small child's fist.

Holding onto her stomach for all she is worth, Avril hobbles over to the door and makes one last ditch attempt to wrestle it open; but this time the handle comes off in her hand. Because she's beat and she knows it, Avril cowers in a tiny ball on the floor and sobs her heart out. It's all too much. She is really quite sick of it all. Even the precious life in her belly can't make her get up from the floor.

'Let me go, please,' she begs hysterically. 'Let me go.'

All at once the laughter stops and the door clicks open. After a few seconds of stunned silence, Avril scrambles to her feet and makes a dash for it. As soon as she reaches the landing her anger gets the better of her again.

'I won't let you hurt my baby,' she rages, kicking out at the door, until a split appears in it. At first it is no worse than a run in a pair of tights but by the time she has finished with it, the door is hanging off its hinges. Feeling exhausted, Avril takes a breather and wipes away angry tears from her eyes. She's so furious something like this keeps happening to her that she hardly pays attention to how dark the landing is as she gropes her way toward the stairs.

In the claustrophobic darkness, Avril stumbles onto one knee. She's about to pick herself up again when out of the corner of one eye she sees Tommy's fire truck scooting along the landing. Where it came from, she has no idea. But it seems to have a mind of its own; lights flashing and siren wailing. 'Fire alarm. Let's go. Out of my way,' it insists.

Terrified by its spine-chilling robotic voice, Avril makes a run for it; arriving at the top of the stairs at the same time as it does. The fire truck intermingles with her ankles, rubbing against her leg like a cat might. Spooked by the feel of its scratchy metal against her skin, Avril kicks out at the truck and misses. Instead of making contact with it, she finds herself tumbling forwards. As her legs go from under her, she feels a sick rush of nausea spread through her body and her world spins momentarily as she somersaults. It happens so quickly, Avril barely has chance to reach out and try to stop herself from falling. By the time she's halfway down the stairs her elbows, arms and the back of her head have impacted against the walls several times. Protectively cradling her tummy, Avril is one step away from the bottom when her head gets knocked sideways against a wooden post. There is a sickening crunch of bone followed by a spray of blood as she lands heavily on the tiled floor.

The house is as still as it's ever been. *Muzzled in fact, like a savage dog,* Avril thinks dazedly, *listening to the creaking and sighing of its walls.* She is reminded of how different houses sound at night when everybody is asleep. *Except*

I am not asleep. Just dazed from the fall, I guess. And too frightened to move in case I am paralysed.

There is pain everywhere. She can taste blood in her mouth and fears swallowing in case she should choke on it. She's on her back, that much she can tell, but everywhere is in darkness and she cannot feel her fingers. There is something heavy pressing down on her chest and she wonders if it is *him*, mauling her. On that ominous thought, her eyes fly open and she manages to free a trapped hand from underneath her. She then becomes aware of a tingling sensation in her hands as blood starts to rush around her body. Her next thought is for the baby. She raises her neck to see if there are any signs of obvious injury but she is too weak and her head flops down again.

The sound of muffled sobs has her opening her eyes again. The sound reminds her of a child snivelling snottily in a corner with his hands covering his face. She cricks her neck slowly to one side and hones in on where the crying is coming from. Just as she thought, there is a child's shadow silhouetted on the wall. He appears to be sitting on the bottom step of the stairs, just a few feet from where she landed. He holds his head in his hands and has his face turned toward the wall.

Go away. Leave me alone. I will not look at you. I will not give you the attention you want. Avril blinks away her own tears and closes her eyes again. After a few seconds, she feels a shadow hovering over her face and her skin prickles with fear. Even though she can feel his hot breath on her face, she still refuses to open her eyes.

'Avril? Avril,' she hears a distorted voice calling to her from what seems like a long way off and it lures her back to the blackness she has always feared; only this time she is grateful to be swallowed up by it. As she drifts in and out of consciousness she conjures up a familiar face – Tommy's – and reaches out a hand for him. But he evades her and runs on without her. Wherever he is, he is smiling and happy. Knowing this makes her own mouth twitch into the weakest of smiles. Finally, she sees him... the crying boy... Don Bonillo... and he is coming for her with eyes blazing. As soon as he touches her, she is on fire. She can feel the flames flickering up from the hem of her nightdress, engulfing her. Once again she is burning, burning alive.

Chapter 86

In a room very like the one Mrs Mills was admitted to, Avril's arms and legs poke restlessly out of austere sheets that would otherwise pin her down and her head moves agitatedly from side to side. There are bruises on her exposed limbs and one cheek is the same colour as a rare steak. Drifting in and out of consciousness, Avril's puffy eyelids flicker in protest at the harsh overhead lighting.

Although she doesn't know it yet, she's in the maternity ward at Airdale General Hospital, where the smell of stale breast milk, Johnson's baby lotion and new-born skin is starting to revive her. She is conscious of a sharp needle-like pain in her right hand and a feeling of hot sticky plastic beneath her skin, but is otherwise completely in the dark as to her surroundings. Despite feeing weird and woozy, she is tempted to open her eyelids, but fears they are stuck together. Then, becoming aware of the soothing gurgle of water being filtered close by, Avril chooses instead to sink back into the welcoming oblivion of sleep.

But when the sound of a small boy crying reaches her highly sensitive ears, her eyes flash open and she finds herself sitting bolt upright in bed. It's him. The crying boy. He's come back. Eyes blinking stickily, Avril stares in disbelief at the walls of the sterile hospital ward and holds onto a mouthful of fear-induced vomit. *Where am I? Is this a dream? Am I sleep walking?*

Slowly, gently, she tests her arms and legs. They're killing her, but she *is* able to move them. She can even wiggle her toes. Realising she wouldn't be able to do any of these things if she was suffering from sleep paralysis, she doesn't yet know if this is a good thing or not. If she can't blame the sound of the boy crying on her sleep terrors, then he really must be here, somewhere, and *this* really must be happening. *Am I back in the looney bin? Did they send me there after the fall? The fall! Yes, that's right. I had a fall. Down the stairs. Somebody pushed me. Something pushed me. The fire truck. The Crying Boy. And I was burning. I was on fire.*

Avril opens her mouth to scream but vomit piles out instead. Wildly thrashing her arms, she tries to put out the flames rising up from her body but when she next looks down she realises they were never really there. All the while holding her breath, in case she gives herself away, she listens out for the crying boy again, but is greeted with silence. *Where is he hiding? Where has he gone?* Avril can't face the thought of him hiding under the bed, waiting to grab hold of her ankles. If that happens, she will surely die of fright. Her eyes dart around the room, at first not taking anything in, but gradually her mind focuses on what is real. At last, she is able to make the distinction. On the wall, to her left, there is a water filtering machine and a bottle of grapefruit squash has been placed on a bedside table next to the bed. Leaning uncomfortably forward, *everything hurts like buggery*, she peers around a curtain and sees a production line of cots with red-faced babies swaddled inside.

In the next bed, a mother cradles her new-born baby. One glance at the cluster of pink balloons, soft toys and cards surrounding the bed identifies its sex. There is a dad in residence too and every time the baby suckles at its mother's swollen nipple, he grins like a fool. His happiness is catching because, in spite of the pain, Avril finds herself smiling. Then, taking her completely by surprise, another head pops up and Avril realises that this is not the couple's first child. They have a son too. Aged about four or five with blond hair. *Tommy!* But, unlike his parents, he is clearly not happy with this new addition to his family. In fact, his face is awash with petulant tears.

'But I wanted a brother. Not a stupid sister. It's not fair.' He cries openly at his misfortune and Avril recognises that it was this child's innocent crying that woke her up and nothing more sinister than that. Grimacing in pain and feeling suddenly exhausted, Avril slides down in the bed, comforted by the knowledge that her hallucination was probably a result of whatever drugs they must have given her.

Until now, she has been putting off thinking about her own baby but now faces the very real possibility that she may have lost it in the fall. It's not uncommon for women who have lost babies to be stacked side by side in wards where others have given birth to theirs. Her body is numb and there is no way of telling if any loss has occurred. The only sensation in her stomach is one of soreness. Could they have scraped the remains of her child out of her while she was unconscious?

At this early stage of her pregnancy, Avril is aware her baby might *look* human but would still be treated as clinical waste by the hospital. *Is my baby a bloody clot of nothingness that has been thrown out in the trash?* is a question she never thought she would have to ask herself. Choking on tears, Avril realises that if her worst fears are founded, she will never get a chance to mourn this child as she did Tommy. *Perhaps that is a good thing,* she tells herself.

Closing her eyes, Avril starts to count down from one hundred and waits for the blackness to settle on her. It can't come soon enough. Anything is preferable to waiting for a doctor to bring her the bad news.

Chapter 87

Clayton stands in the vast kitchen feeling like an awkward visitor in his own home. Come to that, they both have the same misplaced air about them as they shuffle their feet and gaze vacantly at the walls. He offered to book them into a hotel for a few nights, anything to avoid coming straight back here, but Avril had surprised him with her response. 'I'm not going to run away anymore, Clayton,' she had told him. Although he had his reservations about coming back here, and the effect it could have on her, he had eventually agreed. Besides, it was obvious she wouldn't be talked around. He wonders why she won't talk about what happened. She hardly gives anything away at all.

'I expected it to look different.' Avril says quietly, her eyes darting around the unchanged room. He wishes he could do something about the frightened, wide-eyed stare that hasn't left her face since the day of her fall. Seeing how badly beaten up she looks makes him feel useless.

He watches her scoot a finger along the worktop, idly checking for dust, and then finding none, her eyes settle on a bunch of red and white flowers propped up in a vase.

'Blood and bandages,' she says, touching the velvety petals of a red rose. But he has no idea what she's talking about, so he shrugs and pulls a dumb face.

'They still have the cellophane on,' she complains in a whiny voice.

'I put them in water. But I didn't know what to do with them after that.' He is apologetic. Neither of them care two hoots about the flowers. But after what they have been through this kind of small talk is all they can handle.

Avril glances at the writing on the card and pulls a face. 'From The Chief?'

'I know. I got the shock of my life when they arrived.'

'He's got a nerve.' Avril's lip curls into a snarl. A few weeks ago Clayton would have held this against her. Not anymore.

'I don't suppose we should knock him for it. Perhaps he's genuinely sorry and wants to make amends.' Either way, Clayton isn't bothered and this comes across in his voice, which is enough to placate Avril; but he can tell she isn't falling for his explanation.

Clayton turns his back on her and flicks on the kettle; glad to have something to do.

'I'll make us a nice cup of tea,' he says, grabbing two matching mugs out of a cupboard, but when he turns around again, Avril has vanished.

***

Avril stares at the empty space above the fireplace where *The Crying Boy* portrait used to hang and wonders why she doesn't feel anything. She should be angry. She should be demanding explanations. She should feel *something*. It hits her then that, along with the picture, the fishy smell has also disappeared. The static she usually experiences in her hair, whenever she stands in this spot, is also absent.

When Clayton enters the room he chooses to stand right behind her; reluctant to come any closer. She can sense his unease. He must have been dreading this moment.

'The psychiatrist thought... what with your hormones being all over the place– it would be better if–' he stutters.

'It's not still here is it?' Without turning around, she knows that her response has surprised him. He'd obviously anticipated having a real ding-dong with her over this. She feels, rather than sees him, shake his head.

'No.'

Avril's gaze hardens as she continues to look at the empty space on the wall. Subconsciously, her hands go to her stomach; forming an unforgiving mound.

'Good. I hope you burned it.'

Chapter 88

Sinking into a lavender-scented bathtub, Avril realises this must be her third bath in as many days. Normally she enjoys an invigorating shower first thing but she has to admit these long afternoon soaks are helping with her recovery. They certainly soothe away her aches and pains, and help with the bruising too.

In comes Clayton with an armful of towels. She knew it wouldn't be long before he followed her in here. Since arriving home, he hasn't left her alone for one minute.

Opening one eye, Avril grins. 'There's room for one more if you're interested.'

'The doctor prescribed rest, remember.' Clayton places the towels strategically around the tiled floor, so she won't slip when it's time to get out. He seems to enjoy fussing around her. 'Besides, it's already pretty crowded in there with the two of you.'

Avril could listen to this kind of talk all day. They had come so close to losing the baby that they had almost accepted the inevitable and a great depression had landed on them all. This had been hard to shake off, even when she was given the all clear. For a while, it really had been touch and go, but her unborn child has proven to be something of a fighter.

Suddenly noticing that Clayton has changed into his work polo shirt and trousers, she sits up straight and frowns.

'You're not going back to work?'

'Two hours tops. I promise.'

She watches him pause, as if considering whether leaving her alone, even for two hours, is really advisable.

'You don't mind, do you?'

'So long as you don't mind coming home to a horribly wrinkled wife,' Avril holds out her hands, palm upwards, revealing water softened skin.

He attempts to kiss her on the nose, but misses, and she can tell he's already fretting about getting the job done so he can race back to her.

'That's something I'll look forward to thirty years from now.'

'I may just stay where I am until you get back.' Avril tells him, leaning further back into the water. She loves the way the slight curve of her belly bobs above the water line; making her look further gone in her pregnancy than she is. The look on Clayton's face as he pauses in the doorway, drinking her in, lets her know he's thinking exactly the same thing.

'I thought I'd lost you back there,' he says, with a break in his voice and she can tell he's in danger of welling up. She's never known her husband be quite so emotional. Although these last few weeks have taken their toll on both of them, Clayton seems to be the most altered.

'I was certainly missing for a while.' She is playful. 'Some husband you are.' She flicks bubbles at him. 'You didn't even file a missing person's report.'

'You tell jokes too? As well as being beautiful and pregnant? It doesn't get any better.'

Avril laughs and then, holding up her right hand, she extends her little finger, thumb and index finger and closes the remaining two digits. This is sign language for "I love you" and it's clear that Clayton understands the gesture, because he blows her a kiss and calls out, 'You too,' before walking out.

Avril sighs, trying not to mind that Clayton still refuses to use the most basic of sign language skills. He could never cope being around her and Tommy when they were communicating with each other. He will never admit it, but he blames himself for failing Tommy; getting him off to the worst of starts by passing on his faulty genes.

***

Wading through the dense gravel drive toward his work van, Clayton whistles cheerfully – not a trouble in the world – except perhaps for a minor niggle about leaving Avril on her own. But he'll be back in no time and she'll probably enjoy having a break from him. Not for the first time, it occurs to him that his obsessive behaviour might be too suffocating. He tries hard not to mollycoddle her; but just can't help himself. Given the choice, he would spend the whole day with his arms wrapped protectively around his wife's belly.

With the painting finally gone, he feels such a weight lifted off his shoulders. It's not that he ever believed any of that 'cursed' nonsense; but all the same, why run the risk of having it in the house when others suspect it of having supernatural powers. He still can't believe he got away with its removal so lightly. He had braced himself for a huge row on the subject once Avril found out what he'd done. But he had misjudged her. By then, she was well enough to understand that the picture was a bad influence on her and she seemed relieved to hear it had been disposed of. Odd though, that she's never once asked what he did with it; only commented that she hoped it had been burnt. Although he *had* considered burning it, he'd decided against this idea. Once again, he'd been ruled by fear of the unknown, which was so unlike him. But even he couldn't avoid thinking *What if there is any truth in the curse?* So again, he decided, *Why take any chances?* And instead took it to the recycling centre at Keighley where he left it in a commercial skip full of other unwanted items. *What Avril doesn't know can't hurt her*, he tells himself.

Feeling the fine blond hairs on the back of neck prick up, he comes to an abrupt halt in the driveway. If he didn't know better, he'd swear someone was watching him right now. He's not prone to picking up on this type of 'feeling' but the sensation is so strong he can't ignore it. So, he turns and looks toward the house, noticing once again how hostile and oppressive it appears. *Shit. Why the hell didn't I see it for what it was before I bought the place?* In his frustration, he kicks out at the gravel, sending a shower of stones spiralling toward his van. Squinting against the sweltering sun, his eyes search every window, not entirely sure of what he might be looking for. *There. See.* He knew he was right all along. Up there, in the middle window of what would have been Tommy's room, is a shadow. *A shadow that could be just about anything,* he reminds himself cynically. *I won't do this. I won't let what happened take its toll on me. We've been through enough already. This is madness.*

***

Beep, beep, beep. The sound of the smoke alarm going off downstairs causes Avril's eyes to fly open and in her hurry to sit up straight she almost overturns in the water.

'Bloody hell.'

The water is warm and soothing, like a giant massaging hand, and she is reluctant to leave it. But the sound is distracting. She won't be able to ignore it. There she was, not five minutes ago, daydreaming about last night when they'd had their first pillow fight in ages, and Clayton had been the first to surrender. For once, he hadn't made a fuss about the mess; which was a good thing as there were feathers everywhere – in their hair, in the bed, on the floor and stuck to the ceiling. The bedroom fan had seen to that! Afterwards, they made love – gently at first and then more passionately and she'd experienced her first orgasm in months. Avril can feel her face redden just thinking about this.

They have many more such nights ahead of them, but right now she must do something about that bloody alarm, because the din is doing her head in. Avril gets to her feet.

'Just my luck,' she grumbles, stepping carefully out of the bath. She feels indebted to Clayton for sensibly placing a carpet of towels on the slippery floor.

Wrapping herself in one of the warm bath sheets that he thoughtfully left out for her she shuffles toward the door; trailing a wedding like train behind her.

None too pleased at having to face the same staircase she fell down only a few days ago, with a bulky towel flapping around her ankles, Avril is not in the best of moods when she reaches the kitchen. Tugging the towel tightly around her chest, she grabs a sweeping brush from out of the boiler room and aiming the handle at the faulty smoke alarm, smashes it into smithereens. So pleased is she when the beeping stops, she almost looks around for someone to high five. Avril puts the brush away and dusts her hands together in a self-satisfied way. *Exactly what Clay should have done ages ago,* she gloats; not wanting to be reminded of the times Clayton has come home from work complaining about people who remove smoke alarms and never bother to put them back up again, only to pay for it with their lives.

Avril exits the kitchen leaving a trail of wet footprints behind her; ignorant of the fact that child-sized footprints mysteriously appear on the sodden floor behind her and continue to follow her out of the door.

Chapter 89

The kitchen is gutted, burnt beyond recognition, with exposed wires dangling from where overhead lights used to hang. The first floor ceiling remains intact but the downstairs living area is water-damaged, having had fire hoses trained on it for the best part of 12 hours. All that's left of the kitchen cupboards are burnt out frames but the odd charred pot or pan survives; handles poking out like tombstones in the black ash. Although the house fire took place more than five days ago, there is an unmistakable fishy smell in the air, caused by burnt wiring. The kitchen walls are stained black and the window holes have been boarded up, adding an extra layer of gloom.

Armed with a note pad and pen, Clayton wades through the debris, following the shuffling backside of Mrs Danes from one room to another. She is a talker. Earlier, on the phone, he'd had to shout to be heard, because Mrs Danes is deaf in one ear, or so she'd told him. In person, it is quite a different matter.

'You don't have to shout, young man,' she'd pointed out crabbily, removing the handkerchief from her nose in order to do so. 'There's nowt wrong wi' me right ear. And I can hear you if you stay close.'

For a full five minutes he'd done exactly that, listening to her going on about how they had bought the three-bed semi from the council 30 years ago and filled it with three strapping rugby-playing sons. But eventually, he decides to do his own investigating, whether Mrs Danes likes it or not. Swinging open the melted door of an old consumer unit on the wall, Clayton pulls out a handful of frayed wires. For one minute, he thinks Mrs Danes is going to object, judging by the sour face she's pulling – but she covers her mouth again with the handkerchief and breathes deeply into it; fretting about coming into contact with the scorched interior.

'This consumer unit is pre-1985 and still uses aluminium wiring,' Clayton says excitedly. It's a long time since he's come across anything quite this antiquated. Then, remembering where he is, he coughs and explains more fittingly, 'They easily overheat and are nowhere near as safe as copper. But don't worry, we'll soon get that sorted.'

He pauses to look at Mrs Danes, who has her wrestler's arms folded over her bosomy chest. 'I take it the fire did start in here?' Clayton asks.

'You're the electrician. You tell me.' She snaps, her eyes darting through to the adjoining front room; a space Clayton hasn't yet ventured into. Then sighing, she tells him, 'My husband likes to cook chips the old fashioned way in a chip pan. I told him to get with the times and use oven chips like everyone else but he wouldn't listen.'

'The whole house will need rewiring, I'm afraid.' Clayton tells her, pointing out more melted wiring.

'That's what I told Mr Danes.' She takes this news surprisingly well and moves toward the front room, gesturing for him to follow. 'Thank God for insurance, that's all I can say.'

Trailing after her, Clayton notices that the next room hasn't fared much better. Here though, there are remains of black sooty furniture but the walls are badly blistered.

'And thank God nobody was hurt,' Mrs Danes is saying, all the while looking up at the fireplace wall. 'It could have been a lot worse.'

As soon as Clayton glances up at the chimney wall, her voice becomes a monotonous drone; echoing and distant like a swarm of dopey bees flying past his ears, and he finds his feet won't move. He can't listen. Can't see anything except what is immediately in front of him. Can't move. Not even to open his mouth in astonishment.

Noting his strange behaviour and thinking she understands the reason behind it, Mrs Danes comes to stand next to him. 'It's the only thing that survived the fire,' she whispers conspiratorially. With similar expressions on their faces, they stare up at the untouched Crying Boy portrait. It is identical to the one that up until a few days ago hung on the chimney wall of Swallow's Nest.

'Funny thing is; Mr Danes was only the other day talking about throwing it out.'

He feels her hot breath on the side of his clean-shaven face and for the scariest of moments imagines it to be a flicker of flame licking his skin. When she opens her mouth to speak again, Clayton notices that her spittle smells of fish and this is enough to break the spell he has been under. He feels a wave of nausea pass over him. *Please God, don't let me collapse here*, he prays. At last, he remembers to breathe and the panic and terror gradually subside.

'Didn't like the way the eyes kept following him about the room, he said.' Mrs Danes adds dramatically, her own eyes flicking speedily from side to side.

Chapter 90

Weighed down by the bulky towel, Avril struggles back up the poorly-lit staircase; extremely mindful of where each foot is. By the time she reaches the landing she is not as wet as she once was and her damp hair clings to her pale skin, making her feel deliciously cool. She's on her way back to the master bedroom, intent on finishing her bath, but finds as always that her eyes immediately go to the door at the end of the long corridor. Her bedroom door is to her right. She is just a few feet from safety, yet she feels compelled to approach the door of what would have been Tommy's room.

Clayton has made a good job of repairing the damage to it, she notices, and has boarded up the broken lower panel so nothing is visible on the other side. *It's like I'm having a bet with myself. Daring myself to open the door; just to prove there is nothing going on inside.* She rests a hand on the wall, steadying herself, and listens. *For what? You know if you stand here long enough you'll start to imagine all kinds of things.*

'Avril... Avril...'

There. See. Now you're imagining a whispered voice coming from inside. Her hand reaches for the doorknob and hovers over it. *Don't open the door, Avril. On no account.*

Do not go into that room. The warning comes in Clayton's voice, and she heeds it, backing off. Then, congratulating herself on making the right decision, she continues on her way to the bedroom.

Knocking her bare toe against a knot in the wooden floorboards, Avril painfully hops into the en suite bathroom, trying her best not to swear. It is steamy inside and condensation drips down the tiled walls. She goes over to the bathtub and dabbles a hand in the water but it is not warm enough to tempt her back in. She pulls out the plug and smiles to herself, safe in the knowledge that there is no one waiting behind her to push her in and hold her head under the water. Yet she cannot help feeling a little spooked and has to look over her shoulder, just to be sure. After all, it is the first time she's been left on her own in the house since the fall. *This house tried to convince me it was my friend,* she reminds herself sternly, *I must never be fooled by it again.*

Diverted by the rude sounds the plughole is making as it greedily sucks water out of the bath, Avril is unaware that steam collected on the bathroom cabinet mirror behind her is changing into a haunting image of *The Crying Boy*. As the steam starts to evaporate, the child's smile thins to a sinister sneer and then fades completely… just in time… as Avril chooses exactly that moment to walk over to the cabinet. Wiping away the rest of the steam in order to see her reflection better, she casually inspects her face; looking for imperfections and seeing plenty.

***

Driving faster than he should, Clayton keeps glancing over his shoulder, as if terrified he is being followed. His muddled mind is rather vague as to who or what may be following him, but after what he witnessed at the Danes' house he's expecting the unexpected, put it that way. There is no air conditioning in the van and he's sweating buckets, but with one hand on the steering wheel and another clutching his mobile phone, he hasn't a spare to wind down the window. Meanwhile, shadowy stone cottages and old buildings speed by in a blur; with splashes of green moorland thrown in here and there. He's sure the speed limit is forty miles per hour but nothing is going to stop him reaching home as fast as he can.

'Come on. Come on. Pick up.' He barks frustratingly into the phone, all the while grinding his teeth.

***

Legs dangling off the side of the bed, Avril perches on the very edge of the embroidered patchwork quilt. She has stretched the electrical cable as far as it will go and her head is tilted at an awkward angle. The heat from the hairdryer is making her all hot and bothered. She enjoys the sensation of her long hair whipping her bare shoulders and wonders if this is because of that saucy book; the one she keeps in her secret drawer. She may not have touched its pages in a long time, but the very thought of its erotic passages is enough to bring colour to her cheeks. Clayton would be dead surprised if he knew what she was reading and takes pleasure in this thought. It makes her feel a little more daring and liberated than she actually is. *Avril Shaw! Who would have thought it?*

Over on the other side of the bedroom, Avril's mobile phone begins to light up and vibrate, moving of its own accord across the scratched surface of the dressing table. Facing the other way, with the heavy-duty whirring of the hairdryer in one ear. Avril does not see or hear it.

***

With the phone still pressed to his ear, Clayton doesn't pay as much attention as he should to what's going on around him. But when he hears a distant police siren, he panics and drops the phone. *Fuck*, he swears between gritted teeth. By now, his face is bright red and sweat runs freely down it. There are wet patches under his arms and on the back of his polo shirt. Without taking his eyes off the road, he rummages blindly for the phone; convinced it has fallen underneath his seat. When his eyes dip low and he still can't see the phone, he groans out loud. *It's no good, I'll have to stop and retrieve it. I have to get hold of her. So I can warn her.*

He's about to indicate to pull over when he sees *it*. Swearing under his breath, he slams on the brakes, and comes to a skidding stop just a few yards away from a pedestrian crossing. CRACK. As Clayton's head whacks against the steering wheel, a gash opens up on his forehead and starts to bleed. Fighting off a sudden woozy feeling, he looks up dozily, convinced he has hit someone. Through blurred vision, Clayton can just about make out the silhouette of a child standing in the middle of the pedestrian crossing. A shock of adrenalin runs through his veins; making his knees go weak. *Thank God he's okay. Thank God I didn't kill anyone.*

But then he notices that the blond-haired child stands at a funny angle with a slightly crooked neck. Too late he realises it is the crying boy. *I should have recognised the peasant-style clothing straight away.* Eyes on fire, the boy is glaring right back at Clayton. *He is coming for me. I can sense it. Feel it.* Unable to look, Clayton buries his face in his hands. *Pull yourself together, man. This can't be real. Get a grip.* When he glances up again to see if it is still there – he sees a fair-haired, blue eyed schoolboy standing in the middle of the pedestrian crossing. *A regular, normal child! Thank God!*

Blinking in disbelief, but relieved at the same time, Clayton watches the boy's mother appear from nowhere to throw a protective arm around her son. When she's through mouthing obscenities at Clayton, he belatedly slips on his seatbelt and waits for them to safely cross. His heart is in his mouth and he feels as if he has been spared a fate worse than death. To have killed a child would have been the end of him. He's sure Avril would never have forgiven him. He wouldn't want her to.

For the first time, he considers how unfairly he may have acted towards the lorry driver who killed Tommy. *He* hadn't been driving too fast or without due care or consideration the way Clayton was just now. At court, the man had appeared broken, even though he was acquitted of any wrong doing. At the time, this had made Clayton mad as hell. He'd even considered giving him a good pasting on the quiet.

Driving at a more sedate pace, Clayton decides that once they are away from *Swallow's Nest* and the baby is born – he might just track down that driver and let him know he doesn't blame him anymore. That way, they can both get on with the rest of their lives.

Chapter 91

Avril steps out of the master bedroom wearing ripped jeans and one of Clayton's oversized shirts. Her hair is fluffy and flyaway and her skin pink and glossy, having been exfoliated to within an inch of its life. Feeling fresh and regenerated after her bath and looking forward to Clayton's return, she is about to go downstairs to scout around for a snack – *pickled onions and a packet of Monster Munch would go down nicely right now* – when her eyes are drawn yet again to the door at the end of the corridor. *Tommy's room.* There's no escaping the craving to go inside. Deciding she can handle it; that she can always change her mind, turn around and beat it back down the stairs… she tiptoes toward the door, keen not to make any noise and give herself away.

Don't open the door, Avril. On no account, do not go into that room. She is reminded once again of Clayton's warning. *Since when did I listen to Clay, anyway?* she thinks wryly. *Besides, I'm not going to let this thing beat me.* She is strict with herself; stricter even than Clayton had been.

She reaches for the doorknob and pauses, recognising that after what happened it will always be hard for her to do this. *I do not have to go inside*, she reminds herself. *I just want to look. To know it's definitely gone.* And with that, she throws open the door.

***

Having left his work van parked haphazardly in the drive with the engine still running and the driver's door wide open, Clayton bursts into the kitchen, shouting 'Avril,' at the top of his voice. When he sees she isn't here, he throws his weight at the door leading into the hall and looks first one way, then the other, as if deciding where to search first. 'Avril?' he shouts from the bottom of the stairs, looking down on the gruesome spot where she was found unconscious less than a week ago. He can't begin to describe how relieved he is not to find her there again.

Checking out the sitting room, he sees that she is not in here either and he's about to charge upstairs when he notices blood smears on a half open window. He goes over to the window and traces the fresh blood with his finger. Something bad has happened to her. He can feel it. Why doesn't she answer?

'Avril. Avril.'

Out of his mind with worry, Clayton sprints up the stairs, taking them two at a time. Knackered before he knows it, he heads for the bedroom, all the while praying she is asleep on the bed with her earplugs in, listening to music and unable to hear. One quick look inside reveals otherwise. He checks the bathroom and sees that everything, including the towels on the floor, have been tidied away. Back in the bedroom he spies her mobile phone on the dressing table and a quick glance at her call log confirms she hasn't seen any of his missed calls. The only evidence of her having been in this room, he realises, is the sunken patch on the bed. *Had she been taking a rest, reading her book, when she got disturbed by something?* he frets.

A snivelling sound behind him causes him to slow up. There is something so malevolent about the childish crying that he's almost too scared to turn around, but when he does, he does so very slowly. Although there is nothing standing immediately behind him, as he feared, he hears the sound of crying again, and something else – a clunk, scrape, whirring sound that he can't quite identify; even though he knows he's heard it before. It's a sound that belongs in his past.

Swallowing hard, Clayton comes out of the bedroom and approaches the door to the spare bedroom. Pressing his ear up against it, he strains to listen. He may have warned Avril not to go in there but right now he is more fearful than she has ever been. His legs are a dead weight. He can't get his breath properly. The fear is deadening. His terror intensifies when the crying grows louder. It's as if *it*, the owner of those tears, wants him to know it is there, on the other side of the door, waiting for him. *It* wants him to follow it inside. *Perhaps it wants to show me something. Make me understand...*

But on second thought, the sobbing does not sound as if it emanates from a ghostly or spiritual being; although he's not sure how he knows this. It sounds as real as any other child he has heard crying; including his own son. In fact, the crying could be that of Tommy's. It is at once both similar and familiar. *But how can that be?* When Clayton throws open the door the crying stops immediately. Except for the rocking chair and an upturned fire truck on the floor, the room is empty. *Wait a minute!* His eyes swing back to the fire truck. Tommy's truck. The one he himself had taken to the tip along with *The Crying Boy* painting and all of Tommy's other things. Noticing that the wheels of the fire truck are still spinning, as if a child had just been playing with it, his mind cannot grapple with the reality of what he is seeing. He knows it to be impossible.

Feeling suddenly exposed and vulnerable, Clayton bends down and picks up the fire truck. It feels normal. Just as it is supposed to. He can remember how some of the scrapes and dents in it got there. Tommy hadn't exactly been the gentlest of kids when it came to playing with his toys. Although he never allowed himself to smell Tommy's blue knitted sweater, the way Avril sometimes did, swearing she could still inhale her son's scent, Clayton does breathe in the musty metallic odour of the truck and his eyes fill unexpectedly with tears.

There is a creaking of floorboards not more than a few feet away and Clayton spins on his toes to challenge whatever it is that might be creeping up on him. He doesn't see anything physical but a fleeting shadow that is not his own falls onto the wall. It disappears as fast as it arrived.

'Tommy?'

A soft giggling sound surrounds Clayton. It feels gentle and comforting, like a cosy blanket.

'Is that really you?'

Laughter reverberates around the room. His boy sounds happy, at peace. Clayton has never been so moved.

'Tommy? It's me, Daddy. I'm so pleased you found us. That you're...' Clayton's sentence falls away. *If it is Tommy, he won't be able to hear me*, he realises dismally.

At that moment, a swallow hits the outside window pane, making Clayton jump. Holding his hand to his pounding heart, he watches the stunned bird flop down onto the windowsill. Putting down the fire truck, Clayton moves closer to the window, sensing that he is once again alone in the room, that Tommy has gone. *Will I ever see him again?* he wonders. Close up, he sees that the bird is not dead. It is still breathing, if a little rapidly. That's when Clayton sees the silhouette of a person out on the moor.

Chapter 92

Avril turns her head into the welcoming breeze and notices that the sky has suddenly gone grey and threatening; reminding her of the night of the storm when they first moved into Swallow's Nest. For a moment, she wonders if it is an omen and then quickly dismisses the idea. Having found the courage to open to the door to the spare room, *I will no longer call it Tommy's room*, to find no demons lurked there; that it was just a room painted sunshine yellow – she has finally found peace of mind.

Even after she'd closed the door and gone downstairs, only to pause on the last step because she heard an unusual sound coming from the sitting room – she was sure nothing else could touch her. When she'd gone into the room to investigate, she found she was no longer afraid – just inquisitive. That's when the swallow came out of nowhere to dive bomb her, making her squeal. But as soon as she saw the terrified bird land on the fireplace, she'd laughed at her own cowardice. Afterwards, she managed to half open one of the sash windows and shoo it out, but wasn't able to close it again. Reminding herself to have words with Clayton about the stubbornness of their windows and the persistence of the confused birds, she'd finally noticed the blood smears on the glass and suspected the bird must already have crashed into it in its panicked attempts to escape. Lord knows how much longer it would have survived without her intervention. Pleased to be able to give it its freedom, she decided she had earned the right to some of her own and that's why she came up here. To the moor.

The view is spectacular. All around her, she hears the chirping of grasshoppers and the noise reminds her of a classroom full of whispering children. She will miss the way the moorland dips and plunges in every conceivable direction, cutting a path of rock, water and heather across the landscape. Breathing in the distinctive moorland air while she still can, she wonders if she will ever come back here again. That's when she sees Clayton running toward her and even before he reaches her she notices the cut on his forehead; where dark red coagulated blood has formed.

'What happened to you?' At first, she is not unduly worried but this changes when Clayton falls into her arms, knocking the breath out of her. He's just like Tommy in that way, she recalls, completely unaware of his own strength.

'You were right all along and I didn't believe you,' Clayton garbles excitedly, hardly making any sense at all. 'I'm so sorry, Avril.'

'Woah. Slow down there. What on earth are you talking about, Clay?' Squirming to be free, Avril glares at him as if he has gone mad.

'The picture. The curse.' Finally, Clayton releases her. He does so only to look into her eyes so he can gage her reaction. 'It's all true.'

Avril lets this information sink in and then a playful smile appears at the corner of her mouth. 'That must have been some knock on the head,' she says, laughing.

'I'm serious, Avril. We've got to leave. Get out of here today.'

'What are you talking about?' Avril is instantly cross. Trust Clayton to spoil things. Just when she was starting to get over everything. She thought he was joking, but now, realising he is deadly serious, she watches him drunkenly stagger backwards before sinking to his knees. However he got that bump, it's clear that it's knocked him for six.

'I heard him. Felt him… in that room,' Clayton pauses as if he is finding it difficult to go on and then starts to cry into his hands. 'Tommy.'

At last Avril gets it. In response she shakes him hard. Very hard. She can be pretty fierce when she wants to be.

'It wasn't Tommy you saw, Clayton. You've got to listen to me. It wasn't Tommy. It just wants you to think that.'

'It?' Clayton looks up through his tears, confused.

'*The Crying Boy*. It's just as you said, the curse is real. I've always known it. And it will do anything to come between us…' It hits her at last what *The Crying Boy* really wants from them, 'and prevent us… me… from leaving.'

With Avril's help, Clayton clambers unsteadily to his feet. His face is pale and sickly and it's obvious he's suffering from mild concussion. Ideally, they should get him to the hospital, to get it checked out.

'I'm not going to hospital. We don't have time.' Clayton protests, reading her mind. 'And we can't stay here, Avril.' The authoritative part of her husband returns; instantly assuming command.

She shakes her head in agreement. Of course he's right. They must leave straightaway. But she can't resist one last sweeping look over the moorland. Then, her glance comes to rest on the desolate exterior of Swallow's Nest and a familiar frown settles back on her forehead.

Chapter 93

Struggling with a couple of holdalls containing clothing and emergency household items, Clayton comes out of the front door, leaving it open behind him as he makes his way to his work van. Having already reversed the van right up to the main entrance, he throws their personal belongings any old how into the back of it. It's clear he's got several more journeys to make and that he's in a hurry.

Overhead the sky is black and ominous and he hopes it heralds the end of summer. He'd like nothing more than to see this place shrouded in snow and ice. Whatever compelled them to buy this Godforsaken house, he'll never know. His plan, his dream of 'a fresh start' had escalated into a nightmare and he can't wait to put distance between them and *it*. *It* being the house, the boy, the curse… whatever – he just wants shot of *it*. The realisation that *it* isn't a physical thing means he can't fight it; a fact that makes him feel utterly worthless. *What sort of man can't protect his own wife and family?*

'Looks like I was right then… about you not being able to stick it out.'

Clayton swings around and does a double-take when he sees The Chief standing there, not six feet away. Today is not a good day to catch Clayton unawares. In fact, the old man would do well to take that twitchy smile off his whiskery face. The way Clayton feels right now, he's likely to hit out first without asking any questions. He has not given them permission to do so, but his hands have already balled into angry fists.

'What do you think you're playing at? Creeping up on people and scaring them half to death?'

'Wasn't intentional.' The Chief raises his hands in mock surrender and backs off a step or two as if he means it; but Clayton no longer trusts him.

'You've been wanting us out ever since we first got here. Why?' Clayton doesn't mince his words.

'What's this all about, Clayton?'

'The curse of course. What else?'

'There is no curse. It's all superstition. A story made up by the tabloid press.' The Chief sticks stubbornly to his story, making Clayton even wilder.

'That's what you told them in the interviews... but it's not what you really believe.'

'The least you know the better,' The Chief looks away uncomfortably and swallows. 'It's a bad place this. Not fit for man, woman... or child. You should have left long ago.'

'So you were doing us a favour?' Clayton laughs cynically. 'All along you had our best interest at heart! Is that what you're saying?'

'You could have avoided a lot of trouble if you'd told me you were planning on going.'

'You mean Tommy's things, don't you? You bastard!'

'Think what you like.' The Chief shrugs innocently, as if this was nothing to do with him, but he still can't look Clayton in the eye. 'It's clear you're going to anyway.'

'You were there when they burned them, you said.' Clayton stabs a finger in the old man's direction.

'That's right.' Mumbling unconvincingly, The Chief begins to fiddle with the emergency cigarette behind his ear and Clayton finally makes the connection between this gesture and his duplicity. The old man has been caught out in a lie, good and proper, and he knows it.

'They don't burn. I've seen it for myself.' Clayton insists.

'Why let the facts get in the way of a good story?' The Chief mimics Avril's words from many nights ago, trying to make light of the situation.

'The facts are… we could have lost the baby.'

'Nobody wanted that to happen. I wouldn't wish that on my worst enemy.' The old man leans heavily on his walking stick and drags his boot from side to side.

'You were there. But you never saw them burn,' Clayton finds himself shouting.

At this, The Chief's face undergoes a transformation. His yellow eyelids clamp shut and he rocks from side to side, almost whimpering. Judging by the pained expression on his face, he is remembering something terrible. When his watery eyes open at last, they seem to speak the truth.

'The warehouse caught on fire before anyone got the chance to burn the paintings,' The Chief comes clean. 'After that, they were moved to a secret location where they've remained ever since.'

'We're done here.' Clayton fumes, turning away in disgust. 'Stay away from me and my family,' he warns over his shoulder.

Heading back toward the house, an ongoing battle is taking place in Clayton's head. *I don't know why I didn't see through him right from the start? He was never my friend. He only ever pretended to be. Suzie too. She was just as bad. And I fell for it hook line and sinker.* Clayton has never been so angry with himself. By fair means or foul, The Chief had wanted them out of Swallow's Nest, not caring about the consequences, and the fact that he now has the nerve to claim it was for their own good, makes his blood boil.

Clayton comes to an abrupt halt at the main entrance when he finds the front door is shut. Feeling a strong sense of unease, he pulls out a keyring from his pocket and frowns. *I could have sworn I left it open.*

In case the old man is up to his old tricks again, Clayton's glance swings back to the driveway, but The Chief is already beginning his long limp home across the moor. There's a sullenness to the man's bulky shoulders that doesn't speak of much regret, Clayton decides, yet he is somehow reminded of a very old man who has just had his favourite dog put down.

Inserting the key in the lock, Clayton gives it a good twist but the door doesn't budge. He tries it again but it still won't open. *Damn it.*

Chapter 94

Avril sweeps the dead swallow into a dustpan. The rubber gloves she's wearing make her hands hot and sticky. This is a lot like the rest of her feels. There is a humidity to the air that won't let up and rain is imminent. The sky is blacker than she's ever seen it; making the house even less welcoming than usual. In the distance, she can hear the faint rumble of thunder and is reminded of the night of the storm when her baby was conceived.

Fearing that the dead bird is a bad omen, she notices that its feathery tail pokes out rigidly behind it in the early stages of rigor mortis, yet the rest of its body is soft and floppy. Its beak is tucked under one wing and it looks to her as if it is sleeping. She has seen hundreds of children at rest assuming this same pose, with their sleepy faces tucked into their elbows. But the bird's deadpan stare tells a different story. As do the blood smears and feathers stuck to the glass. *Poor thing. Why did you persist in flying in here?*

A black thunderous cloud bullies its way over the house, dominating the sky line and causing the sitting room lights to flicker. This is quickly followed by an ear-splitting crack of thunder and lightning, which lights up the space on the wall where *The Crying Boy* portrait used to hang. *Better get a move on and stop day dreaming,* Avril thinks jumpily.

Braving the elements, she goes through to the kitchen and exits the back door; emptying the dead bird in the bin.

'I'm sorry,' she tells it, quickly closing the lid. Then, looking up at the dark vortex of cloud circulating overhead she wonders why it hasn't rained yet. Surely it is an anomaly for the sky to be this cast over without shedding a single drop of rain. *What is it waiting for?* Feeling panicky, Avril wills herself not to be afraid. *Everyone knows babies pick up on their mother's anxieties from within the womb and I don't want my baby to have a single scary moment in its life. I must do my bit. Besides, the storm is the least of my worries at the moment,* she reminds herself dryly.

Shuddering anyway when she hears another clash of thunder, she darts back inside the house, locking the kitchen door behind her. Avril is dreading driving in this storm; especially along those pot-holed lanes which can be a death-trap in the best of conditions.

Talking of conditions! Avril takes a photograph out of her pocket and looks at it for a second or two like she could just eat it. She kisses it, many times, before putting it down on the hob and smoothing it out. It's getting creased in her pocket so she'll come back for it in a moment.

Going over to one of the cupboards, Avril stands on tip toes and manages to knock down a box of Yorkshire tea and a packet of biscuits. She places them on the kitchen table; then takes out a large jar of pickled onions and a multi pack of Monster Munch, adding them to her emergency haul. *I'm not going anywhere without these little beauties.* She slides open the jar and fishes out a pickled onion, popping it into her mouth whole. Her face screws up in mock disgust when the acidic taste hits the back of her tongue.

I'd best shut the sitting room curtains and put some lights on, she decides in response to a sudden brainwave.

Otherwise passers-by will know the place is empty. The last thing we need is to be broken into and robbed.

As Avril walks out of the room, letting the inner door close quietly after her, one of the rings on the ceramic hob starts to glow red. The edges of the baby scan photograph, taken at the hospital, curls up under the heat.

Clayton chooses exactly this moment to approach the back door. For now, he appears unruffled, but when he tries the handle and it won't open, he grimaces. He rattles the door even harder but it still won't open, so he peers in through the kitchen window, looking for Avril.

'Avril!' He shouts, knocking on the glass. 'Avril.'

Clayton then sees something that really disturbs him. The photograph on the hob is on fire. He doesn't know it's the baby scan photo. He only knows something is burning and that flames are already reaching up to take hold of the kitchen curtains. When he spots the broken smoke alarm on the drainer with its wire innards poking out like intestines, he knows something bad is about to happen. Already he can smell smoke. *My God what has she done to the smoke alarm? How many times have I told her never to interfere with things like that?*

'AVRIL! AVRIL!' He hollers at the top of his voice.

Chapter 95

Everywhere The Chief looks, he is reminded of the connection between himself and the moor. This is where he grew up and all his boyhood squabbles had been fought here. His first kiss, first shag even, took place right over there, by that ridge. One minute, the rocks and moorland are above you and the next they're below you, he notices for perhaps the hundredth time. Up and down like people, he reminisces. Up and down like pain. His own shadow on the grass is not as impressive as it once was. Despite being thought of as a giant by the bairns around these parts, he is in fact only half the man he used to be.

A bad smell follows him everywhere. It's not the earth, the stagnant water nor the rotting carcases of sheep that get up his nose – it's the bad meat smell emanating from his leg that's the problem. Today, it's giving him real grief so he's going no place fast, even with the aid of his walking stick. The antibiotics and other meds are doing bugger all to improve the septicaemia, and they're making him crabby as hell. By heck, his temper doesn't half increase with each new morsel of pain. Every day it seems there is something new to get over; testing his patience if nothing else. On days like this, he's not sure how much longer he can go on.

As he ambles back to what he calls home, each painfully slow step is spent thinking about the Shaws. His entire relationship with the young couple has been based on lies, some worse than others. But taking a shine to Clayton isn't one of them. He was... is... genuinely fond of the guy, even if he did have a face like an itchy arsehole just now. If The Chief had fathered a son who turned out to be only half the man Clayton is, he'd have been right proud. He supposes even Avril is alright when she isn't being all uppity, as is her wont.

As usual, he hadn't been telling Clayton the whole truth about the incident involving the warehouse; because the building hadn't just caught on fire: it had burned to the ground. What he'd witnessed, he never wanted to relate to another human being as long as he lived.

After the fire, grey ash fell on them like summer rain as they stood gathered around the hundreds of untouched Crying Boy paintings stacked one on top of the other. The crew had taken off their sooty helmets, not as a mark of respect, but out of disbelief. The Chief can remember thinking they looked like a line of coffin bearers at a funeral.

Every firefighter had gone home with his tail between his legs that day; none of them daring to look the missus in the eye. And if any were unlucky enough to own such a painting, they made sure it never got passed on. None of them would mention the curse again. This became an unspoken oath, but rather than hold them together it caused friendships to drift apart. From then on, people changed shifts and joined neighbouring fire crews to avoid each other. It was easier that way. And if they did come across the cursed painting in another mysterious house fire, they kept their gobs shut; as he did when his own brother became a victim of the 'curse.' Being the only one left of the original crew… the last man standing, as it were, The Chief feels all the responsibility for what happened now rests with him.

A noise, unnatural to his surroundings, intrudes on his memories; bringing him back to the present. More than ever these days, he finds it hard to let go of the past. But eventually his ears twitch in the direction of Swallow's Nest and he recognises Clayton's voice echoing over the moor.

'Avril. Avril.'

The Chief looks in the direction of the house that once belonged to his brother, where he is no longer welcome. There is only one reason he can think of why Clayton would be screaming out his wife's name at the top of his lungs.

Chapter 96

Immediately feeling how much darker and chillier the sitting room is since she was last in it, Avril shivers and hugs her body for warmth. She then goes around the room switching on table lamps, conscious of the fact her hair is once again full of static electricity. *It must be the storm,* she decides. *I hope the power doesn't go off again. At least not until after we leave. It can do what it wants then.* Once the room is well lit, Avril crosses to the windows and starts tugging the heavy curtains shut.

The loudest clap of thunder booms over the house. To Avril's ears it seems angry. The room shakes and their whole collection of family photographs topples over. Most of them end up face down but some crash to the floor. The splintering of glass only adds to the terrifying cacophony of sound. Avril clings to the curtain until the rumbling and vibration subsides. She's never experienced anything like that before. Surely that had to be a mini earthquake rather than a storm?

***

With the storm raging above his head, Clayton races to the back of the building, all the while protecting his head in case he should be unlucky enough to get hit by lightning.

Up ahead, he can see the curtains in the sitting room have been pulled to. Just one glimpse of light remains at the furthest end of the room. He makes his way there now but as soon as he reaches the last window, he sees the pale whiteness of Avril's hand tugging the curtain shut. If he'd been a second earlier she would have seen him, but for now the whole side of the house is in darkness; just a tweak or two of light peeping through odd gaps in the curtains. Swearing under his breath, Clayton begins to pound on the glass, and then gets thrown off balance when the biggest clash of thunder he's ever heard takes hold of the house; making it tremble.

***

Scanning the room in case there's something important she's forgotten to pack, *I won't worry about family photos for now. We can always make more memories,* Avril's eyes come to rest on *The Crying Boy* portrait on the chimney wall. At first nothing registers… she's so used to seeing it there… and then her eyes widen in disbelief. *He's back!*

Slowly backing away from the painting, vaguely aware that of course everything now makes sense. The storm. The static in her hair. The fishy smell in her nostrils she'd been oh so cleverly pretending wasn't there. Her heart hammering in her chest is so loud in her ears, she can barely hear the storm outside. Then, perhaps due to the heightened electricity in the room, the recording she's been listening to on her MP3 player begins jumping all over the place.

'During the third month of pregnancy your baby's bones begin to harden and he is already moving spontaneously. Eyelids will form later but external ears have already been formed. EXTERNAL EARS HAVE ALREADY BEEN FORMED.'

Tugging the earphones from her ears before the crackling can damage her own hearing, and allowing the cord to nestle against her neck, she locks eyes with *The Crying Boy*.

At first the child in the portrait doesn't look any different, but on closer examination Avril is able to detect a reddening of the eyes. His skin is greyer than ever, lacking the sheen of a healthy child. If possible, the rags he's wearing look even more crumpled than before. *Oh God. Oh God. Oh God. This cannot be. This is impossible.* Avril shakes her head from side to side; all the while admitting to herself that it *is* possible. And it *is* happening.

'What do you want from me?' she whimpers.

Does the portrait move ever so slightly? Tilt gently to one side to peer at her from a crooked angle? She can't be sure. *Do your worst*, she wants to scream at it. But she is afraid. He is her enemy. He has always been her enemy. Even when he was her friend, or rather *pretending* to be, he meant her harm. Only now does she get this.

There is crying now, all around her, an injured pitiful sound that is supposed to appeal to her heart strings and she feels his putrid breath against the back of her hand. Whipping her hand away, she sees his shadow flitting around the room, moving at a pace her eyes can barely keep up with.

'Stay with me.' She senses rather than hears its attempt to communicate with her and her eyes roll upwards in terror.

'I can't,' at last she finds her voice, croaky as it is. 'I can't.' She repeats, more firmly this time. It doesn't like it. She can tell. The floorboards beneath her feet start to scrape and groan. *Good God is it, he… beneath me now?*

'Stay with me, Mummy. Don't go. Don't leave me here on my own. It's me. Tommy. I'm here.'

Despite telling herself not to cry, no matter what happens, her eyes instantly fill with tears.

'Tommy!'

Looking down at her open palms, which are busy collecting her tears, she cannot resist a sudden overwhelming desire to stretch out a hand in front of her.

'Tommy. My baby.' She takes one slow step toward the painting, and then another…

'Stay with me.' It pleads again and Avril nods her head to demonstrate an obedience she doesn't altogether feel. *It's okay. I'm coming,* her heart betrays her. Realising she can no longer fight the painting's magnetism, she experiences sudden exhaustion and her eyes close for a second or two as she sways on the spot, in time with the painting. It would be so easy to keep on walking into the nothingness he is promising her but a small part of her continues to resist his influence.

She is unaware of what that small part of her is until she feels it – the first fluttery feeling that all expectant mothers long to experience – too soon to be a real kick but felt all the same and not imagined. The connection between mother and baby is instantaneous. *I am alive,* it reminds her. *And you and I have a bond that nobody can break.* The unexpected interaction with her unborn child immediately clears Avril's head.

'You are not Tommy,' she says in a hate-fuelled voice. 'You're not him,' she is shouting now. 'Tommy couldn't speak. And Tommy wouldn't want this.'

Avril looks for something to throw at the painting but stalls when she feels the cord around her neck start to chafe against her scarred skin. She glances down, mesmerised by the loop that slowly forms a hangman's noose. She feels it curl its way seductively around her neck before nipping her skin. She doesn't attempt to stop it. Couldn't even if she tried. Her fingers are numb. Her legs don't work. Her heart feels as if it has stopped and the blood that had been circling around her veins comes to a trickling stop. Even the storm outside appears to pause, waiting to see what happens.

I'll never be yours, she thinks rebelliously, closing her eyes and waiting for the inevitable to happen. As the noose tightens further, cutting off her airways, her legs start to jangle and she finds herself choking. Her tongue fills her mouth and has no place left to go. Then suddenly, she hears Clayton shouting from somewhere outside; his voice so loud it drowns out the storm and frees her from *The Crying Boy*'s grip.

'Avril. For God's sake, open up. The house is on fire!'

Clawing at the constricting cord around her neck, Avril wrestles it free and flings it to the floor, simultaneously choking, coughing and trying to get back her breath. Keeping one eye on the portrait, she dashes to the nearest window and attempts to open it. But this time it is well and truly stuck and no amount of shoving is going to free it.

Chapter 97

Clayton watches helplessly as Avril struggles to get the window open. It breaks his heart to see her crying and mouthing his name when he can't do a thing to help her. She may not know it yet but already smoke from the kitchen is creeping into the room. However, he can tell this isn't what is making her splutter and cough. He looks around for something, anything, to break the glass but there is nothing in sight.

'Break the glass, Avril. Find something to break it with.'

He's hardly started his sentence when the hi-fi suddenly lights up in the background and Soft Cell's 'Tainted Love' spews out at full volume, drowning out his voice. Avril covers her ears with her hands and silently appeals for help. Even from out here, the noise is unbearably loud, so God knows what it's like for her trapped inside.

'Break the window. Find something.' He yells, watching her trying to lip read through the window. Next, he sees her press her face up against the glass so that her pink skin sticks to it, leaving a breathy imprint behind. 'I can't hear you.' She mouths back at him as obviously as she can and finally he gets it. Doing the one thing he never thought he'd be able to bring himself to do, Clayton uses sign language to communicate with his wife. He might not be very fluent at it but he's seen Avril and Tommy use it enough to have some idea of what to do. All those times she'd accused him of not taking any of it in, she'd been wrong. He may never have wanted to admit to feeling helpless in the face of Tommy's condition but he overcomes his awkwardness now and wills his hands to move faster.

'Break the glass. Find something,' he signs to her and she immediately nods to show she has understood. Clayton watches Avril's eyes dart around the room, before settling on one of the table lamps. *Good girl*, he praises silently, noticing that she has picked the heaviest. Willing her to move faster, Clayton watches her pull it savagely from the socket and hurl it at the window, but it simply bounces off the glass, landing close to Avril's feet.

'Shit.' Clayton runs an agitated hand through his hair. The frustration is too much. At last, he has an idea, *a better idea*, and signals to Avril to 'wait' realising there is very little else she can do: the smoke and flames are now visible in the sitting room doorway.

Off he goes, running as fast as he can, tripping into obstacles he can barely see – a plastic watering can, a wooden bench – it really is as black as night out here. He finds the spade where he left in, in one of the vegetable beds. He tugs it out of the soil and heads back to the house with it; the metal blade striking him against the thigh with each stride.

Back at the window, he can see Avril wringing her hands, desperate for a glimpse of him. As soon as she spies him, her face fills with hope but Clayton has only to take one look at the smoke and flames curling their way into the room to know time is not on their side. Already the blaze has picked up momentum and is engulfing anything that gets in its way. *Shit. It's taking hold quicker than I thought*, he panics, realising his terror will be nothing to what Avril will feel when she eventually turns and confronts it.

Clayton gestures for Avril to back off and taking aim, he hurls the spade at the glass. It strikes full on, or at least it appears to, but then bounces off again as if the glass were protected by a supernatural shield. Before he's even had chance to digest this phenomenon, the hi-fi explodes into a ball of flames, causing Avril to scream and cower down. Through the glass, Clayton glowers at *The Crying Boy* portrait.

'You, bastard. I won't let you do this.'

Balling his hands into fists, Clayton flays them against his own head. *Think. Think. I must think.*

Chapter 98

From inside the back of his van, Clayton rummages through a variety of tools and electrical equipment, all the while crouching low so his head doesn't come into contact with the roof, *again*. It looks as if the entire contents of the van have been spilt onto the drive, but he isn't done yet. Ignoring the fire extinguisher hanging on the back of the door, *I'll need that soon enough though*, he thinks, making a mental note to come back for it, his hand finally grasps what he has been looking for. *Thank God.*

Armed with a cordless drill and a torch, he heads for the front door. Getting stuck in right away, he drills into the lock, but he can tell by the diminishing sound it's about to run out of power. *Bloody batteries.* With his heart in his mouth, he wills it on, praying the tiny amount of remaining power will do the trick. This time he's lucky. The lock snaps and immediately the tinny whirring of the drill dies in his hand. *So fucking close. Now to get the door open.* Throwing his considerable weight at it, Clayton is relieved to find it caves in as easily as a rotting tooth.

He's about to go back for the fire extinguisher. Lord knows he will need it, when he hears Avril screaming. Realising there is no time to lose, he enters the building, battling against smoke and flames. By now, the kitchen has been completely devastated by fire but the carnage is gradually spreading to all areas of the ground floor. He tugs his polo shirt out of his trousers, spits on it and covers his mouth with it, before getting his bearings. This will help him breathe for a short time. As soon as he approaches the door to the sitting room, thick black smoke engulfs him.

He finds her hiding behind the sofa, shaking and crying and freaking out when he lays his hands on her.

'It's me, Clayton. I'm here and you're going to be okay.' Although she can barely hear him above the roar of the fire, she leans gratefully into his body, almost unbalancing him.

Grabbing hold of her hand, Clayton pulls her to her feet, gesturing for her to stay low. By fault rather than design, he guides her toward where the sitting room door used to be but by now the frame is on fire too. He tugs her toward a gap in the fire, convinced this is their best chance of escape, but when they close in on the gap a ball of flames suddenly appears in front of them, blocking their exit. After that, every way they turn the same thing happens – the flames beat them back, at all times herding them into the centre of the room. Staring up at the untouched Crying Boy portrait, Clayton feels every muscle in his body tighten.

'This is my family. You can't have them.' He yells, refusing to be beat; but he soon finds himself on his knees coughing and gasping for air. Avril is right next to him, patting him in an awkward placating way, as if she doesn't know what else to do. He can see from her blackened face that she has already given up. Knowing this destroys him.

In the darkness, Clayton reaches out for Avril and pulls her into a half sitting, half kneeling position and they curl up together on the floor; heads touching. No amount of stroking it out of the way can prevent Avril's frazzled hair from falling over her face. She is terribly still and her body slumps heavily against him, as if she were already dead. He grabs her floppy wrist and feels for a pulse; relieved to find her heartbeat is surprisingly strong. Pressing his blistered lips to her sooty fingers, he is amazed to discover she is wearing his ring. He has no idea when she started wearing it again but his tongue recognises the familiar metallic taste. *It's not fair. We have already been through so much. We are still young and have a baby on the way*, he grieves. When Avril places his hand over the soft curve of her stomach, he realises she is prompting him to say goodbye. Not just to her. But to the baby too. They look at each other and smile. Yes, they really do smile. 'I love you,' she's thinking. He doesn't have to hear her voice to know this. With his free hand he signs to her in the dark 'I love you too.'

Seeming outraged by this outpouring of emotion, the sound of petulant sobbing fills every corner of the hell hole that was once their home; but it cannot touch them now. Clayton doesn't waste any more energy calling out to let *it* know this. That's when he sees the white mist descending on him. At first, he thinks it's part of the dying process; because by now the fire has grown into such a giant it has consumed all the air around it. What little is left, is so hot, it burns his throat. Although his eyes are smarting, he can make out a bulky shadow in the doorway that wasn't there a minute ago.

'Get up. Come on.' The Chief barks in a foghorn voice, drowning out any other background noise. Clayton can hardly believe it. It really is him. And he's come armed with the fire extinguisher from his work van.

Stirred into action, but still feeling light-headed, Clayton sits up groggily and gives Avril a shake. *Thank God, she's still alive*, he can't help thinking. Then, through streaming eyes, he watches The Chief spray foam on the flames all around them, quickly extinguishing them. He then makes a pathway through the building that is to be their escape route.

This might not be the time to express relief but when he feels the old man pulling him unsteadily to his feet, Clayton can't help holding on to his hand longer than he ought.

Chapter 99

Although the air outside is scorching from the fire, it feels deliciously cold on Clayton's lungs as they all three burst from the house onto the driveway. Pausing only to cough, splutter and inhale clean air, they are soon on their way again – each of them supporting the other – because by now The Chief is struggling to keep up.

They head for the protection of the giant ash tree and hear an explosion behind them as they hobble toward it. Glancing over his shoulder, Clayton sees that every pane of glass in the house has shattered and glass shards are now raining down on them. The Chief screams in agony as a fragment of glass impales his leg, causing him to stumble to the ground. Between them, Clayton and Avril manage to get him on his feet again and drag him toward the solitary tree where all three collapse at its base.

Exhausted, parched and filthy, they turn their blackened faces toward the burning building. By now the flames are reaching up to touch the dark sky and a vibration along the ground is felt as the attic floor collapses. Screams can be heard coming from inside the house but none of them get up again. They all know who is responsible for those sounds. Nobody, not even *The Crying Boy*, could escape an inferno like that. When Clayton catches sight of Avril's horrified expression, he follows her gaze all the way up to the upstairs window that looks down on the tree, *Tommy's room*, where a child's silhouette can be seen. Unable to watch any longer, Avril buries her head in his shoulder but Clayton wouldn't miss this for anything. He's only glad Avril doesn't have to witness the sudden clawing of small hands behind the glass. From here, Clayton is sure he can see a look of tormented longing on the boy's tear-streaked face.

Throwing a comforting arm around his wife, Clayton nods approvingly. *'Burn you fucker,'* he says, but not loud enough for anybody else to hear. Even after all she's been through, he's not sure Avril is ready to hear that kind of talk yet. He on the other hand, has enough anger and hatred inside him for the two of them and it will take far longer to fade than it will this house to burn.

As soon as the screaming stops, the rain comes, bringing with it the weak rays of a setting sun. Dusk is already upon them, Clayton realises, and soon it will be properly dark. He ruffles Avril's hair and she looks up at him; half smiling. Her face is so black he hardly recognises her. The rain is tepid but refreshing against their skin and Clayton catches drops of it on his tongue. Nothing has ever tasted quite so good. Not even the finest Queen of the Moorlands whiskey.

Chapter 100

The midday sun is high in the sky and rays of silver light reach down to pat the earth's crust; as if to thank it for a job well done. The Chief is kind of in agreement with the sun on this, because now that Swallow's Nest is gone, he feels the landscape has been cleansed. Truth is, that house was always a loner and wanted no company. It was built by a sick, troubled man – his own brother – and didn't belong here anymore than Ted or the Shaws had.

The giant ash tree now has room to stretch out her branches and soon the land around it will form part of the moorland; overgrown with heather, grass and the like. Sheep will graze here again and probably a few years from now all traces of the house will have disappeared.

On the deceptively gentle slopes of the surrounding moorland, picnickers have come to gawp at somebody else's misfortune; smug in the knowledge their own houses are still standing. They have no idea how quickly the weather conditions up here can change. How many times do these holidaymakers need reminding they don't belong here? As far as The Chief can tell, only birds and wildlife were ever intended to live and die on these wild, untameable moors.

Unaware that he too might be classed as a voyeur by the firefighters doing a sterling job of making the place secure, he watches them reel in hoses and chat amongst themselves. It's been a long night and they are almost done. He doesn't know a single man amongst them and they all seem impossibly young. They've allowed him to remain on site, on account of him being an eye-witness and a friend of the family and all, but he can tell they don't really want him here. He will not go down the road of bragging about who he is– who he *used* to be, just to fit in. He'll fit in soon enough, where he's going.

Hobbling on crutches with a make-do bandage wrapped around his leg, where that hot piece of jagged glass got him, The Chief searches among the still-smouldering rubble; using the end of one crutch to flip the charred remains over. Only him and two other people in the world know what he's looking for, but he can find no evidence to suggest there ever was a Crying Boy portrait.

His face twisting with pain and disappointment, The Chief straightens up and notices a flight of swallows gathering on one of the sagging electricity cables. He studies them thoughtfully; one crooked arthritic finger stroking the stubble on his chin.

'The fire must have unsettled them.' It's the Fire Chief speaking; having somehow crept up on The Chief without being spotted. *I must be getting old*, he reckons. A few years ago he'd have broken somebody's fingers for doing just that.

'Getting ready to fly home more like.' The Chief is churlish. He doesn't like the way this younger version of himself looks at him with kind, pitiful eyes.

'But they'll be back again next year. You can bet your life on it.' The young Fire Chief's authoritative way of speaking grates on The Chief and he deliberately turns his back on him; hell-bent on ignoring him.

Chapter 101

As Clayton pulls into the driveway of his former home, he can hardly believe what he is seeing. Although he was here till the early hours of this morning, the daylight reality is something else. He gets out of his van and gapes incredulous at the wreckage. All that's left of Swallow's Nest is a scorched smudge. He spots The Chief over by the tree, the same one that offered them protection from the fire last night, and ambles over to join him.

They meet up as if by accident, each avoiding the need to greet one and other, and they stare in companionable silence at the ruin. Clayton expected to feel more. A little heartbreak perhaps? Instead, he feels nothing but relief at the outcome. All that matters is Avril and their unborn child are alive. That they got out in time, thanks to this man here.

'I hope that's the very last time I see that house burn,' The Chief says flatly.

'What house?' Clayton raises his eyebrows.

'You know what insurance people are like for rebuilding.' The Chief eyes him bluntly.

'Not this time.' Clayton shakes his head, tired of how dark and depressing everything is. Bizarrely, he feels like celebrating, not commiserating. 'At last you're starting to sound like a *retired* Fire Chief,' he smirks.

At that, the old man's head bounces up and for a moment he looks offended, but seeming to have a change of mind, he gives a nod of approval. As if by agreement, they fall silent again, each man's thoughts their own. Clayton is starting to feel things couldn't be more awkward between them.

'I told him not to mind the curse.' Out of the blue, The Chief comes right out and says it.

Clayton catches a glimpse of tears in the old man's eyes and he feels his own jaw tighten. *Get a grip*, he tells himself, *if The Chief wants to tell me his story, that's up to him. He's earned the right and I won't judge him for it.*

'Your brother?' Clayton questions softly.

'Aye.' The Chief's head keeps on nodding. 'And I ended up scattering his ashes right here under this very tree.'

At this, Clayton's toes curl and he feels his weight shift from one foot to the other. He really doesn't want to walk on dead men's graves. And he *definitely* does not want to mess with any of The Chief's dead relatives. When it's clear The Chief isn't going to add anything more to this sentence, they both concentrate on their boots.

'I just wanted to thank you,' Clayton spits it out before he can change his mind. 'For not staying away.'

'This part of Yorkshire has always been my patch. My responsibility. I didn't want to take no chances.'

'And that's why you tried to scare us away?' Clayton still hasn't forgiven The Chief for not coming clean sooner. Even though the man saved all their lives it still bothers him. *Christ. How petty am I?*

'I hadn't counted on how obstinate the pair of you could be.' The Chief chuckles unexpectedly.

'You've got Avril to thank for that.' Clayton joins in with The Chief's laughter.

'Tell her I was wrong.' The Chief is once again deadly serious. 'I've always been wrong. I should have looked truth in the face and spit in its eye 'stead of hiding from it.'

Try as he might, Clayton cannot think of anything else to say.

'You want to know something else, Clay?' Here, The Chief grabs hold of Clayton's hand and holds onto it for all he's worth; his whole face welling up with emotion. 'There's no such thing as a *retired* fire chief.'

Chapter 102

His fingers don't shake as much as they ought to, he realises, as he slides open the rusty bolts to a pair of steel reinforced doors. He'd like to enter the building stealthily, but the massive clank of the doors will alert anyone inside to his whereabouts. In the darkness, his torchlight picks out an abundance of high visibility warning signs. 'No Smoking', 'Danger', 'Highly Flammable' and 'Authorised Personnel Only.' With this much security in place, anyone would suspect the warehouse of containing lethal poisons, but he knows better than that.

Once he's inside, every sound he makes is intensified. He shuffles slowly, breathing heavily as if everything is too much effort. In the silence he can hear his bones move. Click. Click. Click. The sound puts him on edge and he can feel the silvery hairs on the back of his neck stand up. As he moves further into the building he feels giant cobwebs brush against his face; a reminder that nobody has been inside for a very long time. Worse though is the sudden warmth he encounters; when the hot air fills with static electricity and of course his torchlight fades almost at once. It doesn't matter. He's prepared for this sort of thing happening.

Behind him, he imagines whispering and childish laughter but he knows it's just his imagination running riot.

It's too soon for that, he reminds himself. The light switch is just where he remembered it to be. He flicks the switch and after a reluctant second or two, the sleepy fluorescent lights flicker on. They take their time to flood the building. It has been thirty years since they were last required to do any work.

Shielding his eyes from the sudden glare, The Chief looks around him and puts down the petrol can he has been carrying.

'You and me are going to have to have a little talk,' he says conversationally, never taking his eyes off the hundreds of Crying Boy portraits stored inside the building.

To his knowledge, there are dozens of different types of Crying Boy designs, all painted by the same artist, and he reckons most, if not all, are represented here. But the most popular one by far is the same version that had been owned by his brother Ted, which had unintentionally been passed on to the Shaws. He goes to stand next to an identical painting and peers into its cold, lifeless eyes.

'Why didn't you take me instead?' He wants to know.

The building trembles ever so slightly. Could just be the result of passing traffic; the motorway is none too far from here – but The Chief doubts it. Turning abruptly, he walks over to the petrol can, twists off the lid, and begins sloshing it over the paintings; stopping only when the can is spent.

Exhausted, The Chief drags himself over to a pile of wooden pallets and takes a pew. If he was expecting anything to happen immediately, he doesn't show any surprise. The curse will not be dictated to. It will react only when it wants to. But he's not going to wait around for that to happen. He slides the emergency cigarette out from behind his ear and inhales it. The smell is like a little bit of heaven. He then takes out a lighter from his pocket and immediately hears the scurry of childish footsteps behind him. Sensing that shadows are creeping up behind him, he wills himself not to turn around. This is no time to be frightened. Hadn't he planned it this way, all along?

Not for him, the hospices for the dying where all anyone can talk of is piss, shit and wind. There was never any chance of that happening to him. He'd have put a bullet in his mouth first; but now finds he doesn't have to. Aside from Suzie and the boy, nothing much matters to him anymore; except perhaps for his bit of wild garden.

Mean spiteful laughter starts to surround him and it feels as if a red-hot poker is pressing down on his chest. Quickly, before it's too late, he pops the cigarette into his mouth and lights it. *Time for one last smoke.*

Chapter 103

Sitting at her desk, beneath a large sign language clock on the wall, Avril flicks through a pile of homework and occasionally narrows her eyes at a vase of ugly chrysanthemums which were a present from one of her pupils. She cannot wait for them to curl up and die. Their cloying aroma only adds to the sweltering temperature of the classroom, making her feel nauseous.

Avril can hardly believe it's late summer already. Although she had secretly been dreading its return, it has crept up on her without her noticing. One year after the fire, the haunted look has vanished from her face. There is a sheen to her yellow hair that is new and she may even have gained a few extra pounds. She appears happy; except when her glance happens upon the flowers.

Looking from one drawing to another, she comes across a house with two chimneys that has a big tree outside and she is instantly reminded of Swallow's Nest. The artist, who she suspects is six-year-old Walter, currently seated at the back of her class, has also drawn a man, woman and child. But there is something wrong with the family he has drawn; in that the characters have upside down smiles. She wonders why Walter would draw something like this. Is he unhappy? Are things not as they ought to be at home?

Glancing over the top of the other children's heads, Avril seeks out Walter's rather small blond one at the back and her face falters when she sees a pair of cold cornflower blue eyes glaring back at her. Walter has vanished and in his place sits the crying boy; tears streaking down his dirty urchin's face. It has been so long since Avril last thought of him that his presence takes her completely by surprise.

Jumping to her feet, and attracting the attention of the rest of her class, Avril wrings her hands and edges away from her desk; her eyes on the door. *Please don't let him be real. Please don't let this be an omen of some kind.* Only when she realises how nervous she is making some of her pupils do her hands drop down by her sides. When she seeks him out again, she sees that she was mistaken. The crying boy is nowhere to be seen. All along it was Walter sitting there smiling back at her. Avril smiles back uncertainly and sits down again, gesturing for the children to continue with their crayoning.

***

It's home time and schoolchildren, wearing summer dresses or shorts, rush out to greet their parents waiting in the playground. They all have adventures to tell and do so with sign language and laughter. Exiting behind them, oblivious to the sound of the school bell ringing in her ears, Avril watches them go. The smile on her face won't be chased away by the darkening sky, which drops sinister shadows on the tarmac. No wonder it's so muggy. A summer storm is imminent. The trees guarding the playground are very still and even their branches wilt in the heat.

Glancing up at the family of swallows flying overhead, Avril realises they will soon be beginning the long migration home. She wonders how many will survive the journey. On that thought, she counts the heads of the people she cares about and notes who among *them* is missing. They both feel the loss of The Chief, but as she walks toward Clayton, the only other person she wishes could be here, is, of course, Tommy. She hasn't forgotten him and never will.

Clayton might have a baby-carrier strapped to his chest but he's still the hottest man at the school gates. He wears a tight-fitting T-shirt that shows off a new slimline physique and golden tan. He's been going to the gym and has given up alcohol; hence the return of his strikingly blue eyes. He's that gorgeous most of the mums here can't resist a peek at his profile. These days Avril doesn't mind.

'I told The Chief here you wouldn't be long,' Clayton says jiggling the baby up and down in a bid to keep him awake.

'Stop calling him that.' Avril laughs, climbing on tippy toes to kiss him very modestly on the cheek, so as not to shock her pupils. 'If he hears it enough, he'll start to think it really is his name.'

She then brushes her lips against the baby's cheek. He's only three months old, but already he is big and strong, with piercing blue eyes and a wad of white hair.

'I'm just happy he can hear,' Clayton says, grinning.

Chapter 104

Clayton's workshop is on the ground floor of their smart new townhouse and opens onto a hallway with a glass and chrome staircase going off. He likes to keep the door open, so he can see Avril and the little one moving around from room to room. She takes young Jamie everywhere with her; even to the toilet. It must have been hard for her returning to work so soon after having him, but their shared way of parenting seems to be working. Second time around he's more determined than ever to be a part of his son's upbringing. No opposition from Avril to date, he's pleased to report.

Since moving back to Leeds, they've come on leaps and bounds. He's still not sure about the house though. After nine months it hasn't grown on him the way Avril promised him it would. Minimally furnished, in Avril's preferred style of course, with white walls and glossy Ikea furniture; he is reminded of an expensive showroom whenever he sets foot in it.

The coffee table he made out of a door has been banished out here along with other unwanted stuff. Avril is insistent that it doesn't fit in here and he is inclined to agree.

'You and me both, old friend,' he says out loud.

Although he doesn't take himself seriously, he *has* refused to get rid of it altogether. He's even decided to give it a bit of a makeover in the hope that Avril will eventually relent. A bit of a rub down and a coat of white gloss, *perish the thought*, and she won't even recognise it.

Slipping on a dust mask, Clayton picks up a large hand-held sanding machine and is about to get stuck in when he hears the sound of his son's crying coming from the baby monitor. He has made sure there is one in every room, including the workshop. It's not that he's paranoid. He just doesn't want his son to wake up crying and not get picked up straight away. He can't think of anything worse.

On that thought, he puts down the sander and pulls down his mask. He's about to dart upstairs when he hears the sound of a door opening and realises Avril has beaten him to it.

'Hello baby.' He hears Avril's voice crackling over the monitor and almost at once his son stops crying and starts to make more contented gurgling noises. Imagining them together, in their cosy nursery world, fills him with joy.

'So you're awake, are you?' Avril's voice is calming and musical, all at the same time. He can understand why babies and children respond so well to her.

Although he could listen to the sound of his wife and child all night, he decides to crack on. The sooner he's finished, the sooner he can go join them. There's a storm brewing and he'd rather be around his family when it breaks. Thanks to the air conditioning, he doesn't feel the oppressive heat; not even when doing something physical like this. Neither of them ever want to experience another summer like the last. When he switches on the sander, its powerful whine drowns out all sound coming over the monitor but he is reassured by the flickering red sensor which lights up whenever it detects sound or movement.

***

Avril leans over the sleigh-shaped cot and holds onto the chubby finger of her son. He is wide awake and lies on his back, staring up at her with intelligent, brilliant blue eyes. She can tell that his balled-up fists are itching to grab at the sheep cot mobile that dangles enticingly over his head.

'You want to play with the sheep?'

As soon as Jamie hears her voice again, he turns his head in her direction and she tickles his multiple chins. At this, his cheeks grow pink and he blows noisy bubbles from his mouth. He smells of fabric softener, talcum powder and a certain something she can't name. Whatever that secret ingredient is, it's worth its weight in gold.

'Too yummy for your own good,' she laughs. She never tires of looking at her son, or watching him sleep. He has the cutest button nose and china white skin. Tonight he's wearing a soft blue romper suit with an adorable penguin print on it.

She winds up the sheep mobile and listens to the gentle strain of Brahms' Lullaby fill the room. It really is an enchanting sound and her son listens to it transfixed. She's lost count of how many times she has fallen asleep to it herself; dozing off in the armchair next to his cot.

The nursery has a beautiful arched window that runs the width of the room and a plush white carpet that her bare feet melt into. Subtle touches of blue mean the all-white room doesn't feel cold or sterile. The new house, one of a dozen in their gated community, makes the perfect home. Avril has made it her business to fit in here. There has never been a safer neighbourhood to bring a child into.

Watching the sheep circle above her head, she is reminded fleetingly of the eyes of a dying sheep that once pleaded with her for help; but she quickly suppresses this thought and stares at her fuzzy reflection in the window instead. The rain is relentless and shows no sign of letting up. Outside the pavements glisten black and a single thread of lightning pokes at the moon's belly. The grumble of thunder is too far away to concern her. She has more reason than most to be scared of storms, but these days she is better at coping. At least that's what everybody tells her – Clayton, the in-laws, doctors and the like. People who should know better.

The rain drizzling on the window pane is even more soothing than the music and it makes her feel sleepy. Neither she nor Clayton get as much sleep as they used to. Closing her eyes, she feels her body sway involuntarily and treasures a moment of perfect calm. Her eyes soon flash open again when she hears the crackling of the monitor behind her.

Beep, beep, beep.

This is not a sound she has heard in a long time. But she recognises it immediately. How cruel that the monitor is able to detect a noise from somewhere outside and allow it to imitate the reverse warning lights of a lorry.

Beep, beep, beep.

Her eyes widen in alarm when she sees the flickering sensor climb higher and higher, until eventually it lights up all five bars. When she glances down at her son she sees that he is scowling and this takes her mind of the unruly monitor.

'It's okay, little one. There's nothing to worry about. It's just the storm.'

That's when the fluffy sheep above his head start to jump angrily about. Something isn't right. She can feel it in her bones. She's about to call out for Clayton when she sees a refection in the window pane that *isn't* hers. A pair of cold, cornflower blue eyes and a shock of unruly yellow hair.

It can't be. Please, God. Don't let it be him.

Avril's heart is in her mouth as she spins around to confront whatever is behind her, but there is nothing there. Not even a shadow on the wall. She turns back quickly, her eyes anxiously skimming the glass. This time he's nowhere to be seen. *Did I imagine it? Oh please. Let that be the case.*

When she hears the menacing sound of a child's footsteps coming from somewhere above her, she places her hands over her ears and wills herself not to listen. But nothing can shut out the muffled sound of laughter that seeps through the walls. A cold chill settles on the room but she is burning up. Her clothes stick to her body, making her feel claustrophobic. The wretched fishy smell has returned and her hair is full of static electricity. The urge to scream is overwhelming.

She's about to open her mouth to do just that when the side of the cot starts to jerkily slide down; as if a small invisible hand is struggling to open it. Fear grips Avril, leaving her immobile. When she tries to uncurl her fingers, she finds she cannot. The cot seems to move further away from her. *How is that possible?* Only her eyes move, tracking the sinister movement of the bottom rail being lowered.

It kills her to know that Jamie is seeing this too; except his eyes are trusting and innocent. He is anticipating being picked up and lifted out of the cot.

Don't you dare touch my baby. Her eyes are blurry, she cannot see. An enormous weight presses down on her chest; making it hard for her to breathe. Making it impossible for her to do anything. Other than watch. *I must not pass out. I cannot allow it to…*

'Stay away from him.'

As soon as she finds her voice, the movement around her stops. She knows from experience he is not that easy to get rid of and in the next second she is proven right. The ceiling light above her head starts to judder and one of Jamie's soft toys falls from a shelf onto the floor, squealing in protest 'I love you. I love you. I love you.'

He is in the shadows behind her. Without turning around, she can sense him scurrying devilishly from corner to corner; wanting her to come play.

'Please don't hurt us,' she begs and he goes quiet again; as if sulkily mulling this over. While he keeps a suspicious eye on her, Avril's eyes never leave the cot. Jamie is just a foot away.

'What did I ever do to you, except try to love you?' She pleads, playing for time. But when she does eventually edge closer to the cot, she recoils in horror when she sees the corpse-like thing that has taken Jamie's place. This baby, were she to pick it up and shake it, wouldn't have any pulse. Its skin is grey and lifeless and the black bloodied eyes staring back at her are bred of evil. Even worse, it wears Tommy's blue cardigan, by now so torn and dirty it is barely recognizable. This is not her child. This thing is not human.

'No. No!' she screams, wondering why Clayton doesn't come to their rescue. He must be able to hear what is going on.

A small sad shadow appears on the floor next to her. His sniffling is meant to pull at her heartstrings but she is confused as to which child this really is. Is it Tommy? Or *The Crying Boy*? When his cold, clammy hand slips into hers, she does not shake it off. There is no longer any point resisting. All along she has known what is expected of her.

'I would never hurt a child. Any child. Let alone my own child. You know that,' she says hauntingly.

But how do I know this is really true when I can no longer remember what happened. People get hurt around me; that's what The Chief said? What if he's right? What if I really did hurt Mrs Mills? Lord knows I wanted to that day I caught her spying on me on the moor. And what about Suzie? Didn't I pray for something like that to happen to her boy? As for my parents. Isn't it just as likely the fire wasn't an accident? That I deliberately put the cigarette back between my dad's fingers, hoping he would burn. I can remember being angry with the kitten for scratching my hand and making me bleed. Perhaps I left it behind on purpose to punish it.

Avril's confusion increases when she glances down to see a pink cheeked baby lying in the cot. Who it belongs to, she cannot tell. The child looking back at her has the bluest of eyes. They make her think of Tommy and *The Crying Boy* and her hand tightens around the grey lifeless fingers curled up inside her hand. She senses that he is still angry with her. He will go on sulking until she does what he wants her to do.

'Nobody ever took your place. You don't have to make me do this to prove it,' she says in a faraway voice. But even as she says this, her hand is reaching out for the blue silk cushion resting on the armchair. Something about her expression makes the baby's bottom lip drop and he starts to cry. Avril knows these are not real tears. They are a cruel trick to fool her into thinking he means something to her, when he does not. This child is an imposter. Sent by the blackness of her mind to torment her.

Noticing that someone has hand embroidered the name 'Jamie' onto the cushion, she wonders who made it and where it came from. The name means nothing to her. *Where have all of Tommy's things gone and why has my confusion come back?* is what she yearns to know. The only thing she *is* sure of is what is expected of her. Until she does his bidding, there will be no peace. He will never let her go. She has no choice but to accept this and do what he wants.

Her face awash with silent tears, Avril slides the bottom of the cot rail all the way down, but does not attempt to pick the baby up; not even when he raises his podgy little arms in anticipation of this happening. She is not repulsed by him but she does not know him. 'I let you go,' she whispers, holding the cushion above his face. In a second it will be done. In a second it will all be over.

About the curse

The 'curse' of *The Crying Boy* began in September 1985 when over 50 mysterious house fires were thought to have been caused by the paranormal painting. In most cases the houses were completely destroyed and only the portrait remained untouched.

There are a lot of myths surrounding the curse and various explanations were given as to why the portraits didn't burn, but it's also rumoured that there wasn't a fire fighter in Yorkshire who would have allowed one in their home at the time.

The Painting

Back in the 1980's my parents inherited one of these portraits and as a child I remember being fascinated by the myths and folklore that surrounded it. Being a superstitious type, my mother was one of the thousands of anxious owners who sent their copy to The Sun newspaper for a mass bonfire.

I love the fact that the paranormal activity surrounding the portrait created such a stir in the UK and even made worldwide news as mass hysteria, generated mainly by the tabloid press, grew.

What the 'curse' inadvertently does is explore human nature in its simplest literary form: - the need for storytelling, the desire to embellish facts and a craving to create legends. Hence the well-documented 'eye witness' accounts that hold the portrait responsible for so many deaths and supernatural occurrences as well as the mysterious house fires.

Today, I own two of the *Crying Boy* portraits. The one on my study wall helped inspire me to write this story and I am rather fond of him. The other is best kept hidden away as I fear there is something malevolent about it. Its eyes have this sinister and somewhat unsettling habit of following a person around the room; leaving me to suppose it would be dangerous to destroy it or even attempt to part with it. A revengeful creature if ever you saw one!

Acknowledgements

Huge thanks to my publisher, Bloodhound Books and to Fred and Betsy for all the support they have given me. Betsy, you are awesome! Thanks also to editor, Clare Law, for meticulously wading through three hundred plus pages of *The Crying Boy* and hunting down my mistakes. Being accepted into the 'formidable fiction' Bloodhound Gang and receiving such a warm and generous welcome from my kennel mates has to be one of my favourite moments of 2016.

I would also like to thank Sign Language Teacher, Sandra Waldin-Walker, who helped improve my understanding of deaf awareness, which proved invaluable when it came to writing about the characters in this book, whose lives are overshadowed by profound deafness. Learning to communicate through sign language is one of the most worthwhile new skills I've picked up in a long time; made all the more enjoyable by my fellow students at Stamford New College who made night classes such fun.

Special mention goes to our brave Firefighters, especially those based in Yorkshire who first came across the cursed 'Crying Boy' painting in the 80's and to Kelvin MacKenzie, former Sun Editor at the time, who covered the stories, and who very kindly agreed to provide the foreword to this book. Kelvin has been very supportive of my work over the years and I am extremely grateful to him.

I can't go without mentioning Jacqui from my local Waterstone's branch (Peterborough), who has long been a champion of my work. From the bottom of my heart, thank you for your support, and for helping to launch both of my books in store.

As always, I would like to thank my hard-working hubby, Darren for taking care of all the practical things so I could concentrate on my writing. A great many sacrifices have been made during the last two years (including time spent together) so I could find the time to complete this book. He is of course my Alpha reader, harshest critic and best friend all rolled into one. As ever, I couldn't have done it without you!

Finally, thank you to my lovely readers and author friends who have supported me along the way; especially to those who enjoyed my first novel 'The Long Weekend' and are eagerly anticipating this one. Sorry I've kept you waiting for so long. I love you all.